SERENDIPITY:
THE GAY TIMES BOOK OF NEW SHORT STORIES

Edited by Peter Burton

First published 2004 by GMP (Gay Men's Press)

GMP is an imprint of Millivres Prowler Limited,
part of the Millivres Prowler Group,
Unit M, Spectrum House, 32–34 Gordon House Road,
London NW5 1LP UK

www.gaymenspress.co.uk
www.gaytimes.co.uk

A CIP catalogue record for this book is available from the British Library

ISBN 1-902852-48-6

Printed and bound in Finland by WS Bookwell

Distributed in the UK and Europe by Airlift Book Company,
8 The Arena, Mollison Avenue,
Enfield, Middlesex EN3 7NJ
Telephone: 020 8804 0400
Distributed in North America by Consortium,
1045 Westgate Drive, St Paul, MN 55114-1065
Telephone: 1 800 283 3572
Distributed in Australia by Bulldog Books,
PO Box 300, Beaconsfield, NSW 2014

By the same author

Gay Portraits
Amongst the Aliens: Some Aspects of a Gay Life
Vale of Tears: A Problem Shared (with Richard Smith)
Talking to… Writers Writing on Gay Themes
Parallel Lives
Rod Stewart: A Life on the Town

As editor

Death Comes Easy: The Gay Times Book of Murder Stories
Bend Sinister: The Gay Times Book of Disturbing Stories
The Mammoth Book of Gay Short Stories
The Art of Gay Love
The Boy From Beirut and Other Stories
Some of the Things Said by or About Kenny Jones and The Faces
Some of the Things Said by or About Ronnie Lane and The Faces
Some of the Things Said by or About Ian McLagan and The Faces
Some of the Things Said by or About Rod Stewart and The Faces
Some of the Things Said by or About Ron Wood and The Faces
The Black Tent and Other Stories

For
Neil Bartlett and James Gardiner,
John Haylock,
Francis King,
and
Tony Warren
with
professional regard and
personal affection

Contents

Introduction

Writers have for years been mourning the demise of the short story but, if the number of anthologies and single-author collections on the shelves of bookshops and libraries is anything to go by, like the reports of Mark Twain's death, those reports of the death of the short story have been grossly exaggerated. What has undeniably happened is the almost complete banishment of short fiction from magazines and newspapers, thus destroying what was once a flourishing market for both new and established writers (often the first step towards a literary career) and leaving a large void that is unlikely ever to be filled.

The rise of the short story coincided with the rise of the middle class, the rise of literacy, the rise of the working class's desire for self-improvement, the spread of the railways and the appearance on the station platforms of W H Smith's book stalls which supplied newspapers and periodicals for edification and entertainment to a wide range of travellers. The twenty-first-century equivalent of those publications seems to be those ubiquitous puzzle books that accompany so many people on flights or rail journeys.

Perhaps the most famous of those nineteenth-century periodicals was *The Strand Magazine*, founded in 1891, in which Arthur Conan Doyle's Sherlock Holmes made his first and so many subsequent appearances. Over nearly sixty years (*The Strand* closed down in 1950), the magazine published stories by everyone from Conan Doyle and H G Wells to P G Wodehouse, thus covering the complete spectrum of genres and thereby satisfying a reading public with a voracious appetite. However, short stories didn't just appear in magazines: publications such as the long-defunct *London Evening News* ran a story in every issue, each of these stories running to around two thousand words. I well remember the excitement with which I read a tale by Kenneth Martin, whose first novel, *Aubade*, written when he was sixteen, published when he was seventeen, is now something of a gay classic.

Magazines like John Lehmann's *New Writing*, which became *Penguin New Writing* and ran between 1936 and 1946, and Lehmann's *The London Magazine*, which he founded in 1954 and edited until 1961, and Joe McCrindle's *Transatlantic Review*, which ran between 1959 and 1977, allowed writers a little more space to breathe, though few were as generous with their space as *The New Yorker*, which gave complete issues to such celebrated *nouvelles* as Truman Capote's *Breakfast at Tiffany's* (1958) and Muriel Spark's *The Prime of Miss Jean Brodie* (1961).

Of course, the brevity of both the Capote and Spark *nouvelles* does raise the question of just what constitutes a short story. Christopher Isherwood is another novelist whose reputation was built on *nouvelles* ('Sally Bowles' being the most famous) that could easily be classified as short stories. Sometimes I think that words like *nouvelle* and *novella* are simply the posh alternatives to 'long short story'.

When contributors ask me to what length they can write when planning a story for consideration in one of my anthologies (this is the fourth I've edited), I tend to suggest that a story take as long as it takes. But that's not entirely true and is possibly too flippant a response.

The short story is a particularly difficult discipline and, before setting metaphorical pen to metaphorical paper, the writer must be certain that the tale they are about to tell really is a short story and not something altogether different: a novel. One contributor to this present collection found that the short story he was writing for inclusion had somehow turned into his next novel. Other submissions that didn't make the collection included pieces which strained uncomfortably at the constraints of the short-story form and pieces that were of the requisite length but were so underdeveloped as to preclude inclusion.

That said, there are long short stories in *Serendipity* and there are short stories that are as neat and happily anecdotal as any of the shorter magazine or newspaper pieces by the likes of O Henry, W Somerset Maugham or 'Saki' (H H Munro), all of whom were masters of the brisk and neat tale.

These days there are specialist publications for just about every interest, though it is surprising that so few (if any) of the world's gay periodicals have any interest in publishing short ficion. But in the past things were rather different. Intensely important in promoting homosexual literature were a number of essentially literary magazines, including *Horizon, New Writing* and *Penguin New Writing, The Windmill, The London Magazine, Evergreen Review* and *Transatlantic Review*. And there were a small number of gay publication which percolated throughout the world: *Der Kries*, founded in 1932 and running until 1967, Swiss-based, published in English, French and German; *One*, the magazine of the American homosexual law reform group The Mattachine Society. In all but the latter two titles, gay writings were eased into print because of gay publishers, gay editors or editors who were gay-sympathetic. Magazines over which John Lehmann held sway were a welcome haven for writers as distinguished as Paul Bowles, Christopher Isherwood and Denton Welsh. Writers who are gathered together in this collection, Hugh Fleetwood, Francis King and myself among them, were published in *Transatlantic Review*. *The Windmill*, co-edited by the lesbian Kay Dick under the pseudonym Edward Lane, published material by T H White, James Hanley, Sylvia Townsend Warner and the New Zealander James Courage, whose *A Way of Love* was a gay hit in 1959.

For anyone who enjoys short stories there are plenty to investigate (from the past, from the present) and many of the finest writers have themselves been gay. The interested should look out for collections from Clive Barker, Alan Bennett, E F Benson, Truman Capote, Noël Coward, Rhys Davies (a forthcoming biography of this Welsh writer who in his heyday was a *New Yorker* stalwart should bring about a revival), Hugh Fleetwood, E M Forster (all his gay fiction was published posthumously), Patrick Gale, Adam Haslett (his debut collection *You Are Not a Stranger Here* cannot be too highly recommended), L P Hartley, Christopher Isherwood, Henry James, John Sam Jones (especially his second slim collection, *Fishboys of Vernazza*), Francis King, Robin Maugham and his immeasurably superior uncle, W Somerset Maugham, Donald Rawley (two superb collections, one novel, an untimely death), David Rees, Peter Robins,

Frederick Rolfe, 'Saki' (H H Munro), whose influence has extended down the generations, Lawrence Schimel (a prolific anthologist), Gore Vidal, Tom Wakefield, Denton Welsh, Peter Wells, Patrick White, Thornton Wilder, Tennessee Williams and Angus Wilson. And that list is a mere taster.

The world of the short story is a world of infinite variety and endless diversion and I hope that *Serendipity* will give readers as much pleasure to read as it gave me to compile.

As usual, I must thank Simon Lovat for all his assistance with getting the final manuscript into shape.

Peter Burton,
Brighton, 2004

The Trouble with Dreams
Hugh Fleetwood

The Trouble with Dreams
Hugh Fleetwood

What he's really like,
that handsome young man on the beach,
that young man you pass on the street
with the broad shoulders,
the flat stomach,
the interesting bulge in his pants,
you neither know, nor care.
Perhaps his voice is shrill.
Perhaps his views are narrow.
Perhaps he's merely
a bore.
No matter.
What counts is what you see,
and
what you imagine him to be:
yourself in a different guise:
the boy with the laughing eyes

Of course it's only part of you
that wants to be that rough –
or smooth, accorting to your taste –
young man,
and could you have him for an hour or two
even part might say: enough!
For the thing about dreams is,
night or day,
one wants to entertain them for a while
then with a smile,
send them on their way

Hugh Fleetwood

If you let dreams stick around
They tend to do damage.
And history's taught us,
On a wider scale,
That if you take them in,
Allow them
To pitch their tents
Permanently,
They're capable of laying waste
Whole continents

1949
Tim Ashley

1949
Tim Ashley

I can picture the room, though of course I cannot see it. It is white in a clinical way; this is after all a hospital, and a private one at that. It has floral curtains, designed to hide the dirt. One or two pastoral or still-life prints on the walls. The sheets, though I cannot feel them, must be cheap, crisp cotton. I cannot imagine that any of my visitors would bother to ensure that I have my own Irish linen.

The one thing of which I am unbearably aware is the machine. It measures my heart with a slow and underconfident electronic beep and drives me mad. I frequently think that I have died at last, so faint is the sound, though always when I strain it is there. I can imagine how it looks. Cold grey with black rubber buttons and chromium edging, a small screen in the middle with a thin green line that spikes rhythmically up and down to reaffirm my continued presence to the faint of heart and the greedy that gather by my bedside from time to time.

I have lost track, totally, of how long I have been here. It is very difficult to follow time when you cannot scratch the comings and goings of the sun on the walls of your cell, when the only thing on which you can rely to measure the passing hours is the electronic imitation of the feeble pumping of your own heart. I am not yet sufficiently bored to will the final blip on the graph, the last, valedictory beep or peep, but I am close.

The reason must surely be the lack of bedside entertainment. Let me clarify: some time ago, possibly a week or so, I heard a doctor explain – to gasps, but few tears – that I was effectively a cabbage. Close examination of the functions of my brain had demonstrated that I have no awareness, and probably no remaining capacity for awareness, of any kind. No sense of touch, taste, sight, hearing (and there, of course, he was wrong) or smell. Completely deserted by the famous five.

I am still puzzled by the desire of my visitors to visit, given that they are all aware of these facts. Possibly they have read that the reassuring sounds of loved ones can miraculously reconnect the severed strands of thought in a damaged brain. None of them, in my view, is likely to have this as his main aim. Not, that is, unless they want to ask for money, or for forgiveness. I am not certain yet to whom I would choose to give either, though I suppose the question is now likely to remain academic. I have not made a will.

None of them is aware of this fact, and they must therefore be waiting, in their different ways, for the traditional denouement. At first, they were rather shy about discussing the matter in front of me but that has begun to change over the past few days. I'm starting to get a feel for what each of them hopes or expects to receive.

Well, I have disappointed most of them for years, and it would be churlish to stop now.

I must say, though, that their discussions are not yet candid enough to make me into a true fly on the wall. Rather, I am reminded of one night (it must have been 1947) when I was dining with Max. We were in an hotel restaurant in France, somewhere on the Cote d'Azur, and I really cannot remember if it was Nice or Cannes or Saint Tropez because we were so hungry for pleasure that we went to them all. Possibly it was Cap Ferrat.

We had a terrible, though very quiet, row over dinner, and Max left the table. Determined to indulge my taste for understated drama, I carried on eating alone. There were only two other diners in the room, and they occupied the table next to mine. They were Italian, and simply assumed that I could not understand them. Nonetheless, I could tell that they were perturbed by my presence. For half an hour at least, they affected nonchalance, discussing all manner of subjects as if privately; but they did not once talk about anything which they would only have discussed in private.

This is the uncomfortable compromise which my visitors feel compelled to adopt. They talk about me as if I were here, though they believe that I am not. It is really very frustrating. The only member of my entourage who would express her opinion without reserve will certainly not visit. As for the rest of them, I know what they think and for once I would like to hear them say it clearly. I have no desire now for dignity or respect: this feels like a time for truth.

It must be night-time, for I have heard no human sounds for a long while. At some point, a nurse will come in to check on me, though I am certain they have the ability to monitor my vital signs from an office somewhere, as if I were part of a transport network or a power station. When she arrives, she will check the machine, change me if I need it – that will be the first I know of it if I do – and she will also change the drips and tubes that keep me drugged and fed.

I know all of this only from what I hear, of course. Part of it is guesswork, resulting from a piecing together of clunkings and gurgles and rustlings and foldings. Part of it I know from changes in the apparent direction of sounds as I am moved. My hearing, like your own, is binaural. My brain, however, has become more acute at sorting and interpreting the three-dimensionality of sound, since this is the space in which I now exist.

My main guide to events is the nurse who tends me most frequently. She is called Sarah, and we have a deal, struck by her for us both, but entirely acceptable to me. She talks me through everything as if she knows I can hear. The weather, the state of my bedding, medications, appearance, even edited highlights from the news. She warns me in advance of my visitors' arrivals and afterwards tells me what they were wearing and whether or not she liked them. In return, I listen to her troubles and reminiscences. Sometimes when she has finished whatever task she is about she will sit by my bed talking, until suddenly she remembers some other obligation and hurries off. She is intelligent and kind and lonely. Why did I not understand the value of people like her until now? I would have considered her a worker ant, and left it at that. Much of the arrogance and stupidity of my life is becoming clear to me now.

Some time ago, Sarah did not come for a few days. Another nurse or nurses took over her duties, with a terrifying silence. I would hear the door open, footsteps, breathing but no words. Suddenly there would be an earthquake in the landscape of sound as I was moved. Elements of noise would swill around and in my disorientation I tried very hard to retreat further into myself until it was over. That was the hardest time for me. I could not prepare myself for my visitors at all. I was elated when Sarah returned, and returned to me the little power I have, which is advance warning of who will visit. I need to prepare my thoughts a little before they come.

At night, when I have heard nothing but my heartbeat or the wind for hours on end, I become confused. Often I am not certain whether I am awake or not, or even whether I ever sleep. It reminds me of a philosophy course I once took. Questioning the nature of reality seemed such a waste of time then, when I knew perfectly well what was real and what was not. Max, and the sun on my face as he drove me to Brighton. These were the real things. I could shut my eyes and my mind to everything else. The hardship of the post-war years, for example, did not become real to me until Max had gone and it became hard to come by certain luxuries. I am certain that I am not the only person who has ever exercised selective perception of reality; surely it is how everybody must live. It is a question that never bothered me until now.

Curiously, death itself poses me no concern: on the contrary it will be a relief when it comes. I am a Roman Catholic, have been for years, and have therefore never worried about that side of things. I am sorry for the bad things I have done in my life and I have said so in the right places and at the right times. A priest has already been brought to give me the last rites. I have been given absolution, and I do feel that I have been absolved. This was the deal I accepted long ago, when I converted. I have kept my side of the deal, and I have no doubt that God will keep his. I do not claim to be good, but I have always been honest. At least, I have always been honest since 1949.

Back to the *dramatis personae* that cluster around my bed. There is my brother Piers, of course. A man who has spent his entire life apologising for me – sometimes even denying our fraternity. Oh, the middle-class shame he has suffered! Though how anyone from a family as old and venerable as mine could have turned out to be as middle class as he, is a mystery. He is very ordinary, always has been, and now he wants my money. Ha!

When he visits with his vulgar wife 'Val' (I can't help but summon her from memory as mothball and cheap scent) and his oafish sons, they bring grapes. Grapes! Can you imagine the stupidity of the man? They sit and whisper, skirting around the subject of the will as if it were a whore they want to possess, but would not choose to be seen with. I do wish I were to be here when their disappointment strikes, but by definition I will not be.

But Piers and his dull brood are positively considerate when compared with Johnny. He is my middle 'friend', the one that came after Max. Consequently he is my age, which is seventy-five, though his devotions to the knife and various lotions and potions have ensured that he always looks ten years younger. What in God's name is the point of looking like a sixty-five-year-old rather than a seventy-five-year-old? Is the game still worth the candle when so little wick remains?

In any event, Johnny believes that I have willed him a tiny Picasso sketch that Max bought for me in Antibes when these things cost very little, though now its value has risen dramatically. Johnny has always coveted it, and has so many times said, 'You'll leave it to me, won't you, darling?' that I think he has convinced himself I will. The fool. But his salivatory response to the little patch of paper is so strong that he comes here at least twice a week to monitor his progress towards it. Sometimes he brings that vile little Moroccan, too, though he knows I have never been able to bear the sight of him.

Harry, my most recent 'friend', has been by far the worst of my visitors. I suppose I should have expected it, should have been suspicious of his apparent affection for someone thirty years his senior. He never explicitly claimed to be a gerontophile but I supposed it was either that or the money, and now I know which. Harry came here not two days ago with a twittering, effeminate man who sounded half his age and with whom he seems on more than merely friendly terms. They sat here for a whole hour discussing the steps involved in having me 'turned off'! Well, I have news for you, Harry. You have been turning me off for years.

This gallery of grotesques is entirely of my own making of course. Actually, that's not true – I chose my friends but not my family, so we can leave Piers and his lumpen offspring out of it. But the others? Yes, my own fault, through and through. The punishment I have designed for myself.

If only Max had lived... though of course, he would probably be dead by now, even if he had.

Max. I wonder if I'll see him soon? When one of these buffoons has me disconnected, or when the moment comes naturally. What would I say? What would *he* say? Could he possibly have forgiven me?

I think not. I think that only God has the power to forgive a crime of that magnitude.

Max. So handsome. So very, very handsome.

I had a thing for older men, or so I thought for a while after Max.

I was too young to join the fighting by a matter of days – I was sixteen years old when the war ended. Max was thirty-five when I first met him later that year. He was one of those incredibly glamorous creations of war – a wheeler dealer with contacts in the government, abroad, in business, everywhere. A Gatsbyesque figure in that no one quite knew where he was from or who his people were. But when a flower is that beautiful, lush, exotic, heady – when its colours are that bright – no one bothers to look at its roots. And so it was with Max. He was just Max, and that was all he needed to be.

Maureen, my twin sister, had seen him in the *Picture Post* before she met him. She was ready to fall in love – it was, after all, nearly her nineteenth birthday. And, when Father brought him to our Mayfair townhouse for dinner one evening, Maureen contrived to have us introduced.

I knew it at once. I could see the cogs turn in his head. He took one look at her, one look at me, and figured it all out. Max always was quick with sums.

They were married in under a year but Max and I had made love many, many times before he came close to intimacy with my sister. Marcus and Maureen, Maureen and Marcus. How he kept his moans discrete I will never know, but Maureen had no clue of what was going on. It was simply too delicious.

What could be more natural? The older husband takes a semi-paternal interest in his teenaged brother-in-law. When his young wife is heavily pregnant and he has to go to the South of France on business, of course he'll offer to take the young whippersnapper along for the ride. Show him the Continent. Play a bit of tennis. In those days, no one thought a thing of it – there was none of the prurient suspicion you see so much of these days. It was the perfect cover. What could be more natural?

Oh, Max, Max, Max. How long did you think it could last? What plans did you make for our future? Of course, you didn't know of my raging jealousies – of how I'd wished pins in the heart of my own father for showing Maureen more favour than me. Mother, dead in the Blitz, would have been more careful, but Father never could hide his heart. And neither could I.

I began to divide Max's attention more insistently – to want more gifts and treats, more time, more signs of his dedication. When the child was stillborn, and Maureen's womb with it, Max pledged to stop our liaison; but he could not. I was simply too tempting for him, and he knew it.

Sarah tells me that I have visitors now. Harry, again, and his atrocious little hairdresser of a friend. They are waiting outside, and Sarah says that she doesn't like the look of the younger one. He looks 'venal', she opines, and I trust her judgement.

After a little plumping and smoothing, she ushers them in.

'Hullo, Marcus. How are you feeling?' asks Harry. The fool.

I beep at him a few times, trying to slow my heart rate or at least to make it irregular, so as to excite his hopes. But the machine has a mind of its own and the sounds remain constant.

'Here, Kelvin, sit down. No, not there...'

I hear the scrape of a chair being pulled closer and then the rustle of bedclothes as Harry (at least I hope it's Harry and not the creature) sits beside me.

'Grape?'

'Nah.'

Silence, apart from the beep.

A few moments pass, then I hear a violent and uncovered sneeze from across the room.

'Bless you.'

There is a snuffle, followed by, 'What's the point? How long do we have to stay here for?'

'Now, now, Kelvin. He was my partner for ten years or more. It's only right. Besides, I want to keep an eye on how he's doing...'

'On whether he's any closer to pegging it, you mean.'

'Kelvin, that is disrespectful to both Marcus and myself. Please.'

'So how much d'y'reckon the house is worth, then?'

'This is not about the house.'

'How much.'

'This is not –'

'A million? More?'

'Rather more.'

Like foraging rats, shy at first, they have finally become brave enough to scamper after my leftovers in public.

There's a whistle, then the cheap one says, 'Why don't you just unplug him, then?

'I've told you. That would be manslaughter. We have to wait. There are wheels in motion – they're considering turning the life support off, but they insist that it's a matter for his next of kin. Besides, we have no idea what the will says.'

'But if he's brain dead and the family want their share of the money, why don't they just sign on the dotted and get it over with?'

'It's not as simple as that. There's a brother, who's been to visit a few times. He's all for turning everything off, even if it means risking me getting the house. But there's a sister too. The hospital won't agree to anything until she's been contacted. She lives in South Africa or something. Anyway, they're trying to get hold of her.'

I am pulled back from my memories by the conversation being held over my head. They are trying to contact Maureen!

Harry and Kelvin babble on for a short while until Sarah comes and bustles them out.

'Tried to get a consent form the other day, he did,' she informs me.

'Partners' rights or something. Hospital legal wouldn't have any, though. Damn cheek. Don't you worry, Mr Sanderson, I'll keep him away from the plug.'

It is night now, and I'm drifting through the past again. Now that my physical life is so attenuated, it seems that my only real existence is in memory. But there is one year in which I don't exist, because it is a year I cannot visit.

1949... the year I cannot make myself remember.

But 1948 is clear, as clear as spring water. 1948 was they year in which I had everything I wanted, in which I forced Max to give more than he had to give. It was a triumph of manipulation, to get Maureen out of the way and me ensconced in her place, all the while appearing to be the concerned brother. Her terrible depression after the stillbirth had to be treated after all, and Switzerland was the best place for it, even though it was so far away from home.

And so for this one year Max and I lived almost as man and wife. We lodged, ate and slept together. We travelled, entertained and were entertained and everybody thought, how wonderful of Marcus to keep Max company while poor Maureen is... being... is taking a... 'cure'.

And so for a while I had the life I wanted. And, most importantly, I had it at Maureen's expense. The fact that Max was so uncomfortable, so guilty, only made things more exciting for me. I loved him, of course, but at the time that was not the point. Owning him was the point, and own him I did, eventually to the point of blackmail.

Morning. Sarah is changing me, and I wonder what she must think of my shrivelled and soiled sexual organs. Can she imagine that the wrinkled bottom she has to wipe was once a peach so sweet that a man was willing to throw himself away for it?

I am sure that she imagines no such thing.

A while later and without warning from Sarah, Johnny arrives.

It was when I first took up with Johnny that I came to understand that I did not have a 'thing' for older men. Rather, I liked my men to be around thirty-five, which was the age that Max was when I first met him and the age my father was when I was a toddler. The psychology is clear.

When Johnny reached forty-five, I left him and eventually found Harry, who again was thirty-five at the time. Johnny never forgave me, but he wants that damned Picasso so he's still hanging around. How sweet, he's often said, that we've been able to remain such close friends. Ha!

'Good morning Marcus. It's Johnny.'

Bully for you. Now get lost.

But, of course, he won't go for a while. He has to drivel on. Talking to a patient in a coma is second nature to him, since that is the state into which he habitually drives his conversational partners. How did I ever, ever stay with him for so long? Just listening to him makes me want to pull the bloody plug out with my own teeth. His rheumatism. What the chancellor has done to pensions. The size of his gas bill. I swear I can feel my blood pressure rising.

I can feel my blood pressure rising! The machine has started to beep faster, and to emit a peculiar whine, as if trying to drown out my fool of a visitor.

Within moments, Sarah is ejecting him from the room and 'there there-ing' me until my vital signs return to normal.

'I didn't like him either,' she says. 'He looks shifty. And I'll tell Doctor about this. I have a hunch that you're in there, somewhere. That you're listening.'

I hear nothing more of this for what I estimate to be a period of two or three days, when Piers next visits.

'But Val,' he drones. 'The doctor insists it was just random. No connection to the stimulus of having a visitor. The tests were one hundred percent conclusive.'

'I don't care, Piers. If there's a chance they're wrong, it would be terrible to turn him off. And it's not as if we need the money.'

'Of course we need the bloody money. We always need the money. Do you think shoes like that grow on trees? What about the Jacuzzi bath? What about Mallorca?'

I lie here – transformed into a pair of shoes, a suburban bathroom fitting and somewhere in the sun. Finally I know my worth.

They moan on at each other for a while, and then I hear the one thing I never thought to hear.

'Still, it'll all be over tomorrow. Maureen'll have been and, assuming she signs, they'll... do it. Soon.'

So, the Last Act is upon me. If Maureen is to visit me, I must visit 1949 in preparation.

It is night again, and I am alone with my heart. The journey begins.

Maureen has made something of a recovery. The Swiss clinic are confident that as long as she 'takes it slowly', she can return to her home and husband. But I will not be displaced, usurped, banished by the whim of her fickle mental health; it is time for me to play my hand.

I suggest that Maureen should stage her recovery by spending a quiet summer with a companion at Cove House. She always loved it there as a child, I whine. The sea air will do her good and, besides, it would be best not to throw her into the whirl of the season. I know her – she is my twin, after all.

My plan is intended to establish Maureen as a permanent invalid, like one of those shadowy members of the royal family that one hears of but never sees. If that fails, at least I will have another few months with Max, another string of weeks in which to burrow deeper into his psyche. Or am I lying to myself now? Was there no real plan, merely a desperate playing for time?

Max seizes on the idea, but not in the way I had hoped. He persuades Father to close the London house and remove himself, chubby little Piers, Cook and Mr and Mrs Stour to Dorset. Maureen will have her family about her. And as for me?
I am handed tickets and an itinerary. Europe, the grand tour.

I rip up this dry, papery handful of rejection in a fury. I will not be elbowed aside. Rather, after an appeal to Father, I am myself established at Cove House. What could be better for Maureen than to have as her companion a mirror image of herself, gay and carefree? Someone to remind her of the fun she used to have?

Max is furious and threatens to intervene but I warn him not to. I don't exactly threaten him – not exactly – but that is the implication. The nature of the threat itself is not mentioned and neither, in Max's case, is it understood. He thinks I intend to reveal our little secret discreetly, to Father or perhaps to Maureen. How little he can have observed my ways!

Maureen is delivered to Cove House, wrapped like an egg. She is fragile and brittle and the dull, absent glint in her eye convinces me that some fundamental change has occurred. She smiles a lot and is taken for walks. She eats what is put in front of her, nods when addressed, makes thin conversation; but the very light of her seems to have gone. Whatever shared spirit or soul we had has been extinguished.

Part of me is distressed to discover this – one is never as close to another human being as one is to a twin, however much competition that closeness may engender – but part of me is triumphant. There is now only one me.

After a few days of *froideur*, I imagine that Max and I will return to our habitual ways. We will have to be careful of course – Father and the servants are around and Piers is always exploring. But it is a large house and there are miles of cliff and woodland in which to get lost. Max, however, has different plans. He tries to treat me like a brother-in-law. I become petulant.

It would be tedious and embarrassing to detail my tantrums and sulks, my pleadings and attempts at seduction. Besides, I have repented of them all. I was just a boy, not twenty-one years old, playing at adult love without realising that adult love is dry, and that young love is the spark.

Days turn into weeks and still Max remains resolute. Often he is away, tending to his business affairs, and each time he returns he seems a little more distracted, more focused on his invalid wife and more distant from me. Whatever threats I make are ignored – whoever would listen to the hysterical claims of a chap when that chap's twin sister has already displayed such mental fragility? That seems to be his implication. And Max is a gambler by nature. He is at home with risk.

August is hot, and night after night there are violent storms which seem to suck the electrons out of the wires and switches and systems designed to tame them, so that we live much of the time without power.

Oh... oh! I am lost now. Lost in time, which is the only space left to me. Lost in the heat and the darkness of this memory. I am beginning to feel that I must not go further, or I will lose all chance of finding my way back. There is so much of this that Maureen never knew – that no one apart from my confessor has ever known. Perhaps it is best to leave it buried? For when my sister visits me tomorrow, I will have no means of confessing it to her. Nor would I, even if I could. I would be too ashamed.

But I was shameless then, and it is this memory that drags me back, forces me to observe myself.

The boy, watched only by a mute elderly ghost from the future, creeps down a moonlit passageway. He places his hand on a brass doorknob and turns it soundlessly, entering the room and closing the door so quietly behind him that even he cannot hear the click of the latch.

On the bed in front of him, drenched in a waterfall of sweat and silver light, lies an older man. The sheets have been kicked from him in the heat. He is tall, tanned, muscled. His limbs glisten like veins of mineral in a cave. Through the window, the gentle sea whispers, 'Ahh, shh, mmm...'

The man's penis is loose and heavy, lolling, waiting for the shadow of youth to creep over it, waiting for the feather-light tongue to descend in silence, waiting for those longed-for lips to perform their miracle of resurrection.

The stiffening is slow, powerful, steady; and so are the lips. Soon a silent rhythm is established and, soon after that, a hot torrent gushes and a gentle moan escapes. 'Maureen, oh... Maureen...'

But the man does not wake – or rather, does not wake enough to open his eyes and see a cunning shadow move back towards the door.

Before leaving the room, the boy takes one last look at the figure on the bed. The sleeping, sweating man has moved a little now, has shuffled an inch nearer the white statue that lies next to him, his young wife, lost in the sleeping-draft her doctor has provided.

Over kedgeree, Marcus fixes and holds Max with an unambiguous gaze. Max blanches, recollects, works it out.

With this seduction, the affair starts again. Max is too full of longing to resist, is too deprived, by Maureen's illness, of every kind of congress. But he is very, very careful. The only place he will make love is in a cave on an island, when he is quite sure that no other boats have made their way to it. And his lovemaking is rougher now, more urgent, the tenderness gone, wordless and resentful. Affection has deserted him and he fucks as if he is punishing them both. So when Marcus suggests to him that Maureen be sent away again, that the two men resume their bachelor life in London at the end of the summer, Max does not reply. After all, the summer is almost over and things will surely take their course. He shrugs off the hints of blackmail until they become more than hints, and then he ignores them. He is at home with risk, and has no sympathy for the hysterical.

It is the last weekend of the summer. On Monday, while the servants close the house up, the invalid and her family will be driven back to London.

Marcus arranges one last tryst. They will row there separately, each with a little food or wine and meet on the far, sea-facing side of the island where the mouth of the cave lies waiting.

After Max has set off, Marcus persuades his father and his sister to join him on the island for a picnic. They will surprise Max, who has already gone there with the intention of reading quietly for a few hours. Piers can stay with Mrs Stour, and Mr Stour can ferry father and daughter out together in time for lunch, when Marcus has already got a fire going on the beach on the far side of the island, with its lovely view of the sea.

But, when their skiff sets them down on the beach, there is no fire. They arrive in time to see Marcus run screaming from the cave, blood and semen spattered across his naked rump, shouting 'No, no, how could you? I am not Maureen. I am not Maureen.'

The longed-for revenge has been enacted.

Days later, with Max released on bail, he tries to see his wife but is turned from her door. That night, his house catches fire – how, no one ever discovers – and by the time the blaze is brought under control his remains are charred to such an extent that he can be identified only by his wedding ring. His manservant later reports that Max spent the evening in his library, smoking cigars and drinking heavily.

Maureen returns to her clinic. When her father dies some months later ('of shame'), she appears briefly, veiled in black, at the graveside. Then she vanishes.

It is daylight now. Sarah has talked me through my morning routine. I am terrified.

When will Maureen come? I cannot understand why she wants to visit at all – she has not responded to even one of my letters or cards in more than fifty years and she has only spoken to Piers through the family solicitors. Perhaps, like me, she wants to face the past. We are twins, two stamps from the same die, so perhaps it was always meant that we would have to do this together.

Maureen does not arrive until the late afternoon. Sarah announces her, leads her into the room, deposits her by the bed, leaves. I am terrified still, and my terror does not diminish as the silence lengthens, punctuated only by my electrical heart.

Is she touching me? Her hand folded over mine, or placed on my brow? I have heard no rustle of clothing to indicate that she has extended an arm, but then she always could move silently. Like me.

Then she begins to weep and I think that I cannot bear it, cannot bear what I have done to her. I would give my soul, now, to be able to comfort her.

But I am mistaken. What sounds like crying is in fact a quiet chuckle. Finally, she speaks.

'Quite the vegetable now, aren't we, Marcus? A stroke, I hear. Oh, dear. How awful for you. Brain-dead, they say. And they want to know if I'll agree to have you switched off. Mmm. I'm just not sure.'

Maureen laughs again. I am chilled. It is my voice, my laugh, the coldest one I reserve for bitter irony. My God! I had forgotten that we shared this same cruelty.

'Let's have a little chat first, shall we?' she continues. 'See how I feel afterwards? Yes! Yes, I do think that's the best idea.'

She pauses for a while, listening to my heart monitor, tapping her finger in time with it.

'And now we'll find out if you really are brain-dead. I'm going to share a few little secrets with you, Marcus. See if you respond.'

She laughs again, and then I hear her cross the room. The beeping of my machine grows louder and I suppose that she has found the volume control. She has turned my life support machine into a lie detector.

'Now. Where should I begin...?'

It doesn't take her long to decide.

'I knew, of course. From quite early on. Certainly before Max and I were married. I smelt your nasty cologne on him, saw the guilt in his eyes.'

I listen for the beep, frantically trying to control it. I do not want her to know that I can hear this.

'I didn't say anything,' she continues. 'That would not have suited my purposes. I needed to be married, to get away from home and from your suffocating presence.

'It was a pity about the child, in a way, but I'm not really the maternal type. Besides, it gave me an excuse to leave you and Max alone together. I had the most wonderful time in Switzerland. Spent very little time at the clinic, of course. They were most accommodating!

'And my performance at Cove House was really rather wonderful, don't you think? Doped and docile. But my God, was I laughing inside! Sometimes I had to go to the laundry cupboard to let it out!

'Poor Max. Trying to be faithful. And, talking of laughter, you have no idea how difficult it was to keep myself from giggling that night you paid your ridiculous visit to our bedroom. I didn't dare open my eyes unless you saw. All I could hear was sighing and slurping and Max moaning my name. *My* name! Ha!

'The next day, I told him I'd seen it. Forced him to admit the whole thing – presented various other little bits of evidence I'd collected. He told me about your weedy attempt at blackmail. Oh, poor, poor Max, falling in with us! Finding himself blackmailed from two sides! The terrible twins!

'Business wasn't going well for Max at the time – he was far closer to broke than you ever knew – so when I, with far more intelligence than you, presented him with a form of blackmail that suited his needs, he accepted. Grudgingly of course, but he really had very little option. And all we had to do was to wait for you to strike.

'Are you with me now? Can you hear me, Marcus? Oh, I do hope so.'

I can hear her, but I am straining, whilst listening to every word she says, to control the beep. She must not know that I can hear her. She must not. I will not give her that.

'Your performance on the island was pathetic. What a little drama queen you were. What a silly little fairy. If Father and Mr Stour hadn't been so shocked, they'd have caught the smell of greasepaint. Cheap greasepaint. The smell that has pervaded the rest of your career, from what little I have heard.

'And did I mention that, in the meantime, Max had drastically increased his life insurance? In case anything should happen to him – to provide for his poor invalid wife!

'Of course, he hated the whole thing. But there was to be money at the end of it. Money he no longer had. Besides, he had no choice. And how I loved his well-deserved humiliation – what poetry it was, that piece of justice.'

The machine – and therefore by implication my heart – has begun to speed up! Oh my Lord! The difference is marginal, is very slight, and I hope that it is apparent only to me. But Maureen pauses, listens, then declares, 'Marcus! So you are there after all! How utterly wonderful! Shall I tell you the rest? Let's monitor your reaction – after all, it may help me to decide whether to have you switched off!

'Max and I found some Burke and Hare types. Shady characters, East-Enders. They provided the corpse. All Max had to do was pretend to get drunk, put his wedding ring on the finger and set the fire. Then he slipped away. Quite brilliant, don't you think? The arrangement was that he'd just disappear and that I'd wait a while before sending his share of the insurance to a bank in South America. I never did of course – and what could he do about it?

There is no doubt about it, the beep has increased in frequency quite dramatically. It is racing now, and I cannot control it. Max did not die! He may even still be alive, somewhere. I cannot bear it. Cannot bear to think that for all these years he has been somewhere, somewhere where I might have found him.

I am furious that Maureen knows I can hear her. She will take more pleasure in authorising my termination now, I am sure of it.

'Good,' she says, her finger tapping faster, matching the rhythm of my beeping heart. 'Now we have each other's attention.'

She pauses, in order to let my tension build.

'Your little machine is such a clever thing,' she eventually continues. 'So here's what I'll do. I'll call the nurse – the plump one that showed me in. She's already quite convinced that you're not as dead as the doctors say. Then I will express my firm conviction that, since you are a Catholic, it would be quite wrong to switch you off whilst there is any doubt.

'And I'll pay you a few more visits, Marcus. Oh yes. I'll stay in London for a few weeks – how I've missed the shops! – and I'll come and sit with you, try out a few ideas for your will. Shackleford & Hurtmore tell me that you haven't drawn one up. But I'll "find" one later on. I always could do your signature.

'So I'll be here, on and off, listening to your machine whilst I throw some ideas around. I'll ask that pathetic string of ex-lovers and hangers-on what they're hoping for if you ever die. Oh yes, I've met them already. How solicitous they've been! That will give me a good starting point. Then we'll see what your little beeping heart has to say.

'What a wonderful idea, to have an invalid to care for – just as you tended me all those years ago. I shall perform with equal diligence. And in a few weeks, or months, I may change my mind about just how brain-dead you are. I may or may not give you some warning, possibly even some false alarms! What fun. Another game of bluff! Just like the one you played with Max. The game of bluff that killed Father.'

There is a scrape and scuffle as Maureen stands, then heads towards the door.

A minute later, Sarah comes in.

'What a lovely woman,' she says. 'I knew she'd get through to you.

And do you know, she is absolutely beautiful. So well preserved. No one would know you and her were twins, you wrinkly old thing! Now come on, let's get you changed. It smells as if you had a little accident while she was here. The excitement, I expect.'

Tim Ashley

Collecting Remains
David Patrick Beavers

Collecting Remains
David Patrick Beavers

When the night is long and the spirit is low, he seeks solace and comfort in the chiaroscuro of surrounding shadows. A room, bright and cheery by daylight, can be a tomb at night. A fragile tomb where moonlight invades and thoughts are borne out of curiosity and fear. Solitude. Singleness. Aloneness. No more a part of the connected world, but an alien spirit free-floating through time and space – through memory, real or imagined. Solace isn't found. Comfort is evasive. So he looks for familiarity in the blue of black shadows. A chair. A lamp. A desk in the room. A window where it has always been. A window that shines as black as polished obsidian. A polished void. There is no moonlight beyond. Only lunar paleness, there in his room. The shadows take form. They move.

Some called him James. Some called him Latham. He lay in his bed, buried beneath a checkerboard comforter, acutely aware of every cell, every atom buzzing the insomniacs' song. A dull ache plagued both legs. His neck and shoulders – a mass of loose knots screaming to be unbound. He lay there in his bed, surrounded by the shadows in the room, watching these simple specters of matter, dark and diffuse – move slowly at first. Glittering parachutes of dandelion seeds alighting a breeze.

James Latham wanted to rise up from his bed. Wanted to stand naked in his room to let the ebb and flow of this moonlit matter wash away the fatigue in his body. Indolence, lethargy, something more than mere exhaustion kept him there on his back, watching the pale shadows move faster. Faster still. A whirlwind, whizzing all around him soundlessly, converging at the center of their immediate universe there before his bedroom door, until the blur of the blackest shadow held fast. A huge cell, growing.

Now James Latham needed to move. The sight of the shifting, inky form seized his lungs. He couldn't breathe. Could only feel. His tensing muscles. His heart beating rapidly. His coursing blood rushing inside his skull, beating his temples, rap-rap-rapping to break through a dense bone dam.

As James Latham bolted from his bed, the door exploded open with such severe force, the doorknob slammed through the wall. James Latham's naked form slammed against the window frame; his hands fumbled and banged up against the window sash. It would not budge.

"James! Please! You might break the glass!"

James Latham whipped around. There, in his doorway, he saw a young man in khakis and a plain, green shirt. The man stepped into the room and flicked on the light.

"You're naked, you know. Not wise when you're near a window." The strange man gently tugged the stuck door, freeing the knob from the wall. He removed a handkerchief from his back pocket, dusted the knob, then closed the door. He returned to the hole in the wall to inspect the damage. "Well," he said, "doesn't look too bad. I had thought about installing a doorstop there at the baseboard. Should've done that."

The man's calm demeanor, his mere presence, sent a bristling shiver down James Latham's spine. The man wiped his hands with the handkerchief, then returned it to his pocket. "Maybe I could affix a brass plate over the hole. Have to anchor it down to the studs, though." He looked directly at James Latham. "Think that would work?"

James Latham said nothing. His eyes fixed on the eyes of the intruder before him. The man returned James Latham's steady gaze. Finally he sighed a quiet, resolved sigh. He stepped a bit closer. James Latham backed himself against the wall, right at the window casement, wanting to hurl himself through the glass into the abyss of the dark void outside. The man stopped moving.

"Charlie? Remember, James? I'm Charlie. Charlie Fosdick."

James Latham felt his knees weaken. Felt himself slowly sliding down the wall to the floor. He never stopped staring at the eyes of the man.

"You're not Charlie," he said flatly as his seat hit the floor. He hugged his knees to his chest and shivered again.

"I am, James. I am."

James Latham remained in his spot, there beneath the window. Out of the corner of his eye, he watched the man who claimed to be Charlie go to the small closet. He slid one of the two narrow sliding doors open, picked through the few articles of clothing hanging within, then pulled out an old flannel bathrobe. This man posing as Charlie took a few hesitant steps closer, stopped, then proffered the robe to him.

"You're cold." The man's voice was soft. "Put this on."

James Latham sprang like a wild cat out for the kill. His prey's reflexes were just as swift. The man calling himself Charlie pounced forward, slamming into James Latham's sternum, sending him skidding and flying onto his back on the bed. James Latham hit the mattress hard. It slid to the side, crashing into the nightstand. The man was upon him, straddling his chest, pinning down his arms and shoulders with knees and hands.

James Latham let loose a primal scream as he bucked and thrashed to throw the man off. The man was strong. He held his ground. Held his captive down.

"Stop it! Just stop it!" he screamed into James Latham's ear.

James Latham suddenly ceased to move. The man atop him was panting red. Perspiration beaded on his forehead. He stared through the curtain of disheveled bangs into the eyes of his captor. He felt the heat of exhaustion exhaled from his lungs.

James Latham took a deep breath. He held it for a moment, then let it explode from within him. He laughed. Laughed to himself. Laughed at the man staring down at him. The man didn't laugh. Didn't move. James Latham stopped laughing.

"You're not Charlie," he said quietly. He sucked down another deep, deep breath. As he slowly exhaled, his entire body went limp. His head rolled to his right. He could see the clock on the rattled night-stand. The digital display read 4:44. He whispered the time.

"Yes, James. Four forty-four in the morning," Charlie whispered back.

James Latham felt his throat constrict. Felt the heat of unwanted tears fill his eyes. He stared past the clock. Stared at the wall. The words crept out of his mouth.

"Why are you keeping me here?"

The man, Charlie, released his grip. He eased himself off of James, then sat up beside him. "Where would you go, James?"

"Home."

Charlie eased the blankets up, covering James's nakedness. "And where is home?"

"I've told you! I've told you night after night!"

"Then tell me again."

"I live at eleven-thirteen Lincoln Street! In a town called Watsonville!"

"That was forty years ago, James. When you were a little boy." Charlie's voice was hoarse. Exhaustion was catching up with him.

"Where's Charlie? Charlie will tell you!" James pleaded.

Charlie abruptly gripped James Latham's face and drew the two eye to eye. "I'm Charlie! I'm fucking Charlie!"

James stared blankly at him. Charlie wanted to slap James. To slap him hard again and again. To knock memory back into the neuro-network of his brain. Charlie couldn't slap him, though. He just released his grip. He finger-combed the hair off James's face.

"Your hair's greasy," he whispered.

James Latham stared into the void that lay beyond the window glass. "Why am I here?"

"What do you remember, James?"

James Latham lay still. He strained his mind to recall. To remember where he had been, before he was here.

Charlie relaxed a bit and leaned against the headboard. "There was a rally. Outside of City Hall. Do you remember that?"

James Latham closed his eyes. He tried to remember. "A rally? What for?"

"Doesn't matter now," he said absently. "There were lots of people." He placed his right hand upon James Latham's chest. He could feel the pulsing heat within the man next to him.

A vague image flickered in James Latham's mind. "Lots of angry

34

people," he said.

The slight recollection gripped Charlie's attention. "Yes. Lots of angry people. Those for... Those against..."

James Latham could only hold onto tatters of images in his mind. Faces. Confusion. His head started to throb. "I'm tired..."

"The police came in droves. Others came in droves. Trash cans were set on fire. Cars were overturned. Bottles and rocks and anything not nailed or cemented down seemed to be flying like shrapnel."

James Latham again stared at the wall. "I'm tired," he groaned.

"You haven't slept much for weeks now."

"My head hurts..."

"Like it's going to explode." Charlie flexed his left hand. Stared for a moment at the glint of gold on his ring finger. A simple band picked up while on vacation in New Orleans. He let his hand drop into his lap.

"It wants out..."

"Tell me about 'it,' James."

"I can't..."

"Can you tell me about Charlie?"

A flicker of a smile played upon James Latham's lips. "Charlie?"

"You remember Charlie?"

"He made me laugh." James Latham turned toward Charlie, but stared at the door. "He... He liked me."

Charlie removed his hand from James Latham's chest, then slipped down on the bed to lie beside him. "What did Charlie look like?"

"He... He..." James Latham couldn't go on. He couldn't remember just then what Charlie looked like. He could never remember when this man who claimed to be Charlie came into the room. He turned away from the man, back toward the wall. "I want to go home."

Charlie raised himself up on his right elbow, persistent in talk. "Was Charlie at the rally?"

"Dunno..."

"Charlie was at that rally, James. At that protest. There with you when the people all erupted."

"Go away!" James Latham yelled at the wall.

"I can't go away."

James Latham shot to his feet, violently kicked away the covers, then pitched himself over the foot of the bed and slammed into the window casement again, screaming, "Leave me alone!" over and over and over again until his voice cracked. Exhausted, he sobbed quietly as he slid to the floor.

Charlie calmly came over and sat beside him. He gently eased James Latham into his arms, soothing him. When James Latham's tears ran dry and his breathing calmed, Charlie spoke again.

"When the riot broke out at City Hall, you and Charlie were caught in the thick of it. You grabbed Charlie by the arm and the two of you tried to get through the crowd. Reports later said there were only about five hundred people, but it seemed like millions at the time."

"No..." James Latham weakly protested. "I don't remember..."

"Some guy swung a broken bottle at you. It was made of clear glass. Had dirt and some part of a red label stuck to it. At that moment, all I could think of was someone's tire getting flattened by some drunk's trash and why didn't they outlaw glass liquor bottles? Well, anyway, you caught the guy's hand and somehow got his weapon from him, but, just as you did, he knocked you off balance and you fell back. Right into Charlie. The broken bottle slammed into his neck. Charlie didn't see it coming. Didn't really even feel it happen."

James Latham suddenly raged. He pushed himself hard, away from the man. "Liar!" he screamed. "You liar!"

"Charlie didn't die right away! He –"

James Latham pitched himself forward, his fists flying. "You bloody fucking liar! Charlie's not dead! Not dead!"

Charlie caught James Latham's arms and held them fast. He pushed James Latham back to the wall. "Before Charlie passed out, he saw someone swing a pipe – a stanchion from the street barricade – and smash it into your head, James! Your head!"

James Latham fought his way loose. He turned to the wall, palms plugging his ears.

"He smashed your head, James!"

James Latham whipped around and bolted to the door. "Get me

out of here!" He kicked and pounded and yanked at the knob, but it would not turn. The door would not open for him. "Let me out! Let me out!" He slammed himself against the door, again and again until his bruised body could do no more. He slumped to the ground.

"James..." Charlie crept closer to him. "When the riot ended and the angry people fell away, they came, collecting remains. Seven dead. Hundreds injured. You suffered a brain injury."

"Charlie..." James Latham whispered.

"I'm dead, James."

"No..."

"This is your home. This was our home. Your sister, Laura, sleeps soundly down the hall. She's been with you since the incident." James didn't respond. Charlie continued. "I wanted the marriage, James. I wanted us to fight the government. I was why we were there. But that's all changed. Now, I can't go unless you let me go."

"You're not Charlie! You're not!"

Charlie sighed again. He glanced at the window, then gazed at James Latham. "Let me go, James Latham. Let me go so that you can stop these visits night after night. Let me go so that you and I can move forward."

"No!"

Charlie walked to the window. "Dawn's breaking."

James Latham refused to look at Charlie.

"It's time, James." Charlie lingered for a moment, then walked through the window into the abyss.

"Don't go..." he whispered to himself as the sun bled in through the window.

A Triptych
Geo C Bourne

A Triptych
Geo C Bourne

1
Auntie's Tale

"Ah, there you are. No, I haven't been waiting long, but I ordered myself a coffee because I don't like just sitting here. It looks bad, even though they are not busy at the moment. I didn't see you coming of course, because I couldn't get a window table."

"Shall I get you another coffee?"

"No, dear, thank you. But you can get me one of those cream doughnuts."

"Really, do you mean that?"

"Yes of course, otherwise I would not have said it. Do you object?"

"No, not at all, but elderly aunts are not supposed to go in for things like cream doughnuts. A sponge finger or a small fairy cake would be more in character."

"Not my character, it wouldn't. Any case, get your coffee and things, I want to hear how my favourite nephew is doing."

The favourite nephew, Douglas by name, returned to the table with coffee and two cream doughnuts.

"Well, how is business?"

"You mean my firm's business?"

"Yes, naturally, unless you have some other business going on that I don't know about."

"As far as I know, it is much as usual. All I have to do is routine maintenance on what someone else has sold. We do have another machine here which I have to look after. So business must be fair enough. And you, dear Aunt, are looking quite well. Not that you don't usually. What have you been up to since I saw you three months ago?"

"Well now, let's see. I get up in the morning and I go to bed at night. And..."

"And you visit the travelling library on whatever day it comes to this neck of the woods. You are stalling. What juicy bit of scandal are you working up to?"

"Scandal, dear? A single woman of my age doesn't get involved in scandal in a little place like this. Not if she has any sense at all."

"Perhaps she doesn't. But she could notice someone else's involvements, no?"

"I do have another lodger."

"By 'another' do you mean more than one?"

"I mean a different one from the last one."

"Really! I find it difficult to keep up with your boy friends. I presume it is male. All the others seem to have been. Another student? How long are you likely to have this one?"

"Somewhere between five and ten months. He has ten months to do whatever it is he has to do, but hopes to take only half that. They all hope that. They never achieve it."

"How old is he? What does he look like? What's his name?"

"Trust you to ask that! I don't know how old he is but he is much too young for you. Or, to put it the other way around, you, Douglas my dear, are much too old for him. He has bright red hair, and his name, his first name –" she dropped her voice to a conspiratorial level –"I had an awful job to keep a straight face when he told me, is Rufus. I gather he often gets called 'Red' or 'Rusty', but he doesn't like that."

"Rufus, the red-headed reindeer. What does he do?"

"I will ignore what you could mean by that, and tell you only that he is an ethnographer or something, which I gather is some sort of geography. All I have ever seen any of them do is play with the computers they bring with them."

"Don't they ever go out?"

"Oh yes, they go out and interview people or something."

"They just use the granny flat for living in, they don't use it for interviewing?"

"True, though I suppose he could have said something like that."

"Who could have said something like what?"

"Rufus."

"Auntie, do get on with it. I'm all ears, but I don't have all afternoon."

"Well. He seems to be one of your friends."

"Oh, I don't think I know anybody called Rufus."

"I didn't mean in that sense. I mean generically."

"A poofter!"

"I'm glad it was you who used that word, not me, but yes."

"What makes you think that?"

"As I said, he does not like being called Rusty. He had a friend in one afternoon. I don't think they realised I knew he was there. I heard the friend ask him what his surname was. When Rufus told him there was shrieking girlish laughter. I think that will be a one-shot friendship."

"Auntie, just because his visitor has girlish laughter I don't think you should assume Rufus is gay. In any case, I thought you were supposed to be hard of hearing. You can hear when you want to."

"No, that is not true. It is just when I especially want to hear that I often can't. If there is no background noise I can hear as well as most other people, better than some."

"I still think you are jumping to conclusions."

"At least I had warning."

"Warning? Of what?"

"Two weeks ago I took Rufus in his early-morning tea and there were two of them. I don't mean two teas. There were two of them in the same bed. And, as you know, it is not a very large bed. And it was a hot night."

"A she?"

"No, another he. So, thinking quickly and hoping to appear plussed, if that is the opposite of nonplussed, I asked: 'Would your friend like a cup of tea or coffee?' They were quite asleep. And, both waking at the same moment, shot up, or as far as was possible in such a confined space and then, I suppose, properly waking up, shot down again. I, trying to look all calm and collected and not to burst out laughing – only grin like a Cheshire cat for, remember, the rent money is very useful – just waited for the answer. It is not the first time I have seen all of a man, even get it on the telly these days, but I think it is the first time I have seen a rusty one. Eventually the friend said, or rather muttered, that tea would be fine. So I went out and made him a cup. While I was pouring it I realised who he was. It was the vicar!"

"Auntie! The vicar is sixty if he is a day! Do you mean your lodger is a call-boy and the vicar was renting him?"

"No, you silly boy, Rufus pays his own rent, the vicar has nothing to do with it. At least not as far as I know. In any case, it was not the old vicar: it was the young one. We used to call them curates in my day, but they don't seem to like that now. What made you think the vicar was paying the rent?"

"Auntie Caroline dear, there is something you should learn. A call-boy is a, a, a sort of prostitute. The money one pays for such, erm, shall I say, things, is called in the vernacular 'rent'."

"Oh, well, I'm always willing to learn. To continue with my little bit of scandal. It seems they both had gone off to sleep unintentionally. It was by then broad daylight of course, and for him to be seen leaving my place, or indeed walking down the road at that time of the morning, would have caused more tongue-wagging than I felt I could cope with. So I put him in my car – Rufus has only a bike – and dropped him in the road behind the vicarage, from which he thought he could appear indoors without any trouble. He told me I was an amazing woman. I like to think that too. I purred to myself all morning. Still, I will be seventy next year and although young people think we oldies have never done anything, and don't understand anything, we have, and we do."

"I see. Well that was a very enthralling bit of gossip. If that's the assistant priest I think it is, he is rather cute. So you have got yourself a gay lodger! Have you told him about me?"

"Heavens no! I wouldn't do a thing like that. I would get a name in the village for tittle-tattle!"

Douglas paused with the last of his doughnut halfway to his mouth, sat smiling to himself for a moment but only allowed himself to comment, "I think I had better go and do some work. By the way, what *is* this Rusty's other name?"

"Ball."

II

Miss Fanshaw Entertains

Miss Caroline Fanshaw had been down to the shops and bought a selection of small cakes. She did very little baking these days and in any case had never been good at anything fancy. A good square meal, yes; fancy cakes, no.

It was Wednesday, and that morning she had answered the phone to find that she was listening to "the assistant priest", who had said that he would be visiting parishioners in her neighbourhood that afternoon and wondered if perhaps he might call on her; he realised that she was not a church attender but that perhaps provided a good reason for calling on her. She had the distinct impression all that had been said in one breath. She would not have been surprised if he had written it down and read it into the phone.

"I hope you don't think this too much of an intrusion, but I would be interested in learning a little of your – how can I put it – background?"

"I'm glad you didn't say 'history'," replied Miss Fanshaw. "My history is very long, gets longer every year, you know. It would take very many visits indeed to tell you my history."

"Well that situation would not be impossible. I expect, however, that you might find too many visits from a clergyman quote, Doing his Thing, unquote, boring and –"

"Do you class enquiring into backgrounds of elderly ladies as doing your thing?"

"In a way, yes. It seems to me, from my small acquaintance with your understanding of people discovered in, shall I say, unintended circumstances, but please don't quote me in public, that you (who never go to the church) might be more used to the church than some who do."

"Flattery will get you nowhere. And I can assure you of something else. If I find you tiring I shall tell you politely to stop coming."

"It would not be the first time I had been told that impolitely."

"Why? Were you so persistent?"

"No. At least I did not get the chance to be persistent. But that story would be telling tales out of school."

"I could tell you a tale out of school but I don't expect the same method would work with you."

"I don't think I should hear any tales like that."

"Ah, this one is a real tale about school. I was sent to a very high class girls' school in the South of England named Roedean. There young ladies were taught the classics. That was fifty years ago. I wonder if they still are. Now a few years ago, before I came here, I lived for a while in Auckland. I had the inevitable visit from two Mormons one afternoon and because I knew very few people I invited them in. They came every week after that until I got fed up with them. I was not interested in what they talked about. As far as I was concerned it was a lot of rubbish. Even more rubbishy than what I would hear in your church. But I couldn't get them to take the hints I gave them to stop coming. Then one week they were trying to persuade me that theirs was the only true translation of the Bible and handed me their Bible. When I looked at it I saw that it was in two columns, one in English and the other in Greek. Well, back in Roedean we had to learn the first chapter of John's Gospel in the Greek by heart and that was the place it was open at. I don't quite know what made me do it, perhaps it was unconscious hankering after schooldays again or something, but I started reciting the Greek. They took the book back, closed it, thanked me and left. Never to come back again."

"And do you read New Testament Greek?"

"Oh, no. Not now."

"I'm relieved to hear it, because I can't."

"That was just something I had learned by heart donkeys years ago and it has stayed with me. That happens with increasing age, they tell me."

"So you have not lived in this town all that long. I would not know that, of course, because I have only been the assistant priest here for about a year. I would be interested to hear why you came, apparently from England, to end up in this rather small backwater."

Caroline laughed quite openly at that. "Excuse my laughing. But I haven't, I think 'taken on board' is the expression you young people use, the idea that I have 'ended up' here, as you put it. It is not impossible that I may yet move on somewhere else. Old I may be, but dying, I hope not yet. To answer your question as to why here, the plain answer is that property prices here are within my reach. I have lived in this country for some years. I had a sister who married a New Zealander, an airman, just after the war. She moved out here with him after a while and a few years ago she was ill and I came out her to visit her. Not long after I had arrived her husband died. It was discovered that she had cancer. I decided to stay here to be with her. By the time she died I had found I liked the country and was working in a position with a company I liked which was supposed to be a temporary position The company did well and I stayed with them until I retired. Then I moved to Auckland but found it so expensive. In this town I have my little house, my garden and a spare room which I can let, which gives me a little pin money. I can get from here to Auckland occasionally to visit friends. So... was that what you wanted to know?"

"It certainly answers my question."

"Good, and now I want to know how a young fellow like you ends up in a place like this. I would have thought that one of the larger centres would have been more to your liking. But before you answer I will put the jug on. I presume tea would be fine."

The tea and cakes duly appeared on a tea trolley. They were served on run-of-the-mill china. The tea cosy was hand-knitted. No more was said until each had settled into the ritual of afternoon tea.

"Right," said Caroline, "your turn. What are you here? Is thin your first posting?"

"No, it's my second. I was first sent to a parish in Auckland."

"How many do you have, that is, how many times do they move you before you become a vicar-in-charge, or something."

"There is no fixed rule. It depends on all kinds of things. The age of the person, how well they get on with the priest they have worked under, how well they are liked by the parishioners."

"I suppose if they get on too well with the parishioners that could go against them."

He thought for a moment about that, then suddenly asked, with the uneaten half of a cake in his hand: "You mean if he gets on better with them than the priest-in-charge does, that would be a black mark against him?"

"No, that wasn't what I was thinking, but I can see what you mean. I was thinking if he was too well liked by one or more particular people, who his church might, shall we say, disapprove of."

"– Yes." He was still holding the piece of cake.

"So you were sent here because you were an embarrassment?"

After a pause. "Yes."

"And how many people here know that?"

"Two. You and Reverend Collins."

"That's the vicar?"

"Yes. Didn't you know?"

"No. Why should I? I never go near the church, and have no intention of doing so. I assume from your not mentioning him that the student who boards here doesn't know about Auckland."

"Oh Rufus. Yes, he does. It was he who was the person disapproved of. So I don't count him, he won't blow my cover, he is well aware of the risks."

Caroline sat looking at the young priest, her visitor. He sat looking at his feet. Then he slowly and hesitantly asked whether or not "the other morning", when she had been so understanding, was the first time she had met men "in that sort of situation".

She, not wishing to increase his embarrassment, permitted herself a slight smile as she replied: "Not quite like that, but I do have a gay nephew who I am very fond of."

Caroline stood up and started wheeling away the tea trolley. Her visitor also started to get up, as though to leave.

"Stay there. I haven't finished asking questions yet. Unless you have to be somewhere else. I just need a minute to think." She sat down again. "What would happen if it were found that you were... 'getting on well' with someone who was disapproved of, here?"

"I don't know. I would probably get thrown out."

"Would that matter to you?"

"Sometimes I think it wouldn't. Not to me. But I would have to disappear. My father would kill me."

"Metaphorically, I presume you mean?"

"No. When I was in college and I first told him about myself, he skidded a loaded pistol across the dining room table to me and said: 'Why don't you use this. It would solve all your problems and many of mine.'"

"Good God! You do take risks, don't you!"

"Yes, but you, I mean I, don't think about it at the time."

Later that evening Caroline Fanshaw could have been heard on the phone, if there had been anyone near to hear it.

"Yes, dear. No, Douglas, dear. I am quite well, thank you, but I have a problem. I had the young priest call on me this afternoon... No, dear, me this time. I wished he had called before. He is known. Yes, dear, by the church. It seems it is not the first time, that's why he has been sent here. If it happens again there would be terrible trouble with his family, real trouble, and I know you would not want that... How is that my problem? Well I don't want to, as I think you say, 'blow him'... Why are you laughing? Oh, that's not the right word. What's wrong? Stop laughing. I can't hear while you are laughing, and this is serious. Oh. 'Out' him. That is the right word. Well, whatever. So promise me you will not say anything about what I told you to anyone. Promise?"

III

Miss Fanshaw Remembers

Archie Cox was the senior partner of Cox, Wishbourne and Keane. The firm had been founded by his father, who, with Messrs Wishbourne and Keane, had long since retired to his eternal rest. The firm now consisted of a number of young to middle-aged people of both sexes, a situation his father would not have comprehended, let alone condoned. They mostly concerned themselves with the legal affairs of many of the businesses, small and large, that had grown up in the town during the last fifty years. Archie was supposed to be semi-retired. He visited the offices on more or less regular occasions. He attended some of the more important meetings with long-established clients and took on some small work, which prevented interrupting the schedules of the other staff. Some of the younger solicitors were known to remark that, since the firm was still in his name, they had to let him come in occasionally. In fact they had some affection for him and genuine respect. That was especially true of those who were grateful for his considerable memory of events long past, when he had saved them from embarrassment by advising them, "Ah, but I think if you look up so and so you will find the situation agreed to was not quite as clear-cut as is here stated", and things like that.

So it was he to whom the receptionist referred when Miss Fanshaw called into the office to make an appointment to ask advice on a matter, the nature of which she did not state.

"Is that the Miss Fanshaw who we advised over a house purchase?"

After a few seconds' delay, the receptionist confirmed that it was.

"Bring her in to me."

After greetings and courtesies, he had established that all was well in the house she had purchased, no problems there.

"Another matter has arisen, on which I thought I might save myself, and other people, trouble, if I sought professional advice."

Archie, being of the old school, sat behind his desk, with his chair pushed back a little as though to remove himself from the several papers neatly placed on its top and, with his elbows on the arms of his chair, had his fingertips together in front of his chest. He nodded.

"My nephew has a problem trying to obtain a British passport. He has a New Zealand passport. That was no great problem, though it took rather longer than usual as there were a certain number of formalities that had to be rechecked. He has been asked by the firm he works for if he would go to England and, with others, represent them in some way. If he has a British passport that would allow him to travel in Europe much more easily."

"He is British?"

"He was born in London."

"When?"

"1945."

"Ah. Wartime. And the problem is he does not have the requested documentation?"

"That is right."

"Ah. How do you think we can help you?"

"I thought perhaps that if I were to explain the circumstances to you, that you may know how to persuade the Wellington British High Commission, or maybe London Passport Office, that Douglas is who he says he is."

Archie parted his hands and took a pen and paper from his desk. "Tell me what you know. I may need to take notes and we will look at where that gets us. I assume that you have come to us because your nephew Douglas does not remember his birth and you do. Have you told him you were thinking of seeking advice?"

"Oh, yes. In fact he has rather pushed me to do so. I hesitated to get involved. But his people, my sister Annie and her husband Roger, are both dead. I am the only one left who knows the story."

There was a pause. Archie placed his fingertips together again. This time his elbows were resting on the desk. He had time to wait. And this Miss Fanshaw was obviously an educated woman and could be safely left to tell the story without too much prompting or guiding back to the point. "You wondered about getting involved?"

"Mr Cox. It was two generations ago. The waters then were very muddy. Looking back to them now, they seem no cleaner."

"Ah. Douglas was truly born in London. How do you know?"

"I was there. I will never forget that day as long as I live. He was born in the basement of 115 Leighton Road, Kentish Town. In the back room, if that makes any difference."

Archie's face did not move. He knew when a witness was telling the truth.

"My sister and I were visiting a friend there. It was expected that the child would be born in Russell Square, where we both had rooms. It was arranged that the birth would be attended by a student doctor from University College Hospital. That was the system in those days. One didn't go into hospital. It was expected in a week or two. But Douglas decided otherwise. We were having a cup of tea. I have no clear idea of who did what. There was no doctor of course. But that was not unusual in a working-class district. But there were several neighbours. I saw a policeman. It was he who fetched a midwife from up the road somewhere. But it was all over by the time she arrived. I remember she threw everybody out. Then we had the problem of getting back to Russell Square. She arranged for Annie and me, and the baby, of course, to stay in a house round the corner by a big church for a few days."

"Who issued the birth certificate?"

"The midwife gave us a note. That should have been taken within fourteen days to the registry office and a certificate of registration issued. I suppose someone must have done that. But that is what cannot be traced."

"Ah. Where was the father? Would he have done that?"

"Annie's husband, Neil, was RNZAF and was on a ship somewhere between England and the Far East at that time. He didn't find out about all that until much later. The Blitz was over before then, but chaos was pretty much the order of the day. Offices were moved round from building to building. There was much of that sort of thing, and the central registry known as Somerset House was moved for safekeeping. Something must have been recorded, because the child had an identity card and ration book, which could not have been obtained without. The next relevant happening was that Neil was demobbed in New Zealand and Annie eventually was allowed to bring the child out here. Shipping was in very short supply in those days. Douglas would have been nearly three by then. He travelled on Annie's passport, and was given a travel document for the shipping line. That he still has. It is the only thing he does have. He has sent a photocopy to the High Commission in Wellington. They want the original. Douglas has said he will take it there but not send it. It is too precious. I have a copy here."

"And can I take it that Neil is not the one you referred to as 'his people' who have died?"

"No, that is true. Neill and Annie broke up fairly quickly. Usual story. Wartime marriage; three years apart. Annie met Roger and had a very successful marriage, until Roger died some years back. Then Annie died. It was her becoming ill that decided me to come out here to live."

"You have certainly satisfied me that Douglas was born in England. You and your sister were, presumably, since you have not said otherwise, born in Britain. Is there documentary evidence for that?"

"Yes. I have my registration of birth and Douglas has Annie's. We also have the approximate dates and places of birth of my parents. Both were in England. Douglas has a photocopy of their wedding certificate. I have the original. It was found in Annie's belongings. She was older than I. There has to be some explaining done, whenever they have been produced in New Zealand, but not in England."

Archie did not ask why. He asked: "You have a British passport?"

"Yes. Though it has expired. I also have a new Zealand one. I am a new Zealand citizen."

"Do the names agree?"

"No."

"Ah. I wondered. And how do you spell your family name in England?"

"Featherstonehaugh."

"Ah. I thought maybe."

Archie made a note. Then put his fingers together again: "So we have established that your sister and your parents were English. I noticed, though I never made a written note, that you never actually said his father was a New Zealander. Was he?"

"Yes."

"So the father can be dismissed from our suit. Not being British, he does not help our case. Now I have also made a written note," here he smiled ever so slightly and leaned ever so little towards Miss Fanshaw, "that you have referred, when a mother has been mentioned, to Annie. But you have never said she was his mother. Was she?"

"No."

"Who was?"

"Is."

"Is? She is still alive?"

"Mr Cox. When you become a parent it is a lifelong relationship. You may disown your child. You may neglect it. You may forget it. You may kill it. But you will still be the parent of that child."

"Miss Fanshaw, I have heard that sentiment several times, but rarely expressed so eloquently. Therefore I don't think I need to ask you who she is. But I suppose I should. You?"

"Yes."

"Ah, now. This travel permit is for a Douglas Neil Hopkins. So at that time your sister was Mrs Anne, or Annie, Hopkins? What was Douglas's father's name?"

"Hopkins. Douglas Hopkins."

"Brothers?"

"Yes. They were in the Air Force together. Douglas was killed in a flying accident. Just a pure accident in bad weather. Nobody's fault. It still seems a shame. Even after all this time. He had been through his tour of ops. He was the younger."

"And he was killed even before he knew he had a son?"

"Yes. It was all arranged by mail between him, Neil and Annie, that they would take my baby and bring it up as theirs."

"And presumably arranged with you as well."

"I had no choice, Mr Cox. I had no choice. That was not what my parents wanted. I was still Miss Featherstonehaugh, you see. Douglas and I were to marry after we knew that a child was on the way. The idea had been mooted, but my parents were against it. And I was underage, as the law then was. I needed their permission. As soon as a child was due, that was the end as far as my father was concerned. Of my mother's private views I have no knowledge. Her public views were not permitted to vary from those of her husband. They wanted the child to be put into the Waifs and Strays Home in Dulwich, south London. My father paid for the confinement to take place in Russell Square. After that neither my mother nor he ever spoke to nor had any contact with me again. Neil said no way was his dead brother's child going to be brought up in a Home, with a capital aitch, if that could be avoided. My parents had no direct contact with him and little with Annie as long as they were together. My father was a pillar of his church, Methodist, financially comfortably off. He was a lithographer. Sent us to good schools, we both went to Roedean. And to the day they died, they both bewailed that they had no grandchildren."

"None?"

"Annie knew she would never have any. There had been some sort of illness when she was a girl and children were not a possibility. There was no secret about that."

"Ah." And after a pause: "Ah. Now. Let's see. We have Douglas's full name. I take it that it was never changed to match his stepfather's."

"Never."

"I have your statement as to the place of birth. You were a witness. That is all that needs to be said. It is quite true. We have documentation as to his grandparents on his mother's side. All those people being English. We have documentation as to his arriving in this country. Indeed that was sufficient for this country's authorities to issue a passport, which is extant. I think if I write a letter to the British High Commission, stating those points, in support of Douglas's application, that should satisfy their queries. If he is then granted a British passport, it would be well to warn him that, even though it eases his travel round Europe, he would be very unwise to travel back to this country on it. He might find the immigration people in Auckland wouldn't let him in. They can be every bit as officious as the English. We will have to make a small charge for this service. But it is a simple matter, and I will make it as small as possible."

"Oh. Yes, that is quite all right."

"Tell me, Miss Fanshaw, why have you not shared all that with Douglas?"

"When Annie and Roger were alive, it was not my business to do so. And in any case most of his life we have lived on opposite sides of the globe. After Annie died there did not seem any point. He looked on them as his mother and stepfather, and loved them and they him. He and I get on very well. He comes to see me when he can. If I needed him, he would only be a phone call away, as the phone advert says. It could not improve the situation for him to know. So why tell him now?"

"Will he not have children?"

"Mr Cox, he is approaching middle age. He has never been the marrying kind."

Archie nodded as he rose and escorted his client to the front door of the building, in the manner they were both used to from a former age. When back in his own office, as he closed the door he permitted himself to remark to his desk, "So that is the woman my grandson's boyfriend thinks is 'an amazing woman'. I am inclined to agree with him. But I still think it is a pity Douglas does not know he is her son and not her nephew."

A Small Triumph
Perry Brass

A Small Triumph

Perry Brass

At five o'clock on a glum, wet Thursday in mid-October, Peter Brogan, a thirty-eight-year-old, not very successful writer who lived in a run-down, mostly rent-controlled building in Chelsea, started out toward the old McBurney YMCA on West Twenty-Third Street.

Rain had washed the sidewalks clean and a setting sun warmly outlined every building as he walked east. He was happy for a change after handing in a big feature piece ("Downtown Cabaret Surfaces Once More"; sidebars plus photos) for the *Village Eye*, a trendy paper that listed him as a "Contributing Editor," thus giving him some recognition among New York's always hungry writers. As he walked, he saw currents of silver light hitting the old buildings and felt once more that magnetism in New York's air that charged and excited its army of movers, shakers, con men, and creators, always drawn to the city, who in some form found their dreams there.

At the Y, Brogan, in gym shorts and a T-shirt that he could never get "spanking" white no matter how much bleach he spanked into it, rolled himself out for ten minutes in a downstairs stretch room, then climbed up to the fifth-floor Nautilus room where long lines of buffed, impatient body-builders waited in front of each machine. Peter's body resisted muscledom the way his T-shirts resisted bleach, but he could admire the pumped-up, plastic bodies of the mostly younger Nautilus addicts around him.

He waited his turn at a punishing shoulder machine, then at one that imprisoned his forearms and exerted an elephant's pressure on his wrists. He eased off the machine's seat, then waited in front of a third that was geared towards thighs and upper legs. There he noticed, already on the machine, facing away from him, this beautiful expanse of a broad, flat back on a short young man. The back was met by two nice shoulders, and then a pair of firm, silky-smooth upper arms.

The back was covered by a pristinely white T-shirt. Peter was close enough to sniff its freshly bleached whiteness. Tapering smoothly, the shirt disappeared into a pair of loose, lightly faded blue gym shorts; these in turn revealed the calves of two dark, downy but muscular legs. The boy (he had to be a boy, certainly not a man) had thick, black, short hair, cut straight across at the back of his neck, which was endearingly thick and which seemed slightly out of proportion to his head.

The backs of the boy's ears appeared like innocent little pink seashells, fairly translucent in the bright light of the gym. Peter wondered what his face looked like. It was a natural curiosity, but it felt, to Peter, easily open to suspicion, now that any curiosity about anyone else seemed to be exposed painfully to labeling.

"We havin' problems?" a bull-necked man behind Peter grunted. With a growing line for the machine's use, its weights and gizmos were not speeding up and down, as the boy sat hesitating. Starting to sound like a New York driver sitting on his horn, the big geek muttered loudly to himself about idiots not being allowed in "de Naut room." The machine, with its gear chains, foot plates, arm rests, and safety warnings printed in several languages, was actually fairly complicated.

"Are you all right?" Peter asked.

The boy in a light, nervous voice that Brogan would have expected from a twelve-year-old, answered : "I'm not sure."

"This ain't a trainin' session!" the guy behind Peter fumed. "If you don't know what'cha doin', get the hell—"

Then the boy did that: he got up, hurrying out of the room before Peter could look at him. Peter felt terrible: the kid must have felt miserably ashamed sitting there, unsure how to spoonfeed his body through the Nautilus's gears. Suddenly it occurred to Peter that he might have been blind, since there was a home for the blind close by and several of its residents used the gym. The thought of the kid's possible blindness upset Peter, and that some Cyclopean bully had made a stink about the delay and Brogan had said nothing, not even a word to support the boy, pained him.

Peter closed his eyes for a moment, trying to empathize. He stumbled out of the line, tripped on a barbell, and then his eyes snapped back open: the world of the blind was dangerous. Then, at the door, he closed them again and stood there. Suddenly a man got so close to him that he could feel his breath on his face, producing a sensual charge he'd never felt with his eyes open in the dismal atmosphere of the gym.

"Hi, Peter. Headache?"

He re-opened his eyes directly on Arnold, a tall, skinny-legged, thirty-two-year-old fellow writer who was so plain-looking that he reminded Peter of a boiled chicken. Arnold, always in the middle of huge things that never panned out—a simply fabulous new boyfriend, agent, or editor at Knopf who was crazy about him. Peter answered he was just resting, and Arnold started bragging about his new novel and new agent. A new editor, at Random House this time, was crazy about it, too. Everything about Arnold was always new, hyped, and huge. He was round-shouldered but Peter was aware, like a lot of other people, that Arnold did have a tremendous dick. But even that didn't help him. Secretly, Peter referred to it as Arnold's "boiled chicken dick," since it was on display so often in the steam of the showers. Peter smiled, then walked away, ready for a shower himself.

The shower room downstairs was crowded and silent, with men eyeing each other while they mushed soap through their crotches and armpits. He waited for a free shower head, then turned on the water as warm as he could get it. The spray released some of his Nautilus-knotted muscles as he turned his face to the wall, closing his eyes again. Darkness. Warm water. No one there but Peter—and the blind boy from the weight machines. He started to massage the boy's beautiful back, suddenly kissing the back of his neck.

But where *was* he?

Peter became aroused by the warm, almost palpable aura of the blind boy. Luckily, the showers had emptied, but were refilled a few minutes later when guys came back in in groups. "Over here!" a man's deep drawl called from the other end of the room. "Shower time!" Peter looked over to his left, and there, six shower heads away, were two naked figures, except that one, obviously older, had a towel draped around his neck. He was taller, in good shape, slightly thick-waisted but with no paunch. A mat of graying hair rose from his upper chest to his throat. The top of his head was bald but surrounded by ring of black hair. "I'm going to get the soap," he said. "Stay here, okay?"

The boy, still facing away from Peter, approached a shower and began to turn it on. Peter instantly recognized that broad back and could not keep his eyes off the lovely round forms of the boy's ass and muscular legs. He was having problems again, this time with the shower knobs, which were often stuck or reversed so that a hissing stream of hot water jumped out of the cold knob. Peter approached him. "Can I help?"

"Thank you," the same light voice replied. He turned around and Peter saw that the boy was not blind, but had Down's Syndrome.

He smiled at Peter with a face that was small, unguarded, and serene. Peter tried to look back at him without staring, but with a similarly open expression. This was difficult because he wanted so much to take in all of the boy, to drink him in deeply: the face, the slightly almond eyes, the small, high ears; the open, childlike "archaic smile" Peter remembered from illustrations of early Greece or the faces smiling back at him from travel pictures of jungle-deep Cambodian friezes. It was a face from Peter's earliest childhood, now delivered to him without self-consciousnss or, on its part, troubling doubts.

"You were upstairs?" the boy asked.

"Yes, I was," Peter answered. He tried simply to smile, to be as open and guileless as the boy. But he was too self-conscious; it was impossible. It was easier to talk. "I'm sorry I didn't help you with the machines. They sometimes confuse me and I've been coming here for years."

He managed to adjust the shower to a soothing warmth, and the boy, who barely came up to Peter's shoulders, got under it. Peter got back and watched the water drift down the kid's naked body. It was beautiful and well defined, with an almost perfect chest, marked by small dark nipples. Peter thought he was more developed than his age, then wondered what his age might be. Seventeen? Eighteen? It was difficult to say. His chest had an early light dusting of hair and his stomach was as neat and inviting as a warm loaf of bread. His pubic hair was black, curly, and shiny with dampness. Peter looked at the boy's sex organ, which appeared like the bloom of a small orchid peering out of a marsh. He tried to read it for any clue of the boy's age, religion (he was circumcised), or thoughts. Then Peter realized he was staring; he shook his head slightly.

The boy looked up at Peter and smiled again. A voice that sounded deeper, less embarrassed, but still like something from a ventriloquist, announced, "My father will be back in a minute."

Peter tried hard to keep some kind of smile frozen on his face, but his dominant impulse was to rush back to his own shower. Being with this kid was unbearable—he wanted so much to touch him. And yet nothing could make Peter move; he felt like he was nailed to the tiles.

"My name is Andrew," the boy said. He looked directly into Peter's eyes, and that smile that seemed to be permanently carved into his lips said, "You're a nice person. I feel good with you."

Peter swallowed hard. What could he say? He started to tremble a bit, knowing he was becoming enwrapped in the boy's own sweet energy. But a small dot of excitement, like the focused eye of a white penlight, shot through him. He felt exposed by it, illuminated vein by vein, thought by thought. Where could he hide? His own shower was now miles away. Other men walked into the wet room. "Peter," he said softly. "My name's Peter."

The boy reached up and touched Peter's shoulder. "Can I wash your back? I always wash Dad's back. He likes that."

"All right," Peter said, trying not to smile. He turned his face to the wall and began counting backwards from a hundred to keep his mind off his genitals, which were responding to the young man's stroking.

"I couldn't find the soap," Andrew's father said, and Peter immediately snapped his head around, feeling guiltier than he'd ever felt in his life. "Is he washing your back, too? I bet without soap! Andrew likes to do that, soap or not."

Peter stumbled for words, but nothing came out. He was a writer, with nothing to say. But at least Dad had not interpreted anything out of the way.

"Thanks for looking after him," he said. "Andy's a nice boy, but I guess you can see he has his limitations."

Suddenly Peter hit on the right words: "You're welcome to use my soap." He hurried back to fetch his large bar of Ivory, then handed it to Andrew's father.

"Thanks. I see you've met my son."

Peter nodded and they exchanged names. Dad was Tom Allister, who seemed casual about his son. The three of them dried off together in a small public alcove in front of the showers. Then Arnold came, calling "Hi, Peter!" while giving him a very knowing look that said, "Sure!" But Peter wasn't sure if the look was for Tom, Peter, or who.

Peter turned aside; Arnold disappeared. Other dripping men passed by them, which only made Peter dry off more slowly. He wanted to look at Andrew, who seemed more self-contained, warmer, and open than any other person he'd ever met. His eyes would meet Peter's and they would both smile, until Peter's old self-consciousness returned and he would have to turn his head. "He is something, isn't he?" Tom announced, tightly wrapping a towel around his middle. "He's like a strange gift. My wife and I already had two kids when we had him. Then, would you believe it, we had another one? I wasn't sure what to do with him, but he's been a real joy. I'm still not sure what to do..."

"Next?" Peter asked.

Tom nodded his head. "Precisely."

"Why don't we go into the sauna?" Peter suggested.

Tom smiled. "Good suggestion. Hot room, Andrew?"

The boy nodded his head in Peter's direction, but looked lost. Tom pointed him a few feet over into the small, redwood-lined room with a stone furnace in it. The sauna was empty and the two men sat down on their towels on the top tier of redwood benches, with Andrew sitting on his, one tier below them.

"You like this room?" Peter asked Andrew. The boy didn't answer. "Andy!" Tom asked. "Tell us. You like it here?"

"Sure!" he said energetically. He waved his short legs up and down, and then sank down so that his genitals flopped over his taut stomach. Then he sat straight up and smiled again. "Sure, I like it."

Tom laughed and ran his hand over his son's head. "He likes coming to the Y. He loves the workout room, but can't understand some of the machines."

"Neither can I," Peter said, and suddenly found himself touching Andrew's hair, too. The boy turned his face up to him, and then closed his eyes while Peter stroked his hair.

"He goes to a sheltered workshop during the week. The idea is to integrate him into the world."

"Does he have any friends?" Peter asked, looking at the boy but not at Tom.

"Some. But friendship is different when you're like Peter."

"How's that?"

"You see, it makes no difference whether you're a child, an adult, an animal, whatever. The idea of a 'best friend' or an adult friend—well, I think it's foreign to them. I keep wondering what he's going to do when he finds somebody. You know, like a girl? But so far he hasn't seemed to land on anyone. It just doesn't make a difference with him. See, I don't think he understands real adult friendship."

"Maybe he's afraid to have someone who'll make a difference," Peter said, keeping his hand on Andrew's head, trying hard to contain himself. Then he removed his hand.

"To tell you the truth, I don't know what I'd do if he did. We've had lots of friends for him, but kids outgrow him. When he was twelve or thirteen, he had kid friends who were nine or ten, and they'd start out loving him, but then get tired of his limitations. Kids don't have that much patience. Now that he's nineteen—"

"Nineteen?"

"Yeah, he just had a birthday last week."

Peter put his hand back on Andrew's head. "Happy birthday," he said. Immediately Peter felt so natural being naked there in the sauna with Andrew and Tom; he had never experienced feeling that way with anyone before at the Y.

"What do you say?" Tom asked him.

There was a second of silence, and then Andrew got up and placed his towel on the bench next to Peter. He sat down next to him and smiled. "Thanks, Peter," he said. Then he turned and shook Peter's hand.

Peter looked at him. They smiled at each other and Peter thought that he would not be able to contain himself. He swallowed hard, then counted to ten and, and then said to Tom, while looking into Andrew's sweet face, "What about friends who are like him?"

"No. He gets too bored with them. Andy's I.Q. is quite high. He's at a fairly good reading level. He can't read the *Times*, but he can make out street signs, has books of his own, and he's great with restaurant menus. He's amazing at math. In fact, he can add up a restaurant bill faster than I can."

"It's getting too hot," Andrew said, and then climbed off the bench.

Peter agreed, and Tom said, "I think he's had enough."

"I have!"

"Do you want to shower a bit more?"

Andrew hesitated, then looked at Peter. "Will he come, too?"

"Sure," Peter said, and then he got up.

"Wait a second," Tom said to Andrew. "Why don't you go into the showers and we'll be there in a minute."

The boy smiled, then quickly closed the sauna door behind him. "That's what I mean," Tom said. "He just latches on to anybody. Kids like this are very friendly, but they don't—"

"It's okay, I don't mind it," Peter interrupted.

"No, wait a second. I mean, they don't form what I'd call a real attachment. They kind of just float. It's been difficult having him to myself for two years."

Peter asked him where his wife was. The question just popped out. It seemed like a terrible breach of privacy, but the situation—the Y, the two of them naked and completely alone in the sauna; then Andrew himself, childlike, beautiful—seemed so naturally intimate that Peter did not hold back from asking it.

Tom's thick fingers drummed the redwood bench. "We separated a few years ago. We're not divorced. It just stopped working for us together. We're still friends. Funny idea, don't you think, husbands and wives as 'friends'?"

"I see," Peter said, looking down at the floor of the sauna and then at Tom's older but attractive body, and wondering, at the same time, exactly *what* did not work.

"I'm not what you *think* I am," Tom said.

Peter raised his eyebrows.

"I'm not some dirty old man who left his wife for a younger woman. No, but I had this chance to work in New York—I'm in energy financing. We make the decisions about where to drill for oil. It's not just any dumb job. Governments fall on what men like me say, although they don't always listen to me, let me tell you that. But I had this chance to hit the big time in the big city and the girls were already grown. Two are married, so they have their own lives back in Tulsa. Sometimes I feel kind of betwixt-and-between. I mean, I wasn't meant for Tulsa and all the fundamentalists back there, but I'm not completely sold on New York, either. I told Gwen that I'd take Andrew. It just didn't seem possible to leave him. I'm nuts about him, you have to understand, he's my only son."

On the way home, Peter thought about Andrew and his father, so that the boy's gentle face followed him, like a face you might see in a cloud or at the bottom of a coffee cup. He got back to his small orderly apartment, filled with well-chosen pieces of furniture and lay down on his bed with a new Saul Bellow novel. He opened the book, but none of the sentences made any sense to him. It was as if his mind had become suddenly too clear, too simple, too basic. As if Andrew, smiling, were watching over his shoulder, asking him what he was doing. He missed him.

But how could he just call Tom Allister and say, openly, that he wanted to "come over and play" with his son?

For the next week he returned to the Y every afternoon, hoping more than anything that he'd see them. But he didn't. He had more work. Some short articles for an antiques magazine, some garbagy public relations work, and some movie reviews for the *Eye*, since their regular reviewer was out of town. The "money work" was easier to write than his creative efforts, the work that he felt made him a writer. Short stories or a poem were a harder to bring off, reminding him of the difficult loneliness of writing. The commercial stuff was closer to the top of his head, but his creative writing came from something deeper within him.

Amazingly, this top-of-his-head fluff fooled the editors. "You have a real *voice*," a self-important moron at the *Eye* told him, as if he were bestowing a medal upon Peter, along with a payment voucher for Peter's small check. Any beginning accountant made more than he did, although he had two college degrees and years of experience. But the money wasn't it. The writing, that was it.

But the other stuff: the stories that he sent off to pretentious literary magazines that had more submissions than subscribers; the poems he beat his soul into; the play that he liked so much but that never got beyond an amateur production at a church in the West Village—they were killers. Why couldn't he simply be a "natural" genius like Saul Bellow? In truth, few writers were geniuses. Some were lunatics, borderline psychotics. Even so, what they all wanted to do was find a way to connect with that deep pool of words the human race collected, but was too frightened to use.

Sometimes Peter did connect. But the connection was so rare, and when it did happen, when his brain finally poured out its words with no distance between itself and the paper, when the brain itself talked; it made the awful, everyday agony of writing only a preparation for the most intense pleasure he'd ever known. A perfect, sparkling, directed pleasure that touched his deeper self even more so than sex had.

Peter desired that connection very much, but every night after writing the money stuff and then searching for Andrew at the Y, his brain (which he wanted to open up and write) shut down. Leaving only silence.

Finally, a week later, at ten o' clock at night (too late, he was sure), Peter decided to try a different approach. Finding Tom's name in the Manhattan telephone directory, he dialed nervously. "Hello, uh, Tom?"

"Who's this?"

"It's Peter Brogan from the Y."

"Yeah?" Long pause, then in a dead tone, "How's it going?"

"Good!" Peter tried to shove some enthusiasm into his voice. "Tom, I was, uh, wondering if you and Andrew ever went out? I've got some movie passes. A new Steve Martin picture's on Twenty-Third at the Multiplex. Would you be interested?"

"... Uhhh?" Another dead tone. Another pause.

Then Tom instantly shifted into what Peter felt was his "on" voice. "Peter! Sure! Yeah! Listen!"

Peter exhaled. A little light must have switched on in Allister's head as his voice got warmer. "Listen, Peter. Andrew might like to see you anyway. See, I haven't had a lot of time for him lately."

"Oh," Peter said, matter-of-factly. "I haven't seen the two of you at the Y."

"Been up to my ass in work, son. My company's getting ready for a big kill in the Mid East. Oil talk, see? Doesn't mean much to you probably. Listen, Pete, I hate to ask you this, but would you feel real bad about taking Andy all by yourself?"

Peter almost dropped the phone. He tried to sound casual. "No, not at all."

"Good! I'd sure love to have some time to catch up with you. I mean, I know I'm not being fair. Sometimes it's hard for us adults to talk to him—but he's really good company. Just do me a favor: don't treat him like he's dumb, that's all."

"I won't," Peter promised.

"He loves to go out to restaurants, especially Chinese. You should see him with chopsticks. He's a pro."

"How about tomorrow night?"

"Just a minute," Tom answered. "I'll let you talk to Andy."

"Andy'll be right out," Tom said in the hallway of his apartment. They lived on Seventeenth Street, off Seventh Avenue, in an older, 20s-style building. The living room was moderate-sized and very spare and cold. It was definitely a "bachelor" apartment as opposed to a gay one. That is, the man in it had little connection with its furnishings, and might at any moment abandon it. There were cheap rugs, drab pieces of discount furniture, and museum posters of Impressionist paintings in prefab frames.

Tom walked Peter over to his desk, which dominated a large corner of the living room. On it were several rolled geological survey maps and some books on geology, oil law, a bible, and a dictionary. There were no other books in the living room. Tom unrolled a section of one of the maps for Peter. "Turkey's *waaay* over here," he said, pointing to someplace actually off the map, "and Iran is *wa-aaay* over there. Now this little place is up for grabs. Oil's a crap shoot, but we think we got something here." His forefinger zoomed in to a spot, and Peter nodded his head, pretending that the here Tom referred to meant something to him. "That is," Tom went on, "if the locals don't blow each other apart first. What are you guys going to see?"

There was the Steve Martin movie and a new Bruce Willis flick. Neither seemed spectacular. "I'll leave that to Andrew."

"Do you need some money?" Tom asked and reached into his wallet. "I mean, I don't want you to think you have to pay Andy's way all the time."

"Tom, I'm not babysitting for your son. It's all right."

Andrew came out from his room. He was dressed in a white dress shirt, a brown corduroy sports jacket, and jeans. His face was freshly washed and his hair combed back in a kind of spunky, tough way that kids on TV favored. A bit of hair tonic made his hair look silky, dark, and glistening. He looked grave, shy, and unexpectedly, perhaps to anyone except Peter, very handsome.

He smiled and offered Peter his hand. "Hello, Peter."

Peter shook his hand and felt a momentary trembling through his own body.

"What will we see?" the boy asked.

"I'll leave that to you."

"You will?" Andrew smiled and then looked over at Tom, who only shook his head and said, "You're going to spoil him!"

"I'm not spoiled," Andrew said and smiled at Peter.

They said good-bye to Tom and went down in the elevator. The doorman smiled at Andrew and then looked suspiciously at Peter. The cold look hurt him. It was like saying that nothing he could do with Andrew would ever be above suspicion.

It was still early in the evening out on the street, and people had that tired, hungry, after-work look. It made Peter feel how lucky he was to be walking to the movies with this beautiful boy, and all he wanted to do was just touch him, on his shoulder, his arm, his hand.

They decided on the Steve Martin movie. It was a broad comedy about raising kids and, about half an hour into it, Peter realized he couldn't pretend to be interested in it. There weren't many people at this early showing on a weeknight, and he and Andrew had a row to themselves. He looked over in the darkness at the boy and saw flickering, colored lights from the screen reflected and moving across Andrew's eyes. A lovely grin opened on his face. Peter drew closer to him until he could smell Andrew's warm breath, clean hair, and cologne. Was it Old Spice? Probably. Probably Andrew had borrowed it from Tom. Peter smiled. He could imagine Andrew in the bathroom getting ready to go out with him; the thought made him feel warm. He stopped thinking about the silly movie. There was no way he could review it; he'd have to come back to see what it was all about. He settled back and let his thoughts wander; then, as Peter's attention returned for a moment to the silliness on the screen, Andrew leaned into him.

"Can I hold your hand?" he whispered.

Peter felt suddenly flushed, then answered, "Sure."

The boy took his hand and twined his smaller fingers in with Peter's larger ones. Peter felt incredibly self-conscious, although no one could see them. Then he relaxed and returned the affection of Andrew's pressure.

Then Andrew turned to him and said, "Let's go. I'm tired of this."

"Where?" Peter whispered.

"Your place. I want to see where you live."

It was much darker and colder outside now. Although it was only a fifteen- or twenty-minute walk to his house, Peter decided to take a cab. They found one crossing east on Twenty-Third Street and grabbed it. "Get in first," Peter said and Andrew did, sliding like a little boy across the backseat. Peter got in and told the driver his address. The driver scowled at such a short, out-of-the-way fare, but took them. Peter tried to make normal-sounding conversation in the back with

Andrew, but found it almost impossible. After a moment, he shut up and saw the driver's shifting eyes watching them in the rear-view mirror. For a second, he wondered whether everything about Andrew was rubbing off on him: that hurtful mixture of curiosity, benevolence, distrust and even fear people might have of Andrew—was that rubbing off? They got to Peter's tenement building and got out. Peter overtipped the driver, while Andrew waited on the curb. "Thanks," the driver grunted. "I guess you gotta watch out wit' kids like that, don't you?" He tried to smile. Peter shut the door, and he drove off.

"It's four flights up," Peter said and they began walking up. Andrew had no problems with it, but Peter's heart was pounding by the time the two of them were at his landing.

"Nice!" Andrew said, his eyes opening wide, once they were in. "You read a lot. All these books!"

"I'm a writer," Peter said.

"Ohhh!"

Peter asked him if he wanted something to drink. A Coke, or some orange juice.

"Do you have any wine?"

"Do you usually drink that?"

"No. But it would be fun. Right? Can I?"

Peter got two large Beaujolais glasses from the top shelf of a china cabinet in his kitchen. He dusted them off quickly with a dish towel and brought them into the living room. "White or red?" he asked. Andrew looked at him, then glanced around the small living room. He sat down on a day bed, where Peter often stretched out to read.

"White or red what?"

Peter chuckled. "White wine or red wine?"

He shook his head softly, then shrugged. "You decide."

Peter re-opened a bottle of red Italian that had been on his kitchen counter for a few weeks, left over from a spaghetti party he'd had. He was not much of a drinker, but the wine smelled fine without any vinegar fumes. He poured a little into both glasses and handed one to Andrew.

"Thanks, Peter. I'm not sure if I can do this."

"Do what?" Peter asked, after taking a sip. The wine was still fairly smooth, with just a wink of acidic tang to it.

"The glass... I don't want to spill any of it on my shirt."

Peter understood the situation. "Just drink from it slowly, and tilt your head back a bit. That way you get to smell the wine while you're drinking it."

"Okay," the boy said, as if he understood and the glass hadn't been designed with some underlying sadism to it. He tried again, but was still scared to tilt his head back far enough.

"It's all right," Peter said. "Now just tilt." He caught the back of Peter's head in his free hand, and tried to guide him.

"If I spill it..."

Then the words tumbled right out of Peter: "Why don't you take your shirt off?"

Andrew smiled mischievously, placing the glass carefully on the floor next to the day bed. It looked liked a large transparent tulip with a small pool of blood in its throat. Andrew began to unbutton his white shirt.

"Let me help." Peter undid some of the bottom buttons, then he opened the shirt tails up and free while Andrew wriggled his shoulders loose. With his shirt off, the boy looked brown and small and lovely. Peter handed him his glass back and then, showing Andrew that he wanted him to feel all right, took his own shirt off and they sat down together on the day bed, which was pressed against a wall.

"This is nice," Andrew said.

"Yes."

Andrew drank some of the wine easily now, tilting his head back so that his small nose fitted perfectly into the waiting mouth of the Beaujolais glass. Peter drew his arm around him.

"Thank you," Andrew said. "I like this."

Peter smiled. He felt as if his body were going to burst out of his pants, just as his soul itself might burst from his body and float, finally, for the first time, genuinely free and delighted above the room.

"I like you," Andrew said, drawing closer to him, and then, without thinking another thing, without trying to come up with one more appropriate, pointless word to fill the space between them, Peter kissed him on the mouth, tasting a bead of red wine left on Andrew's lips.

Now it was darkly calm and warm in the living room.

The two wine glasses sat barely touched but safe on the floor, while Peter and Andrew, with all of their clothes tossed about, slowly kissed on the day bed. With his whole self, with his hands, mouth, genitals, face, and eyes, Peter explored the marvelous amber terrains of Andrew's body. Their faces often met and Peter felt himself happily, gaily swimming into Andrew's opaque eyes, which seemed as dark and wise as an underground grotto guarded by a powerful river god. He smiled and took Andrew's soft, childlike hand—the palm almost creaseless—and raised it to his lips, sucking his fingers, then licking and kissing the back of Andrew's wrist.

"I don't know what to do," Andrew said.

"What would you like to do?"

"Stay here with you."

"All right. But you didn't mean that, did you?"

"No."

"You've never been to bed with a man, have you?"

"I'm not sure what 'to bed' means."

Peter smiled, then kissed him. "That's all right, too. You'll find out."

He didn't say anything else. Neither did Andrew. Andrew made Peter not want to talk, not want to use words, at least regular words, the words of money writing, or crafted "literary" stories in small magazines, the words of walking around New York, of being afraid of eyes on the street, the loud words of men at the gym, the words of being dead.

Dead in a world of so much "intelligence."

There had to be new words for loving Andrew, for holding him, feeling him breathe, kissing and sucking the small, doll-like nipples on his surprisingly large, smooth chest; for kissing his stomach and groin, for holding his cock, kissing, licking, and sucking it; for holding his testicles, for stroking his downy ass. Fabulous, wondrous words for everything Peter did, just as Andrew needed no words for marveling at the dark hair on Peter's chest; Peter's genitals, their weight and skin texture; and the loose sac of Peter's balls.

Andrew smiled, experiencing all of this.

Then sex itself drew closer, guiding them both, bringing Peter to it, and Andrew also, holding them in its ecstasies, its inner music, dropping Peter for a moment into an early silent movie he'd seen at the Museum of Natural History: dark naked men tramping noiselessly through a marsh, splashing black water against the camera, with Peter leading Andrew with his hands, mouth, and heart, touching the boy's completely unguarded face and body, until he found himself returning to a place so raw and refined at once that he'd never hoped to find it in New York.

"You'll call me again? Please?" Andrew asked.

Peter told him he would. "Do you have everything?"

Andrew looked around. He was now dressed and he checked his pockets to make sure he had his house keys and a wallet.

"I should take you back," Peter said, and kissed him once more, holding him so close that he could smell Tom's Old Spice on Andrew's clothes, not wanting to release him.

"You don't have to. I can take a cab back. I can even walk. I know this area very well."

"Your father won't let me see you again if I did that—let you walk by yourself."

Peter looked at him; suddenly his mouth dropped as he saw in the light, for the first time, Andrew's real face. It was no longer that strange, placid, tribal face—stamped with the archaic Down's features—but a real face, distinctly his, shockingly wise. He swallowed very hard, then asked Andrew, "What do you think you are?"

Andrew paused. He shrugged his shoulders. "I don't know the word for it yet."

Peter smiled and zipped up a light windbreaker. "Maybe there isn't one yet." He kissed Andrew once more.

He went downstairs and put Andrew into a cab. He felt very guilty about that while he walked back up to his apartment, but he wasn't sure how he'd face Tom Allister that night. Or even the next time he saw him.

He called Andrew the next evening. Tom answered the phone. "Andy told me he had a great time with you! He said the movie was fine—Steve Martin is one of his favorites—and then he said you went out for a snack afterwards. I really have to thank you for doing what you did. When did you become interested in kids like Andrew?"

"What do you mean?'

"You know, with Down's Syndrome?"

"I guess it just happened," Peter answered.

"Let me tell you, there's a lot to learn about them. My wife and I went to special classes in it. We put him through all those early childhood programs. He surprises us!" Tom's voice became more enthusiastic: "He sure does! You know they used to put boys like Andrew in homes and lock them away."

"Could I speak with him?"

"Sure!"

Andrew came to the phone. His voice sounded distant, almost drugged. Was he pretending detachment in front of Tom? He'd lied to Tom. That was good, Peter thought. It was adult. The boy understood at least for the moment the dangers and boundaries of the situation. He was handling this adultly, but somehow it did not amaze or surprise Peter that Andrew would. Peter suggested that they go out for Chinese food the next night. Andrew relayed the request to Tom, who got back on the phone. "This time I can make it," he said. "It'll be my treat. How about Hoy Sin on Seventh Avenue and Nineteenth?"

Peter tried to sound extremely enthusiastic as he said, "Fine!" Tom decided the time—seven—and Peter hung up. He went back to his typewriter to do some more work. But his concentration had gone completely. All he could think about was Andrew, and when he thought about him, every word that he had evaporated.

Hoy Sin was a small garden-variety Chinese joint, more for take-out than an acceptable restaurant. Tom ordered for them a very usual take-out Chinese dinner, except that they ate it in. Egg rolls, shrimp with broccoli and something called General Yen's chicken, which arrived drenched in catsup. "Show Peter how you use chopsticks," Tom said.

Andrew smiled and picked up the chopsticks. He was very good at it, easily lifting the rice to his mouth. After he put the chopsticks down, he said to Tom, "I can show him a lot of things."

Peter suddenly felt the blood burning at the rims of his ears.

"His mother and I started taking him out to restaurants very early," Tom said, trying the chicken. He looked up at his son. "Looks like you got some of this on your shirt, Andy." For the first time, the boy looked embarrassed. His face darkened. There was an ugly-looking red spot on the blue polo shirt that looked so good on him.

"It's nothing," Peter said. He dunked the folded corner of a linen napkin into a glass of ice water and leaned towards Andrew to dab out the spot. He wanted so much to kiss Andrew right there, right then; suddenly the boy had become his child as well as his lover. Andrew turned away from Tom.

"Thank you," Andrew said, smiling.

Peter stayed close to the boy for a moment, then realized that Andrew's left hand, under the white table cloth, was discreetly investigating the area between Peter's legs.

Peter leaned back and put his hand under the table and held Andrew's hand. He closed his eyes and realized Tom had been going on for a while about the Middle East. "It's the land of the bible, where civilization began," Tom said, "and now it could easily end there, too."

Tom's eyes were on Peter's, but Peter was hardly sure what Tom was saying, because, at that moment, Andrew had managed to evade Peter's hand, unzip his pants, reach inside his boxer shorts, and totally exposed him. Peter, too nervous to have any reaction down there other than surprise, softly grabbed Andrew's playful fingers once more, trying not to smile.

"Who you side with in that part of the world," Tom went on, "is of paramount importance. See, they don't like each other much more than they like us. I think we're about ready for a check, aren't we?"

Peter gulped, as Andrew managed to put Peter's equipment back in. Immediately, the waiter brought the check and Peter made the perfunctory movement for his wallet.

"No, let me get this," Tom said. Peter was happy for that for, while Tom looked away at the check, Peter zipped himself back up and then looked at Andrew, who only smiled at him. A moment later, they were outside. It was very dark out. One of those nights when October was freezing already into November, and it brought a chill right through Peter. He looked up at a crisp autumn moon in the sky and shivered. It could have been any October wintry snap really, but it wasn't.

"Well, we're going to have to be off," Tom said, extending his hand to Peter. "I've got some damn day tomorrow."

"Thanks for dinner," Peter said. He looked over at Andrew, and tried to pull himself back from his desire to really hug the boy. His shoulders and elbows squared and stiffened like a French lieutenant about to make a salute, while he pretended to smile in his most casual way.

"Gwen and two of Andy's sisters are flying in this Friday. It's the youngest girl, Andy's younger sister, and the next one—she's married already, but her husband's going off on business—so Gwen said why not do New York? Not a bad idea, right? I want to spend as much time with them as I can. Gwen is—well, I think I told you about that. Are you looking forward to them, Andy?"

Andrew did not answer. He was looking at Peter, with the same real face that Peter had seen in his apartment, until the masklike, simple smile that he normally wore returned.

"Andy? Andy?" Tom repeated.

"I want to go home with Peter," Andrew said.

"What? *Why*? Peter has his own things to do. He's a grown man, Andy. He can't always take care of you. He took you to the movies this week. Now he has to go back to *his* home, Andy, and we have to go to ours."

"I want to go with him," the boy repeated.

Tom stopped for a moment, while people walked past him. Peter could tell Tom was embarrassed by all of this happening on the sidewalk. "Is this because your mom and sisters are coming? I know you might feel a little bad about it—you've had me all to yourself for a long time—but it'll be all right. You're always my boy, Andy. Always."

"That's not it," Andrew said. "I love Peter."

Tom looked dumbfounded. Peter tried to pull the situation together the best he could. "He's become attached to me," Peter said. "It's okay. He can stay with me for a while. I'd like that."

Tom's eyes narrowed. "What do you mean, you 'love' Peter?"

"He's my friend!"

"Oh, now I see." Tom looked completely relieved and drew Peter aside. "Now I feel better. He had me scared for a moment. It's like I told you, they can't differentiate between one kind of feeling and another. I guess he loves you the way he loves me or a puppy or anything. Sure, if he wants to go home with you for a while and you don't mind it, maybe you can get his mind off Gwen and the girls coming. I know he feels he going to be left out."

Peter shook Tom's hand. "I'll put him in a cab in a few hours. Myself."

"Do you really want me with you?" Andrew asked. He was lying naked on Peter's chest, while Peter kissed him over and over on his cheeks and face.

"Yes, I do."

"Why?"

"Have you ever had someone love you?"

"Dad. My mom. But nothing like this."

"Then you can tell the difference between the way I feel about you—and the way you feel about me—and, let's say, your father?"

"Of course, Peter. I'm not stupid. Just because I have Down's Syndrome doesn't mean I'm an idiot. Sometimes I have to play stupid to my father, because it's the only way he can look at me and still feel good. He wants me to stay his little boy forever. He gets upset when I'm not. But I can't. I want to spend the night with you."

Peter smiled. "Why?"

"I want to dream about you, and wake up and find you here."

"What will you do about Tom?"

"I'll tell him that I love you, and you're not some puppy to me. Isn't that what he said, that I can't tell the difference between one thing and another?"

Peter turned away suddenly, nodding For a second, he was close to crying. How could he ever get himself out of this; or, better yet, allow himself the wonder of going further with it? The word would get out and all of his friends, his sophisticated, literate, cutting, New York friends, would whisper. They'd wink about him. How could they ever understand what Andrew meant to him, when he was only barely beginning to understand it himself? Suddenly he felt sorry for Tom, whose image of his own son would soon be shattered.

He held Andrew closer to him and said, "Your father will have to understand what I mean to you, but I don't know if he can do that fast. Do you know what I mean?"

Andrew looked at him. "Yes."

"You'll have to call him and tell him you want to spend the night. We'll pretend that nothing different is happening. It's just cold and I want you to spend the night here. If he wants, I'll speak with him."

Andrew dialed the number and spoke with Tom. Peter got next to the phone, so he could hear Tom's side of the conversation. Tom took it amazingly lightly, then asked to speak with Peter.

"Hi," Peter said. "Is it okay?"

"I don't know what you're doing with my son, Peter. But I have to tell you it worries me."

Peter tried to smile. "It's like you said, he doesn't know the difference between me and anyone else. He's happy here. We're going to watch TV, and he'll be asleep soon on my couch."

"Is that it?" Tom asked warily.

"Yeah, Tom. That's it."

"Okay, if that's it, I can accept it. I just can't figure out why you're interested in my son."

Peter paused; he knew he had to say something, and fast.

"Well, I guess he's a real story in itself," Peter said, casually as possible, while Andrew smiled wickedly and ran his fingers over Peter's body and then placed his genitals next to Peter's free hand, tempting him to pet him there. Peter shook his head, and covered the mouth piece. "This is important, Andy. I've got to make him trust me."

Andrew nodded his head.

"All right," Tom said. "That makes sense. So that's been your angle all along? You want to do a story on a kid like Andy?"

"I'm not sure," Peter answered. "But he's different and I certainly think there's a story here."

"Good enough!" Tom said, cruising back into his blandly emotionless voice. "Just get him back tomorrow early. I don't want him to feel that he's camping out on your doorstep for good!"

Peter hardly slept that night. They woke up to make love several times—the boy was insatiable and amazingly skillful at sex, without the sort of inhibitions a kid his age might have. Really, he was a story in himself: it was true. There were times when Peter just wanted to look at Andy sleeping, and there were times when he'd wake up and find Andy's face watching him.

Then at nine o'clock, they got out of bed and Peter made some coffee and some bagels and Andrew had a bagel and a glass of milk. Then they showered together and Peter walked him home. He said good-bye to him in Tom Allister's empty apartment and kissed him and then left. Back at his apartment he had a lot of work to do and he tried as hard as he could not to think about Andy. The whole situation seemed so impossible. So undo-able. Yet he knew that he would have to do it, have to find some way to be with Andrew, no matter what. He did not call the Allisters' apartment for the next several days—it seemed too soon to jump back into that pool of feelings, then again on Thursday, he saw Andy at the Y.

They were both in the locker room, and Andy, wearing his gym shorts and a clean tee, ran up to him. "Why haven't you called me?" he said, his voice carrying across the room.

Peter released his breath. "Would you lower your voice?" he whispered. Boiled-chicken Arnold was only a few feet away, ostensibly drying himself. Arnold looked over at Peter and suddenly grinned like the wolf in a cartoon.

"I can't talk here," Peter said. He had a towel wrapped around his waist, but felt more naked and exposed than he'd ever felt. That grin from Arnold chilled the hell out of him. He could see Arnold staring at them and he knew Tom Allister could not be that far away.

"I don't know what to do," Andrew whispered. "I don't know how you go about these things... isn't this sort of like... being friends? I wanted you to call me."

"I will," he said. "Let's walk a bit." They walked down a short hallway towards the sauna. "Where's your father?"

"Downstairs with the machines. He said he needed a little more work." Andy smiled, then whispered very shyly: "I'm getting hard looking at you. Other men don't do that for me."

Peter nodded his head. "I'd better get out of here. I'm doing the same thing. I thought we shouldn't give your father any more room for suspicion."

"He doesn't suspect anything. He can only see me as his little retarded boy."

"You shouldn't say that," Peter said, suddenly putting his hand on Andy's shoulder.

"You don't think I know? I can't be an idiot *and* queer, too. It's not in the books, is it?"

Suddenly Peter kissed him, quickly, impulsively. There was no one around. "Andy, it's hard enough being queer and normal. Whatever that means. Now I feel like a real shit. I thought you'd understand that I shouldn't see you for a few days."

"He doesn't want me to call you. He says I'm getting in your way. That's not true, is it?"

Peter shook his head. But it was true: Andy was in his way, and that was the way he wanted it. He told Andy that they would spend the weekend with each other, no matter what, and then, leaving Andy there, he walked back to his locker. The first person he saw was Arnold.

"Curious," Arnold said, a smirk wrinkling his face.

"What are you talking about?"

"I think the idiot has a crush on you."

"What did you say?"

"I said... I think that kid has a crush on you."

Peter's face hit the cracked floor tiles. Then he looked back up at Arnold, who had not changed his expression at all. "Why don't you go to hell?" he said. "Why don't you just go to hell."

"Sorry," Arnold mumbled. "Didn't realize it was reciprocated."

Peter turned away from him. He didn't want to look at Arnold again. He was afraid that he'd hit him, slap the shit out of him if he had to, and he didn't want that to happen right there in the locker room. When he turned back, he saw that Arnold was still there. His expression had changed, though. It was now filled with what looked like concern or pity, which Peter hated even more.

"I'm sorry," Arnold said slowly. "I was just being stupid, I guess. I mean I know they have feelings like other people... I just never think of them as being the sort of people I'd know."

Peter began to open his locker to get dressed. He'd calmed down now. There was something he'd always wanted to say to Arnold and now seemed like a good time to do it. "You're a fake, Arnold. I have to tell you this: you are a *real* fake."

That was all he said, then Arnold left him.

Peter could tell that Saturday evening when he entered Tom Allister's apartment at six that something had happened. It was not so much that a trap had been set for him as that the velocity of the story had changed. When he had called Tom on the phone that Thursday evening, after the Y, Tom had accepted that Peter was now a part of Andy's life, an adult friend in some way, one that he hardly thought his son would ever have.

But Tom now looked at him differently in the hallway and quietly asked him to come in. "I should introduce you to Gwen and the girls. They're Laura and Lorna," he said and chuckled to himself. "My wife believes in monogramming the kids' stuff, so she figured they wouldn't go to waste this way."

Peter smiled hesitantly, and then they walked into the living room, where Gwen, the two girls, and Andy waited. The room looked somewhat brighter. There were supermarket flowers in juice jars on Tom's desk and on a coffee table, and the Allister women were dressed in those kind of bright flowery mall clothes that girls in New York don't wear. Tom introduced him and Andy smiled at him nervously. Gwen got up from the couch where she'd been sitting.

"You're Andy's friend!" She extended her hand and looked him over nervously. Her thin mouth formed a cautious smile, but her eyes did not. They were trying very hard, Peter could tell, to read what sort of person he was.

"I like Andy," Peter said.

"We all do," Laura interjected. She was the older girl, amazingly pretty, blonde, and tall. "I guess we should thank you for taking him out tonight. I know he's tired of being with us girls. He's already told us a lot about you."

"I said he was my friend," Andy interrupted. "That was all."

"That's not all you said," Tom added.

"Do we have to talk about this now?" Lorna, the younger girl, who looked about sixteen, asked. "This is just crazy! My brother's got a boyfriend who's old enough to be his father. It's nuts. Dad, I thought we were going out to eat."

Peter sat down. "What did you say?" he asked Andy.

"Okay. I told Mom I'm in love with you. I'm not good at secrets. The girls found it out. Laura thinks it's just cute. But Lorna is ashamed of me. She always has been."

"That's not true," Lorna said. "It's just not easy to be the younger sister of someone with Down's. Everyone thinks I should be that way, too."

"So you're not." Andy said. "That should make *you* happy." He turned to Peter. "Let's go. I don't want to be here anymore."

He grabbed Peter by the arm, and they both walked through the hallway towards the door, while Tom and his wife and the girls looked on blankly. Then Lorna said to her father, "Daddy, don't tell me you're just going to let them walk away like that?"

Tom shook his head. He looked flustered and for the first time really under attack. "Wait," he said, as the two men opened the door. He ran after them, and said to Peter, "If he spends the night with you—and I guess he will—I can't stop it, but I'll worry every moment. You'll be careful, won't you? You'll be sure it's all safe? Okay?"

Suddenly Peter felt himself ready to collapse, he'd been so tense. All of this had happened so fast. "I will," he said to Tom. "I'll do everything I can to make sure of it."

"Good."

*

They were in bed, and it was eleven o'clock. Peter had called Tom and told him that everything was all right, at least that evening. Tom had told him that he wanted to have a real talk with him. "There's so much I've got to know now," he said. His voice did not have that backslapping quality Peter hated. "I just never thought it would happen like this, that I would lose him this way."

"I'm not sure you've lost him," Peter said and a moment later hung up. He turned to Andrew and the boy got closer to him.

"Tell me the rest of the story," Andrew said. He was lying on top of Peter's naked chest, but with his face turned away from Peter's.

"Let's see," Peter said. He always felt more comfortable dealing with things in stories—and now it seemed that this was one. "There was once a writer in New York and he was trying hard to be successful. But he felt that he just wasn't doing the right thing. He's only going through the motions, trying to write stories that really weren't a part of his life, until finally this story happened to him. And then, the words eluded him."

"Eluded?" Andrew asked.

"Escaped."

"Oh... that must be terrible," Andrew whispered into Peter's ear. "Trying to find the right story. Then it finds you. And what do you do?" He smiled his wonderful pure smile. "Sometimes I look at words and they don't mean anything to me, either. I forget that this is the way the world works: through words."

"Not with you," Peter said.

"Even with me."

"I didn't think you needed words."

"Because of the way I was born?"

"Yes."

"No," Andy said. "I need words. But mostly I need courage."

Peter lifted him up and kissed him. "Maybe that's what the story should be about, courage?"

"Yes, the story should be about courage. Listen, when I write *our* story, it's going to be about that. And about something else."

"What?"

"The importance of small wins."

"Like a small triumph, every day?"

"Yeah... and listen, Peter, I know how the rest of the story should go, too."

"You do?"

"Yes."

So this time Peter closed his eyes and held Andy in his arms, while the young man told him the rest of the story and the words came tumbling right out of Andy's heart, or brain, or someplace that Peter had forgotten about in his own need to be clever and intelligent, a "somebody." But the story was really so simple that Peter wondered why he hadn't thought of it himself. "I want to write a story about a kid and a writer and they sort of... fall in love with each other. Isn't that correct?"

"Yes," Peter said. "It's correct."

Andy smiled. "Well, then, the writer has all these problems because he's sure that nothing's going to work out—in a big way—and everyone's going to laugh at him and kick him around, but the kid's already been through all of that, and he knows what it means to be ignored and have people talk about him like he wasn't there."

"I won't do that," Peter said.

Andy nodded his head. "That's good. You know, you may get tired of me... or who knows, I may... Anyway, in this whole big world, we're kind of like a small, wonderful thing—don't you think? It's like if there really was a big war and we were the last 'gay' couple in the world, we'd still be happy with each other, right?"

Peter nodded his head. He suddenly loved Andy so much that the sheer power of it was painful to him. "It really is a triumph, isn't it?"

"Triumph?"

"Yes, that small triumph of just us?"

"Yes," Andy said, and he hugged Peter closer to him, until Peter realized then that the boy was crying.

Mysterious Ways
Scott Brown

Mysterious Ways
Scott Brown

Always remember that you should never be complacent: life has a nasty habit of taking away everything it has ever given you without thought or consideration. The simple but honest truth is that we know nothing about life except that death will occur. In fact there are no certainties in life no matter what you do. How reassuring. How refreshing.

Not knowing what's around the corner – isn't that what makes life fun? A discovery, a journey, an experience – didn't someone sing the line 'life's a laugh and death's a joke, it's true'? I never thought about what was around the corner, I really was too busy. Too busy fucking, sticking shit up my nose and enjoying being loaded in every sense of the word. I was in control of my own destiny and, although I never knew what was around every corner, I knew that it would never be anything nasty. I had, shall we say, taken control of my world and its surrounds. You could argue that perhaps I had pissed off God by not playing to his rules, but then I don't play to anyone's rules. I was untouchable, and I really believed that. The champagne lifestyle... it was good... so very fucking good. A regular life followed by a predictable death? Not me. I would live life to the full and I would kill myself at fifty before I suffered from a long disease or grew old and couldn't help pissing my pants as I sat alone in an armchair watching daytime TV. I was in control of every aspect – life, death and taxes. There was no need for God – let's call it cutbacks. Streamlining. But, as with everything, there was a glitch in the works. Sometimes things don't always go according to plan. In simple terms, I know who I blame for the fuck-up, but that is the problem – you can't blame him. But I did, and that's another part of the fucking problem. In fact I called him a cunt. Still, we all say things in the heat of the moment, don't we?

I'm no flash twat, I'm not a poser and I don't want to brag, but I always acknowledge the fact that I had it all. I was the man everybody wanted to be, and of course the man everybody wanted to have. And I really was not grumbling. They called me 'The Man', and by God I was. Life was a party, one big long party. Agent to the best the football world could hold up, TV interviews on a daily basis, press eating from the palm of my hand and a passport to wherever I wanted to go. I was shitting money, dripping class, and style was synonymous to me. Name a football star and he was mine. I had every one of the best – yeah I was a bastard, but I got the goods. I got the goods and I did what it takes. Everyone's bent and I don't mean gay. Life's a game and the sooner you learn to play the better – I was a player, one of the very best.

As I said, I was the man – and of course the clothes make the man. And, fuck me, the clothes were good: Armani, Gucci, Prada – they paid me to wear them. The lifestyle? I got eight o'clock reservations at Claridges for the same night and I was VIP'd into any club I cared to venture. The girls hung off me and I pushed them away; the boys hung off me and I... let them hang. If you were one of Bobby's boys, then you were well looked after: fine food, the best clothes, and holidays in the Maldives, the South of France and Dubai. I had it all. I was thirty-one and I had it all. And, whilst I had it all, I had also had them all. Fucking footballers, team baths and communal changing. Pop-star wives, supermodel brides, kids in nappies. None of it mattered as they all came around to Bobby's pad for a little action. Around to Bobby's place, where they could take as much of anything that they cared for whilst enjoying the kind of fuck they could only experience with me. Yeah, they stayed over, yeah, there were sex parties, and yeah, I had had more cocks than I knew what to do with, but it went with the champagne lifestyle. As I said, everything was good. Power and money, I had them both and therefore I had it all. No love for me, but I was never looking for it. Why would I need love when I could have the England football captain handcuffed to my bed, pumped full of speed and letting me fuck him bareback? That was the power that I enjoyed. It was a little fun, a little perk of my job.

You know how it is. That was my life, and how fantastic it was.

And so, I begin to question why it was that one day I suddenly fell for a boy I managed. He said no to my advances and that threw me. Nobody had ever said no to me, especially not some seventeen-year-old apprentice who was not even that talented. One thing was for sure, though: he may not have been a seventeen-year-old superstar, but he was a seventeen-year-old kid who I was suddenly in love with – a seventeen-year-old kid who had taken over my mind. The truth was that he didn't want me and, harsh as that may be, I really couldn't handle that. The upshot was that for the first time in my life I prayed to God to help me out. It was the first time in my life that I had ever asked God for anything. Suddenly faith had an attraction, albeit a limited one. For the first time in a long time I wasn't in control of mylife, and that really pissed me off.

Luckily enough, though, the infatuation (which it now was) was a substate of mind, and so the rest of me continued to function normally. I had fallen in love, it would pass. That is what I told myself. My life was too big for this little boy. Besides, when I had fucked him (and it was a 'when'), I would realise there were plenty more fish in the sea, and in the river, and in the pond, and in the shop... Pretty boys are ten a penny and soon become fat twenty-something queens. At least my boyfriend had no clue about my infatuation. Mind you, to be honest, I actually didn't care if he did. He was boring, but a real beauty, one of the boy-band types, you know the sort: nineteen, pretty, long floppy blond hair and firm muscles. Thick as shit, goes like a train, do you need anything more? You never want anyone in bed who's more intelligent than you are – unless of course you are the one who is thick as shit but who goes like a train, in which case you don't need to be clever, just content in the knowledge that every older man wants to fuck you.

Anyway, I suppose you think this is one of those hard-luck stories: the twat gambled it all away, got banged up, is dying of an illness or is a recovering drunk or druggie. Well, I'm not. My life was fucking good, and I would never have given up the clubbing until six am, the bottle of vodka I drank each day, the piles of drugs that I took or the anonymous sex with any number of strangers. I liked sex, I liked drugs and, fuck if it's predictable, but I also liked the rock and roll. I didn't fuck my life up, he did. Actually, they both did. Cunts, the pair of them.

So there I am in the Ivy, England football captain sitting beside me, his wife opposite me and my boyfriend beside her, cosy table for four. The England captain was discreetly wanking me off under the table and I had noticed that her from *Coronation Street*, who was sitting at the table beside us, was clearly watching me receive a hand job. I smiled at her and she turned away in stunned silence. They all do. It's a taboo no one can address. Oh, gay life, it is an unspoken sin. I come at some stage into his napkin, all clean, all relieving, all very... pleasant. I was going to have the cheesecake. I tune in and then back out. The shooting of my load seemed to have tired me out without warning. For some strange reason I stand up and instinctively raise my hand to my heart. What followed was quick, painless and perfectly peaceful: I grab at my chest, fall to the floor and die. I'm thirty-two and I die of a fucking heart attack. I die in the middle of the fucking Ivy, celebs all around, paparazzi already flashing light bulbs at my dead body before I am even cold. What a kick in the nuts. I guess I hadn't looked around that particular corner.

Understandably, I was seriously pissed off. One minute I had the life anyone would envy; the next minute I am dead. As I said, I didn't fuck this up, he did. Him, the fucking puppet master in the sky. I am now content that I have been fucked up the arse in life, fucked up the arse by the tax man and now fucked up the arse by death. I have learnt the hard way that being fucked up the arse is not always a pleasant experience.

Now, Heaven is not as you would picture it to be: the pearly gates, the angels with harps, the white fluffy clouds – none are apparent. In fact, it is like a doctor's waiting room. You go through a door and you take a number from one of those machines that you get at the Tesco meat counter – the red ones, with the numbered paper tickets, which you tear off – and when it's your turn the number flashes on a digital display behind the counter. I took a ticket.

What else should I have done? Number 354 was printed in smudged ink. I looked to the digital display which showed number

101 being called. That just about pushed me over the edge – and I never thought anything would piss me off more than dying, but I was wrong and things were only going to get worse.

I looked around heaven's waiting room, but it was empty, plain and barren, there was just me and one receptionist in a room no bigger than an average council flat – not that I had ever been in a council flat, mind. The impression I am trying to create is that the room was small, small for what I pictured Heaven to be. I wandered over to the receptionist, suddenly curious to know what happened next now that I really was in the waiting room in the sky. The balding man with a shaven white goatee who sat at the reception desk didn't speak, and was a very long way from giving a reassuring smile – in fact, all that came from behind his paper mountain was a scowl, followed by a grunt. The guy looked like shit. Poor bastard, dead and still working. He must have been a real bastard on earth – I didn't ask; I thought it impolite. It turned out he was St Peter. A quick glance at his name badge told me so. It read, 'St Peter – Gatekeeper'. He also had a badge on the other side of his white suit jacket, which read, 'Lose weight now – ask me how!' I didn't ask. I was dead, what the fuck did I care about any more?

Pete ordered me to take a seat and wait; he did this by way of barking the word 'sit' the same way that Father Jack in *Father Ted* would bark the work 'drink' – so I did as I was told.

Contrary to belief, St Peter actually looked like a mean old bastard but, fair play, he was St Peter, a top dog in the sky – he commanded respect. He was one of the bitches up here. For some reason it reminded me of *Prisoner Cell Block H* – no idea why, just odd observation, probably the same flimsy kind of set and those horrible plastic chairs.

As I sat down, and had already taken note of St Peter's white suit; I noticed that I was wearing one too. It also dawned on me that I was the only person in the white waiting room. In fact it was just me, St Peter and a couple of doors. Where were the rest of the people? There should be at least a couple of hundred others if the ticket numbers were right. Mind you, I'm not sure where they would all fit – must get busy here sometimes, like at war times or something. I was sure that I couldn't have been the only person to die so far today, and so quickly came to the conclusion that Heaven was a weird fucking place. There was no reasoning behind this: it was just a gut instinct. With not much else to do I stared at St Peter, and thought about breaking the ice, but instead decided to just watch him as he wrote some details in a book, his white suit ill-fitting and uncomfortable-looking, and Peter himself sighed and groaned at the swelling pile of paperwork that appeared in his in-tray. For a bizarre moment I thought I saw him mouth the word 'bollocks' before getting out some Tipp-Ex, but then I couldn't be sure – he was St Peter; he wouldn't say 'bollocks', would he?

He caught me staring at him and said, 'What the fuck are you looking at, cunt?' His stare burned right into my head, those cold blue eyes I will never forget. Stunned at the outburst, I looked at the floor, not quite sure what the answer was to that question, so instead I inspected a little stain on my white trousers. It then dawned on me that when I had died I had been wearing a black Armani shirt with some dark Armani jeans and a pair of Gucci loafers – where the fuck had they gone? Heaven, it seemed, had converted me into a Don Johnson look alike in a TopMan suit. I thought about bringing this up with someone, but there was only St Peter to complain to – and he had just called me a cunt. The day was just getting better and better.

A buzzer rang as I sat staring into the middle distance thinking about my death, how painless, unexpected and easy it was. How vulnerable and fragile human life really is. Light stuff, you know. However, I concluded that I had probably taken the piss out of God one too many times, and that my early death was indeed my punishment for such blatant disregard for authority. I had been rehearsing my sincere apology to God when the buzzer had rang and brought me back to the very depressive present with speed. It was the very same buzzer that you get in the doctor's surgery, the one that scares you shitless and fills you with excitement and dread as your turn draws near. That short sharp shock of a buzz. The number display flicked leisurely from number 101 to number 674. That kind of threw me, and when it buzzed again number 27 came up. Now I was even more pissed off than I had been before. St Peter didn't take kindly to being called a wanker, despite having happily called me a cunt, yet when I pointed this out and offered to take him outside and sort it out 'man to man' he summoned two angels via the PA system, who quickly turned up and proceeded to take it in turns to slap me around before strapping me into the chair and taking it in turns to punch me in the face. Fucking angels? They were no fucking angels, let me tell you – and I have the bruises to prove it.

It was seventeen hours before number 354 flicked up and the 'angels' released me from my forced imprisonment. If I were ever reincarnated then I would inform the NHS that they have no fucking problems. In heaven you have to wait seventeen hours to just be seen. But then if I was reincarnated, I probably wouldn't mention Heaven. They would think I was a loony and lock me up for my own safety, or release me as one of those care-in-the-community cases. Either way, I was hanging on to the coat-tails of this all just being a really bad trip. I've had worse, a lot worse. Eventually, the angels begrudgingly released me, but not before giving me a couple of sly digs on the way and then holding my arms as St Peter gave me his best shot in the nuts with a full swing from his leg. Nice place, Heaven. I was looking over my shoulder for Matthew, Mark, Luke and John to turn up and mug me. There seemed to be a cartel in residence.

Understandably, I wasn't in the best of moods as the doors to God's office opened. And, in hindsight, my first words of 'Are you some sort of cunt?' may have set things off on a bad footing. It certainly isn't an opening to a conversation with God that I would recommend to anyone else. Funnily enough, though, I wouldn't speak to anyone about talking to God because it really does come with a stigma of insanity attached. Ironically, sadly, amazingly and pitifully, dying wasn't the worst thing that was going to happen to me that day; neither was being roughed up by a couple of angels. This had to be a trip. The most surreal trip of my life. I think I had taken some of those cat-worming tablets again. I would cut my dealer's bollocks off when I came down.

Now God also wasn't as you would expect him to be, although I would expect nothing more with the way Heaven was shaping up. The Lord our God wasn't wearing a white suit like everybody else I had seen, no, of course not. God was wearing black Prada. I know Prada when I see it and that was it, black Prada head to toe. Fat Cuban in his hand, smoke gathering above his head, turkey-like jowls hanging down and resting on the collar of the black shirt. Heavy eyes looking at me over half-moon spectacles – D&G specs, I'm sure of it. His hair slicked back and his pockmarked face looking tired and worn. I guess he must be quite old by now. Old, yes; formidable, absolutely. Either way I was furious.

'Did you just call me a cunt?' His words crisp, his English accented with French and cigar smoke drifting from his mouth as he spoke. I was taken aback slightly as his words came out, firstly, because I never thought I would hear God say the word 'cunt'; secondly, because I never imagined that God would sound like Kenneth Williams, and thirdly, because I never really though I would actually speak to God. I don't know which is the most bizarre but out of the three, I'll plug number one: when God says cunt, it really is offensive. Still there are no certainties in this life, and I was dead. What more could he do? So I just said, 'Yes – and you are.' We had a little row and then six or seven angels came in and had a go at me. Ten minutes later they

walked out, and I was left bloodied and bruised on the floor of the office. His Almighty, meanwhile, sat looking on as he chain-smoked another Cuban. Those angels are tough bastards. Fucking mean punch on them. Must be the arm work they do when playing the harp.

With the angels back in Harlem, God and I were left to continue our discussion and, probably for the first time since I was thirteen, I decided to listen to someone else. That last time that I had listened to someone else, I had ended up being buggered in the showers by my PE teacher, and that had been kind of pleasant. However, that wasn't going to happen here – although it would be the ultimate star fuck. A bit of man-loving with God, what a claim to fame. I really couldn't bring myself to do it, although I was being presumptuous. He hadn't even mentioned it, but if he did... I had already changed my mind and decided to say yes. How many people get the chance to be fucked by God in more than the metaphorical sense? But it was up to him to make the first move. Sensibly deciding to pass over this idea, I told him that I wanted to go home. He laughed. I called him a prick and he told me Hell was worse and he would happily give me a pass there. I asked if there was lots of sodomy in Hell and he said no, and so I said I would stay in Heaven as I kind of preferred the angels and wouldn't mind having a go with some of them. Things got heated again and he, at some stage, rose from his chair in Marlon Brando fashion walked over to me and slapped my face. He was about five foot tall and three foot wide, he wheezed when he walked, and for the man who created the earth he was in really bad shape, but then he was the king of the afterlife and so he could do what the fuck he liked. He controlled the world. He didn't have to do crunches to stay fit, he could just create himself a new body, and so I was beginning to question why he hadn't.

The slap was so powerful that it felt like my skull had been fractured, instantaneous, insufferable pain that was gone the moment I opened my eyes. The pain had gone and I was back on earth – back on earth, back in London, I had been reincarnated, given another chance. Life was still, everything seemed to have frozen. Gradually it thawed and I began to move. Something was odd, though, something not quite right. I felt peculiar, I felt lighter on my feet, all four of them. It was then I realised the bastard had turned me into a cat. This bitch of a death just got worse. How much easier would all of this be if you just died and that was the end. Oh, how I wished. Now if there were some complaints procedure about Heaven, then let me tell you I would be at the front of the fucking queue. Maybe someone needs to set up one of those Accident Group type companies for people who have been fucked over by God by way of a dodgy afterlife. I was more pissed off that I had been reincarnated than I had been about dying – I don't remember any moment of my life when I had ever wished to be a cat.

Not surprisingly, the life of a cat was one I was unaccustomed to. I had to get used to being a fully aware adult male trapped inside a cat's body, but of course, having the instincts of a man but being a cat, the first thing I did was to go down on myself, which was perfect, oh yeah, just dandy – until those razor-sharp teeth kicked in. Cats lick themselves; they do not give themselves pleasure. God is a sadistic bastard, and just because a cat can get down there, doesn't mean it's fun. Just as it gets good, it gets bad – let me tell you that from experience already.

It took a day for me to get to grips with the jumping and the transfer-of-bodyweight thing; I was unsteady and I was being careful. It doesn't matter how many times you see it, falling from great heights has got to hurt. I wasn't going to risk it – purely for the reason I still thought I was tripping and that when I came down I would be stuck up a tree with no clothes on and subsequently on the glittery pages of the *News of the World*. I've been there before and it's not pleasant, it's not clever and it creates a very bad image.

Marc (boyfriend) wouldn't take me in. It's not like I asked him, I couldn't – I was a cat, but he did kick me away when I tried to enter my own apartment – he was too busy with the England Captain. Maybe I should have seen that one coming. I shat on the doorstep and I tripped him up, it's all I had to offer in revenge – kind of pathetic, I know, but I couldn't think of anything else. It was hard. I licked my balls hourly and got aroused, I then got excited, before eventually tearing my scrotum with my teeth. I was still a man in a way and so, just because I could go down on myself. it meant that I really *had* to go down on myself – despite the fact that I knew it would hurt; men are stupid, it's what we do. I walked the backstreets of Soho, and took in the life that I had been seized away from in my prime. I was angry, and after two days of being a cat, I also knew that this was no longer a trip: they *were* really angels, that *was* really God, and I really *did* call him a cunt. That's some heavy shit for a little tabby to take on board. I have some scraps from the bin, although it is the bins from the Ivy – I may be down, but I will never be out.

On my third day in Purgatory, fate strikes me. Or maybe my reality check kicks in. I am hit by a car, and for the second time in a week I die. Or so I hoped. However the car driver speeds me to a vet, where I am resuscitated. God willing, and he was, I make a full recovery, which is aided ever so slightly by the sight of two of the vets shagging on the steel table in the office where recovering animals are kept. It's boy on girl, but you can't have everything. Porn's porn, and he was well hung.

It is when I leave the veterinary surgery that the second bit of fate kicks in and everything becomes clear. The driver of the car that ran me down claims me as his own and, freaky as it is, it is him. The boy. The boy I had fallen for, the boy I had prayed for, the boy I had wanted to give it all up for. Back to his we go. Me, fragile and tired, and sick enough to have to share a bed with him. It is indeed all of my prayers answered.

As the days passed, I got to nestle down and push myself and my nose deep down into his groin, smelling his scent, feeling him, pressing him as he presses me. I was doing what I wanted to do: I was living with this man. It was the two of us, but some things were not right. I was a cat, for starters, but that really wasn't it. It was a mistake – who the fuck had I been fooling when I said I could give it all up for one man? That life's not me, and I know that now. I took a long piss and read the details of my own death in the pages of the *Sun* that lined my litter tray – a glowing tribute to the man I was, the life I led and the friends I had. Marc is there, getting it all, having them all. What a cunt. I don't dwell too long, as a cat reading the paper is slightly suspicious.

That night I couldn't sleep. What had happened began to slowly resound around my head as I started to figure it all out. That next evening when he came home, I knew that God had answered my prayers: I had loved this boy and God had brought me close to him in the only way possible. He had taken my lifestyle and brought me into the life of the only man I ever wanted in the only way possible. It was God's way, his own mysterious way, which nobody will ever be able to figure out. I sat with the boy on the sofa that night and watched my own funeral run as a minor story on *London Tonight*. I saw my friends, I saw my coffin and I saw that soulless, sex-, drink- and drug-fuelled lifestyle go up in flames as my coffin was incinerated. I thought of God and how he had listened and answered all I had ever asked him

for. I lifted my leg up and licked my nuts (which I could now do without hurting myself) – the only good thing to come out of this whole situation. With each long sensual lick I thought of God, thought about that fat bastard in his fat chair. I wagged my tail with pleasure and looked forward to the day when I got through my nine lives and I could get back to Heaven and kick the shit out of that Prada-wearing bastard for doing this to me. In my head I could see him, Peter and the angels all sitting around having a good old laugh – be careful what you wish for, that's what I had learnt. I licked my balls once more, purred and came. I would get the bastards back, every one of them; it would mean an eternity in Hell but I knew that wasn't so bad: I had already been to Heaven, so I was prepared.

Abdul Aziz and the Intifada
Jeffrey Buchanan

Abdul Aziz and the Intifada
Jeffrey Buchanan

The shooting started in central Hebron just after three in the afternoon. Abdul Aziz Al-Mufti lay on his bed in the heat where the feelings of anguish and hatred mixed with tedium. The shooting was near the Al-Mufti household, but the youth didn't get up because the combination of emotions stuck him to his bed in paralysis. On the wall was the picture if his grandmother, whose features were as much a part of his world as the emotions which ate his mind and left him motionless. He looked at the septuagenarian behind the dusty glass and the dark, thick frame. Then a volley of shots went zip-zip-zip through the air and a scream came up from beneath the house, and his heart pounded. He sat up and looked about the stifling room and the sweat came in beads on his upper lip. He caught his grandmother's eye. It was she who had told him to die like a martyr. "Death is a bad moment that passes," she had said to him as she had scoured out a zucchini. It was as if she were there in the bedroom at that very moment as the firing hit the air and the screams burst from the neighbourhood.

The old lady whom he adored in death as much as he had in life was staring at him. He saw her dressed in long dark robes with her bundle of belongings, fleeing down a dusty path as she left her village. "It was like that, as I told you so many times." This was the official history, as if etched into marble tablets and held aloft to the universal brethren for daily worship. His grandmother's wisdom thick and unctuous and inculcated within him like the other great beliefs that people were dying for. But then he wanted to pull down the photo, to rip it up, to run away and be free from this nightmare. A tainted taste came into his mouth. That other world he had seen hinted at on television and in magazines existed to set him free. But it wasn't here in these streets, not in Hebron, where you were born to suffer and be killed off in a hail of bullets. He and Fardi could leave together. He closed his eyes and saw the two of them getting on a bus for Jerusalem, the vision rolling forward like one of those old black-and-white movies filled with static. He and Fardi were at the airport. They were boarding a plane and leaving for a place where there wasn't a perpetual struggle for a homeland. Then the movie flickered and went into a fluster of broken images and bits and pieces of nothing. Only the old woman remained behind his closed eyes as the airport scene dissipated: she was scouring the zucchini and the white flesh was plopping onto the table. The sharp knife she was holding dropped as she looked at him in astonishment at being a traitor. Her fat arms swung as she raised them and shouted, "But you are a Palestinian!"

Abdul Aziz realised the futility of dreams. Dreams only melted. You held them for a moment, maybe even a minute, and then they became absorbed by reality. From further away, a blast of gunfire sounded. He got up from his sweaty bed and went into the living room. From where he stood he could see smoke rising from the nearby school grounds. This attack had been expected but it was the tedium of it that filtered sourly through him. The suicide bomb in Tel Aviv three days previously had been detonated by two Hebron youths. Everyone in the neighbourhood knew it had been Tarik and Hamid Al-Badri, the two cousins who lived behind the mosque on the other side of the school grounds. It had taken the Jews this much time to extract their information and they were there now with tanks and explosives to blow up the cousins' dwelling. Abdul Aziz thought, "Sixteen Zionists dead in that bomb attack. They will need to kill at least sixty of our people." He scratched in his armpit and looked at the smoke rising from the school house. "They will kill three or four today and then leave after they have blown up the Al-Badri house. Then they will come back in two days to kill some more Palestinians." It was an equation he knew like something from geometry or mathematics. A great wave of sadness and ennui went through him. At such moments his grandmother would have raised her fat arms and uttered, "Yeee! Yeee!" She would have shaken her finger at him and told him there was no sacrifice greater than the fight for a free homeland. He shook his head and told her to be peaceful. She was dead and wrapped up in a white shroud and buried in the land she had mourned over for half a century. "Go," he whispered. "Please."

Three shots snapped the air and broke his reverie there in the family living room. Smoke puffed up from the school building. "Where is Fardi?" he uttered. "Fardi, come here." He didn't know what to do. The small espresso pot was on the table and he picked it up. But the effort of brewing coffee was too great and the beverage too expensive. Then he saw the absurdity of making coffee while his people were being hounded in the streets below him. The mullah called from the mosque behind the school grounds, yelling in staccato shrieks at the enemy through his megaphone.

"Fardi," Abdul Aziz said. If his grandmother was there, she would have pushed him out the door and told him to throw stones at the enemy. He gripped the espresso pot in his hand and imagined Fardi out there defending his people. He saw his grandmother looking at him, standing there limply holding a coffee pot. Her look incredulous as if he were simple. "Be a man. Be one of your people." The room smelled of smoke suddenly, as if it had been piped in. "I'll leave," he said. "With Fardi."

Then Abdul Aziz heard the cousins' house being blown up. He couldn't hear the inevitable ululations but he imagined them. Such sounds were so familiar: women crying, men shouting, children screaming; they rattled in his mind and stung him. "You will be honoured by death," he muttered. He promised those who would be killed that he would follow their bodies when they were paraded through the streets on their funeral stretchers that evening. He went onto the balcony and looked out through the glare at the white and grey city of Hebron. Beneath him a group of youths stood in the shadows of the ruined apartment block that Susanah Borno had been shot in. Susanah Borno. With reverence he said her name again and again. Susanah Borno killed by a bullet through her head as she sat sewing her wedding veil.

From the school yard to the right of the dead neighbour's building, a flock of pigeons scattered as another burst of explosives threw up dust and stones as if from a volcano. The cousins' house was being obliterated. He saw it all happening through eyes dazed with something he couldn't decipher. Then, just as the wall collapsed and thundered, Abdul Aziz saw Fardi running down the street with a Palestinian flag waving behind him. Fardi was wearing the tight red T-shirt he had bought at the market when they had gone there together last Saturday. As Fardi ran he shouted: "Soldiers!"

Abdul Aziz leaned over the balcony. He yelled, "Fardi!" The soldiers were storming around the corner. One of them took aim at Fardi. Abdul Aziz shouted, "Fardi! Jews!" He held up his hand, the one holding the espresso pot, and waved it at Fardi.

Ariel David took off his uniform and stepped into the shower. His shoulder blades felt like wooden pieces inserted under his skin and he let the hot water burn into him. The day seethed in his mind. The afternoon he dulled by thinking about what the evening would bring when he was dropped off in Jerusalem for a night of recreation. He was a soldier, a lieutenant. He was a man who had to concentrate on saving his nation; a bad afternoon couldn't be a distraction. He dressed in his best clothes. He put on Bulgari and straightened down his blond hair and went out into the night to get the military transport to Jerusalem. But the image remained inserted into his mind as the bus went through the dusty outskirts of the city. "It's war," he reminded himself. "We're fighting." His aunt had known the woman blown up in the Tel Aviv attack which he had been avenging this afternoon. "Dora Goldberg was my great friend and those animals blew her up." Ariel David heard his aunty; he saw her in her Tel Aviv apartment crying on the morning after her friend had been blown to bits in a bus on her way to work. He bit into his nails as the bus raced through the city's outskirts: This was life in modern Israel. This was what Arab scum did to the Jewish homeland. He pulled skin from his left index finger and bit into the skin on his thumb. The image of the blood spurting from the kid's head. He closed his eyes and saw his mother praying and he heard his aunty weeping because Dora had been cut up in pieces by a suicide bomber. He looked at his nails: they were raw and pink and the moons were ugly. For a long time he stared at his right hand: the index finger was the one that had pulled the trigger that had killed the Palestinian. Ariel David looked out at Jerusalem as it flashed past him: a row of houses centuries old, an azure mosque, a cream-coloured church, the shops where you could buy Liberian diamonds. But the image was there as sturdy as the mosque or shops: the pistol falling, the kid plopping to the ground, the stone-throwers chasing the soldiers back up the street to the tanks shouting "Zionists!"

"This is my life," Ariel uttered. "Don't be morbid." The soldier behind him laughed and said something about his Thai girlfriend. Then another yelled an obscenity and all of the soldiers burst into laughter. Ariel David looked at his colleagues and turned his grimace into a smile. Life was like this. It was bittersweet. It was tribal. You fought. Life continued. You did what was right and you told yourself you believed it because without belief there was the nothingness of self destruction. You didn't sit back and wait to be herded into camps by Nazis. Dora Goldberg was a woman who had been cut up, cut out of life by enemies. He saw her now as the bus flashed past the Ottoman Palace and he winked at her in complicity at what he had done to avenge her. Dora had raised African violets in her small apartment and his aunt had several of them in her own house, gifts from Dora. The African violets in the soldier's mind as the bus sped down the highway to the ancient city; a woman who had raised beautiful flowers, whose only concerns had centred on her family, and her violets had been cut up by Arab nails and shrapnel.

Hannah Al-Mufti lifted the broken head in her hands and kissed the washed hair and then laid her son back on his funeral pillow. Where would the tears come from? she asked herself. How many more tears can there be in this household and in this city? It was the youth's father who was weeping. He stood in the same spot where his son had stood that afternoon dreaming about escape from Hebron. "We sacrifice our children," he thought, "and when we do it's like knives cutting our souls into two pieces." Every father sent his son to the streets to fight and to be killed. This was the moment he had known would occur. The hurt went through his head and his heart. He went to his son and looked down at him.

Fardi stood in the dark beneath the room where his dead friend lay and listened to Abdul Aziz's father sobbing. Then he heard the mother start her crying. It was a sound as frequent and as familiar as the tunes that introduced the nightly Iraqi and Egyptian soap operas on television. His parents would be crying for him one day. It would be the same routine: shot dead, wrapped up in white cloth, laid out in the living room to be wept over, then paraded down the street and popped into a hole in the ground while men fired off machine guns and swore vengeance. It had nearly been his turn this afternoon, but instead it had been Abdul Aziz who had taken the bullet. The darkness wrapped further round Fardi. He lit a cigarette and moved deeper into the room so that he would escape those coming to say goodbye to his dead friend lying directly him. He whispered, "See him as I did when we were together." Fardi slumped down the wall to the floor as the tears began. He saw life for what it was: the lives they led were as predictable as the process of dying and being buried. The snot seeped from his nose and wet his lips and the taste stung his mouth as the sobs struck him. It was not fair. It was nothing but murder. Abdul Aziz had wanted escape from this dust and these deaths. He had dreamed of Paris and not the label of martyr. "I should have been killed, not him," thought Fardi as he got up and went to the old bed against the far wall and lay face down on it. It was in this bed that they had loved each other. "Abdul Aziz," he said quietly into the pillow.

Ariel David stood at the bedroom window and looked out over the city. He lit another cigarette and drew in heavily.

"You smoke too much," Ben said. "You'll die of lung cancer before you're thirty and leave me a widow." Ariel David did not answer. That kind of sissy, camp comment he could not be bothered with. He should have stayed in the barracks with his military companions. Or he could have had counselling with that psychologist who was there for these occasions. He saw her with her bobbed hair and her pleasant smile and he heard her New York accent and he scoffed at her New York mind. He looked at the smoke he had just exhaled and saw that bobbed creature talking nonsense about deaths she had no idea of. She was a Jew, but she wasn't an Israeli. She was a psychologist, but she wasn't a fighter. She had never killed anybody. Cynicism went through him like a chemical. He saw that kid topple over the balcony, saw him fall plop onto the ground below him, the pistol in his hand:"This is avenging Jewish deaths," he told himself. He stubbed out the cigarette and pulled off his underpants. In the mirror he saw his outline: tall, strong, handsome. He got hard as he looked at his image. He climbed into bed and held been and began to kiss him. But the youth with the flag appeared, that one in the red T-shirt, the obvious leader who had thrown stones and taunted them and shouted "Jews! Zionists!" Ariel David closed his eyes and nuzzled his nose into his boyfriend's cheek. Then he began to kiss him. He ran his hands through his lover's hair and his mind was a confusion of African violets and taunts and hatreds.

Fardi had waited a month since Abdul Aziz had been murdered for that blond soldier to return to Hebron. In his head and heart he knew what had to happen. It was no use living this dirt life and thinking all the time, "I will live to see a free Palestine." There was no use being alive and merely waiting for dreams to be fulfilled by others. He sat thinking in the orchard behind the house. The heat beat down on him as he smoked and he saw in his mind the thing he had to do to make sure that he didn't go on being a useless victim. The uselessness of a belief in hope attacked him: a free homeland, a life without poverty, justice from other nations. He lit another cigarette and thought that Abdul Aziz had been right: they should have run off together in the absence of anything positive. It could have been just the two of them, of being together somewhere wonderful like Paris or Sydney. Then he remembered Susanah Borno and the others, the long, long list of martyrs. They were like a template to everything else you might desire. They came back to remind you of what was important. "Abdul Aziz died for the Intifada," he said. That was the legitimacy of belief returning. You fought back. You did what you had to do. He laughed as he stubbed out his cigarette because he had just seen wisdom. He had just understood it. It was all wrapped up like a kernel of something in a tight shell which had just been opened and displayed before him. He looked at his watch. It was that time. There was no way but to go towards it. It was the soldier with the blond hair he wanted in particular but it didn't matter if it wasn't him. A busload of them was worth the ultimate sacrifice. He went up the stairs of his house as a Lebanese pop song burst forth from the kitchen radio. The lyrics were about love and denial. His mother was flicking through an Egyptian magazine with glossy pictures of actresses. She looked up and smiled at him but he said nothing as he kissed her forehead.

Glimmer
Richard Cawley

Glimmer
Richard Cawley

He opened his eyes at last. The chalky-blue ceiling, naïvely painted with birds, olive boughs and wispy clouds, would have enchanted him, a year ago...

He must get up. He had lain in bed with his eyes closed for two hours, suspended in the state of consciousness midway between sleep and waking; the state, which, in healthy people, often induces a feeling of blissful cosiness.

Awakened by the alarm on his mobile phone at eight, he had taken the tiny apricot-coloured pill. He never got up until at least ten, which allowed time for the worst side effects of the Venlafaxine to wear off. On a good morning, if he waited for two hours before getting up, he might avoid the worst of the dizziness and sweats. The awful nausea, however, would remain until at least until midday and the constant sensation of leaden limbs and butterflies in his stomach would be with him until he returned to bed for the night.

Which was the lesser of the two evils, night-time's roller coaster of tortuous dreams or waking consciousness with the accompanying constant feeling of panic and imminent doom? What was the unknown thing he feared so much? Certainly not death, which might even be welcome. He had never actually considered suicide, but for the last six months he had simply not wanted to be alive. Sleep seemed to offer the nearest state to oblivion, but even then he was cheated of a single moment's rest. What kind of diabolic mind scripted his never-ending nightmares?

He showered and dressed painfully slowly. Occasionally he would stop and sit on the bed to try to gather his scattered thoughts enough to remember the next stage in his morning's toilet ritual.

Oh, god! How could simple things seem so difficult? Oh, god!

Would he ever be any better? The doctors promised he would, when the pills began to really kick in. Still, at least he was better than he had been three months ago, he admitted to himself; otherwise his sister would never have allowed him to make the plane journey alone.

It was too late for the Locanda al Leone's generous breakfast, which was included in the price of his room. This was a relief, as he wouldn't have to excuse himself to the large, motherly woman he assumed was proprietress of the hotel. He was well aware that he'd become painfully thin, but the mere thought of eating, of nourishing his despised self, at the best of times seemed, somehow, obscene. He would make himself eat later in the day, but in the morning the nausea made anything more than a sip of water unthinkable.

Eventually, he opened the small drawer in the bedside table and took out a book and a small Buddha's head, which he had bought two years previously in the British Museum. He placed the little sculpture on the polished parquet floor in front of the tall window, then took two pillows from his bed and arranged them carefully about a metre in front of the temporary shrine. On these, he sat cross-legged, forcing his spine upright from its now characteristic stoop. Even on the worst days he had somehow at least gone through the ritual of his morning meditation. It was the one thing that seemed to help a little. He opened the book at 'Prayers to be Said at the Start of a Meditation Session'.

He silently repeated the 'Prayer of Refuge and Bodhicitta' the required three times, then, aloud, 'The Four Immeasurable Thoughts':

May all sentient beings have happiness and the causes
of happiness;
May all sentient beings be free from suffering and the
causes of suffering;
May all sentient beings...

"Fuck all sentient beings!" he blurted aloud, falling forward. He sat sobbing for several minutes, head in his hands, then slowly rose to his feet. He dried his eyes on one of the pillows before throwing them back on the bed, then carefully returned the Buddha and the book to the bedside drawer.

He must stop crying! He must somehow pull himself together.

As he emerged from the hotel's womblike warmth and smells of fresh bread and coffee, the surprisingly chilly morning air in the small alleyway hit him like a smack on the back of the head. It seemed to clear his head somewhat! His thoughts started to be less fragmented and he began to recall the events of the previous day.

It had been the first of this four-day visit to Venice and, on more than a few previous occasions, he remembered, the sheer overwhelming beauty of his surroundings had managed to penetrate the chink in his armour of gloom. The memory of these brief respites caused him to quicken his pace. As he emerged from the Calle dei Albanese, the narrow alleyway that led from his *pensione* down the side of the ancient Ducal Prison, he stopped in his tracks. It was impossible not to be impressed by the majestic beauty of San Giorgio Magiori on the other side of the Grand. Its distinctive outline, blurred slightly as it loomed through the faint grey mist, reflected his sombre mood. Sunshine would have been jarring... Inappropriate.

He turned right and walked over the small hump that bridged the a gap in the broad quayside, where a narrow tributary, the Rio de la Paglia, runs into the Grand Canal. He stopped momentarily on the bridge, peering over and past the huddle of Japanese tourists posing for photographs. The irony of the moment forced a glimmer of a smile across his colourless face. The next bridge to cross the narrow tributary was perhaps the most photographed backdrop in Venice, the Bridge of Sighs, which links the prison with the Doge's Palace.

The prison, he discovered, was now put to rather happier usage. He stopped in front of the open door and read the poster advertising the baroque concert to be performed there that evening. Why not? he thought. It would be a way of keeping himself awake that little bit longer for once. Perhaps if he could stay awake longer he might sleep better.

He turned round again and stared at the softly gleaming stretch of water. Close to the bridge rows of sleeping gondolas, wrapped in blue tarpaulins like hikers' anoraks, bobbed almost merrily in the swell caused by a passing speedboat. Tied to their striped poles, they made a colourful contrast with the pale sepia waterscape and the passing tourists dressed in varying shades of grey, black and beige.

There were, happily, far fewer tourists than he had expected, he noted as he walked back along the quayside, past the imposing façade of Hotel Danieli. Then he stopped, turned and headed back the way he had come. He suddenly decided on a goal for his morning's expedition. He would try to find the food markets, he decided. They were somewhere close to the Rialto Bridge, he remembered.

Even in Saint Mark's Square, there were amazingly few tourists amongst the pigeons and puddles. Of course, it was the day *after* the weeklong Mardi Gras celebrations. This was probably the quietest time of the year in Venice. It began to rain slightly.

He walked around the square in the shelter of its dark stone arcades, draped with their distinctive cream canvas blinds. The windows blazed with all manner of fancy goods, intended to tempt tourists into parting with their yen, euros and dollars. Lace and coloured glass, fake tapestries, a violin, a surreal sculptured naked torso with drawers opening from it, like a Salvador Dali painting.

An elderly woman walking towards him seized his attention. She was wearing a short, straight, knee-length skirt of discreetly patterned leopardskin with an expensive-looking, rust-coloured suede jacket. Had she chosen the jacket to match her short, well-cut hair, or vice versa? What appeared so incongruous, however, was that this smartly dressed and very refined-looking woman was licking a large, dripping ice-cream cone, with obvious unabashed pleasure! He warmed to this elegant anonymous stranger enjoying her simple pleasure with such childlike innocence. He liked her...

As he left the square and zigzagged his way through the maze of narrow pedestrian streets, many windows, he noticed, were still crammed with elaborately decorated carnival masks for sale and eighteenth-century costumes for hire. The windows between dazzled with yet more rainbow glassware, jewellery and lace. Others tempted with expensive designer outfits by Krizia, Dolce and Gabanna and the like. Leopardskin prints, he noted, were definitely *de rigeur* in Venice that season

He stopped in front of the church of San Zulian. He took his guidebook from his backpack. Odd name. Who was San Zulian? It was a local spelling for San Juliano, he read. Who, he wondered, was Saint Julian? He would text Chris, his brother-in-law, when he stopped in a café. Chris would look it up on the Internet. He loved any excuse to be glued for hours to his computer. Lynne complained she was an Internet widow. However, Chris *had* found the ridiculously cheap Venice flight for him in little more than a few minutes!

Should he enter the church of San Zulian? He had been so disappointed the day before with San Francisco della Vigna. It had been so cold and dull and lifeless. He knew there was another big church in Venice connected with Saint Francis. Sam had once taken him there to show him a famous painting of the Madonna by the artist Bellini.

When he could face it, he'd scour the guidebook and try to find it. Sam had always had a thing about Saint Francis. He called him the Christian Buddha. The lives of Buddha and Saint Francis had been so similar. They both rejected their wealthy backgrounds to work with lepers and other outcasts; when they weren't engrossed in solitary prayer and meditation, that is. If Saint Francis had lived today, he mused, his mother might have been like the lady with the leopard-print skirt and the dripping ice cream...

A sudden shower forced him to reluctantly decide. Once inside the church however, he silently thanked the little shower. It must have been organised by Saint Francis, or Buddha or San Juliano, whoever he might have been.

Unlike the sepulchral gloom of San Francisco the day before, San Juliano's memory had been preserved in a glittering jewel box! The church's elaborate ceiling was a patchwork of richly coloured painted scenes framed by panels of dark gleaming wood and faded gilding. The pillars on either side of the countless side chapels were covered in a superb brocaded fabric. This was patterned with baroque scrolls and baskets of flowers silhouetted in ruby silk velvet, against a background of cloth of gold. It all seemed quite unreal. It felt as if he were in a film. He felt invisible, unable to connect somehow. It was stunningly beautiful, but almost too beautiful. He lit a candle for Sam and left. The rain had stopped.

He reached the Rialto Bridge and crossed over as quickly as he could. Even though there were still surprisingly few tourists, the shops on the bridge and the surrounding area were overflowing with cheap ugly souvenirs. He had come to Venice to escape from ugliness.

Once over the bridge he turned right and, within minutes, he entered a totally different world. A world of simple daily local life. A scene where, apart from the fashions of the various characters, life was going on much as it had in Venice for centuries. A world where middle-aged women stopped to gossip between haggling and joking with the various jovial market traders.

Yes, he noted again, leopard was definitely this season's print! And as with women all over Italy, he also noted, Venetian mamas hadn't given up their real fur coats!

How Sam had loved this market. How Sam had loved all produce markets. Anything to do with food, in fact. That's why he had got on so well with Lynne, his sister. They were both obsessed with food and cooking. Lynne missed Sam almost as much as he did.

He suddenly realised how cold he was. A small, very basic-looking café seemed appealing. He ordered a café latte and a brandy. Alcohol wasn't really a very good idea with his medication, but what the hell! He sat down. His hand shook as he held the cup. Would his hands ever stop shaking? Would the butterflies in his stomach ever stop? Still, he must do what Lynne had said. Just take each day as it comes and tick off the good things. Tick off each little achievement. Well, he was here in Venice, sitting in a café, drinking a coffee and a brandy. That in itself was a huge step forward, he mentally tried to convince himself. He flicked through his guidebook. Then he remembered the name of the church he was looking for. Even though it had been built by the Franciscans, it didn't actually have Saint Francis in its name. There it was on the map. Not even that far away either. Santa Maria Gloriosa dei Frari. Commonly abbreviated to 'the Frari'. He took a yellow magic marker out of the front pocket of his backpack and highlighted what seemed like the most straightforward route. He was getting much better with maps. Sam had always been the one who took charge of maps and directions.

Nourished and warmed by the milky coffee and slightly mellowed by the effect of the alcohol, he wandered up and down between the parallel rows of market stalls, which were piled high with an extraordinary variety of fresh vegetables and fruit.

A little further along, the artichokes and aubergines gave way to displays of glistening seafood of every kind, which stared back at him with eyes so fresh and bright, they would surely swim quickly away if dropped back into the lagoon!

Time to text Lynne, he decided, leaning against an empty stall.- "Cold and grey, but still beautiful. No tourists! On veg market. You would go mad! Seen weird lettuce. Cream, finely streaked with deep red. Looks like giant hybrid rose! Who's Saint Julian? Internet! Please! Miss you. Thanks for being you. X."

He started off on his planned yellow-marked route. Follow the yellow brick road. He felt himself smile. He'd just made a joke of sorts. To himself, admittedly. How long had it been since he'd indulged in a humorous thought? He made a mental tick.

He noticed a sign on a wall pointing to the Museo del Arte Moderne. He had never been there, but he remembered how much Sam and he had loved the Museum of Modern Art in Rome.

He quickly found it on the map. Not that much of a detour from the yellow brick road.

How could such an important museum be in quite such an obscure location? The crumbling palazzo which housed the museum was at the end of a tiny dingy alleyway. Inside the building, however, the views from the upper floors onto the Grand Canal, which lapped at the museum's foundations, were quite breathtaking.

The effect of brandy on an empty stomach and the dwindling side-effects of his medication had by now softened his mood considerably. He felt even more as if in a dream. Perhaps a Fellini film?

He wandered around in a daze. Under yet more frescoed ceilings, he drifted past a succession of paintings by nineteenth-century Italian painters he had never heard of. One room was crammed with an assortment of decidedly erotic male nude sculptures. Then more works of art by twentieth-century artists he knew well; Miro, Klimt, Bonnard, even Henry Moore. He could hardly take any of it in. He just wandered quickly from room to room until he came to one filled with a series of strangely haunting white sculptures by an artist called Adolfo Wildt. Each ghostly figure had strange deep hollows instead of eyes. These sightless creatures appealed to him for some reason. Their vacant expressions looked like he felt. Did he resemble a sculpture by Adolfo Wildt? Who was Adolfo Wildt? Another project for Chris and Google!

Suddenly he stopped. He felt the blood drain from his face. The coincidence seemed too weird. The most striking and beautiful of the white expressionless figures was a likeness of Saint Francis! It must be a message. But what was the message? He suddenly felt claustrophobic... Panic...

Outside, as his breathing slowed to normal, he noticed the change in the weather. The sun felt quite warm on his back as he walked briskly away from the museum.

The size of the piazza as he emerged from the narrow street quite took his breath away. He looked up to see its name painted on the wall of one of the tall ancient buildings which surrounded the long rectangular space. Campo san Polo. A tall, thin, sad-looking young man stood against the wall under the sign playing sad music on a lute.

He examined his map. He was still on his planned route. It was really quite warm. He decided to join a small group sitting at tables outside a café. A beer would be good! He ordered a small one from the affable waiter, who replied in English even though he had attempted to order in Italian. The beer came quickly and he sat back, suddenly almost relaxed, to sip his welcome drink and observe his surroundings.

Opposite, a building with arched windows was painted exactly the colour of mashed strawberries and cream, he noted. The windows of most buildings sported window boxes filled with flowers. Sparrows! So rare in England now. The passers-by all walked at a very leisurely pace. Everyone looked quite happy and relaxed.

He discreetly examined the occupants of the two small neighbouring tables. On his left a dumpy woman was engrossed in a newspaper. She wore a skirt and matching shoes the colour of conkers – he liked to put names to colours. Her cream knitted jacket was fastened with gold buttons and she wore small, expensive-looking gold earrings. The rimless spectacles perched on the end of her nose added even more gravitas to the already rather superior expression she wore. It was only her surprisingly bright, glossy red lipstick that added a slight hint of hidden frivolity.

The elderly gentleman sitting at the table on his left was also reading a newspaper. He wore a shirt and tie and a jacket made of the sort of fine smooth tweed he had only ever seen on Italian men.

It helped, observing and speculating and making mental notes about people. It kept his mind occupied. Stopped it from dwelling on his own problems.

An elderly couple with two black dogs on leads stopped in front of the café to examine the menu. A scruffy dog, which obviously belonged to the café and had been sunning himself on its step, stood up, stretched and strolled, tail wagging, over to examine the two newcomers. Bums thoroughly sniffed and obviously approved of, the dog returned to his position in the doorway. A short time later a small white Scotty dog received the same territorial welcome.

On the opposite side of the square a very young-looking and indisputably ugly girl strolled past pushing a huge old-fashioned pram. It had glossy deep-red paintwork, embellished with fine gold scrollwork and large spoked wheels. He couldn't remember when he had last seen a pram like that. Everyone now had a small canvas buggy, which collapsed easily to fit into a car boot or lift easily onto a bus. This pram was like the one he remembered at the back of the garage when he was really young, before his parents moved to London. He even remembered the pram's make: Silver Cross!

Topped with a collapsible canvas hood, this one looked almost like an eighteenth-century carriage, he decided. It seemed to fit in perfectly with the historic surroundings. Rather more, he thought, than the fat ugly girl, who wore very tight jeans with bits of embroidery and sequins scattered here and there and a tight white top, which revealed a section of her large white stomach.

Nevertheless, he decided, he rather liked the fat ugly girl with her eighteenth-century pram. She suddenly disappeared around a corner. How would she cope when she came to one of those stepped bridges which crossed the network of narrow canals? he wondered.

The beer was slipping down a treat. For the first time in ages, he had to admit to himself, he was actually feeling relaxed. The ridiculously expensive counsellor had, in the end, actually been of some use. A friend had given him his number. There was a waiting list of at least four months to see a counsellor on the National Health, he had discovered. Not much help if a patient had suicidal tendencies!

At first, he hadn't been able to quite believe that anyone could charge quite that much for a forty-five minute session. He had been so afraid that he might just sit and cry through the whole of his first visit, without being able to speak, that he'd spent a morning writing a list of all the things that had gone wrong in his life recently. All the disasters that had conspired to rob him of his sanity.

The crash and having to organise the funeral might have been enough in themselves, but the whole drama with Sam's hellish mother would surely have been enough to drive the sanest of beings over the edge. If only they had sorted out their wills as they had always meant to! Then having to sell the house, get rid of so much of their stuff and physically move into the new flat. Finally, the ultimate slap in the face: having been made redundant!

After forty-five minutes, the counsellor told him that time had unfortunately run out for that week, but he thought that *he* would have had a mental breakdown in the circumstances!

At the next session, he was told that what he had suffered was a 'reactional mental breakdown'. These were the quickest to recover from, it seemed. He shouldn't need many sessions. The therapist dropped his professional demeanour at this stage in the session and suggested that in fact he might be better spending the money on a holiday rather than counselling.

Nothing could undo the disastrous chain of events that had occurred, he explained. The best plan of action, therefore, was to let the pills do their work and allow time to play its conventional role.

He'd repeated his conversation with the counsellor over dinner with Lynne and Chris that evening. Chris had been on the Internet the moment he had swallowed his last forkful of Thai green curry. They had both been incredibly kind and supportive all through his illness and after. However, he was sure that Chris would be relieved not to come home to his brother-in-law's constantly brooding presence for a few days. Not to mention the minor havoc he had wreaked on Chris's beloved herbaceous borders, where, as a therapy, Lynne had set him to work weeding one warm afternoon. He had insisted, however, as a means of compensation, on paying for the new batch of the wallflowers he had unwittingly mistaken for weeds.

His reverie was broken by the distinctive little double beep from his mobile phone, informing him that he had received a text message. It read, "Mythical mediaeval European saint. Legend states he accidentally topped his parents, mistaking them for his wife in bed with another man. Spent rest of his life making amends with saintly works! Catholic website. You sound better! X."

He suddenly noticed that the man in the tweed jacket at the next table had been replaced by the girl with the pram, who was also engrossed in her mobile phone, both thumbs adorned with silver rings, tapping away at what seemed like the speed of light. She finished sending the text and shifted her concentration to her burger and Coca-Cola.

Some time later, her meal finished and her text message not replied to, she adopted a particularly sour expression and began examining her bitten fingernails with such intensity that it appeared she expected to discover the meaning of life in their close vicinity. She was beginning to annoy him now. He decided he didn't like her after all and stood up, stepping over the dog to go into the café and pay for his beer.

As he emerged into the now warm midday sunshine, the sad young man who had been playing the lute walked past, carrying his instrument in a battered leather case. Where was he going? Home to some tiny apartment to make himself lunch? Was he going to eat alone? Why did he look so sad? If only he'd the courage to invite the sad young lute player to join him somewhere for lunch! He would never have dared, even when he had been well. How he envied the bum-sniffing café dog!

He knew he really should eat something, but the mere thought of food made his stomach turn over. No, he would eat later, before the concert.

The Frari was just as grand and glorious as he remembered, although he had forgotten the carved wooden choir stalls in the centre of the nave, which the guidebook assured were very unusual for the period in Italy, although quite common in Spain. The church was crammed with the most superb paintings, but he was beginning to feel tired. He really wanted to enjoy it properly! Now he'd found it, perhaps it would be better to come back another day and spend some time there. For now, though, he would just find the Bellini *Madonna*.

She was just as haunting and strangely calm as he remembered. It felt wrong, though, somehow, to be gazing on her serene loveliness without Sam... No, he mustn't cry. He'd been doing so well! He'd go back to the *pensione* for a siesta. Quit while the going was good!

As he left the side chapel, which housed the painting, he slipped on an uneven patch in the marble floor. He skidded slightly, but recovered his balance just in time to stop himself from falling headlong. Somebody nearby laughed. He was shocked. It was a surprisingly loud and rather odd sounding laugh. He looked up.

A young man wearing a red canvas jacket was grinning at him. He then made a small circular movement on his chest with a bunched fist and mouthed, "Sorry". He was deaf. Of course! That accounted for the loudness and slightly odd timbre of the laugh.

No one could have remained hurt or affronted, however, when faced with such an obviously genuine and good-natured apology.

The stocky young man, though not conventionally good-looking, had the kind of pleasant affable face which was undeniably attractive. His cheeky laddish grin coupled with the square angular features gave him a rather impish appearance. Added to this his jaw-length, sandy-coloured hair made him look as if he had just stepped out of a Renaissance painting. A merry friend of Romeo, perhaps? Mercutio?

The young man turned away, with an even more appealing grin of farewell. It was rather the optmistic colour of his jacket, he thought, rather thanhis deafness, which seemed to set him distinctly apart from the group of somberly dressed young people he rejoined.

A middle-aged woman wearing dark droopy clothes was lecturing the young group, in a loud authoritative voice on the particular work of art they were surrounding. As she faced the painting in question, as she extolled its various merits, itwould have been impossible forthe deaf boy to lip-read, he realised. It was hardly surprising, therefore, if his mind wandered!

Just as he reached the choir stalls on his way to leave the church, he felt a firm tap on his shoulder. Mercutio was standing behind him, holding a camera at shoulder height. He grinned again, but this time with a questioning expression and a directional nod, which clearly translated as"May I take your photo?"

Visibly frustrated by the look of incomprehension he received in reply, Mercutio scrabbled in his jacket pocket, retrieved a small notepad and a pen, scribbled furiously for a few seconds, then handed over the note.

It read: "I'm a fine art student. At the Slade. I like your face. Can I take a photo? I want to use you in a painting."

He took the pen from the boy's hand and wrote underneath, "If you like. How did you know I was English?"

Another loud guffaw as the boy prodded the guidebook wedged under his arm.

He left the church feeling...He didn't quite know what this new feeling was. Unsettled, but not unpleasantly so. Then it occurred to him that he had not spoken to anyone, except the waiter, all day. How strange, then, that his first social interaction of the day should be with someone who couldn't actually hear him speak. And yet they had managed their brief encounter more than adequately, he felt...

*

After a deep and what, for once, had seemed a dreamless sleep, he woke just before seven that evening. He felt incredibly groggy and spaced out. It was very difficult to get up. He made himself get out of bed. He felt better after a shower. He didn't feel sick, but the butterflies were still there. The concert was at nine. Could he face going? He needed to do something, however, to occupy himself until bedtime. He must try to keep awake until a reasonable hour.

Sitting in the corner of the unassuming little restaurant a few doors down the alleyway from his hotel he felt quite safe. Every scrap of space on walls was crammed with very bad paintings. It seemed so incongruous that, in a city so brimming with superb art, no one seemed to notice or be bothered that they were surrounded by such truly terrible paintings. The pictures, however, by their sheer number, did give the brightly lit little white room a certain naïve charm. The restaurant certainly had is own peculiar personality. Yes, he definitely felt quite safe there.

He managed to eat almost half of his pizza. He also managed to cram his salad to one side of the plate to look as if he had eaten some of it.

He had finished his quarter-litre jug of "house red" long before his meal arrived and ordered another, which he also finished.

He felt decidedly drunk as he climbed the stone steps to the first floor of the prison building where the concert was to be held.

More carving and gilding and middle-aged, middle-class people in sombre clothes.

The musicians were all men, wearing evening suits and bow ties. The concert was short, predictable and undemanding: Vivaldi, Albinoni, Pachebel.

It was an exclusively string ensemble except for the tiny keyboard instrument. He didn't know what it was called. A harpsichord, perhaps? Or maybe a spinet? It wasn't important. What was important was the colour. It was painted red. A particular red, bright, but with a hint of black in it. The colour of red carnations, he decided. Red seemed to be the theme of the day. Red jackets, red wine, red prams...

He didn't wake up next morning until past ten thirty. He didn't remember having taken his pill, but he must have done, because it wasn't where he always left it in the small pill bottle lid by his bed! On top of which the alarm was turned off on his mobile. He sat on the edge of his bed. He felt a bit sick, but not as much as he normally did. He stood up. He didn't even feel quite as dizzy as usual when he got up. He was still faintly inebriated, he decided. It wasn't an unpleasant feeling! The brandy he had drunk after the concert had knocked him out. He really must try to make himself eat something at lunchtime today, he lectured himself.

There was no one about as he let himself out of the *pensione* an hour or so later. The smells of coffee and bread had almost disappeared. The sky was blue and the sun was shining but the wet pavements signified rain the previous night and the patches of grey cloud hinted at perhaps more showers later in the day.

For a change, he turned left out of the Locanda al Leone, where the alleyway opened onto a small square. This one, he discovered, was named after the saints Filippo and Giacomo and was surrounded by the usual cafés and souvenir shops, but was distinctive in having two kiosks in the middle, selling newspapers and yet more souvenirs.

Only one other table was occupied outside the café where he ordered his first beer of the day. Must eat at lunchtime, he reminded himself as he took his first sip.

He glanced sideways. A honeymoon couple, he decided. Late twenties? Professionals? Definitely not English. Probably Italian. Both quietly and elegantly dressed in black. The man crossed his legs. A small red flash under the heel of his leather trainers indicated they were from Prada. They both appeared so relaxed and confident. So happy in each other's company. He suddenly sensed that the man had become aware of being scrutinised. He quickly averted his gaze, wishing he hadn't been caught staring.

The young man was certainly very handsome, though! How long had it been since he had noticed someone as being attractive? He and Sam had always discreetly commented if they saw someone they judged to be a bit of a dish. They had a secret sign. A little short double cough, which meant 'cop that one'. The young Pradagentleman would have definitely have merited a little double cough!

His thought pattern was interrupted as the young woman walked in front of him and disappeared into the café. She must need a pee, he surmised. After a few seconds he dared to steal another brief sideways glance. Mr Prada was examining his diary, rather too studiously. How he wished he hadn't been caught staring. As soon as the girl emerged from the café, her partner left the table and went inside, presumably to settle their bill.

When they left the café, he watched their black-clad backs, as they walked away across the square and disappeared from view behind the newspaper stall.

Should he order another beer? he pondered. No, he was going to find the Scuola di San Giorgio degli Schiavoni and revisit the stunning series of Carpaccio paintings. He took out the guidebook and traced another yellow brick road.

The waiter gave him a pleasant smile as he walked through to the back of the café's interior to find the toilets. He looked in the mirror. God, he looked thin and pale. He couldn't imagine he would ever warrant a couple of little coughs. He returned to the waiter, who was stationed behind he till.

"*Quanta costa per favouri,*" he braved.

Once again the waiter replied in English. "There will be no cost, signor."

"Why?" He was seriously perplexed.

The waiter grinned knowingly. "The young man who just left with the young lady paid your bill!"

Still reeling from the inexplicable, though intensely confidence-boosting event, he arrived at the Scuolain what seemed like no time at all. The sun had gone in and the sky looked threateningly dark. He must buy himself a cheap folding umbella.

He absentmindedly bought his entry ticket from the man who stood sentry just inside the doorway. His mind was still ruminating about the young man in the Prada shoes. Maybe the girl had been his sister. Or perhaps just his best friend? It didn't matter anyway. He would never see him again. He didn't even want to. He was happy that the strange little scene had taken place. It felt as if a little bit of magic had taken place! Another little gift from some friendly saint, perhaps? Or maybe from Sam, wherever he was?

Once inside the dark ground-floor room that housed the Carpaccio paintings, he instantly forgot all about the young man in the Prada shoes.

He had forgotten how stunning and unusual the paintings were. He spent a good hour poring over every detail. He couldn't decide which was his favourite. Was it the picture of Saint George killing the dragon, surrounded by the gory limbs and other various remnants of half-devoured maidens? Or was it perhaps the scene of Saint Gerome, miraculously taming the lion, whilst behind him his brother monks fled every which way in terror, their pale robes flying out behind them?

He decided against visiting the upper part of the building. He remembered clearly that the paintings on display on the first floor were a total disappointment after the glorious series of Carpaccios.

As he left the building, not only could he feel himself smiling, but he simply couldn't stop. The day had gone so well, so far! It didn't matter in the least that it had rained again while he was inside. It must have been a heavy shower, though. There were several new, fairly large puddles on the stretch of ground which led from the door of the museum to the little bridge opposite. He stopped to stare at a particularly large puddle, suddenly reflecting a patch of clear sky as the clouds cleared. The uneven fragment of blue appeared particularly brilliant against the dark damp stone which surrounded it. It seemed to him like a great palate of freshly mixed painter's pigment. The comparison pleased him. But suddenly his look of pleasure changed to one of surprise as the blue turned to red! Carnation red.

From his almost trancelike state, he wondered what it was that was now obscuring the blue sky from his watery mirror. He felt almost hypnotised. A laugh, however, broke his trance, making him look up.

He returned the grin, as his new friend from the Frari raised a cupped hand to his mouth, then tilted it, in imitation of drinking, whilst raising his eyebrows to imply a question.

He nodded in assent.

Loot
Bryan Connon

Loot
Bryan Connon

I lived with Jeff in Noel Road two doors from where it happened. We had two rooms on the hall floor. The bedroom was at the back and in the front was the living room, with an ancient gas stove and a butler's sink in the corner. There were fold-back doors between the rooms, which made it almost self-contained, but we had to share the only loo and bathroom with nine other tenants, so we usually had wash-downs at our own sink. I'd sponge him and he'd sponge me.

Back in 1955 when we got the rooms, Islington wasn't the posh area it is now, everything was run down and going to ruin. Our street was all working-class like me and Jeff until the middle-class pioneers started buying up property cheap. First there was a lawyer and his wife, who tarted up the dosshouse across the road, and then a theatrical producer and his boyfriend took on the semi-derelict house on the corner. Jeff said if there was much more of it our rent would go up sharpish. I told him not to worry, that he would get work out of it with his carpentry and decorating and I was right.

I worked on our family fruit and veg stall in Chapel Street market with my two brothers, who were both as straight as I was queer. Once a yob called me a pansy tart and they gave him a right kicking. Dad and Mum lived above a tobacco shop around the corner, which he had bought in 1940. Mum and my sisters worked in the rag trade; she was a brilliant presser and she could make our cheap suits from Burton's look like Savile Row. Every Sunday she did a big roast dinner for us all – sometimes up to fourteen crammed themselves around the kitchen table.

In Noel Road you couldn't fart without it becoming public knowledge, so we soon heard about the two boys who'd taken a one-roomed flat up the road. We were told that they were writers. The one called Ken was a bit snooty as if he was deposed royalty forced to slum it with the peasants. The other was Joe, whom I nicknamed "the walk" because he tucked his arse in tight, thrust out his packet and moved as if his balls were too big for him. He seemed quite friendly, but we didn't really see much of either of them as they kept themselves to themselves. We heard they were pretty skint, but we knew for certain when they discovered Chapel Street and turned up for the last knockings on a Saturday night when everything went cheap. Ken picked over the squashy tomatoes and wizened greens like a dowager duchess in Harrods, but Joe spent his time eyeing up the trade. He obviously didn't fancy me – the feeling was mutual – but he tried chatting up my two brothers, who were big-built from weight lifting. They just grinned and flirted back, but it didn't get him anywhere.

We got to know them a bit better when Jeff did a couple of jobs for them, replacing a sash cord and shaving a bit off their flat door where it stuck. I went up there for a coffee; poky little room it was, but they'd done it up in bright colours and stuck pictures on the walls. Ken handed round the mugs as if he was Lady Bountiful doling out charity, but he was completely different when they both came back from doing time for stealing library books. Nobody minded that because there were so many villains round our way that being a jail bird was like joining a club, though we thought they could have nicked something more useful than books! I reckon Joe had a rare old time in prison – he was cockier than ever as if it had made him a real man – but Ken was shattered, all the airs and graces had been knocked out of him and he seemed to be in a deep depression whenever we saw him.

It must have been months later that he came to the market grinning all over his face because they had sold some of their writing but the big break came when Joe did that play about Mr Sloane. Ken was really chuffed; he began shopping in the middle of the week when the goods were fresh and the prices higher. He said he'd get us tickets but we weren't keen on going up West just for a play, besides we'd rented a TV. He often got lonely because Joe was out and about such a lot and took to popping in at night for company. We didn't mind as long as he didn't interrupt our watching the box. If there wasn't much on, we'd have a gossip, though mostly it was us listening to him rabbiting on about Joe and about their plans, how they'd move to Bromley where they could have a little house with a garden. It sounded daft to us when you could get a nice little house and garden round Islington for half the price of Bromley. Then he decided to concentrate on being an artist and he gave us one of his first efforts. It was all bits and bobs cut out of magazines and stuck together like on the walls of their room, but we hung it up so as not to offend him. It must have been about this time that he borrowed a few of Jeff's tools to bang down the creaking floorboards in the flat as part of his plan to do it up and sell it. He even offered it to us! As Jeff said, we'd move to something bigger than our place, not smaller.

By now Joe was getting quite well known. I remember Mum cutting a bit out of the *Daily Mail* about how prison had helped him. Poor old Ken got left out of everything and he moaned to us about it. He once followed me into the caff where I took my tea break and went on and on about how he'd educated Joe, taught him to read, taught him everything and how without him there wouldn't be no Joe Orton. I'd heard most of it before, but that day he had a look in his eyes that reminded me of my Aunty Vi who lived on pills to buck her up and pills to calm her down. We began to dread him dropping in at night to rabbit on about how unfair it was that Joe got all the credit and he got none. One night when we were in bed, he stood outside shouting at us to let him in, until a neighbour told him to fuck off or he'd call the police. Then he turned up at the stall one morning all smiles, wearing a wig that was as obvious as a straw hat on a donkey. Joe had bought it for him, he said; when Jeff saw it he said it proved that Joe had a wicked sense of humour.

We didn't see much of him after that until he and Joe came back from a trip to Morocco. He was still wearing that silly wig and boasting about the sex he'd had with the beach boys. We didn't believe him, I think he told us what Joe had been up to and pretended it had happened to him. He seemed all het up as if he was on something and the look in the eyes reminded me more than ever of Aunty Vi.

*

We were both at work when they found the bodies. Ken had bashed Joe's head in with a hammer and then poisoned himself. Jeff was convinced it was the hammer that Ken borrowed and not returned, but he didn't like to ask for it back. For a few days, people in the market asked me about them, but there was nothing much I could say was there? I suppose Ken was jealous and being on pills or something didn't help.

That's about all I can remember. The picture Ken gave us? It seemed morbid to keep it, so I threw it away. There was a bundle of papers Jeff found under a loose floorboard when he got the job of doing their flat up for the new owners. Some of it was a play; Joe had signed it and written "draft" on it; I tried to read it but it was so weird I gave up, so I dumped it along with the rest or the stuff. No point in keeping clutter, is there?

(*From a taped interview with Mr W H at a retirement home in Bexhill. August 2003.*)

Funeral Rites
Jack Dickson

Funeral Rites
Jack Dickson

'Man, I wish I was a woman!'

In the mirror, I slid the tie's knot up towards the shirt's top button. Over my shoulder, Ray pushed arms into the sleeves of well-cut Armani.

'We get any old nondescript black suit, white shirt, black tie. And what do they get?'

I adjusted the knot, scrutinised it for size, shape and symmetry, then folded the collar down. 'Okay, what do they get?'

Behind me, he turned, well-muscled arms gesturing above his cropped head. 'Hats, of course! Huge, veiled creations. With feathers. Brims. Fuzzy polka dots – the works. That's what women get – and don't even start me on the wee black dresses. Or the understated black two-pieces. With the modest high necks or the plunging décolletage. And mourning jewellery – can you believe it?'

He joined me in the mirror, running a big hand over a newly shaved chin on which the charcoal smudge of five o'clock shadow was already visible. Ray feigned a scowl and sucked in his gut. 'Bette Davis in *A Marked Woman*? More Brando in *The Godfather*!' He blew out his cheeks in a parody of ageing Marlon and clamped his hands to my shoulder. 'Michael, the family is yours now. Don't let me down.'

I laughed and made to turn round. His strong hands held me there, eyes meeting mine in the mirror – for the first time since my mother had phoned with the news.

'You are okay with this, baby?'

I held his gaze, the laugh dying in my throat.

'I mean, I know you were never close...'

Bands of muscle tightened reflexively across my chest.

'... but I also know families...'

Bands of muscle became bands of iron, clasping my lungs.

'... your mum needs you. Your sisters need you, right now, Mike.'

I couldn't speak. I couldn't breathe. Blood pounded in my head. Ray's voice was very far away. In the mirror, I watched him kiss the crown of my head.

'You're doing a good thing...'

Tiny back spots floated over the reflective surface. I felt myself start to sway and fought the feeling.

'... that much I do know. And maybe good can come out of bad – maybe this can heal some wounds.'

I stared at the top of his lowered head, losing myself in thousands of tiny cropped hairs. The tiny black dots slowly faded. Somehow the strength returned to my legs. I managed to take a breath, hold it, and exhale slowly. 'Yeah, maybe.'

The grip on my shoulders slackened enough to let me turn and allow his big Armani-ed arms around me.

The estranged gay son's role at a funeral is akin to that of the mistress. Everyone knows who he is. Everyone has views on his right to be present at such a family-oriented occasion. But no one makes reference to the relationship – either between him and the deceased, or him and the bulky skinhead in designer black at his side. And no one misses the opportunity to have a good look at him.

My mother, sisters, their husbands and assorted brats had already commandeered the first three rows by the time we got there, so we sat at the back of the crematorium, giving everyone else the chance to ogle us on their way in – and Ray the opportunity to elbow me in the ribs and whisper, 'Who's that?' as assorted mourners walked past.

Answering him broke up the monotony of the taped organ music. 'Auntie Jeanie, my mum's sister... Chrissie, she's a nurse and some sort of second cousin twice removed... Jimmy... Cathy... Uncle James, he's a hospital porter, well, he used to be... dunno who that is...'

'Told you the mourning jewellery would be in evidence.'

I followed his wry eyes to where a tiny, hunched figure, escorted by a middle-aged fat boy who might have been her son, was enteringthe utilitarian would-be church. I met Fat Boy's eyes. He looked away. But my Auntie Flora's beady pupils zeroed in on me. She lurched left, shrugging off Fat Boy's restraining arm and waving her stick.

'Michael – ah, wee Michael.'

I got to my feet. She came up to my chest. 'Hello, Auntie Flora.'

She smiled. 'Not so wee any more, eh? Shove along, son, shove along.' She sat down heavily at my side, then leaned forward and beamed at Ray. 'And who's this?'

'Mum, we have places down the front...' Fat Boy hovered, the buttons on his off-the-peg Slater Menswear jacket straining across his gut.

Auntie Flora fixed him with an icy stare. 'I'm sitting here, with wee Michael and his pal, son. Away you go and sit where you like.'

I heard Ray stifle a chuckle. And I watched Fat Boy depart, far from happy. Auntie Flora wedged her stick between our seats.

'Useless article, my Bobby. Always was, always will be...'

She linked her arm through mine and patted my hand. 'Wish I could say his heart's in the right place, but I doubt he's even got one.'

Cigarettes and lavender. Auntie Flora still smelled the way I remembered her smelling. On my other side, Ray gave in to the chuckle and leaned forward, hand outstretched. 'Raymond Molleson, Mrs...?'

She laughed. 'Call me Flora, son.'

'Nice to meet you, Flora...'

'And you, son. Any friend of Michael's...' She grinned and patted my hand again. '... it's good of you boys to come. My brother wasn't the easiest man to love.'

I caught Ray's eye over the top of her tiny form and looked away, focusing on the flower-draped coffin at the far end of the aisle. I could almost read his thoughts:

Family Reunited by Tragedy.

Black Sheep Welcomed Back into the Fold.

The Prodigal Poof Makes Up for Lost Time.

But it wasn't going to happen. Too much water under the bridge. Too many things left unsaid – every cliché in the book, in fact. But Ray was ever hopeful. And ever curious:

'I know Michael and his dad were never close, but he doesn't even talk about the rest if his family, much. To be honest, I thought most of you were dead.'

A forty-a-day laugh. 'Not quite, son. Not quite.'

I was vaguely aware that Ray and Auntie Flora were conducting a whispered conversation around me. Only vaguely. Staring at the box that now housed Michael Dickson Senior, I wondered what he'd make of the son he'd cut out of his life, twenty years earlier.

And I wondered why I cared.

The service was mercifully brief. We sang a hymn no one seemed to know and a minister who'd obviously never met my father said all the wrong things by saying all the right things. A crematorium assistant wearing something suitably funereal stepped forward and removed the best of the flowers from the top of the coffin. Somewhere behind the scenes, someone pressed a button or pulled a lever and what was left of my father trundled a little more noisily than one would expect through a mean set of curtains and out of sight.

There was no following of coffins out of churches into waiting hearses and, as a consequence, the occasion petered out rather than ended, with various people moving down to the front of the area to shake hands with the grieving widow.

An elbow in my ribs. Too bony to be Ray's.

'Go talk to your mother, Michael, son. Raymond and me's going outside for a fag, eh?'

Auntie Flora was hoisting herself to her feet. At some point during the service, she'd unlinked her arm with mine and was now holding Ray's. He smiled, reiterating her advice with a wordless nod to the huddle around the first three rows.

I'd known this was coming. I'd always known, at some point, I'd have to talk to my mother. Standing, I moved into the aisle, watching as Ray and Auntie Flora made their way slowly towards the door. They were deep in a conversation, which seemed to concern everything from how beautiful I was as a baby to where she got her jet necklace and brooch.

I smiled. Watching two people I loved – one who'd known me all my life, the other merely a quarter of it – I slowly turned and moved towards a group to whom my emotional response was somewhat less clear.

Like the good son I'd always tried to be, I hugged my mother, allowed my sisters to kiss me and solemnly shook hands with the men who had married them.

At ceremonies I'd never attended. Because of him.

I smiled at children whose names I knew only vaguely. Because of him. And I wondered for the umpteenth time over the past 25 years if they knew. If any of them knew.

They had to know. Surely...

'You and your... friend are coming back to the house for a cup of tea, aren't you, Michael?'

My mother's voice cut through my thoughts. I blinked, refocusing on the present and the still-handsome, red-eyed woman in front of me. I knew what Ray would say: he'd take one look at the seventy-year-old Mary Dickson and wink. 'I see where you get your good looks,' he'd say.

Other voices chimed in: 'Aye, come on back for a wee while, eh, Michael?'

'What's your friend's name?'

'You're looking really good, by the way.'

'Where are you living these days?'

'Is that your car outside? The Merc?' This from a nephew, whose name I had already forgotten.

I smiled. 'No, that's Raymond's.'

A shy half-smile in return to mine. 'Can we go back to Gran's in it, Uncle Michael?'

'Don't be so cheeky, you.' The admonishing voice of my sister Jean.

'Uncle Michael' – the new title sat uneasily on my shoulders. I didn't know if I wanted to get used to it. Any of it. But there was something in the way the kid lowered his eyes when he asked that stuck a chord.

'He's the image of you, at that age, so he is – aren't you, Ewan?'

My mother smiled fondly. I looked from her heavily lined face to the large smoky eyes of my eight-year-old nephew and back again. Then I looked at his mother.

The fleeting glimpse of a hesitation. Then a tight smile. 'Aye, on you go, son.'

Through half-heard instructions about how to get to the house and who was giving whom lifts back, Ewan and I stared at each other. Then I mumbled something and we walked together towards the door.

It was an interesting car journey. Ewan sat in the front, totally rapt as Ray gave him a blow-by-blow on the subjects of fuel injection and engine litreage. In the back with me, Auntie Flora stroked the black leather upholstery and lowered her voice.

'I thought Mick would go on for ever, know what I mean, son?'

Her voice broke. I stared at this tiny sparrow of a woman. He might have been my father. But he was also her brother – her big brother. 'Yeah, me too.' If she wanted to talk, I'd do the generous thing and let her. Because he was dead. It was over. And it was the least I could do for someone who had played one of the few positive roles in my childhood.

'I was sure he'd outlive me, yon one.' She leant back against the seat, her ashen skin bleached further by the rich dark leather.

I tried to work out her age. My dad would have been eighty-eight in July. Aunt Flora had to be...eighty-five? Eighty-six?

'It's a blessing, though.' Tiny glittering irises matched the upholstery. 'With him gone, and me snapping at his heels, that'll be the end of it.'

I smiled. 'The end of the Dickson line?'

She turned her face to mine. Another of those fleeting hesitations. Something almost said, almost too brief to see. Auntie Flora patted my hand. 'Aye son, that's right.' She looked away, watching the streets speed past outside.

But I did see it. And I could identify it now, for what it was.

She knew.

His own sister knew what he was.

What he'd done.

The bands were back around my chest, tighter than ever. I couldn't speak. I couldn't breathe. I stared at the side of her wizened face, blood hammering in my ears. And as Ray pulled in at the kerb in front of the house where I'd grown up, I opened the door and threw up into the gutter.

Minutes later I was sitting on the low wall that framed my parents' front garden, head between knees. Ray's warm hand rested on my forehead, holding my hair back from my face. 'It was really stuffy in that bloody crematorium, baby... you should have said you were feeling sick – I'd have put on the air-con.'

'Where's Auntie Flora?' I pressed my elbows against my knees, willing my body to stop shaking.

'Oh, don't worry about her – young Ewan took her inside. Nice kid, isn't he? Looks so like you. And he's really good with his... what would Flora be to him – great-aunt?'

The words swam in my head. Through a mist of nausea, I heard various parties stop and enquire about my health, heard Ray reassure them it was just a bit of car sickness and nothing to worry about. And I tried to phrase what I needed to say to the man who had shared my life for a decade. The man who, from only the best motives, had urged me to come here today. The man who, above everything else, deserved the truth.

I raised my head. Everything shimmered a bit, but I locked onto Ray's big blunt face until reality solidified. And I kept the lock on while I spoke. 'He fucked me from when I was... seven till I was fourteen. They all knew what was going on. And no one did a thing about it.'

Ray stared at me. His pupils shrank to pinpricks.

'How could they do that? How could they just all stand by and let it happen?' The bands were still there, pulsing across my ribs. 'I was a bloody kid, for Christ's sake!

The colour left Ray's ruddy face as it rose in mine.

'How could they do that? Why would they do that?' I was on my feet now, pacing the street in front of this ordinary wee semi in this ordinary wee Scottish seaside town. People were turning, looking at me, looking at the queen who was home for the funeral and making a scene. Again. The way he'd made scene after scene at other family occasions, getting drunk, dragging along bemused bits of rough and parading them as sexual partners, seducing his sisters' boyfriends until his long-suffering, much-sympathised-with parents put their communal foot down and refused to have him in the house any longer.

Ray walked towards me. His expression was a mixture of shock, anger and guilt. He stopped less than a foot away and put a hand on my shoulder. 'We're going home. I should never have made you come.' He began to steer me towards the car.

'I'm not going anywhere.'

He looked at me. I looked back. His palm curved, rubbing into tensed muscle. 'Tell me what you need then, babe. Tell me what I can do.'

I had no idea. And even less of a clue about what I was going to do. But I knew one thing: I'd walked away from this house once before, my gut churning with unanswered questions. I wasn't about to do so again. Turning to the very ordinary, very Scottish semi, I stared at a the bricks and mortar that had haunted my dreams for years. I could feel Ray watching me, with questions of his own. I had no idea if it helped, his being there. He was part of a new life. And this was old – so old in a sense it didn't matter any more.

Water under the bridge.

Done and dusted.

Maybe I should have just walked away. But I walked towards the front door, Ray at my side, and into my father's wake. The spectre at the feast.

The house stank of him, even though he'd spent the last two weeks of his life in hospital. And, of course, everyone was on their best behaviour. With Ray awkwardly holding a doily-covered plate of salmon paste sandwiches someone had thrust at him, we chatted politely with my sisters Babs, Vivienne and Alex, discussed football, rugby and hard drives with their respective husbands, and exchanged opinions on the merits of *Buffy the Vampire Slayer*, *Grand Theft Auto II* and Justin Timberlake with their various offspring. If you'd been a fly on the walls of that house, everything would have seemed normal.

But it wasn't. It was unreal. And yet so real. When you're eleven and unhappy, if everyone else around you is smiling you soon get to realise it's you that's out of step. You that's in the wrong, you that's making a fuss about nothing. And after twenty years off and on of therapy, you learn that, while it's not you that's wrong or out of step or to blame, it's still you who has to adjust.

Two choices: let the anger fuck you worse than he did, for the rest of your life. Or let it go. Forgive yourself. Forgive the man who came into your bedroom, put a hand over your mouth and a cock in your arse for more nights than you cared to remember. Forgive those who stood by and watched, who knew and did nothing. Forgive it all. And move on.

I was somewhere between those two places. Maybe if I'd stayed away, things might have been different. But I was here. I had come, raking it all up again. And there was no time like the present.

I finally tracked my mother down in the garden, removing pegs from that morning's wash. Even on the day they cremated her husband, this woman washed clothes. She turned as I approached, startled. That tight smile she wore for awkward visitors fixed itself to her face.

Blood was beating a tattoo inmy ears as I uttered the words. 'Mum, why did you let him...?'

'There's some of your... things upstairs, Michael. I kept them for you. I thought maybe, since... Raymond has the car, you could take them home with you and...'

'Why did you let him?'

She stared at me, arms full of washing, eye full of tears. 'Oh, Michael, I –'

''C'mon, son...'

A voice at my elbow. Then a clawlike hand on my arm. 'We want to show you something, don't we, Ewan?'

I turned. Auntie Flora and my eight year-old nephew stood there. She was holding a small wooden box. Ewan's eyes were huge. He was eating a sandwich. We stared at each other while two women conversed around us.

'It's all right, Joan. We'll bring Michael back to you in a wee while, eh?'

'Flora, I'm sorry, it's just –'

'I know, hen. I know.'

The hand on my arm tightened, gripping on for support. And, as three generations of Dicksons walked slowly back into the house, I caught Ray's concerned eye from the living room window.

It took an age to get her upstairs. Ewan and I each took a side, he carried her stick, I held the wooden box. Auntie Flora's clawlike hands gripped the stair rail, hauling her tiny body ever upwards.

'I was born in this house, know that boys? In the days before your big posh hospitals, most weans were born at home...'

She never stopped talking the whole time.

'... grew up here, till I met your uncle Tommy, God rest his soul...'

As we reached the top of the stairs, memory came flooding back. Auntie Flora grabbed her stick from Ewan, who had produced another sandwich from somewhere and was now stuffing it into his mouth, and took the box from me. I moved ahead, onto the landing and towards a closed door.

'Aye, that was your room, eh Michael? Ewan's, too, if your mum looks after him when Alexandra and Colin are away...'

There was a smell. Or the memory of a smell. Carpets. Cooking. Boots Albany aftershave. Male sweat. The warm comforting odour of shit and spunk.

'... and my room, when I was a wee lassie...'

I paused at the door, with its badly painted white gloss surface. Ewan and Flora stood behind me.

'... in you go, Michael son. Go on...'

I closed my eyes and tried to breathe. My fingers reached for the handle, shaking. I wanted to run. I wanted to throw up. I wanted to kick the door down and wreck the room.

'... do it, son.'

But I did none of these things. Something in her voice let me turn the handle and open the door.

We all went in. The room looked totally different. As I took in the new carpet, wallpaper and *Grand Theft Auto II* posters, Ewan edged past me and sat on the bed. He wiped the last remnants of the sandwich from his lips and exhaled noisily.

'Things change, Michael-son.'

I spun round and scowled at her. 'How can you pretend it didn't happen?' Then I glared at Ewan. 'And what's he doing here?'

'No one pretending anything, son. And Ewan needs to be here. This is his room now, eh Ewan?'

The eight-year-old nodded sombrely. 'How many miles to the gallon does Raymond's Merc get, Uncle Michael?'

Auntie Flora moved slowly to the bed and eased herself down beside my nephew. 'We can talk about that later, son. Just you listen for now, eh?'

The kid nodded obediently.

I glared at them both and opened my mouth.

'And you need to listen too, Michael.'

Maybe her legs were slow but her tongue was quicker than ever.

I took a deep breath and leant against the wardrobe. The same MFI wardrobe I'd once hidden inside, in the vain hope he'd go away. He didn't. He found me.

'I know why you left, twenty-five years ago, Michael. Do you know why I left?'

I knew she'd been a nurse. I knew she'd served in the Wrens, during World War II. But I didn't know what any of this had to do with anything.

'Back then, no one listened to lassies. It was a man's world, right enough. Probably still is.'

As she talked, she opened the box.

'The patriarchy, eh boys?'

Ewan stared at her. I stared at her, surprised she knew the word. Then angry at myself for assuming this tiny birdlike creature was either uneducated or stupid. The band across my chest was back. And I suddenly knew what was coming.

'My father – your great-grandfather, Ewan-son – taught my brother Mick to be a strong man. A hard man. Mick looked after me and your granny, Michael, when our father was away at sea...'

The gorge rose in my throat. I bit back the taste of breakfast and bile.

'... and when your great-grandfather was on leave, your grandpa had only me to look after.'

She stared at the eight-year-old boy. I stared at her ancient face, lined with life.

'He was my big brother, boys. He taught me so much. He taught me how to take his thing in my mouth, at a time when some wives never saw their husbands naked their whole married lives...'

My face flushed up. I blushed for her, because her own cheeks were sallow and sunken. And because she was long past embarrassment.

'... he taught me how to please a man; he taught me what a man needs. I would have borne his child at thirteen had he not kicked me in the belly until the bloody mess poured out of me onto that very floor. We wrapped it in *The Sunday Post* –' her eyes were free of tears, her voice steady as a rock '– and Mick threw it into the dustmen's cart, next morning.'

Somehow, I was moving. Towards her. At the side of the bed, my legs gave way. Her hand rested on my head.

'And he taught me things he maybe didn't mean to teach me. How to look after myself. How to stay quiet. How to keep a secret.'

The calmness in her voice sent chills through my body.

'Tell your Uncle Michael about your grandpa, Ewan-son.'

I stared at the floor, watching the veil of black dots descend over the same carpet on which my Auntie Flora had miscarried.

'I miss him. I liked him. He gave me whisky and said I wasn't to tell gran, 'cos she wouldn't understand. He bought me Playstation II – and an XBox, but Xboxes have crap graphics so we took it back to the shop and got a credit note.'

The voice was unbroken. Like a girl's.

'Tell your Uncle Michael what your grandpa called you at night, son. When you used to stay over with him and your gran?'

'Grandpa said I was good cunt. He said Gran's hole was all loose and dry, cos she'd had so many children and she was so old. Grandpa put Vaseline up my bottom and said I was nice and tight.

It hurt a bit at first. But not much.'

Sweat drenched my body. I was shivering, the veil of dots dancing on the carpet. I wanted to be angry. But the anger wouldn't come. I wanted to feel pity. But it didn't seem appropriate. The guilt came, though, piling on top of the misery.

Maybe if I'd done something concrete, rather than shout and scream and throw things around this room, twenty-five years ago, I could have stopped my father starting in on another piece of his own flesh. But I hadn't. I left. She stayed, though. And I had to ask. 'How long have you known?'

'Known what?' Ewan's childlike tones rang through the room.

'Shhh, son...' Auntie Flora placated him. '... I don't think he's talking to you.' A hand came to rest on my head. 'About you, Michael?'

'About Ewan.'

'Oh... as long as you, probably. Ten, fifteen minutes?'

'How long have you known about... me?'

Clawlike fingers played lightly in my hair. 'A bit longer. But there was nothing I could do. No one knew where you'd gone, son. You never kept in touch.'

My head shot up. 'Do you blame me?' Now the anger came, directed at the wrong target. But it was the only one I had.

I could see the faint milkiness of cataract in Aunt Flora's eyes. Her hand remained on my head.

'I don't blame anyone, son. What good does blame do, especially now?' She removed her hand and set the small wooden box down on the bed between the three of us. 'We're not the first. And we won't be the last. Oh, I know these days it's all about telling people, reporting theabuser. Making him pay. All that kind of malarkey.'

I stared into the box, at the white powdery stuff that quarter-filled it.

'But what good does that do? What good would it have done to take Mick away from me? Would you have been any happier with your parents divorced, Michael, or you and you sisters taken into care, the whole world knowing your business?'

I could almost taste those ashes in my mouth. 'It would have been the... right thing to do.'

Auntie Flora's head shook slowly. 'There's no right and no wrong sometimes, Michael-son. There's just what some people do, and the way other people cope with it. Getting it all out in the open's the modern way of dealing with it. Maybe it's the better way, maybe it's not. I don't know. But I do know this. As long as men have needs, it's never going to stop. But Mick's dead now. For us, it's over.'

With an unexpected and unladylike energy, my 86-year-old Auntie Flora hawked up phlegm from deep in her chest and spat a dark green mouthful into the box containing what was left of her brother. Then she passed the wooden box to me.

I closed my eyes, thinking about all the wasted time, the decades of hate and confusion. The years of sleeping with women in at attempt to make myself straight, only to turn every man who fucked me into my father. Then I thought about Ray, somewhere downstairs, in a room full of people he didn't know, holding his doily-covered plate of sandwiches and making small talk with my family. He was the only man who really looked like my father: tall, broad-shouldered, deep chested, with a constant smudge of five o'clock shadow. And he was the only man who let me fuck him.

'Do it, Michael son. Let it go.'

I opened my eyes and spat my hate into the box, then handed it to Ewan. 'Your turn.'

Huge smoky eyes glances between me and Auntie Flora. And the box of mortal remains. 'My mum says it's bad manners to spit in front of –'

'Your mum would make an exception this time, I think.'

Part of me was only just holding back a weird sort of laughter. Another part was crying, wondering how this calm, normal-looking eight-year-old was handling all this.

Ewan peered into the box, his lips curling with distaste. 'Gross.'

But he managed a fair mouthful all the same before solemnly handing it back to his great-aunt, who closed the lid and patted it.

'This ends here, eh boys? It ends with him. With us. We'll keep the secret. Because now it's ours to keep.'

My nephew and I exchanged glances but nodded. I stood up, reached out a hand to help Auntie Flora off the bed.

'Your mother never knew, Michael. Like mine never knew. Like yours doesn't know, Ewan darlin'. And it stays that way.'

The bands across my chest were still there. A bit slacker. A little lighter. Maybe it wasn't the telling after all; maybe it was the sharing that helped.

As we made our way from the room where three generations of Dickson children had been fucked over, a clear voice piped up: 'Were you good cunt too, Uncle Michael?'

This time I did laugh. 'Yeah – I like to think I was, pal.'

Together, three survivors made their way back down to the funeral party.

Essence
Simon Edge

Essence
Simon Edge

For a long time I would go to bed early. I would read myself drowsy and then turn the light off. Other nights I would put my head down as soon as I slipped under the duvet, retreating into a fantasy world of conversations with my imagined love; I looked forward all evening to these private meetings where I chose the time and place, if not the outcome (not even in fantasy could I get my way). Then, when sleep came, my dreams took off in a different direction.

I tell you this to show the kind of romantic I was before I discovered there were better things to do, in a city of dark corners, than go to bed quite so early. (I have kept my romantic nature, even if my behaviour has become more basic.) Also, I'll admit, it's a way of trying to get away with what I am about to say. Meditate on sleep for a while, and you can fly all kinds of filth under the radar later on; people think it's literary. My namesake did it, and the world turned a blind eye to the buggery and the whips and chains. He described ejaculating in his teenage pants as he pawed his girlfriend on a park bench, and what happened? They named the street after him. The very street where the bench was! Look it up in *Paris Pratique* if you don't believe me.

There is a school of thought that says my namesake (we are both called 'I', you see) meditated on sleep so effectively that most readers were in that state long before reaching the smut. Since they could never admit they had not got as far as the emperor taking his clothes off, they never knew he did. The secret was safe with those of us who stayed the course.

Among the lightweights who dropped off early, the myth endures that, once my namesake had done with nodding off, he focused entirely on the taste of tea and cakes. It was a myth that must have suited him: dunking scallop-shaped sponges was an alibi for a man who would rather play dunk the delivery 'girl'. (He was even dodgier in life than in fiction. Apparently he could only reach orgasm by having a rat killed in front of him. Granted, that may have been the fertile imagination of a housekeeper keen to bid up her serialisation prospects in the *Courrier du Jour*; but it's so bizarre I like to believe it.)

Anyhow, let's forget about the emperor. We'll play the game by sticking with taste, and its sister olfactory sense. You will recall that my namesake claimed to have discovered the essence of being when he realised two things: first, that the memory of certain experiences is always there to be discovered; and second, those experiences are quite random, as are the sensory events that allow us to remember them. In plain English: you never know when a slurp of soggy cake is going to transport you back to a world you had forgotten ever existed; but ,when it does, you have discovered the meaning of life.

I discovered my own version of this long after I had stopped going to bed early, in a way that might even make my shameless namesake blush.

There is a corner I know that is dark by any standards. A railway arch, naturally, and danker than usual. The kind of place you wouldn't want to see in the light: if darkness tells no tales, a lightbulb would recount the kind you wouldn't want to hear. There was a bar, but they never made much money from it. Customers were too preoccupied to drink. They were busy in alcoves and cubicles; lolling on wipe-clean sofas; rolling on the pool table. Those with least to hide stood boldly in the semi-gloom; the more bashful (or realistic) stationed themselves in deep blackness. Talking was unofficially banned, but the noises that came out of the dark were distinctive.

One promising evening I had followed a fellow patron inside one of the darker alcoves. Blonde, pale, slim: she (indulge me as you indulged my namesake) was my type, and I seemed to be hers – at least, the shadowy stranger she thought she could see was acceptable to her as long as no one lit a match. We followed our instincts, and mine included encouraging her to turn her back so that I could pay her the greatest compliment one human being can pay another.

It was not the first time I had paid this compliment – I am a terrible flatterer – but it was the most extraordinary. I was transported, not to Aunt Léonie's kitchen at Combray but – I cannot describe where. All I knew was that I never wanted the sensation to end. It was sweet in a way that it should not have been, and the incongruity of this fragrance made it all the more compelling. When I stood up she was grateful; she turned, and even let me kiss her properly. I wanted to say, 'Do you know you smell like heaven?' Why should she know? We are aware of what we look like, but there is no pheromone mirror. Telling her would be the least I could do. For some reason, though, I decided against it. I didn't say anything. We smiled and parted, without even making up names to swap.

I made my way home trying to keep her from blowing out of my nostrils. But as my namesake pointed out in his own, confectionary, context, you can't make it happen. Within days I had forgotten what the sensation was like.

Time passed, and more late nights. I went back to that place, among others, and a few months later I befriended a fellow patron. We began to visit each other at home, daring to forego the darkness of the arches. She too was blonde, pale and slim (they had to be). Her name was Jasonetta. I didn't stop going out, and I assume that she didn't either (we never actually discussed it). Neither of us had any great expectations from the other; the nature of our first meeting saw to that. But I enjoyed our encounters. When I look back on them now, I am sorry they had to end.

There were dinners, I think, and films. Clubs, too: the alcove-free variety, out of passing respect for one another's feelings. And afterwards we would go to bed.

We were on our fourth of these dates, maybe the fifth, and we had come back from a sweaty dive where we had been dancing. We normally went back to my flat in Houseman Street, but that night we must have been nearer to her place, because that was where we went. We opened a bottle of wine, smoked a joint and talked, and then nature took its course, in its perverse way. I won't bother you with the details, bar one – that way, perhaps you will believe me when I say I do not recount this to boast, or to titillate. I want to tell you because I think you will find it interesting, if I can only persuade you to view it as curiosity, not filth. That was what my namesake wanted too, even if he buried the evidence so deeply that only the truly muscular digger could find it. I love the way he writes: 'Perhaps she was dimly conscious that my game had another object than the one I had avowed, but too dimly to have been able to see that I had attained it.' He meant us to understand he had come in his pants, but he described it so dimly I'm not sure he attained it.

So there we were, on our own equivalent of a bench in the Champs Elysées, which in this case was Jasonetta's bed in her rented room in Dollis Hill (she was new to London, and it was all she could afford). We had been getting on well, and that night I determined to pay her my trademark compliment. She was pleased with it, I could tell. But, as I delivered it, something amazing happened. How shall I tell you? I could string this out over several pages (Marcel would say: 'An exquisite pleasure had invaded my senses, something isolated, detached, with no suggestion of its origin'), but we haven't got all day, and anyway there *was* a suggestion of its origin, a very precise suggestion. You see, this was the very same delicious fragrance from all those weeks ago.

I realised with a shock that Jasonetta and the stranger from the club were one and the same. It had been dark, but the shape of the face I could vaguely remember, the curves of the torso, they were Jasonetta's. For all these weeks when we had been getting to know each other, I had not recognised her. Now suddenly it came flooding back.

I wanted to tell her about my discovery, but how could I? After five weeks, to say, 'Darling, I think we may have met before.' It was indecent. Either she had known all along, in which case it would be ungallant to confess that I had not; or she remained unaware that we had met before, which was a possibility my ego bridled at. How cruel: a funny story, a great coincidence, but I had to keep it to myself. I couldn't tell it to a third party and hope to be understood. The world does not let us talk about these things as observers of the human condition; only as lechers or bores.

I woke in the late morning to find myself alone in the bed. Not one of those daft clichés from the television: I didn't fling a sleeping arm across an imaginary body, waking when it passed through thin air and hit the sheet. I prefer to sleep unencumbered by foreign bodies, so I don't do much arm-flinging. I just woke, sneaked a look to see if she was still asleep, and found she wasn't there. The room was unfamiliar, and it took a while to place the heavy, bedsit wardrobe and the shelves of videos, not books. I had just worked it out when the door opened and Jasonetta appeared, pink from the shower, with slicked-back hair. 'Morning,' she said, unwrapping her thin towelling robe and letting it fall to the floor as she turned her back. 'Like a shower?'

I said I would have one in a moment, and lay watching her as she talced herself. It was evidently the kind of bedsit where nothing could be left in the bathroom, and all her stuff was on a shelf above a hideous chest of drawers which she had tried to disguise with a cloth. She smiled at me, popping the top off a can of spray-on deodorant and raising each arm. She blew a cloud in my direction, and I watched the beads of moisture fizz in the sunlight. I swatted them away, and she laughed. Then she held the aerosol down at arm's length, reaching behind her back to apply between her buttocks. The spray hissed. At the same time the droplets she had fired at me settled over my arms, face and shoulders. Like Marcel drinking tea at his mother's kitchen table, I was transported back to the night before, and to the darkened alcove.

Our friendship petered out after that. It was funny, of course, to discover that the truth had nothing to do with pheromones. I laughed at the private joke I could never share. Nevertheless, my illusions were shattered and could never be rebuilt.

I could not begin to explain to her, but quick-dry, high-performance Right Guard was no match for the essence of being.

Bodily Parts
Drew Gummerson

Bodily Parts
Drew Gummerson

Me and Mickie James were moving down to London together. We were 24. We were going to be pop stars, Mickie James on keyboards and me on lead vocals. Mickie James had a hunchback but that didn't matter. Even I knew it. He was the talented one.

We talked about how famous we were going to be on the train on the way down. "The world is fed up with manufactured pop," I said. I put on my Ronan Keating voice. "I'm a talentless Irish twat," I said. Mickie James laughed at this. He likes it when I'm funny. It takes his mind off his own problems.

During the journey people going to the toilet kept tripping over our Korg keyboard. "It's not my fault it's long, is it?" I said to this skinny bloke. Then this big bloke tripped over it. I apologised to him. You can't be too careful these days, there are a lot of nutters about.

When we got off the train at Euston, Mickie James asked me to take his photo. He wanted a reminder of the time we arrived. I took the picture on an angle, slicing off his hunchback. It was the sort of thing I'd done before. I'd been at Leeds art college for two years. I hoped I'd got it right. To be honest, these disposable cameras are crap.

This guy we knew from a pub in Birmingham had told us to contact his mate who worked at St Pancras station. He said that he would sort us out for somewhere to stay and our first gig.

We eventually traced the guy to the station manager's office. He was wearing trousers that were too small and you could see the outline of his knob. Or it might have been a key chain.

"What do you want?" he said.

"We heard you had a room going," I said.

He shook his head. "This is a bloody station, not a hotel." The other guys in the office laughed at this.

"You want to get some glasses, mate," said another one of the guys.

He added, "What's in Quasimodo's case? Is it a banjo?"

"Come on," I said to Mickie James. "Let's go."

Between us we had over eight hundred pounds. I'd been working in HMV at weekends and Mickie James had been doing stuff for the council. He'd worked in this office but eventually they'd sacked him because he wouldn't take his coat off. He had this coat that he always wore. It had padded shoulders and he thought it made his hunchback less noticeable. It did in a way but then people were always going on at him for wearing a sheepskin jacket in summer.

We were halfway across the St Pancras concourse when that guy from the station manager's office caught up with us. He was a bit out of breath.

"Sorry about that, lads," he said. "Didn't want the other guys to know about the room. Come on, this way."

The guy, Dave, led us through this door that said 'Janitor' on it and then through a room stacked with cleaning stuff. At the back of this room was another door.

"I warn you," said Dave, "there's a hell of a lot of stairs."

"That's alright," I said. "We can do stairs."

I counted them as we went up. I thought this was one of those facts that we could use in competitions. You know, when we were on SMTV in the future they could flash it up on the screen. "How many stairs did Down By Law have to climb to get to their room when they first arrived in London?" Down By Law was the name of our group. It was Mickie James's idea. *Down By Law* was the title of his favourite film. It was directed by Jim Jarmusch and it starred the singer Tom Waits. That could be another question. "Which singer starred in the film Down By Law?"

After the 256th step, Dave came to a stop. The stairs didn't have any carpet here and wallpaper was peeling off the walls. There were two doors. We were all pretty out of breath and I could smell Mickie James in his jacket.

"This is it," said Dave, and he pushed opened one of the doors. "The sink works, and also those two sockets. I'm not asking much for it. Fifteen quid a week. It's not official, you understand. I'll give you both a smock. If you could put that on when you come in or out then people will just assume you're a cleaner. If anyone does stop you then send them to me. I'll sort it out."

But we weren't listening. On one side of the room was this big window. From it we could see what we assumed was the whole of London. It was all there, roads and parks and trees and cars and shops and it was ours for the taking.

"So you want it?" said Dave.

"Sure," I said. I felt this big ball building up and building up in my stomach and it felt great. "We'll definitely take it." Then I remembered something else. "There was another thing. Our mate told us about this gig."

"I'm chairman of the gay train drivers' association," said Dave. "Thursday week, we're having a bit of a do. Last year we had karaoke but this year we thought we'd go for something different."

I looked at Mickie James and he looked back at me. One thing we'd said was that we wouldn't do gay venues. We didn't want to become ghettoised.

"The thing is," I said to Dave, "we could do it, but the next thing you know they'll be asking us to do Pride in the Park. You get a name for yourself."

"They have pretty big names at Pride in the Park these days," said Dave. "I saw Blue there this year. We'd pay you. Fifty quid."

I looked at Mickie James again. He was kind of nodding his head, waiting for me to make a decision. Dave was still standing there. He was going to be our landlord and it didn't make any kind of business sense to piss him off.

"Ok," I said, "we'll do it."

"Yeah," he said and he clapped his hands. He seemed really excited. "I'll let Cyril know," he said. "He does the posters."

The room next to our new home was like this big loft. Actually it *was* a big loft. There were ladders and old rolls of wire on huge spindles and all these iron girders in there. God knows how anyone had got them up here. They had probably been there for years.

It was the perfect place for us to practise in. It was a forgotten urban backdrop to our sophisticated electronic groove. That was what

Mickie James said, anyway. Although he said he didn't like the word groove. Pared-down electronic lo-fi hi-fi beat was better, he said. That sounded too long for me. And what was lo-fi hi-fi?

Our best song was "Manos Sucias". We got the title from this play by Jean-Paul Sartre, *Les Mains Sales*. Mickie James translated the title into English, "Dirty Hands", and then he translated it into Spanish. It had to be in Spanish because the tune we were working on had this whole flamenco section in it.

The song is about a crippled Spanish boy. He lives in a tiny hut with his mother and she is dying of cancer. His only companion is a donkey called Manolo. Manolo was a hard word to find a rhyme for.

Jean-Paul Sartre was an existentialist and he wrote stuff about what is the point of life and all that. That is what our song's about, what is the point of it all when you are a different from everyone else. I think it's about Mickie James himself. 'Manos Sucias' is going to be our first number one.

Our room has one bed in it, one sink and a box that we use as a table. We found this old tin bath at the back of the loft and we use that to bath in.

I love it when Mickie James has a bath because that is the only time I get to see him naked. When we sleep together he always wears at least a T-shirt, even if he has taken off his underpants for sex.

I'd like to take a picture of him when he's in the bath. He looks so vulnerable there. His hunchback is on the left side. The spine curves dramatically to the left and then forms a loop under his skin. Sometimes when Mickie James is asleep then I will run my hand over this lump. I say 'I love you I love you I love you' over and over again. I wish that he would learn to love it as much as me but I don't think that he will. This is the only thing that will ever split us up. You can only pour so much love into something before you empty yourself out.

Sooner than I could believe one week had passed and it was time for our first gig.

Dave was waiting for us at the bottom of the steps. He wasn't wearing his blue trousers now but he was wearing some jeans and they were equally tight.

"I've got this van," he said.

"Is it far?" I asked.

He shook his head. "Just up the Euston Road."

The back of the van was full of tins of paints. I sat on one and Mickie James sat on another one next to me. We had the Korg across both our knees.

"Are there many people coming?" I said. "I wouldn't have thought there were that many gay train drivers."

"Oh, you'd be surprised," he said. Then he added, "We also invite the guards. You done many gigs before?"

"Loads," I said.

Our best gig had been the previous Christmas. Simon Turner had been having this house party. He was a bit of a nutter but we said all right. His parents had gone to Bali and then that bomb had gone off and now he was an orphan. Rumour had it that he had loads of money but the tight bastard didn't offer to pay us.

We did one set in his parents' old bedroom. It went well although during the fourth song Peter Smith was sick and then passed out on the bed. John Cox and Chris Jones jumped up on the bed and crossed streams over him. Trish Rogers said they were gross but she didn't leave the room. *American Pie* had been a big hit that summer and this kind of thing was going on all the time. It was part of teen culture and we were keen to hook into it.

"This is it," said Dave. "We're here."

The pub's name was the Charlatan's Arms. There was a chalkboard outside on which someone had written "Private Party Upstairs". I was disappointed that we hadn't got a mention but I was determined to act professional. I went inside and I asked where we should set up and if our amps had been delivered yet. The landlady was this fat woman and she had this bright red lipstick that she'd only put on the inside of her lips so they looked really small.

"Your amps are here," she said, "but a word of warning. Keep it down, love. We've got ladies' darts tonight and if we play our cards right we could be through to the semis."

I started to walk away.

"I mean it," I heard her say behind me.

It didn't take us long to set up. We flicked on the speakers and Mickie James played the opening notes to "Slow Train to Havana" and I said one, two, three, four into the microphone. Then I went to get us a couple of pints. I wasn't nervous but I was thinking of Mickie James. He hates people staring at him.

By eight-thirty the place was beginning to fill up. When I went to the toilet for a piss this cute guy asked me which train I drove. I said I wasn't a train driver, I was in the band. He said would I like a blowjob, then? I said no thanks and I walked out. I walked the wrong way, though, and found myself in a cubicle. I shut the door and waited in there until I was sure he had gone. I had an erection. He really was a cute guy.

At nine o'clock Dave turned off the jukebox and said it was time for the band. There were some claps. Dave said we were fresh down from Birmingham and we were going to be the next big thing. He said more than likely people would catch us later in the year at Pride in the Park. Then Dave said he was still waiting for subs from certain people. He read out a list. It was quite long. Then we were on.

There were eight songs in the set. Six were our own and two were covers. The covers we did were "Jokerman" by Bob Dylan and Duran Duran's "Rio". Our own songs in this order were "Slow Train to Havana", "Curve", "Ain't It", "Festival of Dreams", "Alien Amore" and "Manos Sucias". We did a cover at the beginning and the end. It is good to start and finish with something that people know.

Everyone says that "Manos Sucias" is our best song. It has this flamenco bit in the middle and during it I go wild. By this time I am sweating anyway and I pull off my T-shirt and I kind of stamp up and down the stage. It's not a pose or anything: this is how I feel.

Sometimes you can perform and not be aware of the audience. Sometimes the performance is all about you but this evening I guess because the audience is so close to us you can't help but notice them. And when I start doing my flamenco routine I find that I'm in the crowd and I feel hands on my body. The whole thing is intense. I spin and I spin and I think this is what I want to be doing forever. It's the best feeling. It's fantastic.

As "Manos Sucias" comes to an end, people go wild. I mean really. They are shouting "more" and "more" and when Mickie James plays the opening notes to "Rio" everyone starts singing right away. "Rio" is a killer song and a perfect way to end our set.

When it's over that guy I saw in the toilet comes up to me again.

"About before," he says, "I didn't mean to offend. I was just having a laugh."

"That's okay," I say.

"I'm Tim," he says, "let me get you a drink."

"Thanks," I say.

The eight-hundred quid we had was soon almost gone and Mickie James and me started to argue. It wasn't as easy to find gigs as we thought. Mickie James said the problem was that we had the right look but before people would book us then they would want to hear us. We came up with the idea of making a demo tape. Only we didn't have any recording equipment.

We went from music shop to music shop only to find everything was out of our price range. Then I had this last-ditch idea.

The woman in Rymans had us over a barrel and she knew it. The Sanyo Dictaphone was just what we needed, she said and at £49.95 was well within our price range.

Back at the rehearsal studio we tried the Dictaphone in various locations. The major problem was that it sounded crap wherever we put it. Not crap because we were great but it was more of a sound quality thing.

Mickie James said that as manager this kind of thing was my responsibility and I said that if he hadn't got sacked from the council then we would have had more money to buy better equipment. He pulled his sheepskin around him and stormed out. I shouldn't have said that.

I sat down on one of the spools of cable wire for about half an hour and then I came up with an idea. I remembered this documentary I'd seen about the whole *Pop Idol* phenomenon. The bit I was thinking of was when Will Young came to record his first song "Evergreen". In my head I could see him in the recording studio singing into a microphone. What surprised me was how big the microphone was; it had this really big head like an afro. That must help, I thought, with sound distortion and stuff. It was the kind of thing we needed.

I took off my left shoe and my sock. I wrapped the sock around the Dictaphone and sang a few notes into it. I played it back. It wasn't recording studio quality but it was better. There was no doubt about that.

I found Mickie James out on the roof. He was crouched down at the edge gazing out towards the British Library.

"I've done it," I said, "listen."

I pushed the button on the Dictaphone. Mickie James stood up and clapped his hands. Then he looked down at my feet and asked why I was wearing only one sock. He told me to be careful that I didn't stand in any shit. This was the part of the roof we used as a toilet.

Armed with the tape we went round a few venues. The guy at the Blue Note was more than interested.

"I haven't got time now," he said, "but if you leave me a tape then I promise I'll listen to it and get back to you. I'm always looking for new talent."

I took the tape out of the Dictaphone and slid it across the bar.

"What's this?" said the manager. He picked up the tape.

Now that I was looking at it with his eyes I could see his point. It was only about an inch long.

"You're having a laugh, aren't you, lads?"

"We'll be back," I said.

Outside it had started to rain. We had £10 left and Dave would want his money the following Tuesday.

"We're going to have to get jobs," I said to Mickie James. "Just to tide us over until the money comes flooding in."

It was Mickie James who saw the sign. It was outside this shop called Bloomsbury Cheeses. The sign said 'Help Needed'. That sounded us to a tee.

As we went in a bell rang above our heads and a fat man with a large moustache came from behind a curtain.

"We've come about the job," I said.

"You'll do," he said to me. He looked at Mickie James. "Not him, though. He'll frighten the customers."

"I wouldn't work here if you paid me," said Mickie James.

"Calm down," I said to Mickie James. I turned to the man. "It's illegal to discriminate."

"Tell that to the Turks."

"Are you a Turk?"

"No, I'm not. Do you want the bloody job or not?"

I nodded my head and I told Mickie James I would see him later. He said was I going to take the job then after the way the man had spoken to him and I said I was. I knew this would make Mickie James angry but I no choice; one of us had to do something. Sometimes I felt that that hunchback was on my back as well.

My new boss's name was Constantine but he said that I should call him Con. He said that he'd been in England since 1976 and that he'd hated it from the day he arrived. I said why didn't he go home then and he said he hated home more. He told me to go down to the cellar and bring up three Edams. I did know what an Edam was, didn't I?

"'Made' backwards," I said.

The job was easy enough, going down to the cellar, cutting up cheeses and then displaying them on these big plates.

Con said that he stayed open late as he liked to catch the commuters.

"That's one thing I've learnt about the English," he said, "you are impulse cheese buyers."

It was nine o'clock and on orders from Con I was about to close the door when someone stepped through it I thought I recognised. At first I couldn't place him and then he reminded me.

"Tim," he said and smiled. "Gay train driver who offered you a blowjob in the toilet."

"That's right," I said.

"You work here now?" he said.

"Well, you know," I said.

"Look, it's my last day of work on Saturday. You want to come up to Manchester with me? You can sit in the cab."

"I don't know," I said. I wiped my hands down the front of the apron Con had given me. Bits of cheese crumbled off.

"Come on," said Tim. "It'll be a laugh. You ever been in a train cab before?"

"I've been on a train," I said.

"Manchester is the home of music, isn't it?"

"I suppose," I said.

"Be on platform 4, then. 7 am. Now, have you got any Camembert?"

When I got home that evening Mickie James was curled up on the bed. He had pulled the duvet over his head. I thought he was asleep and I tried my best to not disturb him but just as I was taking off my underpants he sat up quickly.

"It's because of my back, isn't it?"

"The job, you mean?"

"Everything," he said. "Everything." And then he wouldn't say anymore.

I lay in bed thinking about Tim. I thought Mickie James may have been right. Perhaps things would be easier without a hunchback.

On Saturday morning I told Mickie James that I was off to a cheese convention on behalf of Con. Mickie James looked upset and said that I cared more about cheese than I did about him or our music. I said this wasn't true, although cheese had gone up in my estimation. Con let me try little bits of all the different ones. My favourite was Roquefort.

Tim was where he said he would be and he held the door open for me and I climbed up into the cab. It was smaller than I thought it would be and it had loads of buttons.

"So this is where you work," I said.

"Kind of," said Tim. "Although today is my last day. I've been offered a job on Eurostar. Forty-five thousand a year. At twenty-eight, I'll be their youngest driver."

"Well done," I said.

"You got any more gigs lined up?"

"Not yet," I said.

"You should lose the keyboardist," said Tim.

"He's my..."

"I'm sorry," said Tim. "I shouldn't have said that. It's not because, you know... a lot of the guys said it. I mean he looks so..."

"The Pet Shop Look miserable," I said.

"Yeah," said Tim, "but that's a pose. There's a difference."

And then we were pulling out of the station.

It was more exciting being up front than it was sitting in the carriage. The way the tracks rushed towards you was neat. When you were going fast you felt that you were cutting through the landscape. Everything was on either side of you and you were straight down the middle. The centre of everything.

As we zipped through Radlett, there was a knock on the door behind us. Tim reached behind him and pulled it open. Standing there was a very pretty woman dressed in a blue uniform. She handed us both a bacon sandwich.

"This is Tracy," said Tim.

"Hi Tracy," I said.

"Go on, Tracy," said Tim, "show him."

Tracy smiled at Tim and then she unzipped her skirt. Then she pulled down here panties. Nestled there between her legs was a cock.

"Tracy's a transsexual," said Tim. "Some people deal with their difference."

"I guess so," I said.

It was about a four-hour run to Manchester. Tim didn't talk much but he was easy to be with. He pointed out different sights and he told me their brief history but not in a boring way. He was quite funny really. It was a long time since I'd been with anyone who just spoke.

It was as we were about to pull into Piccadilly Station that it happened. Tim saw him first and he shouted out "Shit! Shit!" and he thumped something on the dashboard and then I saw him too but it was only for a second and then there was a crash against the windscreen and a spattering of liquid.

"Jesus, we hit him," Tim said.

"Do you think he'll be alright?" I said.

"He's a goner," said Tim.

The train hadn't been going that fast, but still it was fast enough.

When we eventually stopped Tim climbed down out of the cab and I followed.

"That's the fourth one this year for me," said Tim.

"What?" I said.

"That's one of the reasons I'm going over to Eurostar. They don't seem to get as many jumpers."

"This has happened before?" I said.

"All the time," said Tim.

We came to the first part of the body as we reached the end of the train. It was a leg. It was under the last of the wheels.

"Fuck," I said and then I threw up onto the embankment.

"You don't have to see this," said Tim.

"I'm okay," I said.

A bit further down we came across an arm and then another one. One of the arms was bare but the other was still in the arm of the jacket that the guy had been wearing. The jacket was corduroy. The bare arm had pretty big muscles.

"He must have worked out," I said.

"There's the head," said Tim. "Don't look."

"I'm all right, I think," I said.

The left side of the head was caved in, like a partially deflated balloon. The right side was still okay. If you'd have come by the head on the right side you would almost have expected it to smile from its lips and say hello. It was a nice face, kind looking, and not the kind of face you'd expect to see under these circumstances.

"We'll have to wait for the police," said Tim. "They'll probably want to take a statement. I don't know if we'll get back tonight."

"That's alright," I said. Despite the accident I was enjoying myself with Tim.

It was past eleven when Tim checked us into the motel. We'd been with the police for hours. Tim booked a double room and I didn't say anything.

"You have a shower," he said. "I'll see if I can get us some food."

"I don't think I could eat," I said.

"Do as you're told," said Tim.

When I came out of the shower Tim was sitting on the bed. There were two plates there as if they were on a table and on the floor was a bottle of wine.

"You want a drink?" said Tim.

I ran a towel over my head. I had another towel around my waist. "That could have been Mickie James," I said.

"What?" said Tim. He was eating a sandwich and I could see it in his mouth.

"On that track."

"How's that?" said Tim. "He in the habit of walking around on train tracks?"

"Mickie James was going to kill himself one night."

"What?" said Tim. "Have a glass of wine."

I sat down on the bed. I took the glass of wine from Tim.

"He said he'd had enough. We'd been in this pub watching a cabaret show when the guy behind us asked Mickie James if he'd move his hunchback. This guy thought he was funny. His friends did as well."

"I'm sorry," said Tim. "He sensitive about it, is he?"

"When this guy said that Mickie James leapt up and he was off. I went after him and before I knew it we were down at New Street station, off the end of a platform, and onto the tracks. He said he was going to jump in front of a train. He did, in fact. He jumped in front of one, but it wasn't moving. It would be funny if it wasn't sad."

"It's funny, anyway," said Tim.

"Yeah," I said.

"And sad. Do you love him?"

"How much can you love someone? I worry, though, that I make it worse."

"In what way?" said Tim.

"I don't know." Then I said. "This whole band thing, it makes it worse. If I'm there, he doesn't have to cope."

"Have some more wine," said Tim.

"Thanks," I said.

"You should come to France with me," said Tim. "I've bought this little house in Bordeaux. It sounded like a good idea and all the other lads are jealous as hell but, thinking about it, I don't know if I want to live on my own."

"What," I said, "just like that?"

"Why not?" said Tim. "There's lots of little bars around there, loads of tourists. I'm sure you could get work."

"Doing what?" I said.

"Singing," said Tim.

I imagined buying one of those little accordions, not one with a whole keyboard but only with those little round white buttons that you press. I'd had one when I was a kid. I was pretty good with it. Mickie James wouldn't let me use it when we started the group though. He said that you can't have us both with instruments.

"I speak French," said Tim. "I could arrange things. Be your manager if you like. Besides it would give this Mickie James some space to sort himself out. You can't love others if you don't love yourself."

"You might be right," I said.

"Me," said Tim, "I love myself. But that might be because I've got an extremely big knob."

"Ha ha," I said. I was joking but I meant it.

"You coming to bed, then?" said Tim.

We lay in bed side by side and we were both naked. Tim had this very skinny but muscular body and his cock was thick and dark brown. I couldn't sleep. Around two in the morning I turned Tim over on his side and put an arm around him. It was a strange sensation not having the bump there and the sensation of skin on skin. I kept thinking of that guy we'd hit. It was a waste but I wondered what went up to that point – was it a waste, too?

In the morning we got dressed. We got a taxi to the station and then we took the train back to St Pancras.

We said goodbye on the concourse with trains grunting all around us and Tim told me to think about his offer. I said I would and then I headed back over to the door that said JANITOR on it.

As I was about to go through it I stopped. I couldn't do it. I stood there for ages until a cleaner pushed past me and went through the door. Then I turned away and walked slowly out of St Pancras station. I wasn't sure what I was going to do yet. All I could see were those bodily parts strewn across the tracks.

Playing It by Ear
John Haylock

Playing It by Ear
John Haylock

Retirement descended upon Clive Danks with the suddenness of a clap of thunder. Of course he had thought about it, but each time he postponed making a decision. He had been teaching English in Tokyo for fifteen years. He knew he would miss Japan sorely. Regular visits to England had not endeared him to his native land. He felt a stranger there and found he had little in common with his old friends. Tokyo was not a place to retire to, certainly not one to grow old in, not for a bachelor, anyway, and it was extremely expensive. Clive had resisted the temptation to share a flat with his Japanese lover, as he felt it was important for Tatsuo to have a life of his own; they met at weekends and went on holidays together to other Asian countries and to Europe. Clive knew that he would find leaving Tokyo a great wrench; it had to be. Where should he go? An English friend suggested Thailand. "It's not outrageously expensive like Japan or Europe," he said. "It's not so far from Japan, so Tatsuo could visit you and vice versa, and the Thais, unlike the young English, respect the old; also, the doctors, often trained in America or Japan are competent and their charges are reasonable. I'd recommend Chaing Mai, not Bangkok, too big, too crowded, too cluttered with wild traffic; not Pattaya, it's too sleazy with too many foreigners chasing or being chased by kids; so go to Chaing Mai."

With the assistance of a compatriot, introduced to him by a friend from Bangkok, Clive went through the bureaucratic procedure of applying for a residence permit and renting a flat in a block of apartments a mile or so from the centre of Chaing Mai, the second city of Thailand, 480 miles from Bangkok in the northwest of the country, not a great distance from Burma and Laos.

Tatsuo managed to get a few days off and came to help Clive install himself in the furnished flat, which was on the fourth floor. The rent was affordable; there was a concierge; the lifts worked. Together Clive and Tatsuo reconnoitred the district. They found an excellent open market, where, apart from food, all sorts of useful things could be bought, and further off a supermarket geared to both Thai and Western tastes. And then Tatsuo, busy like most Japanese, had to return to Tokyo: another sad departure.

One afternoon Clive came upon a bald, portly man with dark-brown eyes and a pale complexion waiting for the lift. The man exuded bonhomie and smiling said in English, "I'm Stanley Trench. You're also an inmate, I gather. I live on the fifth floor. And you?"

"I'm on the fourth. My name is Clive Danks."

Stanley made a clumsy *wai*, his briefcase dangling from his little finger.

The lift arrived. "After you," said Stanley. "Age before – I mean, Beauty before..." Stanley emitted a giggly laugh.

"Thanks." Clive flapped a hand. "Isn't it hot! And it's November."

"Wait till April." Another laugh and Stanley entered the lift with a slight swish of his well-covered hips.

The flap of the hand, the swish of the hips acted as signals and at once they recognised each other's inclination.

"Come and have a drink," said Stanley. "I'm in five-two-seven."

"When? What time?" It was four in the afternoon.

"Seven. OK?"

"Thanks. OK."

Stanley's apartment was larger than Clive's. It had three bedrooms and was better furnished. The Thai bibelots – ceramic bowls and vases and small bronze figurines of the Buddha – showed that the owner had been in the country for some time. The sitting room had a view of the Doi Suthep, the mountain on which there is a renowned and revered temple. Clive's flat looked onto another apartment block.

When the two had settled into armchairs with glasses of whisky at hand, Clive asked, "What do you do here?"

"I'm one of Bernard Shaw's 'those who can't'. I teach." Stanley laughed.

"I belong or belonged to that group too, but I have just retired."

"Lucky you. By the way, I saw you with a very nice-looking

Japanese man the other day. Lover?"

"Yes. He's been promoted to the status of friend, though, after twenty years."

"Promoted?"

"Yes. It's a firmer relationship now that sex is over, a deeper connection," explained Clive, seriously.

Stanley laughed, giving Clive a quizzical regard with one bushy eyebrow high above the other.

"Do you have a Thai lover?" asked Clive.

"Not really. Having a job I have to be careful. Don't want it known at the school that I'm 'that way'." The eyebrow came down and joined the other in a frown.

"The place is full of foreign teachers, most of them women. I have to be circumspect. The head is English, has a wife here, very straight, religious too, evangelical."

"Oh dear!"

Stanley had a car, a small one, but a car, and Clive had begun to realise that Chaing Mai was a town where a car was necessary. The public transport was non-existent; there were elaborate roofed bus stops, but no buses. One had to rely on tuk-tuks or red vans. The tuks were sort of motorcycle taxis with a low roof; the red vans had two benches inside for passengers. Both vehicles were difficult to see out of, and to mount or alight from a tuk-tuk required the suppleness of a contortionist.

"Yes," said Stanley. "You must have a car if you are going to spend any time here."

He drove in rather a vague way and traffic was heavy and fast-moving. Clive gripped his seat and pressed his right foot on to a non-existent brake pedal. Stanley noticed. "Don't be nervous, the Thais have quick reactions." Motorcycles raced past on both sides of the car.

"They seem oblivious to danger," remarked Clive.

"It's their Buddhist philosophy," explained Stanley.

"Their buzzing bikes are like a swarm of wasps," added Clive.

"I don't mind then when they're in shorts and display their legs and thighs. And when a young cyclist with bare, hairless arms stops alongside me at a traffic light, my day is made."

They dined at a French-style restaurant with glass-topped tables. The young, winsome waiters in blouses and sashes that drew attention to their slim waists outnumbered the customers. Stanley knew them all, some of them by name.

"I don't come here for the food," said Stanley, turning in his seat to eye the waiter who had just placed a dish of roast duck in front of him. "*Korp, koom khrup*, Siria."

"What did you say to him," asked Clive, suspicious.

"Thank you. Siria is his name."

"Such a mouthful."

"Yes, 'thank you' is rather. Wait till you try the tones."

"I don't think I will."

"You know, if you get the wrong tone the meaning can be quite different, sometimes rude."

"So I've heard."

Back in the car, Stanley said, ""I'm going to take you to the Captive."

"Where?"

"The Captive. A gay bar. You might like to free one of them – at least temporarily." He gave a raunchy laugh.

The bar was some distance away: the other side of town, across the river and at the end of a long street off which they turned into a leafy lane and then into a parking space by a Thai-style house.

"It looks like a private residence," remarked Clive.

"It was until a few years ago."

They walked to the entrance, where there was a shoe rack. And steps to the front door. "Shoes off, I'm afraid," warned Stanley.

"I'm used to shedding my footwear, coming from Japan."

"You can shed something else if you find a captive you fancy. There is accommodation."

They entered a large room, dimly lit à la American. The teak floor was partly covered by rugs and cushions; there were no chairs. In various parts of the room customers, some of them foreign, were flirting with bar boys.

"You can stand or sit up at the bar over there, if you don't like the floor," said Stanley, sinking into a mound of cushions.

Across the room there was a stage on which a youth in a brief slip was performing a go-go dance; his movements – kicks in the air, pelvic thrusts, arms outstretched then bent –were automatic; his face bore no expression. A young man came over to the almost supine Stanley. "You li' beer?"

"Yes, please. Want a beer, Clive?"

"That would be nice." Clive lowered himself down onto a cushion with a groan.

"Two small Singhas, *khrup*."

"No have small," said the boy.

"One large, then."

The boy went off to the bar.

"He's Burmese," Stanley informed Clive. "From the Shan States. Lots of them over here. They smuggle themselves into Thailand in search of work, which they can't always find, so some of them drift into bar jobs, which can pay quite well."

"Poor things."

The boy returned with two bottles and three glasses. He knelt down and deftly served the beer. He stayed by the two elderly men and topped up their glasses and his own now and then. Stanley mildly rebuked the boy. "I did say one bottle," he complained.

"*My pen rai*," answered the boy with a dashing smile.

"All right. Never mind, as you say."

After some muttered exchanges with the boy, Stanley, with the boy's help, struggled to his feet. "Won't be long. Therapy," he said, cocking a bushy eyebrow. "There'll be a show for you to watch soon." He disappeared with the boy from the Shan States. The show consisted of five boys in G-strings romping gracefully about the stage and grabbing at one another amid high-pitched squeals; soon they were all naked and a simulated orgy was enacted; it was rather like a frenzied ballet, but it had obviously been choreographed.

Clive could not stop himself from becoming excited by this wild display of slim, lithe bodies. The boys seemed to enjoy themselves.

When Stanley returned with the boy from the Shan States, he said, "Any captive you fancy? I don't mind waiting."

"They're a bit young for me," Clive answered.

"Most of them are around twenty."

"They're pretty, charming, but not really my cup."

"Sorry about that."

The boy from the Shan States helped Stanley on with his shoes and accompanied the two foreigners to the car. He kissed Stanley filially on the cheek, and then, putting his palms together, gave Clive a respectful *wai*.

A few days later Clive found his "cup", or rather his "cup" ran into him. They passed each other in Tapae Road, the main drag, and while passing their eyes met. A few paces on Clive looked round and the Thai had stopped and was looking round too. They advanced towards each other. It was around six in the evening; the rush hour had begun.

"Where you go?" asked the Thai, a slim, handsome young man of, Clive guessed, about thirty. This question in Thai doesn't expect an exact answer. It's a kind of greeting and the Thais reply, "Just round and about". Clive answered truthfully, "I'm going back to my flat."

"Where your frat?"

"Not far. You like to come with me?"

The Thai hesitated, then said, "OK... I go."

As soon as the two were inside the flat, the Thai said, "You gay?"

"Of course."

"No one they come here?"

"No. I live alone. What is your name? My name is Clive."

"Crive?"

"Yes, if you like, and your name is...?"

"My name Sawit, nickname Tam."

After a few embraces, kissings, unzippings and then undressings, they lay on Clive's double bed.

"What do you do?" asked Clive when, sated, they lay still on the bed.

"I work at fron' desk in hotel. You tourist?"

"Not really. I'm retired. Maybe I stay here for a long time."

Their explorative remarks continued for a while. Suddenly Sawit or Tam leapt out of the bed, had a shower, put on his slip, white shirt and black trousers. "I go," he said.

"So soon?"

"I mus' go to work."

"Now? It's eight o'clock in the evening."

"I on ni' shif'."

Clive gave Sawit his telephone number. "Please phone me."

"OK." He kissed Clive on the cheek, gave a *wai*, and hurried away.

Clive, thinking about what had happened during the last hour or so, dressed slowly, playing the scene again in his mind. He felt elated. He rang Stanley.

"I think I've found my 'cup'," he said.

"I'm glad, my dear. I've just had terrible news."

"I'm sorry. Can I help?"

"Hardly. Come up and have a drink?"

"I haven't dined."

"I'll knock up something."

Clive went to Stanley's apartment.

"Sorry about your terrible news. What is it? Not a death, I hope."

"Let me get you a drink first," aid Stanley. He poured out the whiskies – his was clearly not his first of the evening. He sat in "his" armchair. "My wife is coming."

"Your *wife*?"

"Yes. I'm married, have been for years. She has a brother in Melbourne and she's going to visit him, dropping off here for a few days on the way. He's paying for her trip, thank heavens, though I should have thought she could afford to pay for herself. She has a good job with an airline. She lives alone in London. No children."

"Does her coming here matter? She won't be here for long, will she? Doesn't she know about you?"

"No. At least I don't think so. Anyway, I wonder if you could help."

Clive, showing reluctance, frowned. "How?"

"I have a young man living here –"

"He wasn't here when I came for a drink."

"He goes out sometimes in the evening. He's not here now. He's an orphan. He has no home. He's Thai, from the northeast, the poorest part of Thailand. I took him in. He has a key. I can trust him completely. I wondered if you would put him up while my wife is here. He'd be no trouble."

"I'll think it over." Clive did not want his new friend to know he had a Thai living with him. He had told him he lived alone.

"He'd help with the housework and do the shopping." Stanley was anxious for Clive to agree with his request.

"Can't he go to a hotel?"

"He failed to turn up for military service and has no papers."

"Surely there are hotels that don't require papers."

"It'd be easier if he were here in this block. He could go on doing my flat."

"How old is he?" asked Clive. Having someone to do the housework and shopping was tempting.

"Twenty-two. He's called Eed, a nickname."

There came the sound of a key inserted into the lock of the front door which gave directly into the sitting room. "Here he is now," said Stanley. And the young man entered the room. His hair was bronze, his face made up and he was wearing a sort of unisex outfit consisting of a loose grey blouse and wide floppy trousers. He kissed Stanley on the cheek.

"This is Eed," said Stanley. "He likes to dress up a bit. He's a *kathoey*, a drag queen. He says he wants to have the operation, but I forbid him to have it while he's here – can't afford it anyway. He works in a jewellers' shop." While Stanly was talking, Eed, having made a polite *wai* to Clive, examined his makeup in the mirror.

"Eed, we haven't eaten. Please make us a ham omelette and a salad," Stanley commanded in an avuncular manner.

"OK, Papa." Eed went into the kitchen, a cupboard off the living room.

"I haven't told him yet about Mama's arrival. He won't be surprised. The Thais with their vicissitudinous lives are never surprised. They accept events as if they were expected."

The omelette was perfectly made, *baveuse*, which Clive liked. During the eating of it, however, he decided, in spite of its excellence, he didn't want Eed living with him. He told Stanley this when Eed had gone to his bedroom to watch television.

"Oh, all right," said Stanley, displeased. "I don't know what I'm going to do. It would only be for a few days. I shall have to play it by ear."

"I told my new friend that I lived alone. What would he say if he discovered I had a drag queen living with me?"

"As I was saying just now, he wouldn't be surprised. He'd accept the situation."

"I don't want to spoil what promises to be a rewarding affair." Clive rose. "I must go to bed. I'm tired. Thanks for the omelette. It was good."

A few days later Clive had a call from Tatsuo in Japan. He proposed coming over to Chaing Mai for a weekend. There was a national holiday in Japan and he could get a few days off. Clive rang Stanley. "My Number One is coming. What am I going to do about Number Two?"

"Play it by ear," advised Stanley unhelpfully. "Molly, that's my wife, is here, by the way. She arrived yesterday."

"What does your ear recommend you to do?"

"She seems to be getting on well with Eed, treating him like the child she never had, and he treats her like a long-lost parent. She's helping him with his makeup at the moment. She approves of my looking after the waif, which is what she calls him."

"Extraordinary. I'd like to meet her. Bring them both up for a drink tomorrow evening. Tatsuo arrives in the afternoon."

"Thanks. About six?"

"Seven would be better."

On putting down the phone Clive realised that he had only three glasses and a half-bottle of whisky and there would be at least five for drinks. He rang Tam on his mobile phone. "Where are you, Tam?"

"In hotel. I come see you?"

"Yes please, as soon as you can."

"I finish at six. I come then."

Clive felt nervous and conspicuous on the back of Tam's motorbike; however, they arrived safely at the supermarket, where they bought wine, glasses and other supplies for the party the next day. Tam volunteered to bring the purchases the following afternoon in a tuk-tuk. "My bike cannot take," he said.

Tatsuo arrived and soon after him Tam with the supplies for the party. Clive introduced his friends – he had told Tam about Tatsuo, having known him for years and so on. Tam had said, "No problem. I li' second wife." And laughed. The first thing Tatsuo said after greeting Tam with a bow was, "Thank you very much for looking after Clive for me." Tam replied with a *wai* and a deep bow.

While Tatsuo unpacked in the spare bedroom, Tam dealt with the bottles and the glasses and put nuts and crisps into bowls. Tatsuo came out of his bedroom bearing, like trophies, two duty-free bottles: one of champagne (Veuve Clicquot) and the other of brandy (Remy Martin XO). He had changed into a white T-shirt that had ACTIVE on it in large letters, and shorts. He at once began to help Tam with the preparations. Clive found it amusing, if a bit disconcerting, to see the two together.

Soon after seven Stanley arrived with Molly and Eed. Molly was in a blue, billowing long dress and Eed was in his trouser suit. Molly wasn't a bit like the picture he had of her in his mind. She was bosomy, blonde (dyed), fifty and had a jolly disposition, the sort of woman whom gays can get on with. She greeted Clive, Tam and Tatsuo warmly and sat on the sofa with Eed, who, spotting the TV set opposite, got up and turned it on. Tatsuo and Tam vied with one another over to pouring out of the wine and the handing round of the nuts and crisps. Molly held forth to no one in particular about her flight from England: "After hours, I thought we must be arriving soon, so I asked a steward, and to my dismay he told me there were six more hours to go. I was too tired to read and unable to sleep. I just sat. It was torture. And then when we arrived in Bangkok I had to change planes to get to Chaing Mai. A long wait. The Thai airport staff were sweet. I'm glad I decided to break my journey to Australia in Thailand and not go straight through to Melbourne, where my brother is. It's a twenty-four-hour flight from London. Imagine! Twenty-four hours!..." On she babbled. Eed, whose English was limited, had adopted the vacant look of the TV gazer. Tatsuo took Tam aside and seemed to be interrogating him. Molly's monologue continued relentlessly in spite of her having no audience. "I don't like the heat," she informed no-one." It doesn't seem too bad here as it's a dry heat. Bangkok was like a sauna. It's summer in Australia and it will be hot, my brother says. D'you like the heat, Eed?"

Clive managed to have a few words with Stanley. "What does your wife think?" he asked.

"Molly," Stanley replied, "has never thought much. She talks. Never listens. But like most bores, she's kind. Eed seems to have aroused her maternal instincts, which were never fulfilled. She's taken pity on him and he treats her like a cosy aunt."

"We'd better eat soon, Stanley. What'll we do after dinner?"

"Play it by ear, Clive." Stanley clapped to call attention. "Time to eat, chaps. I'll take Molly, Clive and Tatsuo in my car. Eed and Tam can follow on their bikes."

During the meal, which the party had at the restaurant with the glass-topped tables, Molly said to Eed, who was sitting opposite her, in a loud voice, not that she ever spoke softly, "I'd love to go. Listen, everybody. Eed wants to take us to a transvestite show, which is on tonight and includes a beauty contest. Shall we all go? It might be fun."

To Clive's surprise, Tatsuo was interested, but Tam and the two Englishmen were not. With Molly and Tatsuo on the back of his motorbike, like Thais flouting regulations, as they often do, Eed drove off. Stanley rose from the table and said to the two who remained, "I think I'll go and free a 'captive'. Want a lift?"

Clive and Tam declined the offer. When Stanley had gone, leaving Clive to pay the bill, Clive asked Tam what Tatsuo had said to him.

"He ask many questions. He want to know everything abou' me. I told him I was married."

"You *what*?

"I said I have a wife."

"To stop his questions?"

"But I have a wife."

"You're married?"

"Yes."

"You never told me."

"You not ask. I no change. I li' you. We go your flat. No one there now."

Clive tuned himself in to the suggestion and played it by ear.

Aaron Godwin
Randall Ivey

Aaron Godwin
Randall Ivey

I

It's the blond ones, Harris thought, who are the hardest to reach. Blocks of ice. As cold as their lucid skin, their flaxen hair, their icy stare.

Take this one, for instance. Aaron. The Godwin boy. In the far left corner. Three times already that period Harris had called him down for disrupting class, and in no time Aaron was at it again, whispering, giggling, causing others to giggle. Blame the seating arrangement. Aaron sat amidst a constellation of impressionable girls who gave him their attention and laughed at anything he did. After all he was a handsome, college-bound athlete, and they hungered for his approval.

A mere "Aaron, quiet!" didn't work. It would have worked on the others, the dark-headed, pockmarked modest ones, but not this one. This one needed humiliation.

Harris finished writing the chapter number on the board and turned. "Aaron, is there something interesting you'd like to share with the rest of the class?"

A titter. Aaron, his red-white face buried in his bare arms, glanced up. "Now, Mr. Harris, what could be more interesting than you?" Female giggles rippled around him, but it was too late. The bell sounded to end the period.

"Aaron, I'd like to speak to you before you go." Harris sat still as the class emptied, as Aaron came and stood at the corner of his desk. He still smiled, as though it had all been a joke they'd played together on everyone else.

As prelude, Harris crossed his arms and stared at Aaron a moment, because he could, because he had the authority to stare, because it gave him great pleasure to stare.

Handsome? An insufficient term. A horse was handsome, a reward was handsome, a matron was handsome. Aaron was beautiful. Unutterably so. Obscenely so. Those full red lips were obscene, licentious almost in the way they curled and twisted over Aaron's teeth. The same went for those naked, hairless, chocolate-dark arms and that nimbus of fleecy hair. His small waist led up to the broad chest with stiffened nipples showing through his shirt and the Praxitelean shoulders. And, if Harris didn't forever admonish his students against the use of cliché, he'd resort to one himself and call Aaron's eyes limpid pools, but he settled instead for blue storms, dark harbingers, wicked omens.

"Aaron," he began dryly, neither his voice nor his eyes betraying his want, "you know class participation is one of the requirements of this class. Each out-of-turn remark and snicker means a zero in the grade book. And I see and hear every one of them. Why would you want to jeopardize your grade in this class so close to graduating?"

Aaron stood a second, then broke into a very wide grin, the only time he was not beautiful, when his high, blushed cheekbones nearly met his forehead, shutting out his eyes. "I'm a senior, man. I'm on autopilot from here on in."

"But if you don't pass English, you don't graduate." A second bell sounded, halving Harris's voice. "You know that."

"Second bell, man. Got to go. You wouldn't want me failing P.E. now, would you?" A long laugh followed him out of the door into the hall.

For Harris it was cafetorium duty, not P.E., but where he stood, at the beginning of the lunch line, gave him a good view of the football field. Two groups of boys gamboled there under the vague spring sun like a Whitmanesque fantasia realized, dear comrades stripped to shorts and cut-off T-shirts, one playing football, the other baseball. Aaron stood in the first group, luminous, rose-gold among so much pale, unshaped male flesh, his exposed belly flat as a slab of mahogany, his legs girl-smooth. Someone threw him the ball. He ran with it toward the goalpost, toward the sun itself, it seemed, and Harris half expected the sun to reach down with molten arms and steal Aaron from the earth, as rapacious Zeus had Ganymede. Aaron, quick as he was, couldn't make it. Two boys caught him, brought him down. A friendly tussle ensued, a mock fight that left the three of them scarlet and laughing. Harris flinched, envious. That was how he pictured Aaron and himself – in this same Hellenistic grip, like figures in a Grecian frieze. The ancient ideal. The wise man and his smooth youth. Except the wisdom came from Aaron, the ageless wisdom of beauty, from his unblemished throat, his clavicle, his perfect chest, his heaving, barely visible ribs, his white navel, and Harris wanted to drink wisdom from them like a fountain, press his mouth to what was golden and solid and strong.

An hour later Harris ate his own lunch in the teachers' lounge, where everyone was as excited as the teenagers about year's end and talked about graduation and the seniors they were glad to be rid of, the rogues' gallery, so to speak. Harris had suffered many of the names himself and nodded as each one was ticked off; and then someone mentioned Aaron Godwin, and Harris froze, though surely, objectively speaking, he would have added the name himself.

"Why Aaron?" he asked the woman who had offered Aaron's name. A math teacher.

She started behind her cigarette, surprised. "You teach him, don't you?" When Harris nodded, she went on. "Aren't you tired of his smart mouth? His interrupting your class just to impress the girls?"

Harris swallowed and grinned. "He's excited, that's all. He's a senior."

"He's an arrogant bastard," the woman returned, rousing a howl of laughter from the others. "And he was a bastard in his junior year too." A chorus of other teachers joined in to speculate about Aaron's arrogance. They mentioned his position on the football team. His college scholarship. His family's money. Harris listened and seethed and, silently, offered the true reason for Aaron's hubris: He's beautiful, you dolts, you dullards, you plebeians, he's a prince among peons, and you despise anything beautiful.

"His family doesn't have money," the first teacher corrected. "At least not any more. Do you think when Aaron's daddy left town he was chasing after some mistress? No. He was embezzling money from the company where he worked. Now Mrs. Godwin's in a fix. They say she's even renting out rooms in that beautiful house of hers just to make ends meet. That's how bad things have gotten."

"No!"

"Trust me."

In the school parking lot, Harris pretended to rummage and rearrange things in his car, all a pretence which let him wait for Aaron Godwin to come out of the building. There he came. Not alone, though. Some chubby, fluorescent blonde hung off his small hip, and Aaron whispered in her ear. Harris winced and ducked back into the car ,where he could watch them in his rear-view mirror make their way to Aaron's car, a beige Volkswagen Rabbit which sat not too far from Harris's. They lingered a little at the passenger door, embracing, chatting, mouths very close, then kissing. And, when Aaron held the door for the girl and started around for his own, Harris cranked his motor and waited and, when the boy's car eased from its spot, Harris followed, careful to let another car get in front of him so as not to be too obvious.

This intervening car, a blue Honda Accord, shielded Harris for about a quarter-mile before it made a right turn, exposing Harris again, but that was all right, because Aaron had only a few blocks to go before he stopped too, in front of a stuccoed house on Main Street. It was the girl's house, not Aaron's. According to the Rolodex in the school office, Aaron lived in Hidden Hill Estates, a much more exclusive part of Compton; and, while Aaron got out to open the girl's door, Harris kept moving, towards that address. That house, Aaron's, stood back from the road in a mélange of shrubbery, brick, two-storied, with a stately pair of Corinthian columns. Mrs. Godwin's financial state seemed incongruous with this place, but according to school gossip she was determined to do whatever was necessary to hold on to it, even renting out its rooms in a kind of informal bed-and-breakfast. Harris stopped a second to study it then headed back to Main Street, where Aaron's car still sat while he visited with the girl inside.

*

Harris ate his supper that night in town and afterwards went to City Park to walk it off.

More and more these days exercise was about all the park offered him. But not long ago the park virtually teemed with people, even at this late hour. Scampering children. Scolding parents. Lovelocked teens. And men, like himself, in search of collusions in the dark. Young, middle-aged, old, they sat in their cars or on the hoods of their cars, in the park swings, on marble benches, or, like Harris, they walked but in any case hunting for the same thing. Harris knew the hunters from the non-hunters. The hunters fairly vibrated with their frustration and their hope. It was obvious in their quivering greetings to Harris, their uncertain gestures for attention. They coughed like TB patients. They asked inane questions: "What time is it, buddy?" – and a wristwatch clearly visible. They lit cigarettes and prolonged the flame to let Harris see their eyes. And he had made some connections too – with thin, nervous youths, slightly effeminate and very voluble, or middle-aged men, baldly masculine and round-bellied, furry as afghans. He'd gone with them – to the woods, to their houses, to his apartment – and gotten what he could get from the encounter, afterwards chastising himself, depressed almost, not by the act itself or the nature of the act but by his lack of fealty to the thing he really wanted, had always wanted – the athlete, the beautiful, guileless youth with the full mouth and the bright eyes and the lucent skin and sinewy limbs, resolutely masculine, with no, or few, complicated thoughts in his glorious head. Someone he could roughhouse with or embrace tenderly. Somebody to whom he could point out the felicities of Mozart and Matisse. A son, a brother, a pupil, a comrade.

Harris rounded a corner and looked up towards the illuminated tennis court and spotted someone coming through the avenue of inflamed maple trees. A hunter. A solitary figure with his head down and his hands in his pockets. Something flickered in Harris. Anxiety. Hope. Dread. He gave the signal, coughing obviously. The man's head came up. Harris became excited. The man cleared his throat in response. The two men got closer, close enough for Harris to judge clearly. His hopes fell. The man was paunchy and silver-haired. He smiled at Harris with a nod. "Hey, buddy," he said in a thick upstate

South Carolina accent. "You got any idea how long this big path is? You think it's a mile? Got to be at least a quarter-mile."

"I have no earthly idea," Harris replied and moved on.

At home, showered and in bed with a tumbler of whiskey, Harris flicked through the television until the monotony made his head hurt. He flung the remote aside and went to this closet to drag out a cardboard box of pornography, glossy magazines and old videocassettes he'd collected through the years. He selected a tape with a young blond lead, lean if not muscular, fair-skinned with plum-ripe lips, and stuck it into the VCR with some hope of relief. He got irritation instead, remembering why he seldom bothered with pornography any more. It was a virtual genitalia ballet and little else. Why didn't they focus on the head, the face, the mouth, the true source of sex?

Disgusted, he turned off everything and lay awake in the dark, thinking how untouchable youth could be, especially the blond ones. Take Aaron Godwin, for instance. Harris hadn't always been confrontational with him. For a time he had let Aaron have his jokes, his little coups for attention, had even laughed himself at some of them, hoping for – what? Friendship? The same camaraderie he had with the other students, the dark-headed ones, the pimple-scarred ones, the sweet and rotund? After all, he wasn't that much older than they were. Ten, fifteen years maybe. He was still young, and he liked a lot of the movies they liked and some of the music. He liked athletics too and had been an athlete in school and had retained an athletic build. But Aaron remained unresponsive, and Harris, in bed, fumed thinking about it. He could fail Aaron if he wanted, keep him back another year, and what good would his scholarship be then? Never let Aaron forget – let none of them forget, the bright-eyed know-nothings – who really had the upper hand here.

Warm now with anger, Harris kicked off his bedsheets and lay exposed. Soon he had Aaron coming at him, in leonine stride, from the foot of the bed, naked and stiffened, golden even in the dark. Harris was naked too. They embraced, brown flesh on white, smooth on hirsute. Harris bound the boy's hips with his hairy thighs. They kissed. Harris tasted Aaron's throat, his protuberant tits, his omnivorous mouth. But it was more than sex. It was a melding of two things into one great thing – Harris the brain, Aaron the brawn. They were an entity. Then something slipped, Harris lost control: he saw the girl, Aaron's girl, naked on her back and Aaron atop her, moving, moving, moving, his brown back rigid, his white, dimpled rump flexing. They stared at each other and smiled. *They* were an entity. No! Harris cast the image from his mind.

He couldn't sleep. He lay on his back and waited for morning.

II

The Saturday after graduation, Harris braved the interstate for Atlanta, Georgia. An old stomping ground of his. He had taught at a community college in Marietta before coming to Compton, so he knew the area; and he headed toward the city's northeast flank, not far from the interstate itself. He had made motel arrangements beforehand on Cheshire Bridge Road, an old haunt crowded over with barbecue pits, Mexican restaurants, gay bars, porn shops, and a well-appointed but cheap motel.

In his room Harris opened the immense Atlanta phone directory to its yellow pages, the E section specifically, where a maze of similar-themed ads spread out over several pages: GIRLS! GIRLS!GIRLS... ANGELS OF MERCY...FOR THE DISCRIMINATING PROFESSIONAL... ATLANTA'S BEST...mFOR ANY OCCASION...GIRLS! GIRLS! GIRLS! Their similarity blinded him, but Harris kept looking until he found what he needed: JOCKS...COLLEGE BOY ESCORTS...THE BEST IN THE SOUTH SINCE 1979...

"A blond," he told the man on the phone. "Toned. Smooth. No older than twenty-two. You understand?"

"Yes, yes, yes," the man replied between rasps. "I have just what you need. Perfect. Blond as the day. Passive, active, whatever you want. A real sweetheart."

Harris leaned back on the bed to wait the hour he was told it would take. This wasn't a violation of his principles, Harris rationalized over the drone of the TV. This was something practical, a balm for his nerves, a reward for months of abstaining, sustenance for the bleak summer ahead. What came through the door wouldn't be

Aaron, of course, merely a simulacrum, but right then, at that stymied moment, it was good enough. Harris remembered how, previously, in those rare times he had managed some intimacy with his ideal, he had come away buoyant, rejuvenated, happy as a colt in clover, as though the silken biceps, the obdurate pectorals, the purple-pink phallus had been actual wellsprings of renewal. He could live for months on the memories alone.

Someone knocked. Harris mashed down his hair before answering. A young man stood framed in the lurid motel porch light. He was the requisite age, Harris thought, but the light made it hard to judge his suitability otherwise. He was slim and smooth – at least his shorts and short sleeves seemed to indicate so. He had a sullen mouth, pouty and hard, which was all right with Harris, and when he spoke his voice was low and ambivalent, scratchy but not entirely masculine, which caused Harris's hopes to sink some. "I'm Tommy," he said. "The agency sent me."

"Come in, Tommy," Harris said. What else could he do? When the boy stood in the more substantial light of the room, Harris's hopes sank irretrievably. A peroxide blond. A phony. Harris saw a long black crease divide the boy's head into a pair of bleached wings. And he wasn't merely slim but bony, his elbows and knees sharp as flint. His face had a pinched sort of prettiness to it, pampered, indolent good looks exceedingly feminine. At once Harris wanted him out of the room, angry at what he thought was a cheat on the agency's part. But had he specified masculinity? The doubt quieted him inside.

The boy took a seat near the window, setting down some green knapsack he'd brought with him to light a cigarette. "You're lucky, fella. I was headed out of my apartment when Bill called. Bill – from the agency. He said, 'Yeah, there's this guy on Cheshire just dying to meet you. Get over there right now!" The boy crossed his legs on the bed and grinned. "So tell me," he said, opening his arms to display himself entirely, "have you ever seen anything better looking than me?" Harris, who'd moved over to the bathroom door, forced a laugh but said nothing. The boy, unfazed, puffed and through his smoke said, "I started not to come, anyway. Hell, man, I just got screwed last night by my boyfriend, and I'm too sore right now to be touched with a powderpuff, you know what I mean?" Harris recoiled inwardly. "You'd go for Nick. Nick – my boyfriend. Gorgeous beyond belief. Like Tom Cruise crossed with Jeff Stryker. Know what I mean?" He arched his eyebrows and used both hands to describe great length. "Straight till I met him. Oh, yeah. Had a fiancée and everything. Me and him were just good buddies. Then we got real drunk one night and he fell on top of me, saying 'You're the only guy I'd go for.' After that he got rid of the fiancée." The boy laughed. Harris didn't. The boy was playing the old hustler's trick of talking out the hour, going through the numerous items on his erotic résumé, especially the number of heterosexual men who'd fallen to his charms.

"Nick don't like me doing this. He's jealous as hell. But to hell with him. I do what I want. Know what I mean?" The boy finally stood. "Okay, honey, let's get the show on the road. Bill told you how much I get, didn't he? Tips are appreciated. And oh, I never kiss. That's the one thing I promised Nick I wouldn't do. You can kiss me, but I don't kiss back. Although I might with you. You're not bad-looking at all, fella."

Harris choked over his response. "I'm not interested any more."

The boy froze, gap-mouthed. "Say what?"

"I've changed my mind. I don't want to do this."

The boy reddened and drew his mouth into a scowl. "You mean I drove all the way here from Decatur so you could blow smoke up my ass?"

Harris reached for his wallet. "I'm sorry. This won't work out."

"Well, goddamn."

Harris peeled off three twenties, half the agreed rate, and threw them to the boy, who softened at the sight of money, smiling some before he looked up to say, "Tips are appreciated."

"Thank you for your trouble, Tommy, and I'm sorry this didn't work out," Harris said, quickly going to the door and opening it. He closed it again on the boy's ridged back and a whiff of obscenity.

Just after midnight, Harris started the drive back to South Carolina.

III

Harris could see the resemblance at once in the woman. She had the same high forehead, the same small nose, the same blue, unfathomable eyes. And the hair – the same blonde hair, except hers was longer, thicker, and bunned. She had Aaron's coolness as well, because when Harris told her he had heard about her through a friend's recommendation and wanted to rent a room from her, she seemed to look straight through him – as though he'd disappeared or never been there to begin with – before she said, "You're the teacher, aren't you? I believe Aaron was in your class."

Harris confirmed her with a smile and eager nod of his head. "Yes. Aaron. A fine young man."

"You gave him a C, didn't you?" Mrs. Godwin asked, an icy shine surfacing in her eyes.

Harris could only laugh.

"Now why would you want a room here? You must have lots of books and things, being a teacher. You'd be cramped."

"True. Yes. This is a transitional move. I'm looking for another apartment and need a place to stay while I look." He fabricated a story, not entirely a lie, about the number of randy young people in his apartment complex. Complaints to the manager hadn't helped. In fact, the manager, a kid himself, often joined in the antics. So he had no choice but to move. It would only be a month at the most. He wouldn't even bother unpacking everything he had. Just what he needed.

Mrs. Godwin remained unconvinced and then, for the first time, showed some unease, and Harris thought he knew why. Mrs. Godwin's usual tenants, she had informed him, were elderly men and women waiting for rooms in rest homes, and Harris was young, probably ten or fifteen years Mrs. Godwin's junior. It was a small town. People talked. How could he diffuse her anxiety? Offer his practical help? She had a strong young son for that. More money? He opened his mouth to make such an offer when she stopped him.

"A month?" she asked with warmer eyes.

"Yes."

She stalled again. "I need a safety deposit."

"Of course."

Harris spent that evening unburdening his Corolla of boxes of books, record albums, clothes. What furniture he had would be put in storage downtown, he told Mrs. Godwin. Actually, he hadn't moved out of his apartment yet. That was a task ahead. But he didn't tell her that. Mrs. Godwin stayed out of the way, watching with trepidation, as though she were being invaded, as though the intellectualism that had left her and her son untainted for so long finally threatened her. When he was done Harris sat in a chair near the window and listened for what he wanted to hear until he heard it – Aaron coming in, asking about the car in the driveway, being told who it was. Harris waited, a bit jittery, for some reaction, an exclamation of some sort, to the news, but none came. A backdoor slammed. There came the rip of a motor being coaxed into life. The lawnmower. Harris went to the window. Aaron, in shorts and a cut-off T-shirt, was pushing it across the lawn toward the green sunlight. The undulation of muscle and blond hair drew a constriction in Harris's chest. That was why he came here, to be close to that, that chimera, that vision of unfettered carnality. He knew beauty was wasted on the wrong people, wasted on Aaron, but maybe not. Maybe it was compensation for other lacks – curiosity, good humour, manners, imagination – he didn't know or care. He loved beauty more than anything else; and Aaron's room sat right across from his own.

When Mrs. Godwin invited Harris to eat supper with them, Harris felt giddy and nervous at the prospect of being so close to the boy. He imagined Aaron greeting him, his new roommate, his old teacher, effusively, with a laugh or clap on the back. But no such thing happened. In fact, Aaron was still out in the yard when Harris and Mrs. Godwin sat down to eat and he didn't come in until they were done and talking. He was a startling sight in the kitchen, glazed with sweat, reddened by work and the remnants of the hot sun. Harris caught a flash of his torso, an ant-trail of down plunging from his navel to his waistline. His hopes rose. He smiled and said, "Hello, Aaron. Guess who's your new boarder?" Aaron only nodded with a sullen "Hey, man" and got his plate and loaded it with mashed potatoes, turnip greens, a thigh and breast, grabbed his tea, and took off for upstairs.

When Harris returned to his room he unloaded a couple of his favorite books from their boxes and fished for his cassette player and a tape of Shostakovich but decided against music. Instead he would lie and read and listen to the sounds of the Godwin house, to Aaron's movements, his routines. Aaron remained downstairs mostly, watching television, talking on the phone, presumably to that girl, since his voice had the soft, playful sound of intimacy. That made Harris sweat, retaste his supper. He switched on the Shostakovich and let the static lugubriousness of the music drown out all other sounds. When it ended, Harris could hear Aaron move around in his room. Getting ready for bed? Or a shower? Harris's heart shivered at the idea of Aaron's nudity so close to him. He sought, frantically, some excuse to go to the door and look. But no. Too obvious. He stiffened himself against the bed to resist reflex. Then Aaron went back downstairs, not to the bathroom, and resumed his TV show. Harris heard the mother say goodnight and go to her room; and with the closing of her door Harris's imagination ran free. What, he wondered, would attract the attention of an eighteen-year-old fraternity hound in the making? One thing. Harris stood and went to one of the uppermost boxes where he hunted and found a bottle of malt whiskey.

Aaron was in the kitchen scouring the refrigerator, bringing out a pear and searching for something else, when Harris came in, shielding the bottle in case Mrs. Godwin showed up. He tried a pitiful joke to ease the tension. "You don't have to worry about me being here, Aaron. I'm not going to grade you on anything."

He blushed at the silence, before Aaron, still hunting, said, "I ain't worried about shit, man." Aaron settled on orange juice and stood. That was when he saw Harris's whiskey and a smile lit his face. "Mr. Harris, I didn't know you bent the old elbow."

Harris, unbalanced by the smile, recovered quickly. "Oh, yes. How do you think I teach high school and stay sane?"

Aaron laughed his loud, careless laugh. "I hear you, man."

Harris, thrilled by the attention, moved straight into pedagogy, explaining the history of that particular whiskey, its Scottish origins and all, but that left the boy blank-faced, so he said quickly, "Would you like a little? Say you've tried it?"

Aaron thought a second. "Naw, man. Can't get blotto. I start a summer job in the morning. Thanks, anyway."

Harris had gone there partly thinking that if he got this close to Aaron, he could cure himself of his desire. What was the Proustian maxim? "We get through a suffering only by experiencing it to the fullest"? Something to that effect. He thought a daily closeness to Aaron's rudeness, his moodiness, his unfriendliness might overwhelm his want and purge it finally. But day after day Aaron's unfortunate traits were obliterated by sight of him in his lifeguard uniform, tanktop and swimtrunks, as he left and returned to the house in a blaze of blond and honey fire. Harris watched him from his window upstairs and swooned nearly, fretful and frustrated. He'd have to pour a drink sometimes to calm himself, which he did more and more frequently.

At night, with Mrs. Godwin tucked away in her room, Harris came downstairs with his liquor for a glass. He hesitated at the cabinet, waiting for Aaron, who sat watching TV, to come in for a snack. When he did he eyed Harris's bottle with interest, and one night he smiled at Harris, who brought down a second glass and filled it. He nodded at it and at Aaron. "Try it. One shot won't make you blotto. Oh, go on, Aaron. Live a little." Aaron kept glancing in the direction of his mother's room. "Your mother doesn't approve of drinking, does she?"

"Hell no, man. My daddy drinks. She'd kick my ass out of here if she caught me taking a drink."

Harris nodded toward the stairwell. "Let's take it to my room," he whispered and before Aaron acquiesced swept up the bottle and glasses and headed upstairs. To his surprise Aaron followed him, and when they had the door closed and were standing together in the light of one burning lamp, Harris gave Aaron the glass. Aaron sniffed it, took a tentative sip, then gulped it down, stepping back as though jolted. His beautiful face contorted. "God Almighty!"

Harris laughed. "Strong?"

"Hell yes, strong. Like fire. I usually drink beer."

Emboldened by his own whiskey shot, Harris gave a mock laugh.

"Beer. That's like drinking piss. This has hundreds of years of tradition behind it."

"Well, you can keep tradition," Aaron said and handed over the glass.

But a seed had been planted, because the next morning, while Harris poured a glass of orange juice in the kitchen, Aaron came to him and whispered, "Hey, man, do you think I can give tradition another shot?"

"Are you sure?" Harris asked with an excitement he could barely contain.

"I don't like anything to get the best of me."

Harris spent the rest of the morning in a hot euphoria, unloading more and more of his books and cassettes and clothes, feeling more at home and devising some excuse to give Mrs. Godwin for staying longer than the month they'd agreed on. But he was too nervous to think, too agitated over the idea of Aaron's coming to him that night. He couldn't even stay in the house and left in his car and drove for hours – until dark – inside and outside Compton County. But when he got back there was still time, and Aaron was nowhere to be seen. In his room Harris uncorked a new bottle of Jameson's and poured himself a shot. And then another. And another. Until his darkened room had a subaqueous uncertainty to it, as though the air were moving, as though he were under water. He could see Aaron in the waves, moving, coming toward him, naked and tumescent, deeply tanned except for a patch of white hips and thighs. Harris opened his arms to accept him, and Aaron fell into them, and a great swirling commenced. Everything moved round and round. The bed, the room. Harris squeezed his eyes shut to make the swirling stop, but it went on a moment, until someone knocked at his door and the excitement of knowing who was knocking sobered him enough to where he could stand and open it.

It was Aaron, yes, but he wasn't alone. He had the girl with him. The ostentatious one who had clung to Aaron in the parking lot. The one Aaron had driven home. With the lightened hair and the roll of baby fat. They stood together, young and bright and smiling at him. Harris's impulse, fueled by Jameson's, was to slam the door on them, but he couldn't do that, so he stood staring a moment until Aaron spoke, gesturing at the girl. "This is Annette. My girl. She wants to try tradition too. She's a big-time alky."

The girl showed shock and punched Aaron's arm. "Am not! You liar!" They giggled together.

Harris hated their voices in the hall. "Come in," he said and closed the door. Aaron noticed the opened Jameson's and grinned. "Looks like you started without us." Harris filled two glasses and handed one to Aaron. "Sip it. Don't throw it back like beer. It's not beer." Aaron obeyed and his face wrinkled only slightly. Meanwhile the girl protested. "Mr. Harris, don't you believe nothing Aaron says about me being a alcoholic. He's just talking crazy." Harris watched her, her hair, her mouth, her breasts, her thighs, all the places where, in all probability, Aaron's hands and mouth had been, and he wanted to hate her, had hated her until now, when she had been distant, nothing more or less than an abstraction. She seemed unworthy of Aaron, fat almost, and made up stiffer and brighter than a mortuary cadaver. Why did the beautiful almost invariably choose the plain for mates? For security's sake, the assurance of not being cheated on? But now, sitting on his bed, she seemed sweet and demure, a teenage girl, not an ogre, anxious to be friendly to him. It seemed rude to hate her now, unfair.

"I'm serious, Mr. Harris. Annette really wants to try tradition."

Harris nearly scowled at the girl in what was meant to be a look of inquisition. "Are you sure?"

"Well, maybe a little. Don't fill me a whole glass, now."

Harris found a plastic cup among his things and poured it a fourth full. The girl sipped and grimaced, whiskey wasted, as she gave Aaron the cup right away. Aaron dumped it in his glass. Harris asked Aaron what he thought of the whiskey now. "It's better when it's sipped," Aaron replied over a beautiful smile. A sudden panic took Harris, the realization that Aaron would finish the drink and leave, and Harris liked him there, even with his companion. Alcohol, even a little bit, had softened Aaron – he was all smiles and giggles now. Harris stood and gave him more whiskey and asked him how his summer was going, what he had planned. Aaron replied that next week he was going house-hunting in Columbia with some buddies. He hoped to be down there soon. Time to get out of Compton, you know?

"You from Compton, Mr. Harris?" Harris started at the girl's question, almost forgetting she was with them. He was too busy watching the lamplight play on Aaron's hairless forearms.

"No," he answered, not tempted to say any more. Then he said he was from nowhere, he'd lived all over, he wasn't ready to settle down, he was still young.

Aaron laughed at that. "You ain't young, Mr. Harris! You're old. You listen to all that old music, that Beethoven."

Ignorant people thought all serious music was written by Beethoven, as though no other composer existed. "Shostakovich," Harris corrected, but neither the boy nor the girl seemed interested in elaboration. Harris stood – "I listen to all kinds of music" – and went to where his cassettes sprawled on the credenza. He handed a couple to Aaron, from his "progressive rock" collection, but Aaron wasn't impressed. "Naw, man. That's still old. I'll show you some music." He sprang off the bed and left the room and Harris and the girl by themselves. The girl looked at the room, its accumulation of Harris's things, and then at Harris himself. "You not married, Mr. Harris?"

Aaron returned right away with a couple of cassettes, pallid imitations of rock and roll. "Let's hear 'em." Harris feigned distaste but put the cassettes in happily because it would keep Aaron there longer. He refilled Aaron's glass. Aaron sipped. They talked about music. They got quiet. Aaron moved to leave. Harris stopped him with a refill and refilled his own glass. The girl yawned and asked for the time. Aaron said it was late. Harris panicked and went through his liquor collection for something more accessible to the girl and the boy, a dainty chocolate liqueur, sweet as a candy bar. The girl sipped it and liked it. Aaron and Harris stayed with whiskey. Aaron looked at the books piled and scattered on the floor and asked, with gorgeous insouciance, how anyone could read so much. The question irritated Harris, so much so he was ready for the two to go. Whiskey had about blinded him, so it was no use having the boy there to stare at when he was nothing now but a gold blur, a smudge in the lamplight. But, when he made the suggestion that it was time to break up, Aaron said something, declared something, which stopped Harris, stunned him, brought all clarity back to the room:"I love you, Mr. Harris." The words came out slurred, but they wounded Harris like a bullet. He watched Aaron nod and smile affirmation, his young face slackened by booze. "I do, man. I really love you." Something, incredulity at first then gratitude, spread through Harris, sobered him somewhat, but he was still too numb to say, "I love you, Aaron" and go on to say, "Even though you're crass, vulgar, arrogant, rude, ignorant. You're beautiful. And that's all that matters." He couldn't say anything. He could only sit and listen while Aaron went on: "You're the coolest teacher I ever met. Really. Sharing your tradition and listening to tunes you don't really like. I know I gave you some shit in class, man, but you're cool. So cool, you know what? I'm going to let you dance with my girl! Yeah!" He stood and forced the girl up from the bed by the arm. "I wouldn't trust anybody else with her. Nobody but you."

The girl squealed, tottering some; a small amount of liqueur had gotten to her. Aaron himself swayed. "You're crazy, Aaron!" Terror struck Harris as Aaron motioned for him to take the girl. When he refused, Aaron, still holding her, came over and lifted Harris from his chair and posed Harris and the girl so their chests met and their chins very nearly. "The two people I love the most together!" The girl laughed and fell on Harris, who couldn't let her drop. When he lifted her she locked her arms around his waist and moved for the both of them. Some horrible, synthesized treacle poured from the cassette player. Their movements were stodgy and broken. The girl corroborated the farce, cooing and sighing and pressing herself suggestively against Harris. Harris devoured her hairspray and perfume – they and the whiskey set an indeterminate quake in his belly and bowels.

"Y'all kiss! Come on! We always kiss when we dance, don't we, Annette?" Harris blanched at the suggestion; the girl had to catch *him* and keep him steady. She puckered up and looked like a carp, all pink and blue. Harris refused, so she caught his chin and left moistness there. "Faster!" Aaron shouted from the bed. "Y'all dance too slow!" He stood and spun them to a tempo of his liking, and all Harris could see was Aaron's wide, white grin flashing; soon it detached itself and spun ascendant in the whirlpool he and the girl made together.

"That's too fast!" the girl cried. "Slow down, Aaron. It's too fast!" But Aaron spun them and spun them like a spindle. "Stop it!" Finally the girl broke free, hurtling against the wall with a thud. Harris fell to the bed. "Damn you, Aaron!" Aaron laughed. The girl charged at him with closed fists. "I told you it was too fast!" Aaron held her at bay with one hand, but she struck at him, getting his face. A welt appeared on the ivory smoothness. Aaron flung her away. She came back, bottle in hand. A 1982 Bordeaux. She swung it and let go. There might have been a crash; Harris couldn't tell. She threw books at Aaron, cassettes. "Fuck you," Aaron said, trying to constrict the girl in his arms, but she fought free and left the room, sobbing, her face a rouge-and-mascara soup.

The light woke Harris, and the song of a bird. He wanted to rise up to see the light. There was some reason to be glad, which he couldn't name then. A reason for gladness and for despair. He had been deprived of something and saved from something, a disaster, and he had a girl and a bottle of Jameson's to thank. But his limbs were too heavy for movement and his head too ponderous for thought. He went back to sleep. When he woke again someone was mowing a lawn somewhere; and he fought the swirling, the shaking, the chill, the raw eyes to stand. He needed coffee – that might give him the *illusion* of steadiness at least. He stood carefully and saw that his things – books, cassettes, clothes, liquor – were scattered everywhere. His room resembled a battleground. He stepped over things carefully, left the room carefully, took the stairs carefully, and stood in the kitchen door to rest his newly won equilibrium. That was when he saw Mrs. Godwin at the kitchen sink cleaning breakfast dishes. His balance left him again. He caught it and forced some cheer into his "Good morning," but it sounded hollow in the kitchen. Mrs. Godwin took a moment to turn but, when she did, Harris knew, from the firm set of her jaw and the focus of her stare, that she knew what had transpired the night before. Nevertheless he went to the cabinet for a cup and poured himself coffee and stood drinking it, managing to keep his head above shoulders and his eyes open.

The woman wasn't convinced. "I understand," she began in a calibrated tone, "that you offered my son alcohol last night." She paused, for confirmation or confession perhaps, but Harris didn't offer it. "I'm not naïve. I know teenagers drink. But you had no business giving Aaron whiskey. He's only eighteen years old. I thought teachers were role models. He was sick this morning. So was his girlfriend. My ex-husband is an alcoholic. That had a lot to do with the situation this family is in. I'm sorry. I have to ask you to leave this house. Right away." And with that she turned back to the sink, leaving Harris to stand and feel his coffee grow cold.

Upstairs he neither washed nor shaved but stood looking at his things scattered. Books sat with their spines cracked, cassettes lay unspooled, bottles lay on their sides, clothes were everywhere. There sat his Bordeaux, lonely on the other side of the bed but still intact. He went to the still-uncapped Jameson's on the dresser and poured a glass. What if the girl hadn't been there? Then Harris could have touched the thing he loved – the incomparable face, the perfect chest. Maybe, maybe not. But at what price? Humiliation probably, maybe Aaron's vehemence, blunted by whiskey, but still able to do Harris great harm. Or his job. Breath left Harris, replaced by the feeling of having skirted, just barely, some great calamity. Breath returned and with it sorrow, because he still loved Aaron or what Aaron represented: the athletic love of life, the *elan*, unfettered by intellect.

Something got his attention outside the window. A pair of shadows in the grass-green sunlight. Harris stood and glanced out the window and saw Aaron and the girl move across the lawn. Even in he midst of things, desire cut into Harris's heart at sight of the boy in tanktop and shorts, tall, bronzed, smooth. The boy and girl walked slightly apart as though about to diverge. Harris held out some hope they might go separate ways, unreconciled. But then the girl reached out for the boy's hand and the boy pulled her to him in rough-tender fashion. The girl encircled his small waist with her meaty arms and laid her head on his shoulder. They went off together towards the green morning sun, bound forever it seemed.

Harris finished his drink and began the act of packing.

Common or Garden
Alan James

Common or Garden

Alan James

Merlin, the black cat from two doors away, had been digging in the garden again. Or perhaps digging isn't exactly what cats do, but the ground around the newly planted hellebore had been vigorously disturbed, and the plant was leaning loosely from the border at quite a slant. David pushed it back in again, and firmed the ground around it with his fingers, checking carefully for semi-concealed turds. Or then again, do cats try to bury their turds, as dogs do? David suddenly thought that this might be unlikely, and that cats may simply, quite arrogantly, even, leave anything with which they no longer wish to be associated just lying on the ground behind them.

David's garden lay long and narrow behind his old terraced house, separated from similar gardens on either side by much-repaired brick walls, each four or five feet high. They were town gardens, but lush enough, benefiting from the mild south-of-England seaside climate; gulls often flew, screaming, overhead, as did formations of wild ducks, and the occasional hawk, on the hunt for the fieldmice and shrews that had the run of the ragged, old-fashioned plots of marguerites and marigolds, dotted with self-sown feverfew. David's garden had become more overgrown than most, and tailed off into long coarse grass and drifts of creamy cow parsley, shaded by a stand of lichen-grown apple trees. Towards the house, however, the garden was a slightly tamer affair – borders running along under the old walls, with between them a patchwork of paving that David had made from the old bricks and flagstones he had found stacked up in a couple of old tin sheds he had since taken down.

David had dug the borders some time ago, but they too had become weed-run in his absence. A cultivated, thornless blackberry had seeded, and the new shoots had reverted, their stems being covered thickly with sickle-sharp prickles, while their roots had sunk deep and tenacious into the chalky soil. Periwinkles which David had put in as 'caretakers', until he had decided on the eventual planting, had become leggy, greedy, all-devouring bushes which had to be carefully dug out, lest they leave behind them intricate webs of fine, fragile-looking roots, which looked as if they could never again have the strength to throw anything up out of the soil; but every few days, David noticed a furl of virile, slightly fleshy, emerald-green leaves pushing through again.

David was crouching, engaged in uprooting just one such intruder, when he heard the lightest sound behind him – hardly a footfall, more the softest touch of pads on the mossy bricks of the path. He knew what he would find if he turned round: the black cat would be poised there, motionless, interrupted on its way across the beds and borders. And then it would suddenly fly off, shooting up the garden until it reached the shelter of the old orchard. For a few moments, David refused to turn around to meet the creature's unflinching gaze; it was like a curious, possibly one-sided, game. When he finally did swivel round to look behind him, he was completely taken aback: instead of the black cat, there was a boy standing there, staring down at him.

David had so expected to see the cat, that for a few moments he almost believed that some kind of transformation had taken place. The boy, however, didn't look in any way ethereal; he was a thin, rather undersized teenager, sixteen or seventeen maybe, dressed in skinny bleached jeans, and old once-white trainers. His white T-shirt hung from his bony shoulders, and had some kind of logo, printed in red, which draped across his narrow chest. David's mouth felt dry; the boy was obviously some sort of trespasser, but showed no sign of running away. He simply stood on the path, his pale arms hanging loosely by his side, with the hands not quite clenched into fists.

He stared at David unblinkingly, as the cat would have done. His eyes were a clear pale blue, and he was unsmiling; this, and his close-cropped reddish hair, gave his face a small, mean, hard-bitten look. David had no idea what the boy would do, as he showed no signs of being embarrassed at having been surprised on somebody else's property. After a few seconds, during which David had risen slowly to his feet, he asked the boy, 'Can I help you?' The boy looked at him for a few long seconds more, and eventually flicked his lips up to one side, but still he wasn't smiling. Then he answered, 'No.' The word shot out of his mouth with an inflection at the end, an upwards twist which, if written, would have demanded a question mark; it was thrown out insolently, as if David had made an insulting request.

David didn't know what to do next, but suddenly the boy turned, and vaulted over the wall behind him. Without seeming to be in any kind of a hurry, he crossed next door's garden, leapt over their wall, and the one after that, veering off then to the right, where he was soon lost to David's view under some overhanging beeches. The boy's white T-shirt had a scarlet motif on the back, too, and David stood trying to decipher it, until it was absorbed by the shadows.

David was slightly shaken, but kept on pulling at the weeds. Only this time – for completely illogical reasons, as he told himself – he turned to work at the opposite border, so that he could face the way from which the boy had come. However, the boy did not return, and neither was there any appearance from next-door-but-one's cat.

It would be untrue to say that David was able to put the incident of the boy absolutely from his mind over the following few days. Obviously the boy had been interrupted, but whether he had merely been intent on taking a short cut across the gardens, or whether he had intended casing, or actually breaking into, any of the properties along the route, was of course impossible to know. David had been surprised, as he hadn't realised that there was any particular way of gaining access to the gardens, apart from through the houses to which they actually belonged; at their far ends, the gardens backed onto others, which in their turn ran down to the backs of houses facing a parallel street, on the next block over from David's. At one end of the block, facing the town marketplace, stood the old Guildhall, and at the other, facing the now disused quay, stood the new courthouse, partly carved out from handsome old converted warehouses. In between, there were no connecting alleyways, or service lanes.

However, David reasoned that, if such a boy wanted to run around on other people's gardens, sooner or later he would find a way to do so. The boy didn't live in his street, of that David was certain – the houses forming the attractively assorted Georgian and Regency terrace were probably by now too valuable to be lived in by 'normal' families any more, and the boy had definitely had about him what David thought of as the 'council' look – the kinds of boys who were still a bit too young for the pubs, so instead hung around in groups, smoking, outside the sordid-looking, almost boarded-up, Spar-type shops on the one or two estates which fringed the town to the east.

The important thing, David told himself, was not to become paranoid; the town was a small, friendly place, and he was happy to be back living in it. So, almost in defiance, he still kept the back bedroom sash open a few inches at the top, and when he was only popping out to go round the shops for a while, and the weather was good, he kept the glazed back door open, too.

A few weeks went by, and David had more or less forgotten the boy, except occasionally when he was in the garden; but then one Friday lunchtime, David saw him again. He had been to the indoor market at the Guildhall, where the Women'sInstitute sold good fruit loaves, and garden produce which the regular shops almost didn't bother with any more – rhubarb, maybe, or punnets of redcurrants. David always bought as much as he could from these ladies, and he was walking back down the road to his house, fairly laden with plastic carriers and damp, newspaper-wrapped parcels, when he happened to notice the boy walking ahead of him, on the pavement opposite. The wide road sloped gently down towards the quay, so people walking on either side were relatively easy to recognise at a glance, and although David could not see the boy's face, he had known him at once from the white T-shirt with the red circle on the back; there was also something particularly distinctive about the boy's determined, yet skulking, gait.

Whether the boy had also noticed him, he had of course no way of knowing. As he went down towards his house, David kept his eyes on the figure walking ahead of him, on the other side of the road; but, when he reached the quay, the boy disappeared behind a tourist coach which was slowly disgorging a Saga tour group, and as by this time David had reached his own front door, he let himself in. After a moment's thought, he deposited his shopping on the stone flags of the hall, went back out into the street, and looked down towards the quay – but the coach was still unloading, and the boy was nowhere to be seen. David told himself not to be unduly alarmed – the town was after all small, and the boy obviously lived locally, so it was almost inevitable that their paths would cross again at some point; or at least, if not inevitable, then certainly there was a reasonable chance of its happening sooner or later.

David couldn't quite put the boy from his mind – the sighting had been unsettling. Fears – it would not be too strong to call them that – had been awakened. Over the following few days, David threw himself into getting the house back into better shape. A thousand little things needed doing, while the good weather lasted – niggling painting jobs, the cleaning out of gutters. And inside, the place was far from tidy; a long wooden ladder, for instance, was always lying against one side of the hall skirting, as it was too useful to get rid of, and there was nowhere else for it to go, unless it could be squeezed diagonally into the remaining garden shed – which of course meant emptying and sorting the shed's contents. And David wasn't even sleeping upstairs, as he couldn't work out a way to manoeuvre the frame of his heavy Victorian cast-iron bed up and around the narrow, steep old risers, with their delicate wooden banisters. There was certainly enough for him to do.

A few weeks later, though the good weather still held, and the tourists were still coming, the cool of the evening and the mists of the early morning from the quay served as a reminder to David that he must finish the tidying of the garden before winter set in. One of his few extravagancies since his return to England had been the purchase of a Black and Decker shredder, for garden refuse; disposing of prunings is always a problem in an enclosed town garden, and David didn't want to simply push everything into an unsightly pile against the end wall, or have somehow to keep taking unwieldy loads over to the tip; in any case, he was a born re-cycler, and shredded matter could be spread as a mulch, or left in the compost bin to reduce to a fine, organic silt.

The shredder was supplied with a generous length of bright orange cable – easily long enough for David to work at the end of the garden, where the old apple trees began, if he plugged the flex in at the kitchen, just beside the back door. The cable snaked up the garden, a bright streak of colour against the worn grey slabs of the paving. The shredder's only drawback was the noise it produced; a real cacophony of harsh metallic rasping, as with its chillingly efficient revolving blades it gorged itself on the stems and roots it demanded to be fed. The whole thing was admirably designed, though, the sharp metal teeth being well and safely secreted in the body of the beast.

The shredder needed constant attention, like a baby cuckoo in the nest it has usurped; the semi-dried cuttings were fed in at the top of the vertical green metal tube of its body, having to be pushed through thick rubber safety-flaps. Larger branches could be fed through a special pipe nearer to the blades. The tube stood securely on a steel tripod of three sturdy legs; at its base was the cutter, which spewed out the detritus through a wide flattened spout attached at ninety degrees. The whole thing resembled an outsize straight-sided Wellington boot.

By the time David was ready to start, on the day he had chosen, it was mid-afternoon; out of deference to his neighbours, David wouldn't work with the shredder much later than that, although it would have suited him to do so, because of the din it gave out. He didn't want to disturb the shortening, peaceful evenings which descended across the gardens as the shops were shutting, and as the tourist coaches were heading off to the big hotels in the larger seaside towns.

He spread a large, green plastic garden tarpaulin under the mouth of the shredder, steeled himself slightly, and pushed the safety starter button; when he wore his thick red rubber gardening gloves, David felt clumsy, and switching on the machine sometimes took him one or two attempts: suddenly, the thing croaked, and then roared into life. David began to lower in the branches, and the twiggy pieces of vine, keeping the speeding circular jaws continuously fed, and making sure the waste was ejected evenly; the mulch began to build up into a flaky, green-brown pyramid, spilling out over the groundsheet.

After a while the engine changed its tone, and the flow of the shredded matter dried; David stabbed at the Off button, and stood waiting for the last whirring gasps from the throat of the tube. Sometimes the cutter became blocked, if there was too much sap, perhaps, in its fodder; then, the mechanism could easily overheat. When the shredder had quietened, David bent to pull the rubber plug from its socket, and to unscrew the plate which covered the circular blade; as he did so, he glanced back towards the house, and stiffened as he saw the boy, who stood calmly watching him. The boy was in next door's garden, a few yards down from where David was standing. Only his head was visible, and his hands, which were clutching the top of the brick dividing wall. As before, the boy showed no intention of moving.

David knew that he must say something; he didn't quite like the fact that from where he stood, the boy was, in a way, between him and his own back door. As he didn't want to shout, or in any way to raise his voice, which he knew would sound thin, dry and strained, he took a few steps towards where the boy was standing. The boy stood his ground.

That's not your garden, is it?"

"Ain't yours, neever."

"Where do you live?"

"Why??"

The boy's voice was insolent, challenging.

"Well, you don't live near here, do you?"

" 'Oo wants to know??"

"What are you doing around here?"

"Ain't doin' nuffin.' You livin' there?"

The boy tilted his head slightly towards David's house.

"In that house? Yes."

"Oh. Fort that 'ouse was emtee."

"Maybe it was, for a while. But it's not now. Anyway, we don't want you hanging around our gardens."

David was rather surprised to hear himself speaking on his neighbours' behalf.

" 'Oo's we??"

David was discomforted; the boy certainly knew where to attack.

"How old are you?"

"'Ay-'een. Old'nuff. Why?"

David didn't particularly know why he had asked. Or maybe he did; fear came creeping again, and froze his throat, stifling any further words – but in any case, he didn't know what else to say. The boy saved him the trouble; he looked David up and down, and then turned, leaving the garden as he had before.

David didn't feel like making any more noise that evening; he gathered up the corners of the tarpaulin, took the bundle to a back corner of the garden, where he had built a large rectangular brick bin for compost, and emptied it in. He unplugged, opened, and carefully cleaned the shredder, before carrying it back down into the kitchen – it was another thing for which a home had to be found. David rolled the yards of orange cable into a neat coil, winding it over his wrist and elbow, and placed it on the purple-dark quarry tiles of the kitchen floor, beneath the shredder's spreading metal legs. While the light still held, David went back up the garden to his shed, and began to remove its jumble of contents, which he laid tidily on the ground around it.

When he had time, the following afternoon, David went back to the shed, and began to give it a thorough clean. Whoever cleans out sheds? The corners and angles inside the old brick lean-to had long disappeared under accretions of spiders' webs, thick smoke-coloured garlands viscid to the touch. Clusters of ancient grey snails' shells still hung in brittle cloud-like growths from the low, sloping, roughly-boarded ceiling, and small mountains of tiny non-coloured amulets, the pale skeletons of woodlice long ago caught and consumed, littered the uneven dirt floor.

Every way he turned in the narrow confines of the place, dry, dusty things crackled faintly, and attached themselves to him. David straightened up, and went out into the garden for a breath of air; as he was brushing chalky ash-coloured powder from his jeans, he saw the back of the boy disappearing through his open kitchen door. Although dusk was falling, there was no mistaking the red logo on the white T-shirt, and, in any case, who else could it have been? Surely the boy must have been aware of him, working away there, up in the garden?

Of course, David would have to follow the boy who had just walked so arrogantly into his house, but even though he was the householder, and so of course totally in the right, he was strangely reluctant to take any action. He realised that he had begun to shake; he felt cold, but could also feel the prickling of sweat in his scalp, and on his upper lip. Maybe the boy would simply come out, of his own accord, carrying whatever he had chanced on which he thought would raise a quick buck; in which case, David could simply – simply! – challenge him when he emerged, hampered by whatever he had in his hands; although certainly David thought the boy would be well disappointed if his aspirations had risen to expensive stereos, mobile phones or portable televisions – David lived, had to live, a more ascetic life than most. But surely nobody – not even the most arrogant of thieves – would willingly risk an almost certain confrontation with the owner of the stolen goods they were carrying?

And then a sudden thought, a revelation: of course, the boy would simply stroll through the house, perhaps without even bothering to go upstairs, picking up whatever he fancied along the way, and let himself out through the front door.... except that, just for the pleasure of handling and turning it, David sometimes used the large, heavy old key to the mortise lock, which he had found, hanging from a hook on the kitchen dresser, when he had first taken possession of the house. Attached by twine to the key had been an old-fashioned, thick, putty-coloured cardboard luggage label, on which someone had carefully written in rather elaborate black capitals with a fountain pen, KEY TO FRONT DOOR. And only that morning David had used it to secure the house, on his return from the greengrocer's – placing it back again on the dresser, but in an old mug, not hanging from a hook, on display. But, thought David, the old key might just as well have been there for all the world to see – the boy probably wouldn't even have known what it was, having no doubt used a Yale lock all his life.

Still David stood paralysed, dry-throated, in an agonising seethe of indecision. But he knew he must act, and so, after some moments, he slowly walked, as quietly as he could, towards the open back door.

The boy was not in the kitchen; from the doorway that led into the front portion of the house, David had an uninterrupted view down the dark, stone-flagged passage to the front door. Usually, that is, uninterrupted; but, that afternoon, the front door was partially obscured by the boy, his back turned to David, and his cropped head circled by a halo, given by a greenish light which came through the two thick old squares of blown glass set into the upper panels of the solid eighteenth-century door. The boy was fumbling with the Yale lock – turning the catch, and wondering, no doubt, why the door wouldn't open. Sensing, maybe, that he was being watched, he turned. David saw that he was holding something – what it was, he couldn't quite make out.

"The door won' open."

"Oh, yes, it will."

"I carn' open it."

"That doesn't mean it won't open."

David had taken a few steps down the passageway while they had been having this exchange. The boy was, in effect, trapped; David felt his emotions changing. It was an old, and not altogether a comfortable, sensation; when David had identified the feeling, he stopped, still a good few yards from the boy. The surge he was experiencing, he now realised, was that of power.

The boy kicked, but rather feebly, at the base of the door.

"Stop that."

"Open the fuckin' door."

"What have you got there?"

But David could see that the boy was holding a large white china jug – decorative, but nothing special; except special to David, as the jug had been his grandmother's – one of the few family things to have come his way.

"Jug."

"Why?"

"It's old, innit? I can flog it."

"It's not valuable."

"But you ain't got nuffin' else."

"Put it down."

The boy was, in his own way, sensitive; somehow he knew that he had a card up his sleeve. He played with the jug, holding it rather too lightly, passing it from hand to hand.

"Open the fuckin' door."

David moved a step nearer.

"Give me the jug."

"Don't you fuckin' touch me. I'll tell. I'll tell how you touched me an' hit me an' touched my fuckin' dick an' all."

David froze where he stood, amazed. Should he unlock the front door, or should he tell the boy to go the same way as he had come, through the garden? But he didn't want the boy near him, pushing past him, maybe, in the narrow hallway...

"Wait."

David turned, to make his way back to the kitchen; as he did so, he heard a movement behind him. The boy could not have known that David was going to fetch the key that would have given him his freedom; did not even know that another kind of key was necessary. Needing to escape, the boy's only thought was to make for the open back door. Before David could turn again to face him, the boy was upon him, had brought the old china jug down on his head.

As David staggered, falling to one side, the boy missed his footing in the narrow dark space, stepping between the rungs of the long wooden ladder that still lay on the floor, propped against the skirting. Trying to run, he tripped, and fell; the back of his head met the stone flags of the passage. David, dazed, slumped across the hallway, slowly recovered; he knelt, and remained on his knees, his head splitting. Cautiously, he ran his fingers around the back of his skull, feeling for blood, but the skin was unbroken. The boy lay on his back behind him, the white jug still clenched in his right hand.

After some moments, as his head cleared, David eased the jug from the boy's fingers; the flesh was soft and moist – so the boy was living. David went to the kitchen, and placed the jug back carefully on the dresser. The sound that came, though, as it made contact with the wood, was not good, and David flicked at its rim with his finger; it gave back an empty, flat *clunk*, which told him that it was badly cracked; he was immensely saddened.

David returned to gaze down on the prostrate form beneath him. He knelt again, to look at the boy's face: the half-opened lips were pink, girlish, against the pallid, junk-fed skin. David pulled the boy's greying white T-shirt up to his ribcage, and then pushed it further, over the flat nipples; the pale torso was hairless. The boy wore no belt. David undid the stud at the waist of the boy's faded jeans, slid down the zip, and thrust his hand inside the boy's briefs, down into the warmth of the groin beneath. What he found there was flaccid and damp and minimal; the boy stirred.

David could never quite analyse the all-pervasive feeling that came over him when he knew that he had gone past the point of no return, and therefore had no choice but to go further still. He had been so afraid of the boy, right from the first; not afraid of what the boy might do to his home, his few possessions, not afraid even of the harm the boy might do to his person; but nevertheless, afraid. Old, and not so old, memories stirred; half-subjugated desires rose again to the surface.

The boy was no longer lying on the stone flags of the hallway when he awoke. David was sitting beside him, watching for the moment when the boy's eyelids would flicker, and finally rise over each iris of clear baby-blue. It would be good to see the look of pseudo-tough arrogance, which the boy had worn as a permanent mask, seep away, to be replaced by the flat, toneless pallor of fear. Later, of course, there would be other emotions, too. Eventually, the lids did rise, and the pale-blue eyes rolled, then tried to focus; frowned, and focused again... expressed non-comprehension... sought for an explanation... then widened, with some kind of realisation... sought David's eyes in... what – questioning, pleading? – then rolled again.

David was glad he had remembered where he had put the roll of adhesive tape – some kind of carpet or packing tape, silver-grey, strong and fabric-backed; it held well, wound around the boy's jaw, and over his mouth. Hardly a sound came through it – a muffled, grating, throat-bound gagging only, sounds of drowning, if anything, more than screaming. Fabric bindings would never have been so effective, somehow – the modern world did, after all, produce some useful innovations – and the tearing-out of tongues seemed, in this day and age, so medieval. In fact, only recently, David had himself inwardly shuddered on reading accounts of the excesses of Uday Hussein – one of the dead captured sons of Saddam of Baghdad – his razorings, for instance, of friend's tongues, so that tales could never be told. Well, no need for that with this boy. Or, at least, not yet.

It had only been necessary for David to drag the unconscious boy a few yards. His sturdy Victorian iron bed, which had been too difficult to move upstairs, was set up in the small back sitting room, whose French windows opened onto an internal courtyard, and not onto the public street. The boy lay now spread-eagled on the garden tarpaulin laid over the bare mattress – no need to give him the discomfort of being stretched directly over the old iron springs, as, after all, David intended soon to himself share the bed with his young captive, whose ankles and wrists were now firmly tied to the decorative, brass-trimmed frame. The boy was now naked, although he would have to feel this rather than see it, as from the position he was now in he could not, unfortunately, of course, gaze down upon himself.

To give him the idea, David reached over and gently riffled his fingers through the boy's sparse, gingery pubic hair. The boy's body jerked from the bed as if he had been electrocuted; more urgent, muffled barks came through the wide band of silver tape; colour seemed to drain from the sky-blue eyes and, from the bony anus of the boy, a soft, warm, khaki-coloured pellet was involuntarily ejected.

"Tut, tut, tut."

Now this was very naughty indeed, and at such an early stage: David went to the kitchen, and returned with his right hand inside a small transparent plastic freezer bag, on which he had drawn two large dots, using a black felt-tipped marker. He sat down again by the boy on the bed, and made with the bag an improvised glove puppet, with which he made amusing, grimacing, yawning faces, with the black dots as their mad blank eyes. As a finale, the puppet mouth swooped down and gobbled up from the tarpaulin the small turd, which it waved under the boy's nose before using it to plug both his nostrils. All but unable to breathe, the boy writhed and snorted until he had cleared for himself two snotty, shitty lifelines, at which the skittish puppet impishly pinched the boy's nose, which had him tossing his head from side to side, and snorting all over again. Still wearing its plastic sheath, David forced his index finger as far up the boy's faeces-lubricated rectum as it would go; the body again rose in a spasm from the bed, and the eyes became those of a helpless and cornered beast.

The deep subversive joy, the very power of it all – to see the boy so bound and trussed, so wide open and helpless... The little tough-man-bully gone, now just a thing of living flesh to be ravaged and pierced and entered at will, and bones to be... The problem always was, of course, with people strapped to beds, how to change the positions of their sweat-slippery limbs in order to mount fresh assaults on this or that tunnel or cleft or gland or cavity... Free a limb and it would jerk and flail; free two to turn a body over and one could be done for ... Accidents will, after all, in moments of passion, lust and tension, happen. David stepped back to survey the pinioned X of pale flesh spread beneath him.

When, in that prison in Chiang Mai, he had had plenty of time for reading, and especially after he had been placed in a sunken, stinking solitary cell since even the rough, feral-feline street-trade boys had repeatedly complained about him and his attentions, David had found amongst the pile of grubby, dog-eared, old donated paperbacks in the 'library' a copy of *Schindler's Ark*; a moving and memorable work. The picture which came to him now was from a description of soldiers of the Third Reich sacking a Jewish hospital, dragging elderly patients, in the freezing winter weather, down long flights of stone stairs, pulling them by the hair on their heads. The narrative tells of one particular woman patient, being treated in this way, whose leg had become trapped at an awkward angle, protruding through the iron uprights of the banisters. Instead of pausing to free the limb, the stormtrooper had simply carried on tugging, until the brittle femur had snapped, and the then loose and useless leg had eventually worked itself free. David looked at the elaborate head- and foot-pieces of his bed, at the ornate, but sturdy, convolutions of the cast-iron rods and bars which made up its frame. He nodded to himself, slowly.

He sat by the boy again, slipped off the freezer bag and gently caressed the boy's ginger-blonde fuzzed thighs. The boy's body contorted, the best it could, sideways, and then back, and then away again. The boy strained frantically, but uselessly, at his bindings: David had used electrical ties – those ingenious, strong plastic straps with a ratchet at one end, which, once mated with the corresponding loop at the other and pulled tight, can never be undone. And that's the thing: some things can never be undone. David glanced at his watch; it was getting late. Best get on with things.

David worked hard in the garden all of the following day, using the shredder for a little longer than usual, and with the fall of darkness came a great wave of fatigue which suddenly swept over him. Of course, the night before had hardly been restful. There was yet work to be done – the contents of the shed were still spread out, albeit tidily, on the ground around it. The compost bin, however, was full, and neatly piled. Merlin, as cats tend to do with things newly disturbed in the garden, was visiting the spot regularly, and daintily pawing about amongst the brittle twigs and desiccated leaves.

In the end, David had decided that he would keep things close to hand; there were, of course, many stretches nearby of pleasant common land but, in his experience, taking, let's say, a spade to ground not often, if ever, dug over was unrewarding work indeed. And then of course there was always the sea, but what the sea received, it could almost certainly be relied upon, and possibly at a most inappropriate moment, to give back. In any case, the juxtaposition of the domestic and the grotesque had, since childhood, held many fascinations for David. He vividly remembered being taken to the old Madame Tussaud's – before the place had been filled with waxen images of fashion models and ephemeral celebrities – and remembered also the discussion between his father and mother as to whether he should be allowed downstairs to the infamous Chamber of Horrors; in the end his mother had acquiesced, sending his father on ahead to vet, and, if necessary, to censor, the more excessive tableaux.

The image that had stayed with David, though, was of a simple, old-fashioned, domestic interior – a reconstruction of the kitchen at Number Ten, Rillington Place, for a considerable time the most notorious address in London and even now, many years since that thrilling-chilling name was deleted forever from the street map of the capital, a name that many might recognise. David well remembered the worn, homely green-and-cream-chequered linoleum, the simple tongue-and-groove panelling, the chipped white porcelain sink, the commonplace wooden chairs – but all, from their association, imbued with the sordid and the wretched and, hovering about them, a miasma, and the almost tangible stench of fly-blown decay.

David had, in fact, as a kind of overture, or appetiser, when the boy had still been with him, held up within his captive's line of vision a succession of everyday items, holding them one by one for a few seconds, quietly, and without expression on his own face – a blue plastic bottle of strong bleach, a small pot of Vaseline, the coiled orange cable from the shredder, a pair of pliers – without any real intention of using any of them. But the boy's face had blanched, and the eyes had screamed with pain before pain had been given, and in the end had rolled whites-upward in a dead faint, so that eventually, as it happened, the pliers had had to be applied, after all.

But that already seemed a long time ago.

A day or two later, David had finished rearranging the shed. The long wooden ladder had just fitted inside, when placed diagonally, making it an interesting challenge to fit all the other items in, accessibly, around it. From where he was standing in the garden, David could hear the two little girls from next-door-but-one calling again for Merlin, which was rather sad. A beautiful cat in his way, Merlin had unfortunately taken to spending far too much time burrowing down inside David'scompost bin, and scattering the contents untidily behind him.

David returned to the kitchen, and, very thoroughly, using a scouring pad, and rinsing in hot water several times, washed the saucer which had contained Merlin's last taste of milk; he placed it in the wooden rack to drain. He stooped, and, from under the sink, took a newly opened packet of the really rather pretty little forget-me-not-blue pellets to which mice, for instance, have such a fatal attraction, and carefully placed it inside a plastic carrier bag from the checkout at Safeway before going back up with it to the shed. David neatly knotted the handles of the carrier over the packet, and set it down in a little space behind the watering can. After all, it really wasn't the kind of thing he wanted to have hanging around in the house.

Sunrise at Salmon Pool
John Sam Jones

Sunrise at Salmon Pool
John Sam Jones

Gwion hadn't been prepared for the starkness that greeted him. Because he found it difficult to see the rooms the way they had been, the anticipated cascade of memories, which he'd feared might overwhelm him, failed even to leak into his consciousness with the drips from the tap in the kitchen. Each drop echoed through the hollow casing of a spent life, emphasising its emptiness. After his initial disconcertion he began to relax, realising that a house so devoid of everyday trappings was lacking any harbours of memory; the bare walls and scabrous floorboards offered little by way of sanctuary to the ghosts he'd feared might have assailed him.

Exactly what he was looking for in Alltfawr wasn't tangible. Perhaps it was certainty; to know that there was nothing there to arouse the newcomers' curiosity. He'd often wondered if Melfyn's brother and sister-in-law had found the videos and magazines that were stacked in alphabetical order on the shelves that he'd helped Mel put up in the small dressing room off the main bedroom, or whether their disposal had been a part of his intricate preparations.

Mel had always kept that door locked: *We don't want Peggy-Pwllgwyn sprutting when she comes in to clean, do we, Gwi? She'd have a field day telling everyone in Aber about our little fancies.* Gwion smiled as the words whispered in his memory and he laughed quietly to himself hearing Mel say "sprutting"; it was one of his pet words, applied to all manner of circumstances where people poked their noses in.

The splintered dressing room doorframe suggested that the key had never been found. Perhaps that had been the police's doing; they'd gone through the place, sprutting – looking for anything that might explain the why of it all. Mel had certainly planned it with painstaking care, even sending a copy of the note he'd left on the mantelshelf to his solicitor in Porthmadog. None of the letters and photographs linking the two of them had ever turned up and Gwion had been back in college more than a week when Mel drove up to the salmon pools. No one had ever thought to ask him what he knew about Melfyn's death.

He sat on the floor, his back against the fractured doorframe, and tried to visualise the bedroom. There was a stain on the wall above where the bed had once been. He remembered how Mel had laughed at him that first time he'd shot over the headboard. He wondered whether a DNA test of the stain might identify him, but then he remembered that he'd helped Mel strip the walls of those hideous pink roses and redecorate the bedroom; running his fingers over the deeply embossed Supaglypta, he recalled the traumas they'd had matching it up and he gave a melancholy smile. It must have been sometime just after they'd redecorated that he'd managed to persuade Mel – and he'd liked it straight away – but then, Mel was so gentle and he wasn't so big. They'd done it all the time after that, even though Mel complained that it was messy. He'd have been sixteen when it started. He remembered Mel as a reluctant playmate with an imagination disappointingly limited, with such limited experience. On and off, it had lasted for two years and they'd both understood why it had to be a secret. In Gwion's memory, anyway, it was he who always initiated things. He pictured Mel snoozing on the sofa in front of *Wales Today* and saw himself cuddling up for a *cwts* and then nuzzling his face into his lap; Gwion heard him say playfully, "Is that you again, Gwi, sprutting in my fly?" He wondered about the truth of his memory and then remembered Melfyn, sitting on a rock, fishing in Llyn Irddyn.

He cried for a long time.

After he'd stopped crying, Gwion lay on the rough floorboards in the bare bedroom, his head nestled in his cupped hands. With each breath of the room's fusty stillness he felt a veil of a capricious calm settle over him. There was nothing, after all, to fear from Alltfawr: the demons skulked elsewhere. His eyes traced a lazy trail along the intricate embossing of the wallpaper, each loop and swirl of the pattern pulling him back from the edge and leading him to a safer place. Then a breeze of notions billowed beneath the gauzy calm and the waters of the salmon pool gurgled around him, murmuring a call that he knew he couldn't ignore.

He wanted to go up there straight away but Mam had got the Astra and his dad wouldn't let him drive the new four-by-four. Annoyed that his father was treating him like a kid, Gwion swore under his breath and stormed out of the house. When he calmed down he thought about cycling up the valley and made light of the twenty-odd-mile round trip. He checked the old bikes in the far outhouse. One had a buckled wheel; another had a broken spring spiked through the seat. A third, all rusted, looked promising until he thought about the miles of rough track up from the main road. Brychan found him sulking in the orchard; he didn't need much persuading and they set off for the afternoon, to sprut in the rock pools and explore the sea caves in Llanilltud Bay.

Puffed up with importance because he believed he knew something his big brother didn't, Brychan led Gwion a mile or so along the shore to the site of the recent rock fall. The thirteenth-century twin-naved church of Saint Illtud, built (according to the tourist leaflets in the porch) on the ruins of a much earlier monastic site where Illtud was supposed to have come ashore from Brittany in the fifth century, was now left precariously close to the cliff's edge. Parts of the graveyard on the southwest side had already fallen away and the grassy mounds that traced the lines of the ancient cloister had been cut by the jagged contour of the cliff. Gwion remembered the television coverage; the story had even made the main evening news bulletin on the BBC and the newsreader had got tongue-tied with the Welsh names, but he didn't let on to his little brother.

"If there's another big landslide," Brychan said with excitement, "Saint Illtud's head might even get cut off and the church will be on an island; then everybody will have to go in a boat to take flowers to the graves."

"Now there's a nice job for Sam-Pen-Cei," Gwion teased.

"Do you think so, Gwi?" Brychan said, looking curiously at his brother.

"Sam's so old now, he'll probably be dead before there's another rock fall."

"We might *all* be dead before there's another one," Gwion said, remembering the television interview with one of Aber's most colourful characters. "Even old Sam couldn't remember any of these cliffs falling into the sea and he's lived in Aber for more than seventy years."

Realising that Gwion had known about the landslip all along, Brychan seemed to lose interest and thrust his hands deep into a rock pool.

"You can still go in, you know," Brychan said after a few moments. "It was closed for a few weeks but then they said it was safe."

"Perhaps we should go and have a look later," Gwion said. "Just in case it does fall into the sea before I come home again".

"But the cliff path just along here has gone too," Brychan said, pointing a finger dripping with sea bootlaces at the gouged cliff face before submerging his hands again to search through the maiden's hair and bladderwrack for starfish and sea urchins. "That would mean we'd have to walk all the way back into Aber and then go along the road."

"Or we could walk along the beach past Sarn Meirion and Ogof Hir," Gwion said, looking north to where Trwyn Idris nosed craggily into the sea to close in the bay. "The tide is out far enough."

"That's a long way around," Brychan said with no enthusiasm for the walk. "Why don't we just look for sea cucumbers?"

"But it would be such a nice walk, Brychan," Gwion said.

He shielded his eyes from the sun and took in the sweep of the bay.

"We might even get to see some grey seals with their pups off Y Trwyn," he coaxed, trying to bring his little brother around to the idea. "And then we could go up the smuggler's steps by Dant Idris and walk along the cliff path from that end."

"Well, maybe..." Brychan said, pulling a crab from the pool and thrusting it up towards Gwion's face. "Will you buy me a new bike with some of the money you got from Uncle Mel's house, and some new computer games?"

Gwion heard his brother's requests as demands: a set of conditions to be met before he'd cooperate. He saw the grasping claws of the small crab; it looked bigger and more menacing, held so close to his face in Brychan's slender fingers. He overreacted to the sense that his little brother was trying to intimidate and manipulate him, and with an almost reflexive backward swipe, Gwion's knuckles caught Brychan's outstretched arm hard on the wrist. The crab flew into the air and landed in a splatter on a slab of slate; Brychan's fleeting look of taut astonishment crumpled into sobs of frightened confusion.

"It's not fair that you should have everything," Brychan blurted between jerky intakes of breath. "Uncle Mel said that I was his special friend... It's not fair that I shouldn't get anything."

Alone, walking towards Sarn Meirion, Gwion wondered if the fraught little episode with Brychan was a taste of things to come. He'd tried to comfort his brother, to apologise and explain, but red-eyed and inconsolable, he'd run off, back towards Aber. Gwion had watched him go and stayed watching until the wailing strains of "It's not fair" had faded and the boy became a blotch on the cliff path rising over the last hill before dropping into the town on the other side; then he'd set off at a brisk pace in the opposite direction, his mind churning over the debris his life had accumulated from having known Melfyn.

There were no seal pups off Y Trwyn; the sunlight danced, a translucent greenish blue shot through with reddish flecks, on a gossamer oil slick that bled into the crevices and crannies of the jagged-rocked spit. Dant Idris, the towering stack that rose out of the sea just north of Y Trwyn – a rotting tooth, so the myth went, pulled from his mouth and cast into the sea by the giant Idris from high on his mountain throne – was a tumult of noisy, quarrelling guillemots and razorbills, its vertical slabs smeared dirty-white with guano. The cliff path, its verges heavy with primroses and viper's bugloss, brought Gwion quickly to the wall on the northern boundary of Llan Illtud, its dry stones orange with xanthoria and a kissing gate rusted and squeaky from the salt spray.

The old graveyard was blotched red with campion and bloody crane's-bill among the tall grasses. Here, the memorials, on crude slate slabs encrusted greenish-grey, were barely legible: Jonnet – an old-fashioned Christian name bereft of family ties, chiselled deeply into the rough stone – drew his eye, and dates – 1685–1703 – that proclaimed, once upon a time, such sorrowful meaning. Many of the headstones had toppled and lay on cushions of golden kidney vetch; Gwion felt uneasy stepping from one to another, believing perhaps that he was being disrespectful. Coming around the west end of the church, the nineteenth-century cemetery opened out on the south side with its marble angels, ship's anchors and Celtic crosses raised on plinths and pillars, competing in grief for sympathy and attention. In a section that was overgrown, the archangel Gabriel poked his head through the brambles. Even in the tended segments, divided by slate-paved paths, most of these grandiose commemorations were swathed in ivy and few had been adorned with a bunch of flowers at Christmas or Easter since longer than Gwion could remember. Looking west, where the cliff had slipped into the sea, he could see the line of a new fence beyond which the monumental masons' follies were pitched at eccentric angles. He wondered how long it would be until the movements of the earth would send them crashing to the rocky beach a hundred feet below.

The thick oak door of St Illtud's church, its surface so deeply split and rutted – yet worn as smooth as a love spoon – was protected from the squalls off the sea by a deep porch of honey-coloured sandstone. Though facing south it offered shade from the afternoon sun. Gwion sat on the bench beneath the empty notice board and became fascinated by the patterns winnowed by centuries of weather in the ornamentation of the portal's graceful arch. The surface of the stone looked granular and something compelled him to trace what might once have been a band of Celtic knotwork. At the lightest touch of his fingertips, the natural oils and sweat on his skin drew grains of sand from the stone until the pads of his fingertips looked like the strike board of a matchbox. The ostensible fragility of the stones that had enclosed that sacred ground for hundreds of years startled him, yet the urge to withdraw his hand was overcome by a more mischievous thought. He pressed his thumb into the loop of a knot and, as if pushing home a drawing pin, he twisted against the crumbling stone, wondering how much malicious rubbing it would take to diminish St Illtud's to a heap of sand. Suddenly appalled by his act of vandalism, Gwion wiped the gritty sand from his fingers and took a visitor's leaflet from a wooden box that hung next to the notice board. A torn sign suggested a donation of twenty-five pence for the single folded sheet of information; to absolve himself, Gwion slipped a two-pound coin through the narrow slot of the unpolished brass wall box.

As he pushed open the door, the iron hinges sighed into the chilly stillness. Shafts of sunlight from the clerestory windows reflected on the whitewashed walls and filled the sanctuary with a dust-speckled brilliance that ran counter to Gwion's memory of a sullen gloom. Where the light fell directly onto the nave pillars, the roughly hewn sandstone glowed yellow and orange, radiating a warmth that contradicted the goose pimples that had risen on his arms; he sat on a sun-soaked pew and scanned the leaflet. Following the graceful spans of the Early English arches in the nave, he wondered what capitals were. From where he sat he was too far from the altar to see the Celtic cross carved into the sill stone of the single eastern lancet window but he was close enough to marvel at the carving of wheat and vine motifs in the broad arch between the nave and the chancel. It was as he visually traced the centuries-old vine, its grapes overplump, that the sound of the sea encroached upon him, as if someone had put conch shells up to his ears.

There was rush matting on the slate-slab floor and wilted flowers in a tarnished brass vase. Broken-spined prayer books lay randomly abandoned on the rude pews that generations of shifting bottoms, numbed by the hardness, had worn shiny and smooth. Gwion sat in the '... *tense, musty, unignorable silence, brewed God knows how long...*' and Larkin's poem wove through the flotsam and jetsam that had accumulated as he'd walked along the seashore. That he remembered all the lines of "Church Going" surprised him; it was one of the first ones he'd learnt after Bethan had challenged him to a poem a week: "... Learning by heart can give you such a resource to draw on – and it might improve your English too!" He heard her speak as if she were sitting there beside him: "Poems are extraordinary, really... they have a way of creeping up on you when you least expect them to. When you're in the right place and in the right frame of mind, a poem, the right poem, can touch you in a special way and bring you insights and understandings that you might never have thought possible."

The place and frame of mind must have been right – the poem too. Gwion had never allowed himself to think too much about the *"hunger in himself to be more serious"*; that's how Larkin had described it. For so long he'd teetered on the edges of that emptiness and been terrified by their hunger, those demons of despair and dispossession that he imagined – that he knew to be lurking in those depths. And he'd always retreated. Maybe now it was time to face them, before they destroyed his life as they'd destroyed Melfyn's.

Gwion didn't sleep much. Different voices seethed through the darkness in whispers and screams. They'd come back again: the man and woman from the Child Protection Unit. About a week after they'd come into college to run the sexual-abuse workshop for the module in Child Development they'd started to sneak into his dreams. They'd upset most of the class with theories on grooming children over many years and the eventual betrayal of their trust. He'd been more shocked than upset because his understanding had been so informed by recognition. For months now they'd kept coming; they competed with Melfyn for a hearing. None told truths that Gwion recognised. His own inner narratives, constructed to make an untroubled and comfortable reasonableness from it all, made little sense against their squalid testimonies and Mel's pathetic refutations. Once the cockerel at Hendre Illtud farm started to pierce the red-streaked dawn with its defiant, honest crowing, he decided to dress and drive up to the salmon pools.

Through a golden shimmer of dancing morning sunlight the salmon parr rose for a hatch of March Browns, splashing dimples across the water's face. Melfyn reached out to him through the gilded ripples. His beckoning startled Gwion, who pulled back from the edge, slippery with dew.

"Please don't let them do this to me," Melfyn whispered in anguished strains, his hands reaching out for Gwion's. "Don't let them make up such a malicious story about us, Gwi."

The man from Child Protection stood next to Gwion, his arms open wide, beckoning.

"You don't have to do what he wants any more," he said over Melfyn's pleading.

"But I liked it," Gwion protested, clinging to a less grievous account. "I liked doing it a lot... I wanted to do it."

"We were best friends, weren't we, Gwi?" Melfyn offered. "Best friends, that's all we were... isn't that right?"

The woman from Child Protection put her arms around Gwion and whispered her malice, reminding him of Melfyn's interest in the boy once Gwion had gone away to college; reminding him how Melfyn had taken Brychan on long walks across the Llawllech and how they'd fished in the pools... spending time together, Uncle Mel grooming his next special friend. And Gwion collapsed into her embrace, overwhelmed by the antagonistic forces of memory, perplexed by the dissonant veracity of what he'd chosen to believe. Then the apparitions disappeared and, losing his footing on the slick, muddy bank, he went over that edge and sank deeper. The pool, its waters cold and bubbling, drank him into his fears.

Plunging through the salmon pool's refracted sunlight, Gwion forced his eyes open and was dazzled by the coruscant detritus: a teeming galaxy of shooting stars danced in bursting collisions across each retina. He willed himself to see what lurked in those depths, straining for a glimpse of the beasts and demons that would assail him, but only the coldness strafed his body. It pricked at his skin, spiked the muscles in his thighs, and stabbed at the nape of his neck; piercing the soft tissues of his brain, it dulled his consciousness and numbed all fear. In the eternity that was no more than a few seconds, and with the same innate yearning for life that had guided his expulsion from the confines of the amnion and chorion, he kicked unconsciously against the turbid water. Scattering the hatch of March Browns, skittish on the ripples of his own foundering, his head tore through the membranes that enveloped the pool's universe and he dragged himself onto the low bank.

Cradled in a womblike groove on the ice-scarred shelf of rock from

where he and Melfyn had often fished, he caught his breath and
became calmer. The sun warmed his face and arms, but under the
sodden material of his jeans and T-shirt the cold made him shiver. He
stripped, and laying his wet clothes on the deeply rutted rock face, he
heard Uncle Melfyn telling the little boy – now bored and
uninterested from the long waiting for the fish to bite – that Idris,
who would sometimes come down from his throne on the other side
of the valley, must have lost his footing at that very spot, his giant
hobnailed boots scraping at the smooth stone. He smiled at the
memory and lay, naked in the sun.

A stray sentence, carried to him as if on the morning air with the
scents of gorse and bracken, detached from its source and devoid of
any context, cut benignly through the child's memory: "... *the words
which carry most knives are the blind phrases searching to be kind.*" One
of Bethan's damn poems again, he thought, enjoying the sun on his
nakedness. But, as the warmth thawed his numbness, the kind words
slashed at his consciousness and hacked through the calm.

The voices resumed their butchery of his history.

The woman from Child Protection, her lips deaf to the words she
was mouthing, said, "Even if you liked all the things he did to you,
Gwion, and even if you sometimes sought him out to do it again and
again, you were still his victim."

Her colleague, silent and smiling the empty empathy of imposed
care-giving, said, "Even if it did all start when you were sixteen, like
you say, the fact that he was a close family friend, someone you called
'uncle' and had known and trusted all your life, made him an abuser."

The child's voice, from somewhere deep inside him, screamed for
all the times before the time he'd chosen to remember as the first.

Then his mother's words, unsuspecting – pleased even, telling him
on the phone that Brychan had gone hiking, or fishing, or just for a
ride in the car with Uncle Mel.

And then Melfyn's own voice, cracked by the fear of being exposed
and drowned in tears, saying, "Perhaps I should hang myself from the
rafters in the bottom shed or walk out over the dunes and shoot into
my brains through the roof of my mouth so that all this will stop."

And he heard his own last words to Melfyn: "Are you asking me if you should, or are you telling me that you will?"

Voices of a different timbre sent vibrations through the ossicles of his inner ear; barely audible at first, they became progressively louder. Sitting up, he saw two fishermen, their cloth-capped heads and rods above the gorse bushes through which the footpath up from cytiau Gwyddelod climbed. Fearing they would misinterpret his nakedness, he dressed quickly. The gauzy cotton of his T-shirt, dried by the sun, slipped over his head and tickled the fine hairs as it draped over his chest and belly; the heavy denim of his jeans, still damp, clung to his thighs as he tugged them up.

Moving too quickly down the steep, winding gorge, pitching and lurching on the uneven track, the ageing Astra's suspension creaked with reedy harshness, competing for Gwion's attention with the voices that sought to recast his life as the victim of sordid distortions. To distract himself he turned up the volume of the radio voices, crackling with interference from the carelessly gouged landscape's topography.

Dreams
Francis King

Dreams
Francis King

It is the break and ache of day. Yesterday I awoke to those words. They were a fragment of some monument that all through the night I had been struggling to build. The words were no longer only in my mind but now also on my lips. I whispered them. *It is the break and ache of day.* But of the complex construct of which all through my sleeping hours they had been merely a tiny part, I now rememberednothing.

It is in words, not images,that I now almost invariably dream. All my life I have been, above all, a wordsmith. When so many other, less important, of my attributes have vanished or are vanishing, that still remains. In consequence, I am becoming more and more like that old man, a famous jeweller, who was my neighbour in Japan some forty years ago. He could not remember his wife's or children's names or, often, even his own. He could not remember how to knot a tie or fasten his shoelaces or pour a glass of iced tea or find his way to the primitive privy in a wooden shed at the bottom of his narrow, overgrown garden. But each day he sat at his workbench in a contented abstraction not merely from the world but also from eighty-three years' accumulation of memories, now inaccessible to him, while he still fashioned, with all his old consummate artistry, some brooch, bracelet or necklace. Fascinated and admiring, I used to watch him. Occasionally, he would look up and across at me and give me a vague, happy smile.

But this morning it was different. I had dreamed not in words but in images. One of those images remained with me, so vivid that I still saw it in every minute detail even as I felt the battering of the alarm clock and opened my eyes. The image is of a wavelike curve of balcony, constructed of wooden slats, many of which have rotted. It overlooks a clifflike incline, so that the tops of trees all but brush one's feet as one looks over it. Its railings are a greenish blue, the paint cracked and peeling. Behind it is the low annexe to the farmhouse, with its identical rooms each with its French windows. The paying guests in the annexe usually keep their curtains drawn even in daytime, since otherwise anyone on the balcony can glance in on them.

With an effort, I banish the image, so seductive and yet potentially so dangerous. Then I fall, rather than clamber, out of bed and, hand to banister to steady myself, creak down to the kitchen to make my wife's morning tea. Some months ago she moved to the bedroom on the floor below mine to avoid being kept awake by my muttering in my sleep of those innumerable words that all through the night jostle for attention in afatigued, failing brain craving only for the respite of silence. 'How did you sleep?' She stares up at me, as though a stranger were asking some obtrusive question. 'Oh, you know how it is.' Yes, I know how it is, having so often heard how it is. The restless legs. The nag of pain in the back. The mosquito whine of tinnitus in her left ear.

Instead of at once shaving and taking my bath, I return to my bedroom and lie out on the bed. I do not bother to pull the bedclothes over me. I am unaware of the cold. I close my eyes. I entreat the banished memory of my balcony dream to come back to me...

On that balcony a boy of thirteen is sitting on a folding canvas chair. It is afternoon. He can hear, in the distance, his mother tinkling at the upright Pleyel piano in the Ardennes farmhouse. She often complains, even to the Belgian farmer and his wife, that the piano is out of tune. They look bewildered, as though they did not understand her, even though she has spoken in perfectly correct French, albeit with it a heavy English accent. Then one or other of them shrugs, smiles and says something like 'Eh bien, madame...' They will do nothing about the piano, just as they will do nothing about the dripping tap of her washbasin or the curtain that, missing a ring, lets in a narrow wedge of light to prod her awake far too early every summer morning of that holiday. The boy's older brother is out, gun at the ready, with the bearded, taciturn farmer. They will usually return each with at least a brace of rabbits. The boy hates the rabbit casserole that everyone else finds so delicious. He eats a mouthful or two, then pushes it to one side – 'I'm not really hungry,' he tells his mother in a fretful voice when she enquires why he isn't eating.

Now, on the balcony, he is halfway through the *Collected Works* of Tennyson, in a leather-bound copy that belonged to his recently dead father. If his father were still alive, they would be staying in some elegant hotel and not in this farmhouse, recommended to them as 'amazing value' by one of his mother's bridge-playing friends. Already he recognises in Tennyson someone who is obsessed with words – their appearance on the page, their subtle gradations of meaning, above all their initial sounds and then the other sounds that resonate on and on from them – even as he himself is already obsessed with words. His brother, seventeen years old and about to become a Sandhurst cadet and eventually to be killed on a Normandy beach, laughs at this passion for Tennyson. He puts on a voice, melodramatic and comically cockney, as he intones: '*Come into the garden, Maud.*' There is something ludicrous about the name Maud, even the boy can see that.

The afternoon sun is in his eyes. He hears a far-off shot. He winces as he imagines the rabbit leaping into the air and then crashing down on the hard surface of a field baked dry by day after day of furnace heat. A voice speaks behind him. It is deep and resonant, the accent German. The boy has not heard any approach, since the man is wearing plimsolls. 'What are you reading?'

The boy swivels his head. He has already seen this squat, muscular man, with the flat, oddly expressionless face and large sunburned hands, the nails savagely bitten, at breakfast that morning. Having entered the long, narrow room, the man then bowed and intoned with an almost comic gravity: '*Bon jour, messieurs, bon jour, mesdames.*' Much later, his wife, thin and anxious-looking in a pale-blue cotton dress, her face heavily powdered, slipped through the door. She gave no spoken greeting to the assembled company, merely a bow smaller and far more hesitant than her husband's. He extended a hand to her. She took it with a look of beseeching gratitude. Suddenly the anxious-looking face was irradiated by joy. Later the boy's mother learned from the farmer's wife that the couple were on their honeymoon. They came from

Düsseldorf, the farmer's wife said, and both of them were teachers.

The man stoops over the boy. He looks down at the book. 'Poetry?' The man must have realised that from the way that the lines are laid out on the page. The boy nods. 'Who is the poet?' There is an odd formality in the way in which the words emerge from under the man's closely clipped moustache.

'Tennyson,' the boy replies. There is a quaver in his voice He might be attempting an answer to a difficult question back at school. He feels a mounting excitement, as though a swarm of bees were buzzing inside him. 'D'you know his work?'

The man shakes his head. ' Sorry. Heine. You know Heine?'

'Not really. No.'

'He is good. Very good. Genius. You must read.'

'I don't know any German.'

'In English. I am sure there is translation.'

The man is bending even lower over the chair. Suddenly the boy is aware of the hand in the man's trouser pocket. He cannot help noticing it, it is so near to his elbow. As though he has realised that the boy has noticed that hand and what the hand is attempting to restrain, the man walks stiffly over to a distant chair and then returns with it. He places it beside the boy's and sits down, crossing one leg high over the other. They begin to talk.

The man asks about the boy and his family. The boy speaks about his father, brilliant, reserved and never ill before his sudden, premature death from a heart-attack, and about his mother, who is half American and who was briefly on the stage. The man talks about his life as a schoolmaster and his passion for sports. He teaches gymnastics, he explains. He hoped to be chosen for the German gymnastic team for the Olympic games but – he shrugs, his shoulders droop – at the last moment...

'I'm no good at sports. Hopeless. My brother's in the rugby fifteen at our school. And he's a terrific shot.'

The man laughs. 'Yes, yes! Rabbit every dinner!'

Later the man tells the boy that he is on his honeymoon. The boy does not say that he knows this already. The man explains that his wife is sleeping – he jerks his head upwards and sideways – in the room over there. She does not sleep well at night, he says. She needs – how do you say? – her *siesta*. She is a fellow teacher, the daughter of the headmaster of the school. She teaches art. A good artist, mainly watercolour.

Then the man leans forward, hands clasped between his knees, to ask, 'What is your name?'

'Evelyn.'

'Strange name! I never hear that name.'

'There was an English diarist. A long time ago. Evelyn. John Evelyn. My father was writing a book about him when I was born.'

'I am Götz.'

'Götz.' The boy likes the name. It has a monolithic solidity and strength that suit this stranger.

'You look German.'

'Me? German?' The boy is taken aback.

'Blue eyes. Blue, blue eyes. Like the sea. Like the Atlantic Ocean. And hair so blond. *Blond*.' Tentatively he extends a hand. Touches the hair briefly. Touches it again. Ruffles it.

A voice, high and querulous, calls, 'Götz!' It calls again. Something in German follows.

'*Meine Frau*. My wife. You will excuse.' He smiles. He puts a hand briefly on the boy's shoulder. Then he again ruffles the boy's hair, this time forcefully, almost aggressively. The boy's scalp tingles under the alien fingers, as though an electric shock were passing through it. 'Evelyn. Strange name. Good name. I like.' He smiles. Then he strides off to the far end of the balcony and enters the French windows into the room where his wife awaits him.

From then on their meetings are frequent but all too brief. The boy now spends most of his time reading on the balcony. He waits in patience. From time to time Götz appears, usually through the French windows. The chair remains beside the boy's and Götz first stands briefly by it, leaning forward with a supporting hand on its back, and then sits on it. They have so much to say to each other, but all too often the high, querulous voice interrupts them. It seems to the boy that that cry of 'Götz, Götz!', usually followed by something in

German, becomes increasingly plaintive, even desperate. Götz shrugs on one such occasion, then gives an embarrassed laugh as he puts a hand over the boy's and then hurriedly withdraws it: 'Women, women! Difficult!' He laughs as he gets to his feet. Again the woman calls: 'Götz! *Was machst du?*'

One evening after dinner, as the boy's mother fumbles over a Chopin Nocturne on the out-of-tune piano and his brother, perched on the arm of a sagging sofa, flirts with the bosomy, red-cheeked daughter of the house seated on it, the boy gets up, his forefinger keeping his place in the book, and leaves the low-ceilingedroom with its smells of omnipresent dust and of dead flowers left for far too long in a vase on a mantelpiece crowded with small objects and photographs in tarnished silver frames. There is a cramped hall outside the room. Beyond are three doors, one to the rooms in the main building, one out on to the balcony of the annexe and one to a lavatory. Götz is waiting in this small hall. The boy's first thought is that he is waiting there for him. Then he realises that, no, he must be waiting for his wife, who is in the lavatory. Götz smiles. He holds out his arms in invitation. The boy hesitates. Suddenly Götz lunges over and grabs him. In frenzied succession he presses his mouth to the side of the boy's neck, to his forehead, to his lips. The boy attempts to jerk away, then yields, at first reluctantly, then with an access of emotion that overpowers him like some huge breaker suddenly soaring skywards and then crashing downwards in a previously tranquil sea. There is a clank followed by the sound of flushing. The man retreats, pushing the boy away from him. The book falls from the boy's hand. He stoops. The German woman emerges. She stares at the boy, then at her husband. The boy notices that, though her face is, as always, coated with powder, there are raw, red patches on her bare arms and on one side of her throat.

Götz puts out a hand to the latch of the door that leads out to the balcony. He nods at the boy, then bows slightly as his wife, head lowered, passes out before him. He follows her without a backward glance.

The following day the German couple will leave. It is a long drive back to Düsseldorf. As Götz checks the car, a Mercedes but an old one, probably bought second hand, the boy's brother joins him. He is not interested in the Germans but he is interested in the car. He even helps to pump up a tyre. He then asks if he can have a quick spin. The German asks if he has a licence. He shakes his head. The German smiles and says, 'Sorry.' The boy wishes his brother would leave Götz alone. The farmer and his wife are angry with the brother because, unknown to them, he took their daughter to a bar in Han-sur-Lesse and brought her back in the early hours. The brother has described the girl as 'hot stuff' to the boy.

That night, almost at midnight, the boy creeps out of bed and, leaving his snoring brother sprawled across a sheet damp with sweat, tiptoes out onto the balcony. The night is stifling. In any case, he is in such a torment of emotion that he cannot sleep. He leans over the railing of the balcony and breathes in the air. But it does not cool him, even its breath is scorching. From far off a strange creaking sound reaches him. A bird? An animal? There is something sinister, even frightening, about the sound. It is like the creaking of a rocking chair hugely amplified. Behind him he hears another sound. He twists his body round. In the moonlight, wearing only his pyjamas, Götz puts a forefinger to his lips. Then he steps forward and takes the boy's hand in his. 'Come.'

At the farthest end of the balcony, there is a narrow, spiral staircase. The boy has never noticed it before, much less gone down it. Götz descends, crablike, from time to time looking back over his shoulder. The boy follows, in unquestioning submission and wonder. Götz must have explored this region in preparation for what is now about to happen. There is a malodorous rubbish tip, surmounted by a broken sofa vomiting horsehair. There is a wheelbarrow without a wheel. There is a stack of old newspapers, blotched with damp and tied with hairy twine. In the extraordinarily bright light from the moon the boy can at once make out all these things. There is a door, with a glinting handle. Götz puts a sunburned hand with bitten nails to the handle and opens the door. He turns his head and smiles. There is an iron bedstead with a stained mattress on it.

Later Götz says, stooping to tie the cord of the boy's pyjama trousers with frowning attentiveness, as though for a child, 'It is only when I think of you that I can do it with her. Only then. And then it is still difficult.'

At the time these words seem to the boy a betrayal even more cruel than what has just happened on the bed.

Afterwards I asked for his address. At first he seemed reluctant to give it to me. 'I have no paper. You have paper?' I shook my head. 'Can you remember it?'

'I think so.'

He told me the address, then repeated it. 'Say it,' he said. I said it. 'Perfect!' He laughed. 'Oh, Evelyn, I miss you, miss you!' The present tense made the utterance even more poignant. Our separation had already started.

'I'll write to you. Will you write to me?'

'Maybe.' Then he laughed: 'I make fun! Of course, if you write, I write! Yes, yes!'

'I'll tell you my address. Can you remember it?'

'No, no, you write letter first! My memory is bad!'

I stared at him. Then I took a step forward and grabbed his forearm, as though I were drowning and he were my rescuer. He stooped and for a last time put his lips to mine. 'It is only when I think of you – of you, only you – that I can do these things with her.' At that almost word-for-word repetition of what he had said only a short while before, I felt both triumph and a pang of desolation, but now none of that former guilt.

Because the journey was so long, they left early, at five in the morning. I woke and heard their voices, little more than whispers, as they dragged their luggage – so many and such large pieces! – down to the car. I swung my legs out of the bed and thought that I would go down to help them. Then I lay back on the bed again. If he had been alone, of course I would have gone down. But I did not want to see her or even think of her. When I thought of her, that poor creature with the thin arms and over-powdered face, I at once tried to think of him instead.

Eleven days later, the Germans invaded Poland. I wrote him letter after letter but none ever received an answer. His memory became like one of the snapshots taken by my mother during that Belgian holiday: shrivelling, yellowing, fading.

Two years after the War ended, I attended a summer school at the university in Göttingen. There was a student from Girton in our party, beautiful, witty, sexually provocative, fluent in German. I thought that I was in love with her. 'I want to go to Düsseldorf to see if someone I knew before the War is still alive.'

'A German?'

'Yes. A German.'

'Well, why not?'

In normal circumstances such travel would have been impossible. But no circumstances were normal for her and nothing was impossible. With the help of a titled cousin of hers, a colonel in the Control Commission, she fixed our weekend leave of absence from the summer school and the long, frequently interrupted journey across mile on mile of scorched, desolate landscape. She had insisted on coming with me – 'It'll be fun.'

Largely through her pertinacity and charm we eventually found first the street and then the house – with, next to it, a ruined building that had once been a school. It was in that ruined building that Götz and his wife must have taught. The house, their house, was also ruined. In London, where my mother and I had continued to live all through the Blitz, I had often viewed similar houses – their surfaces blackened, their contours broken and jagged, shreds of wallpaper cascading from their walls – with a mixture of dread and awe. I felt that dread and awe, in a far more intense form, now. Perhaps he had died there. I voiced that thought to my companion. 'Or somewhere,' she said, indifferent.

It was she who asked at the lodge at the gates of the ruined school. A shawled old woman, her mouth fallen in around the few front teeth that remained to her and her fingers grimy and greasy, answered our ringing of the bell. She squinted at us from under a ragged grey fringe, in what seemed to be both bewilderment and hostility. She did not know what had happened to the inhabitants of the house, she said. That was before her time. People had died, people had moved. She told us all this as though it had no interest for her.

I have just woken from another night of jumbled words, endlessly recurring, that I struggle now first to rescue from oblivion and then to arrange into some kind of sense. *The ladder upside down.* That odd phrase keeps repeating itself, like a bell tolling maddeningly on and on. I sip my coffee. I put a hand over my closed eyes and then press my fingers onto them until sparks shower downwards behind their lids. Yes, I begin to see what that strange phrase must mean. I reached the pinnacle of the ladder in that Belgian farmhouse before I had even started to climb it. The rest of my life became a descent, precarious rung by rung, until – now an old man no longer desired or even desirable – here I sit sipping coffee from a chipped cup in a kitchen that feels cold even though I have yet again turned up the central heating. *In my end is my beginning.* That phrase also now returns, a piece of flotsam on the reluctantly returning tide of memory. Then, as I did in my dream, I amend the sentence: *In my beginning was my end.* The most important thing that ever happened in my life ended when it had hardly begun.

'Evelyn!' It is my wife calling to me to remove her tray and help her to the bath. 'Evelyn!' The tone of her voice, plaintive, even desperate, is uncannily like that of Götz's wife summoning him back to their bedroom more than sixty years ago. It is only by thinking of Götz – now either long since dead or a man even more ancient than myself – that I can continue to perform for her the tasks that I have to perform.

'Coming! I'm coming!'

Our Last Night Together
Reuben Lane

Our Last Night Together
Reuben Lane

The protesters gather in Parliament Square.

The white-shirted boys with adult tall bodies (or will they grow taller still – and this will be the land of giants?); the CND symbol reborn and painted onto their cheeks. Top buttons undone, school ties stuffed in their pockets. They cover the statue of General Haig with STOP THE WAR stickers – paper plasters to pull together the wounds in his bronze body. Or the boys and girls who drag paper and discarded banners together and make a bonfire on the grass. Embers rising up edged with fire.

Nightfall. Big Ben chimes seven. Drums and trumpets; dancing in the crowd – pushing towards the line of police in their yellow fluorescent jerkins; beyond them riot police mounted on horseback.

The man who has been holding his one-man protest against the sanctions on Iraq opposite the gates of the Palace of Westminster for the past two years lies fast asleep on a campbed – surrounded by the crush of protesters and the belly roar of loud hailers. His eyelids gummed together – tumbling back inside.

Federico Garcia Lorca carries an armful of flowers – soft, waxy, poisonous, creamy lilies – that he's cut from the riverbank with a razorblade. He walks amongst the crowd finding the young – *los jovenes* – and to each he offers a flower. The girls are less shy – they take the lily or they refuse it, but if they take it they attach it to themselves, putting it in their hair or through a buttonhole, practical with safety pins and hair grips. But the boys are less sure. Two go bright red – the CND circle black against their fire-moon skin. One fingers the stalk, turns it in his hands – he looks at the poet; asks him what it means.

'It's a flower for all those who will lose their lives when the bombs rain down, when the war planes loosen their cargo over Baghdad.'

The boy, who is indeed taller than the walnut-skinned, raven-haired man – he hesitates. And then he holds the stalk firmly in the grip of his palm. He thanks the poet. He carries the lily with him all the rest of the evening in the mash of people – and when he goes home sitting on the top deck of the number 38, his throat hoarse from chanting, the lily lies across his black-trousered thighs.

A glass elevator that has the whole of Parliament Square plunge to other floors in time. I think I might have wasted my life between this night and the night, 15 January 1991, when we came to mourn the inevitable opening of a father's war. The twelve years in between. The police dragging the sit-down protesters out of the road that night.

Now they are schoolchildren who organise themselves with emails and mobile phones – who come with articulate minds to the arguments. And the police pull them off the road. And time ellipses.

Lorca walks over Westminster Bridge and dies before any of this begins at the hands of his executioners.

There was a black notch chipped into the cream paintwork on the horizontal bar of my cot. In the small bedroom with an orange lampshade. A window over the drive led to the dark-green-painted gates. On either side of the gates were beds of roses, foxgloves, snowbells, daffodils, weeds – depending on the time of year; all except the weeds that were there any time of the year. Before I knew what the seasons were; before I understood that the snow would melt; that the late afternoon sun that shone in through the windows a scarlet orange and did freaky lovely sad things inside my head – that each would go and be replaced by something else. Getting the hang of days and nights; that the days were better because during the nights I had to lie inside the barred walls of the cot and not cry – and listen: creaking floorboards, wood pigeons cooing and fluttering in the fir tree in the drive, the clatter and tinkle of crockery, of grown-up noise muffled, of laughter; laughter far away and then near – people that didn't hear me if I shouted out – so I gave up shouting and watched the black notch in the paint staring down at me, breathing over me – an eye that at its will could suck me inside and never let me out again.

So that in the morning when Mum came to unhitch the side of the cot she'd find just rumpled blankets and they'd never find me; they'd never hear me screaming from inside the chipped circle in the paintwork – forever trapped inside the bars of the cot.

A bump of coke on a glass dining table before he pulled down my trousers and sucked on me – high up in this block of flats at Baltic Quay – and I said – but can't people see in from over there ? And on TV, these French porn films worn thin and misty. Launderette, the back of an ambulance, a mechanics' garage. His body is completely hairless. But the hair on his head has gone a lot greyer than the last time – the first time I met him – just three months before – 'I just want to suck that cock.' This new apartment that must have cost a fortune in rent. I ask him if he's got a job yet – he's a solicitor and he was out of work a few months back three months ago. Now he must be desperate – living on credit, wired on coke. He says to me, 'You must think I'm like this all the time. But it's just tonight – someone offered me some in Soho – and that other time – I'm not a cokehead.'

Then – by now – we're completely stripped off. I want to kiss him – but he breaks away. 'Hold on; not so fast.' I want him to invite me through to the bedroom. He says as he slurps on my cock, 'Murray –' that's his boyfriend or ex-boyfriend, depends '– would love *this*.'

Then he says, 'Why don't I fuck you ?' Which is a surprise because the time before he'd said how he always wants to be the one who gets fucked. And then I'm on all fours – French flick chattering – and he's got a condom on, and he's getting into me. He says, 'Here, you're too tight; relax.' And hands me the yellow bottle of poppers from the sofa.

The amyl nitrate scatters like cordite from a gone-off gun inside my head.

And now he's fucking me. I want to watch him. But then he pulls out. And says 'I don't want to do any more.'

And I see there's shit on the condom. I go and wash my arse. And then I kneel next to him on the sofa.

And he says, 'I really love Murray.' I ask if I can have a cigarette. He's not talking to me. He wants me the fuck out of there as fast as possible.

I get dressed. I smoke.

He says at the doorway, 'I'll see how it works out with Murray – and then perhaps I'll give you a ring in a couple of weeks.'

And down and round and down and round the stairs. Out – to my bike locked up high on the railings. Four o'clock a.m. Time does my head in. I cycle to a place we'll call home.

There was a precise moment when I was sixteen that I fell in love with Jake Taylor. We were at school in the same year.

It wasn't a good school I went to – or a bad one. A private school for middle-class boys and girls in southeast London. A mix of the progressive and the traditional – strong on music and drama – but also with an army cadet force. Most of my time there I managed to remain invisible. I was always in the bottom forms – where nearly all the girls were filtered out – and there were lots of boys with car dealer or newsagent dads who hated sissies like me. I kept quiet and lay low. In the fourth and fifth years our form teacher was Mr Bruce, who ruled over his class of twenty-five rowdy boys with his army discipline, barking orders which kept even the Michael Stephenses and Matt Calverts in line. Mr Bruce was also our history teacher and he was a fantastic spinner of stories, bringing the Crimean War, the rivalry between Gladstone and Disraeli, and even the background to the Corn Laws and the Education Acts to vivid life. Also he was genuinely fond of his class of underachievers who were constantly getting bollocked by our other teachers. He had a gleam in his eye; a covert message to us: play their game – but rebel if and whenever you can get away with it.

I didn't join the CCF. There was an alternative to dressing up in army uniform and pounding the playground doing marching drill. You could do voluntary service, which meant visiting old folk, doing their gardens and making them cups of tea. Or there was the Duke of Edinburgh award. I realised from who else was signing up for the D of E that this was the mildest evil.

Speed forward to the Lower Sixth. Jake Taylor wasn't someone I'd shared a class with. He was in the top forms – an unostentatiously clever boy. But apart from D of E we also worked on the unofficial school magazine. About ten of us met in the art room on Saturdays to edit, collate and glue the magazine together. I was the film reviewer; Jake Taylor was doing music. This was 1982. Jake liked Joy Division, the Jam, 'Shipbuilding' by Elvis Costello. He had long, scruffy, thick, wiry, brown hair. His green shirt cuffs were blotted with ink. He had a nice smell about him. He didn't strive for an image; he wasn't self-consciously 'cool'. He was friends with Jason Nesbit, Rupert Priestley and Simon Casey, who all also wrote for the mag. The tall, blond-haired, cricket-playing Simon Casey was a boy who, after his A-levels, went to live on a kibbutz where he shot himself with a rifle. Mr Bruce wrote to tell me about Simon's death: 'You might have heard...' But I hadn't. 'Life isn't so easy,' he wrote in his neat clipped handwriting.

It wasn't that I was obsessed with Jake Taylor. He was just there.

And as part of the Duke of Edinburgh silver award we had to go on several expeditions – cross-country orienteering; setting up camp; cooking meals. But the moment I fell in love with Jake Taylor was at the end of a day's expedition in Kent. We were waiting at Sittingborne after a fifteen-mile hike. It was a June Saturday afternoon. We – Jason Nesbit, Simon Casey, Reno Petrides, Jake Taylor and I – were waiting on the grass verge by the side of the road. And some of them had linked arms and were doing the walk that the Monkees did: 'Wey hey, we're the Monkees – we're just monkeying around. We just want to be friendly.'

And then Reno said, 'Who wants an ice lolly?', nodding to the shop next to the station entrance.

Simon, Jason and Jake all went 'Yeah.'

'Right,' said Reno, 'four strawberry Mivis.'

I was sitting on the grass. I knew he wasn't asking me even though Reno and I were in the same form. He and Jake crossed the road to the shop. They were back, doing the Monkees dance. Reno handed ice lollies to Simon and Jason. They tore off the wrappers. I just wanted the teacher to get here so we could catch the train back into London. But then there was a strawberry Mivi held out just above my knee. Jake Taylor sat down next to me on the grass. 'Here,' he said, insistently, shaking the Mivi in the air, 'I got one for you.'

That moment. Then. More than half a lifetime ago. Both of us quietly sat on the grass licking our strawberry Mivis as the other three ate theirs standing up and messing around.

The church fête in Sproughton Village. In the garden of the vicarage. This was the summer of 1972. I was six.

Corn dollies, jars of gooseberry and damson jam, homemade cakes for sale. A tombola, a lucky dip. And in a cage on the grass were three kittens for sale. Each cost 10p.

I put my finger through the bars and an eight-week-old kitten with brown and black mottled fur came up to give it a sniff – and stuck its tongue out to lick it.

'I want one.'

My mum was high above me looking for my four-year-old sister, who was always running off. I tugged the sleeve of her cardigan.

'What?' She peered down to see.

'I want one of these.' I pointed to the cage.

'Hey.' My mum had spotted my sister running under the trestle tables laid out with cups of orange and lemon squash. She was running under, around the side and back again underneath – her face red with laughter.

Mum bent her knees to see what I was looking at crouched on the ground.

'I want a kitten.'

A woman from the church told her, 'They need a good home. There's only the three left.'

We used to have a cat, a big black cat called Suki, but one morning my father, jumping into the car to go to work, had driven over her where she'd been asleep in the shade of the tyres.

'We'll come back later. We'll buy one later. If we buy one now, we'll have to go home with it straightaway.'

But I had already chosen. I wanted the mottled brown and black cat who had said hello to me; his scratchy pink tongue against my fingertip.

Mum tried to pull me away from the cage.

I waved my red purse at her. 'But that one will be gone.'

'It won't be. It will still be there.'

But how could she be sure? The kitten was looking at me as if he was disappointed.

'Mum.' I ran back.

The woman from church smiled at my mother.

'It seems he's *got* to have that cat.'

The woman opened a door in the top of the cage and lifted the kitten out by the scruff of his neck.

'He's a boy. Cheeky fella, isn't he ?'

I suddenly felt sorry for the other two kittens.

'What's going to happen to them?' I asked the woman from church.

'They're his brother and sister. Let's hope they find someone to buy them too.'

I opened the fasteners of my red purse and handed the woman two 5p pieces.

She handed me the kitten.

'Have you got him?'

He was soft. I held him in front of my face to have a good look at him, his legs and tail dangling as he watched me, and then he stuck his tongue out to lick my face.

I laughed.

'He's tickling.'

Mum was pleased I had bought the kitten.

'You'll have to think of a name for him now.'

The woman from church put the money in the pocket of her apron. She waved as my mum led the way through the villagers to pick up my sister, who was crying because she had bashed her head coming up too early from under the trestle table. One of the women was comforting her with a sip of orange squash.

'Look what I've got.' I dangled the kitten in front of my sister. She stopped crying, put out her hand, grabbed the tail and yanked it.

I called the kitten Joe. He was mine. I had to remember to feed him and refill his bowl with milk.

He was a real rascal of a cat. He used to chase, pounce and tear around as my sister, our friends and I roamed on expeditions through the long grass, the ferns and the stinging nettles. He would vanish for

days and nights and then turn up covered in oil, ravenously hungry –
and once he'd been fed he would sleep in the boilerhouse for two
whole days solid.

Then in 1975 we moved to south London. But, because Mum and
Dad could not sell the house halfway between Ipswich and
Sproughton, we went back there every weekend. Joe stayed there –
and the neighbours, the Bellinghams, fed him. The first thing I did
getting out of the car after the two-hour Friday evening journey
through the East End and Essex, my sister and me playing Cheesy Feet
and I-Spy in the back of the car, was to call out for Joe. And sure
enough there he'd be bounding across the lawn or through the
straggly flowerbeds, miaowing a welcome. I'd hug him and tickle him
under the chin. Dad would go off to the shop on Dickens Road to buy
cod and chips for Mum and him, battered sausage and chips for my
sister and me.

One Friday night we drove up to the house and there was Joe
already waiting for us. I jumped out of the car.

'There's something wrong with him,' my sister said.

Joe was limping. He could hardly put any weight on his front left
paw.

Mum bent down to have a look at him. She held him against her
chest and inspected his leg.

There was a raw red gash in the fur the size of my thumb.

'He's caught it in a trap,' Mum explained. Joe's eyes were dirty with
a yellow mucus.

'What kind of a trap?' I asked.

'Badger, rabbit – one that's snapped shut on his paw and then he's
gone and scraped all the fur and skin off by pulling himself free. I'll
have to take him to the vet for a jab.'

Joe took ages after that to get better. The Bellinghams promised to
keep a closer eye on him.

And then eventually, after having to sell off the house with half
the garden – and the rest of the garden as a building plot – we no
longer went to Suffolk every weekend.

This was in 1976, the summer of the heatwave. Mum came into
my bedroom in London. I had been very proud of the flowery plastic

velour wallpaper I had chosen. We had been living there for almost eighteen months. It was nighttime. She sat on my bed.

'You know how Joe is a country cat?' she said to me.

I smiled and nodded, my head on the purple pillow.

'And how he likes to be outside and run about and explore ? Well, he's had another accident; he got his paw caught again. The Bellinghams, they've kindly said that they'll look after Joe now. They'll see he gets better.'

I didn't understand what she was telling me.

'But when he's better – he'll come and live here with us in London?'

'No,' she took a deep breath, 'The Bellinghams are going to keep him.'

'But Joe's *my* cat,' I shouted out.

'Yes, I know he's your cat. But he'll be happier with the Bellinghams – and in the gardens he knows. And he's not well. He needs to get better.'

I understood that this was the world of the grown-ups; that it was unfair; they could decide to give my cat away without even asking me.

I turned my back on my mother and slid deep under the eiderdown. She stroked my hair.

'I'm sorry,' she said. She sat there quietly for fifteen minutes as I watched the orangey-lit shadows from the street pass across the velour flowers on my wall – a wallpaper that I was already growing to dislike.

Eventually I felt my mum lift herself up from the edge of the mattress. She walked over to the door and whispered clearly, 'Goodnight.' Her footfalls going down the stairs to the living room where my dad had the nine o'clock news turned up loudly.

It was only today as I was writing this down that it crossed my mind that actually Joe might have died – been run over or clamped by a trap and bled to death – or just gone missing. And that my mum decided to take the blame rather than tell me the truth.

In a tower block off Borough High Street.

Frilly curtains at the windows and then a view across the Thames to the City of London.

The silence curdles. The man's bubblegum-smile eyes.

'Well what did you come for?' he asks crossly, 'what do you want us to do ? Have a *chat*?'

'If you're going to get angry with me, it's probably best if I go.'

'Fine.'

I button up my flies, pick up my knapsack and jacket and head for the front door. The man swings it open. I push the metal grille gate out. 'See you, then ,mate,' he says sarcastically – not looking at me as he slams the door.

Down in the lift from the eighteenth floor.

Twice. Three times the tears fall down my face as I stand in Battersea Park by the pagoda looking at the mist on the river – the pink sugar icing of Chelsea Bridge lit up. Sleeves of dried snot. The tubas and the euphoniums oom-pahing from the icy stage of the bandstand. All I need is a good night's sleep. All I need is a very modest amount of love and care, taking up the slack. A handful of words from the right mouth to understand.

Film of my mum in her 1968 bathing costume on Swanage beach sitting with a bag of home-prepared sandwiches – waving one at my brothers, who race away in the background towards the frothing sea. She opens her mouth to shout and air funnels out from her throat – it's silent, but even this silence is loud enough to capture the attention of my three brothers who all turn in from the sea to find her.

Film of my street. The plastic punnets of strawberries, the bunches of purple grapes and Jamaican bananas laid out on the fake green-grass cloths. Last night at three in the morning the police loud-hailered the men in the dark underground public toilets opposite to come out in ten seconds before they were raided. I peeked out around the corner of my curtain and nobody appeared up the piss-smelling Victorian steps.

Film of the Bangla lads kissing fists in Altab Ali Park. A plastic wrap of heroin that one of them shakes in his hand – smiling as he looks at it – jumping over the wall.

The days follow each other neat and quiet. I lose myself – taking inadequate responsibility for my freedom. All is offered and all is taken away.

The film snags where it's snapped before and been spliced back together. Burning a hole that craters with brown scorch marks and then snaps again. Stories that always stop just when the hurt is beginning to show through.

Zacharias on Brick Lane at 2.30 on a Saturday morning. I've escaped the gypsy music and the foot stamping of the party upstairs.

'I'll be outside Over Dose On Design.' And there he is – this thin short chap with thick lips and black black hair.

We take off on a circuit. A cup of tea from the all-night bagel bakery.

By Columbia Road he's telling me that he's gay, but no, he's not out.

'Is it because of religion?'

'How did you guess?'

After an hour of wandering, double-backing and chatting we get to the bit of park and we cross it to reach the railway line.

'I'll have to walk over the Bridge of Death to get to my street,' he says. We walk into this Victorian viaduct arch strewn with grey plastic sacks full of rubble and the sooty scorch marks of a fire. I bound up the steps of the footbridge over the railway. The lights are out. I linger on the bridge in the dark.

Zacharias pulls me to him and we start snogging. Those fat lips. I slip my hand in under his shirt.

'You've got mischievous eyes,' he tells me.

'I just want to unwrap you.' I tell him.

I realise, kissing him, the pent-up eroticism inside of me.

On Sunday evening I arrange to meet him at the Vibe Bar. He's twenty minutes late. He makes me uneasy by looking at every man who goes past our table – eyes oil shiny. He says 'I've had the *maddest* weekend' and then spills out a weekend of sex, trips to Kent, ex-boyfriends ('or whatever you want to call them'), cooking for friends, church and church committee meetings. After an hour he leaves to go to Walthamstow to meet a middle-aged woman who's a friend of an eighteen-year-old boy from Cape Town whom Zacharias met and had sex with last autumn and whose brother has committed suicide and the boy wants to come and live in London with Zacharias.

I come home and start crying and don't stop for ages.

Every night for six years, before I fell asleep curled up with Garcia, I would reach over and kiss him on the mouth or on the back of his neck just below his ear and whisper, 'I love you.' Just so that he'd know as he sank into whatever dreamscape awaited him – just in case this was our last night together.

The boy ran to the end of the pier, his conciousness already unsteady. There he unwrapped the Wilkinson Sword razorblade from its waxy paper – like the one that had always been in the bathroom cabinet for his dad. He held it between his thumb and forefinger and slashed his wrist lengthways. Then, before the rush of blood and the belly-wrenching sick pain became too much he swapped the blade over to his other hand and slashed the other wrist – again with the grain of his veins. And then he climbed the railing and, swaying there for a moment, he jumped into the sea. The sea of all his past.

Lantern fish and giant octopi; the rhythmic swaying of a forest of seaweed growing from the ocean bed. Dead men's teeth.

Dropping into the space at the end of the record.

The repetition of lives. In the dressing room, climbing into the costume that's waiting on the hanger – still warm and damp beneath the arms.

The long elastic moments before death as the train slow-motions into the buffers.

The final bubble of air that rises from his lips.

You keep on telling the story until it comes true.

The ice cream van on the promenade. WATCH OUT FOR CHILDREN. Jangling 'Greensleeves'. 'Who but my Lady Greensleeves?'

Fourth World: Notes for the Unauthorised Biography of Andrew Rolliard-Trowe

Simon Lovat

Fourth World: Notes for the Unauthorised Biography of Andrew Rolliard-Trowe

Simon Lovat

1. What the piece looks like:

A section of whiteboard measuring fourteen inches by eight inches, and mounted on the wall at eye level, is encased in a double layer of clear bubble-wrap packaging. Fixed between these two tightly stretched layers of plastic is a piece of card measuring six inches by five, also white, on which there is an inscription set in Times New Roman, size sixteen-point, in black type. The bubble-wrap distorts some of the letters, but the text can still be clearly distinguished. It reads thus:

> *Before you is an installation consisting of a small polished mahogany occasional table, two feet square, height eighteen inches, on which stands a jug of water and four crystal tumblers. The jug is almost spherical, almost closed at the top, upon which a rough map of the world has been etched by laser. The four crystal tumblers are arranged to the right of the jug, in a square formation. Three of them contain water. The fourth, that occupying the top left-hand corner of the square as we look at it, remains empty.*

The piece is entitled *Fourth World.*

The subject of numerous attempts at vandalism whilst on exhibition in London, *Fourth World* is now permanently protected by an armed guard. It currently hangs in Gallery 16, New York Museum of Modern Art.

2. Criticism

a) Sceptics:

i.) Not all reviews were favourable. Morag Cairnustie, the intellectual dynamo behind Channel 9's radical and ground-breaking arts programming, asked Andrew Rolliard-Trowe if he would be willing to submit to an interview as a part of her sceptical *Unmasked* series. Surprisingly, Rolliard-Trowe agreed. This is an excerpt from that interview, which was screened at 11.00 pm on Friday, July 12th 2006:

MORAG: So what would you say, then, Andrew, to your critics?

ANDREW: I wouldn't say anything. My work speaks for me. If people have trouble with what I do, then they have trouble with *the thing itself*, and not me as an artist.

MORAG: But you must be aware that Fourth World has caused a great deal of excitement, and indeed I might say anger, and that you, as the artist who created it, are responsible for that, and therefore must answer your critics.

ANDREW: If we're talking specifically about Fourth World then I'd prefer to be known as the 'author'... (MORAG nods in agreement)... but to return to your point, I simply have to return to mine. I conceived of Fourth World, I made it, it exists. What happens after that is an interaction between that piece and whoever sees it.

MORAG: Genevieve Foulds would claim it *doesn't* exist, though. If I understand her correctly, she claims that its power lies in the very fact that it isn't art at all. That it isn't really anything!

ANDREW: Yet, it is being exhibited in a gallery. Clearly, something exists. Something is there with which Ms Foulds can engage.

MORAG:Yes, but what *is* that?

ANDREW: I can't give definitive objective meaning to my work. I have no responsibility for that.

MORAG(turning to camera): In case there is anyone out there still unfamiliar with this, the most controversial piece of art (MORAG puts the word in inverted commas with a little movement of her index fingers) since formaldehyde guru Damien Hirst, here's another chance to see for yourself.

(A shot of Fourth World appears on screen for over a minute, long enough for even a slow reader to digest the text. Finally, MORAG appears on screen again.)

MORAG: So, what should we make of it, Andrew? What does it mean?

ANDREW: I could only tell you what I intended, not what you should take away from it. And in a sense, that's my point. Who can say where the actual meaning lies – at which precise moment in the interactive relationship between myself, the piece, and the viewer that 'meaning' arises?

ii.) Archie Roberts, 'voice of the people' and columnist for one of the less intellectual tabloids, called the piece "a pile of old crap that my grandmother could have come up with in five minutes over a cup of coffee."

N.B. Neither critic had actually viewed the piece. Each referred to a photograph supplied by the artist, or 'author'.

iii.) Prior to the screening of Cairnustie's interview, public opinion of the piece had been mixed. But judging by the avalanche of email, telephone calls, and letters received by Channel 9 the following day, we can say that art-wary viewers

– bamboozled since the era of the infamous, grant-aided *Twenty-four Soiled Nappies* exhibited in the late 1970s, and those tedious bricks in the 1980s – finally had an inkling that perhaps, at last, they could recognise a joke when they saw one. It was 11.20 p.m., they were tired, and they didn't need to hear any more about it. Thousands of viewers switched off their TV sets and went to bed with a complacent smile on their lips, without bothering to watch the remaining ten minutes of the interview. Obviously, Rolliard-Trowe was not going to defend his work – not because he didn't feel inclined to do so, but because the work was in fact *indefensible*. Everything had settled down. The Englishman's inalienable right to stare at an offering on the wall of one of the most famous galleries in the world and announce that it was artless rubbish, without a nagging doubt that perhaps he just wasn't 'getting' it, that he simply *wasn't bright enough*, had finally been re-established.

b) Champions:

i.) Genevieve Foulds, critic of Modern Art for one of the major broadsheets, heralded it as a work of genius. In an article which itself became the centre of debate, and to which Morag Cairnustie repeatedly refers, Foulds describes Fourth World as "the quintessence of conceptual art, after which simple being will no longer be enough." Her enthusiasm waxes: 'Of course, we have seen artists using everyday found-objects before, beginning with Duchamp, and at the hand of the artist those objects have transcended their intended utilitarian purpose to become objects of lucidity – as with Julia Koolab, winner of last year's Turner Prize. But Rolliard-Trowe has moved even beyond the constraints of matter. Here we have essence without being, profundity without physical shape; art, if you will, outside of itself, and at the same time self-deconstructive. Rolliard-Trowe has effected the paradoxical embodiment of Derridian *Différence*.'

ii.) Carlo Vischenci, famous champion of the much-vaunted 'New Dada' movement in his seminal retrospective, *Visual Art for the New Millennium: The First Ten Years*, has perhaps shed the most illuminating light on Rolliard-Trowe's celebrated Fourth World. 'Would it have mattered,' he writes, 'if Trowe had indeed created the installation? Had there been an actual table, with a real jug and four real crystal tumblers for people to gaze upon, would his meaning have been any clearer? Would we have been any closer to understanding his message? Perhaps not. At best, simply one more layer of the Chinese box which he presented to us in 2005 would have been stripped away. For, surely, by presenting an artefact, an article – his bubble-packed "pitch" – he is asking us still more questions about the nature of the work.

'*Fourth World* is clearly a powerful statement about equality, First World Imperialism and our legacy to the future. It is also a *trompe d'oeil* in a double sense: first directly, in the content of the putative installation itself – those four glasses, what is actually in them? – and secondly, in the presentation of the piece as something which is not a piece at all, yet which now hangs in the Gallery of 21st Century Art in New York. *Fourth World* is a Zeno's Paradox of epic proportions.'

iii.) Martin Duke, Rolliard-Trowe's sometime lover during his last year in London, has been asked many times about the working practices of his famous co-habittee. In a rare interview (*Brushlines*, Autumn 2003, No. 64), he reveals his part in one of the great moments of artistic history.

'I turned up to the studio late one morning and found him sitting perfectly still, staring at the wall,' Duke tells us. 'I asked him what he was doing and he told me he was working. This surprised me, because at that time he was working manically on a series of large pieces made from discarded factory machinery. He had tremendous physical energy, was always rushing around, and constantly made me feel as if I wasn't doing anything – although there was depression there, too, because he thought that his work never said what he wanted it to say. I remember thinking that he looked completely beatific this particular morning, as if he was receiving a message from God. He had a small notebook in his lap, which he'd evidently been writing in, and he waved it at me with a look of exalted triumph. 'I've got it! This will change everything,' he said. I'd no idea what he was talking about then, of course.

'After the completion of what was to become *Fourth World*, Andy was really excited because, finally, he felt that he was freed from the constraints of physicality. Also, he was completely exhilarated by the realisation that he could only do it the one time. You can only make that statement once – a crucial fact that all his imitators seem to have missed. It was his greatest moment, and perhaps mine, too, as I watched that realisation dawning on him. The way I see it, it was all part of his larger scheme to defy labels, tear down all constraining walls – even notional boundaries. It was a direct extension of his politics of sexuality; I mean the idea that we are socially constructed, with no inherent core or centre. That's why he always hated being called a "gay artist". How can an artwork have sexuality? It's inanimate. Therefore, the sexuality of its creator is irrelevant, or even misleading, especially when the content of his work – if it can be said to *have* content – has nothing to do with sexuality. *Fourth World* embodies that. As an artwork it *has* no centre. And of course it also challenges our idea of linguistics, which *ipso facto* deconstructs all labels. I mean, think about it for a moment: sure, there is a sign there, but no *referent*!'

3. From the Horse's Mouth:

a) Rolliard-Trowe, inevitably, *has* been much copied, most famously in Paul Redhead's *Who's Queen?* for which the text, written on the back on an office envelope, runs, 'Here is a segment of crimson carpet taken from the Queen's bedroom at Buckingham Palace, on which a thin patina of dust has been laid. Nearby, stands an Electrolux Royal vacuum cleaner. The dust consists entirely of the incinerated remnants of Princess Diana, taken from the hospital in Paris where she died.' Unjustly, Rolliard-Trowe has been held responsible for this. People blame him for creating a rash of 'art that is not artistic, or very much of anything, except a kind of tasteless undergraduate joke' (*New Perspectives*, Autumn 2002, No. 23).

It was this backlash, more than anything else, that prompted him to move to the United States. At the press conference at which he announced his departure, he told journalists, 'Just as I am not responsible for your interaction with my installations, I am not responsible for another artist's reaction to my work. To link me to Paul Redhead is to blame Alfred Hitchcock for *The Texas Chainsaw Massacre*. When I board my plane an hour from now, I shall escape the intellectual pigmyism embodied by this so-called argument, which has crippled the artistic community in this country for the past thirty years. Clearly, the European *avant-garde* is dead. What began in Paris must continue in the New World.'

b) Shortly before his assassination in Washington DC by fellow New Dada artist Pretzel Pregorak, whose defence of 'artistic statement' did nothing to commute her life sentence, Rolliard-Trowe made some remarks which are believed to have been Vischenci's source material for *Visual Art for the New Millennium*. They appeared in a short article entitled "Philosophy of Ideas", in Washington State University's arts magazine *Quorum*, alongside his obituary: 'Yes, I could have actually made *Fourth World*. Of course. But I chose not to. To make it would have been to turn my idea into a *thing*. Instead, I elected to exhibit the idea of the thing as the thing itself. In this way, the idea of the thing *became* the thing itself, leaving my original conception, my idea, inalienable and intact.

'What many people miss is the idea of actually seeing. When we look at something, what do we see? If I had actually made *Fourth World*, for example, I doubt that many would have spotted that only two of the tumblers were really full of water, the third being full of super-clear resin. People see what they expect to see. And how many would have known that the liquid in the jug, the same liquid that filled two of the tumblers, came from the Chugwa, the world's most polluted river, polluted by a First World chemical plant in Third World East Asia, where there is no regulation? And who might have discerned that the fourth tumbler, unlike its genuine crystal neighbors was a cheap plastic replica made in Mozambique, and remained empty because nobody had chosen to share the resources further – which in any case have been poisoned beyond hope?'

4. Interpretation and meaning:

i.) Vischenci concludes, in *Visual Art for the New Millennium*, that 'Rolliard-Trowe had reached a cliff edge of despair. Were he to conceive of a piece of work and then make it, his meaning would very probably have remained opaque, abstruse. So he chose, instead, *not* to make it; he chose to exhibit the fact that his idea, *de facto*, would remain opaque. And here is the paradox, the great duck-rabbit of this century. What he communicates is that he cannot communicate by means of visual art, so resorts to the exhibition of words. The words are bubble-wrapped, partly but not completely obscuring their meaning. But what they say is not their meaning. For that we must open another layer of the Chinese Box that is *Fourth World*. And here at once is another layer, for what do we have in the Gallery of 21st Century Art? A piece of bubble-wrapped card for all the world to look at. Surely that, of itself, is a work of art?'

ii.) Others have read less into the bubble-wrap. One BBC wit said it was used in the case of *Fourth World* for the same purpose as it was used in the postal service: padding.

Hunter and the Hunted
David Mckintosh

Hunter and the Hunted

David Mckintosh

The young man leaning against the opposite wall, perfectly positioned to invite observation. As far as the scant illumination allows for assessment, he seems rather presentable; handsome, even. He wears a jacket of a rather outdated loose cut, the same default-brown as most everything else under the ambient lights. He wears it without a tie – actually, without a shirt. It is therefore possible to observe how thin he is. It is a thinness that carries no hint of the sickly or (and this is remarkable) of the fashionable. Rather, it comes across as a sign of good health, made more evident by the strong bones and the flat, unassuming but noticeable chest musculature. Hairless, in all likelihood, though it's impossible to see clearly enough for that. In fact, most of what you've observed so far has needed some reinforcement from your imagination.

Everything about the young man suggests someone barely into his twenties, an impression reinforced by the abundant dark – again, as far as the light allows – fashionable hair and bored look on a smoothly chiselled face: this last detail is the one that especially denounces youth, because of the calculation behind it, which he probably believes well hidden but you find transparent. You can read in his expression how aware he is of his attitude, how apposite he feels it is; neither, of course, something a truly jaded person would care for. You can read him, all right; this is what you have been doing for the last fifteen minutes or so.

He has noticed you; acknowledged it even, albeit noncommittally. He certainly isn't discouraging you from looking further; on the other hand, neither is he doing anything to indicate he would like you to continue. A game has been established, in which your role has been set as that of the aggressor. An external observer, though, might find that a hard thing to define; that observer might, in fact, even have some difficulty to realise a game is taking place between you. It goes to show just how restrainedly (not subtly) you are playing.

Based on the same principle, the boy doesn't actively look back, but merely verifies now and then whether you're still looking. You cannot possibly know whether he would be participating if your roles had happened to be inverted; so, in order to keep the game going, to maintain tension and interest, you make sure not to be blatant yourself, which would be a giveaway. Instead, you contrive always to be looking elsewhere, or at least to keep your gaze unfocused, whenever he turns to check. Thus, no real meeting of your eyes ever happens: your eyelines merely cross while shifting away from one another. And that might well be all they're ever going to do.

The objective of this game is rather obvious: one must force one's opponent to surrender. In this, it's no different from most others we all play from childhood. What difference there is resides in that, ultimately, the ideal situation would be to have both players win simultaneously, therefore losing, therefore winning. Such a result can't be accurately described as a draw, for that is reached when the equality of forces at play is such that no result is produced. In your case, the equality of forces *would* produce a result: the very result both players should presumably be going for.

Presumably only, because there is always a chance, even if it's slim, that the other might not be playing at all: another remarkable peculiarity of this game is that it isn't always possible to tell at first who the players are, or even if there is a match going on. Sometimes, not even the players themselves are completely sure. Which may be one of the reasons why this game so often ends in complete forfeit and general frustration. Ecclesiastes would surely have attributed this to *vanitas vanitatis*, maybe even used the example, and no one could accuse the writer of being unfair; however, you are not concerned with moral judgements or edification of any sort. Not at the moment, at any rate. What you want is to force the boy to look at you openly and, by doing so, invite you to make what either of you may later view as the 'first move', according to each one's conveniences and priorities. (This classification may also vary according to time, occasion and aftermath of the encounter.)

A peculiar game indeed, where the word 'no' can cover the whole spectrum from 'yes, what are you waiting for' to 'I'm not quite sure yet, let me think for a while', and the word 'yes' may not signify acquiescence. With more sophisticated players, however, words may eventually reacquire their dictionary meanings. The phrase 'don't get sentimental on me', for example, might indeed mean just what it suggests: a negative request, and not, as one might be tempted to interpret it, following the reverse logic typical of the game, a flat demand for that very sentiment that is apparently being pushed away. (This, of course, without considering the problem of what may be meant by 'getting sentimental'.) Therefore, knowing when to take sentences at face value can be tricky. Nothing is to be taken for granted: even politicians, on occasion (admittedly rare), have been known to mean precisely what they were saying.

Furthermore, a deliberate and not insignificant effort is called for, so that you may successfully ignore an entire universe of concerns that may in fact be separating the young man's attentions from you. For the game to be properly established, it is imperative that you believe him totally uninvolved with any professional, sentimental or study-related situation that may require more than a fleeting thought. He must dedicate his full concentration to you, and any show of inattention or indifference must be purely strategical. Assuming he is playing, he'll expect the same from you. This makes it sound as if you're trailing behind: you *know* you are concentrating on him. But, if he is playing too, he will be in the exact same position as you – provided you keep playing well, and do not reveal too much.

A reduction of this magnitude demands more creative energy than it might seem at first. So it is that an inordinate amount of time is, depending on your shifting point of view, either invested or wasted in this display of pseudo-indifference, this dialogue that does not admit of words, gestures or even admission itself. You are, now, by turns, bored and amused by the game, and bemused at yourself (actually, a combination of the previous two states), and you wonder if the boy might be feeling the same. If that is the case, the boy related to obscure concerns about pride and not allowing one's arm to be twisted. It might also have to do with pre-emptive self-defence, fear of exposure – a remnant from times when it *was* dangerous for men to eye one another out in public? Or, perhaps, it has transformed into fear of a different kind of exposure, that of one's ultimate availability. The unwillingness to let know that one *is* on the look. Or maybe it's just the perversity of denying foregone conclusions. Many strands to consider: but not right now when you're quite tired. No – it's time to sleep now.

As you board the bus that has arrived after a surprisingly short wait, you find yourself pleasantly tired, and expect a lovely sleep tonight. All in all, although no imagination could be stretched enough to call this night satisfactory, it has at least had enough in it to be considered amusing. In this day and age, that's surely no reason to complain.

Stamp Out Your Cigarettes and Pull Down Your Pants

Stuart Thorogood

Dedicated to Misty Woods

Stamp Out Your Cigarettes
and Pull Down Your Pants
Stuart Thorogood

I would like, if I may, to take you on a strange, *but rather fabulous*, journey...

Woooooooo! Rarrrrrrrr! Yarrrrrrrr!

It's Thursday night.

Come on!

Time for the world to come ALIVE again.

We got our fingers on the trigger, so grab your guns and let's go...

Thursday evening, five p.m., and it's time to party. Well, what are you still sitting there for? COME ON!

Spectre, Lance and I are heading home from our BORING day job (hey, we gotta pay the bills, y'know?) and we are on our way! Off we head through Camden Town to Spectre's pad near Euston station. We stop off briefly at Spectre's pal's, the underground Pop Art artist, Nicky Nuklear, who lives above a chip shop. Just to see if he's got any drugs. We buzz. And buzz. And buzz again.

Nothing.

"Fuck," says Spectre.

So we move on. Nicky'll be at the club later anyway. We'll see what's what then.

Back at Spectre's flat, we make ourselves at home – Lance and I, that is. Spectre busies herself in the kitchen and brings out some french toast and a packet of Brussels pâté, along with two fancy bottles of Chardonnay.

"Just to get us in the mood," she trills.

I tell you what, I love Spectre. Her real name is Elizabeth Toods, but she has the nickyname Spectre, which dates back to her childhood. Don't know why; never really asked. Spectre rocks, though.

And Spectre is a queen – queen of the London club scene.

She plays in a band: the X Bomb. And OH! they rock, too! They are gonna be huge stars soon; huge, I tell you. HUGE!

So next we come to Lance. Lance is in love with Spectre; I'm sure of it. Just the way he looks into her eyes, all gloopily. Bless 'im. The fact that she's a lesbian doesn't seem to bother him, or else has completely passed him by. Lance is this cool bohemian type with shoulder-length hair who wears baggy shirts and plays bluesy guitar. A cool customer if ever there was one.

Spectre cracks open the wine and pours us all a glass and we start eating some of the French toast and pâté. The phone rings. It's Nicky Nuklear, asking what we need for tonight. After a quick discussion, it's agreed that between us we'll have two grams of K, ten pills and maybe a bit of speed. Well, honey, it is a school night so we don't want to go TOO nuts.

It's agreed, and Nicky will drop the drugs round later.

Spectre finishes her wine and goes off into the bedroom to sort out her outfit for the evening.

Well, I suppose I should tell you a little about myself, huh? Okay, here goes. My name is Daniel and I'm 25. Originally from a small little town called Newport Pagnell, I moved to London to live with my boyfriend about a year ago. We have a small flat in Fulham. It's really good, y'know.

Unless it was bad.

Now it's bad. REALLY BAD.

The truth is, we're not together at this moment in time. He threw me out this morning. It was horrible: he didn't scream or shout or kick or hit, he just kind of deflated and said although he loves me, he can't go on like this and then burst into tears. I wanted to punch and kick myself, I tell ya.

Then I left.

That was this morning.

Oh, but hang on, I'm getting a tad ahead of myself here. You probably want to know *why* he kicked me out. Well, the simple truth of it is that he came home from work last night and found me crouched over the toilet cistern snorting a quick line of heroin.

Now let me just quickly say this about that: I'm not a junkie. Well, not properly. I don't mainline or anything like that, I don't even chase the dragon. Just the odd line here and there, a little bump or two once in a while, just as a pick-me-up. To me, there's nothing wrong with that. C'mon, it's not as if I'm in the gutter at Mornington Crescent begging for money, swigging out of a 59p can of White Ace cider and fantasising about my next hit.

Huh.

Not yet, at least.

No, it was just the odd line here and there, just for – y'know – when things get too much and I need to calm down a bit.

Anyhoo, while *I* didn't think it was that bad, you betcha Jamie did. Oh, Jamie's my boyfriend, by the way. Yeah, and he hates it, the drugs. When I first met him, I told him about my little habits and he seemed fine with it then. Well, he was new to the gay scene, and I think he kind of thought it was par for the course, y'know? That had been about five, maybe six years ago, before I moved to London and would just come down on the train every weekend, funds permitting.

Christ, when I think of what I was like back then. Oh, *HONEY*! Why, just half a pill and I'd be OFF MY TITS! Heroin? Ketamine? Coke? No way José , you wouldn't catch ME doing any of that shit! Not then, at least...

'Course, a lot has changed since 1998. Well, it would do, wouldn't it? I used to be one of those silly little teen-queens turning up at the Ku Bar in Charing Cross Road at eight o'clock on a Saturday evening, clutching my bottle of Hooch, or Kooch, or Slooch or some bitch-pissy alcopop, giggling like geese with my prissy little clique; waiting eagerly for the bar staff to start selling the G-A-Y Queue Jump tickets 'cos – well, oh Lordy, my goodness gracious, whaddya know...!

STEPS ARE ON TONIGHT, DARLIN'! OOH! AMAZING!

Marvel at their matching outfits!

Sing along to their cheesy tunes!

Try in vain to imitate their simple dance routines!

Cringe in horror as you look back and can't believe you actually liked that bollocks!

But I digress.

Where was I? Oh yes, Jamie's hatred of my spiralling drug habit (but remember, as I said, I'm NOT A JUNKIE).

See, he didn't mind me doing it when we were out together. If we were at Heaven, or DTPM, or Liberation, or (of course) Trade, it would be fine. In fact, he'd go and buy the pills for us. He was in control that way, y'see, and it would ONLY be pills, mind. We'd do half here, half there, but he decided WHEN. That's what was important. But I'd always have my secret stash of coke or heroin or whatever for when I was alone at home in the flat, and needed – as I also said – a little pick-me-up.

But then I'd get sloppy and he'd find the odd wrap of something or other shoved down the back of the sofa (just for emergencies, you understand), or he'd find a couple of tabs of Dexedrine in the back of my designer Chillipepper jeans when he was putting a wash on.

Oh, the rows we would have. THE *ROWS*! Honey, I tell ya. It was like nuclear war in Fulham; just NUCLEAR!

So we'd row and row, and then as usual he would forgive me and I would promise never to do it again and we'd end up having mindblowing sex and that was that.

Till the next time.

Did I feel guilty? Shit, of course! Of course I did, every time.

Jamie was the sweetest, kindest, best-looking, most generous geezer going. Not to mention a red-hot fuck. And I would always crap all over him, every goddamn muthafuckin' time. But I couldn't help it – EVEN THOUGH I AM NOT A JUNKIE – I couldn't help it.

I *can't* help it. No, sirree. Uh uh.

So, that is how it would happen. I would get caught, we'd have a screaming row, then we'd make up... but last night, last night – oh, sweetie, last night was a doozie; yup, a real humdinger, baby.

I'd had a bitch of a day at work and came home and knew that I had a tiny bit of heroin left. Just a sliver, really. Barely even a line. I chopped it out onto the toilet cistern, and – WHOOSH! – snorted it up with a rolled tenner.

Ahhhhhhhh... that's the ticket... mmmmm... yeeeeeehhhhhhhhhhhh...

Buzz, buzz, buzz, baby... like a honeybee... mmmmmmmmmmmmm...

I didn't hear the flat's front door open; didn't hear the bathroom door open. Only when I turned round and saw Jamie standing there. I smiled at him, all gooey and moist. The rush is really hitting me now; feels so good, but the look in Jamie's deep brown eyes makes me feel so bad.

"Hiiii…" I drawled.

"What are you doing?" he whispered, staring at the rolled tenner in my hand.

"Nothin'," I lied.

"You're doing it again," he said.

"No! I've done nothing!"

I could feel blood trickling from my left nostril. Who the fuck was I trying to kid?

"You have to go," he said. Whispered it. And I knew that I had used up the last of my nine lives. This was the end of the road for Daniel.

The end of the line.

Last stop.

All change, honey.

Thank you for travelling on the Jamie Line. Mind the gap.

NO!

He went out then; he went out and I passed out, onto the bed. I don't know where he went.

When I woke up this morning, it was almost seven. My head was spinning and I leaned over the side of the bed and tried to throw up. My stomach heaved, I retched, but nothing. I felt like pure, unadulterated shite and had to leave for work in half an hour.

Jamie was in bed beside me, and he leaned over and wrapped his arms around me.

I thought, *IT WAS ALL JUST A DREAM!*

Oh, sweet merciful Allah, it was all JUST A DREAM!

I snuggled into Jamie's arms, and into my ear he whispered, "I love you so much, you know, Daniel. More than anything. Anything."

"Mmm," I whispered, smiling, suddenly not feeling quite so sick.

"But you know I stand by what I said last night, don't you, babes? You have to go. Today. I can't deal with this anymore. It's not fair on me. You've got a problem and can't see it. And I've suffered enough."

I wanted to scream, "BUT I'M NOT A GODDAMN JUNKIE, GODDAMMIT!"

I kept my trap shut.

"You do understand, don't you, babes?" he said. And I nodded, and got up and went to work still dressed in the same clothes as last night, telling him I'd pick up my stuff as soon as I sorted somewhere else to stay.

"Take care of yourself," he said, as I left the flat.

So, then. That pretty much brings us bang up to date, doesn't it?

Told the whole story to Spectre this morning and she said I could stay with her for a few days. She was pretty much convinced that it was just a storm in a kettle and would blow over soon enough. I have to say, I kind of agreed with her.

Anyway, we'd work it out later.

Right now it's party time, and I can forget about Jamie for a while.

Don't think I'm awful, or selfish. But you probably do.

But DON'T PANIC! Jamie will come round. He has done before.

Anyway, there's nothing I can do right now, and that's what it's ALL ABOUT, sugarplums!

RIGHT... NOW.

Electric blue neon overdrive... DVD twin customised... shoot it up to Saturn Live... all you hot shots can take a ride... I'll see ya honey when the shooting's done...

"Hey, D," says Spectre, coming through the door into the living/dining room area. Lance is busy watching *The Simpsons*. "Can you tape me up here?"

Spectre is a complete goddess. Seriously! She is the *über*-queen of cool and no foolin'. She is the creator of the very-little-bar-a-plastic-bag look and always looks TIP-TOP STUNNING. She tapes this bag around her with the word TRASH emblazoned across it in red. She wears fishnet stockings and these amazing glass-bottomed high-heel platforms. Sooo chi-chi it hurts! When she performs, she wears a blonde bob wig, but tonight she is going without it. No matter. Her hair is a work of art. Shoulder-length, about eight different colours to it. Utterly amazing. Like I said, she is a

GODDESS! She doesn't move, she just glides; doesn't cruise, she just rides... rides... rides...

GODDESS OF THE NIGHT!

Uh huh.

So I help tape her into this creation. She says, "How are you feeling about things?"

I shrug. "Ah, not so bad. Things'll sort themselves out."

"They will," she says. "You just need to lay low for a while."

I nod, and finish securing her. "All set," I say. "Wish fucking Nicky would get here soon, though."

And you know what? – as if by magic, there goes the buzzer.

So we're off! On our way! Now the night can REALLY begin!

I've pushed Jamie to the back of my mind. Like Spectre said, things will sort themselves out, but for now I just have to concentrate on RIGHT NOW.

We've had a couple of bumps of speed just to get us going. I have the rest of the shit, safely ensconced in my sock.

So there's me, Spectre and Lance, in a taxi heading towards Old Compton Street, to Electrogogo's @ Madame Jo Jo's.

(Ooh, that rhymes! Kinda...)

We'll be meeting others there later: there'll be Tash, and, well, obviously, there's Louise As-U-Please, and of course Nicky Nuklear, plus Paul, and David, and the fabulous Bella Blaze... ooh, and let's not forget Deputy Platinum!

There'll be celebrities, too...Lady Miss Kier who is over from New York, Mat Attraction, James St. James and of course, OF COURSE, the main man, the promoter of the event, that's right, ladies and gentlemen, boys and girls: it's Mr Mark Moore himself. YES, that's RIGHT! MARK friggin' MOORE!

Ooh, it's gonna be spectacular.

Jamie??? Jamie WHO?!?!?!

I pull the wrap from my sock and take another quick bump of speed off the end of my key. Lance nudges me and I give him one, too, then Spectre.

WE ARE WIRED, HONEY! WIRED!

We are, after all, Da Da Gods.

Hmm... now. Let's go off on a little tangent here, shall we? Yes, I believe we shall.

Y'see, first there was the Blitz Kids. Doubtless you know of them, have read of them, and so forth. Or perhaps you were there... Yes, Boy George, Leigh Bowery, Steve Strange. Oh, and of course, who could forget dear sweet Marilyn? May the Lord bless his mascara and wiggage.

Gorgeous. Just gorgeous.

That was in London; that was in the oh-so-lovely Eighties.

And then there came Michael Alig.

No, no, no... not *Ali G*.

Michael Alig.

Alig.

A-Lig!

Yes, now you're with me. Or not.

Well, perhaps you've heard of him, and then again perhaps you haven't. Maybe you've read *Disco Bloodbath* by James St. James.

Maybe you've EVEN seen the film *Party Monster*, which is BASED on that book by James St. James.

Either way, I'll give you a brief history here anyway. And, sugars, when I say BRIEF, you can bet Buckwheat Bertha that I MEAN brief.

Uh... From what I know, anyway.

Okay?

So.

Right, well, in a nutshell Mr Alig created himself in Mr Bowery's image. Y' know: crazy club clothes, blue spots on the face, pubic wig's on his head...SOOO unoriginal (of Mr A, not Mr B, that is)... But, hey, you couldn't help but love that little imp. A teeny-tiny queer guy from a shitty small town comes to New York, creates this crazy, magical drug-fucked club scene... Ooh, well according to all sources it was all the talk of the town!

FABULOUS! WONDROUS! FUCKIN' A!

Yes.

Then, of course, as you know (well, if ya'd read the book or seen the film, at least) it all went tits up and the crazy heroin-fucked shit murdered his drug dealer with a hammer and some drain cleaner (don't forget the drain cleaner!) and got sent to prison for fuck knows how long and now... well, now isn't due out for several years.

Ooh, but you know what's really annoying? What's REALLY annoying is all these idiots who now seem to idolise Michael and write to him in prison via his website.

Oh, Michael, we love you! they gush.

Oh, Michael, you're fabulous! they fawn.

You so don't deserve to be where you are! We can't WAIT until you're released.

Oh, well, golly gosh, my oh my. Poor old Michael. Locked up for committing a MURDER! *I mean, is there no justice in the world?*

But...

... well, hey-ho, huh? Not *our* problem, is it, darlings?

For we are the *Da Da Gods*.

Ah.

Yes, mm hmm.

That brings us nicely – again – bang up to date. Doesn't it? Well? *Doesn't it?*

So, you've got the... what was it?... yes, the Blitz Kids (London, 80s); the Club Kids (New York, 90s).

And now... ha! Now, it's come round again.

Da Da Gods (London, 00s – "Naughties").

Why the fuck call yourself that? I hear you ask.

To which the reply would be: WHY THE FUCK NOT?!

Have you shut up now? Good. Because I am trying to tell a story.

Well, here we are: Lance, Spectre and I... we've got a whole load of drugs at our disposal, we are dressed to kill, and we are a long long way from all that G-A-Y shite. Good.

And in we go.

I hate all that G-A-Y crap. The gay-clubbing equivalent of fast food: homogenised, bland and full of shit. Yeah, Jeremy Joseph can kiss my tight, toned, gorgeous little arse. The arse that has been rimmed, fingered and fucked by my honey of a boyf Jamie soooooo many times. Sooooo many times.

(oh jamie oh jamie oh jamie oh!)

But I cannot think of that right now; cannot think of the shit that's going down with my boyf right now. There'll be time for that later.

I told you – it's all about RIGHT *FUCKING* NOW!

So we're there, and we are riding high. The music is pumping: electroclash at its finest. There is a fantastic, up 'n' coming band on later, the Ju Ju Babies. We have all seen them before at Kash Point and Nag Nag Nag and various other *über*-cool London hangouts, and we all LOVE THEM! Far better than watching some Kylie-wannabe prance around lip-syncing to her non-hit on the Astoria stage, or some Z-list boyband that has been formed from the dregs of rejects on some god-awful reality-TV "talent" show.

I've done a couple of pills and a few bumps of K now and I am in the mood, honey.

Yeah!

I'm dancing with Spectre and over the music shout out, "Money! Success! Fame! Glamour!" And she squeals with drug-fucked delight.

The beat goes on, and on we dance. Groove on, brothers and sisters… groove on.

I AM FEELING SO GOOD RIGHT NOW.

(*Jamie? Jamie who?*)

Ooh, here comes Ruta! Fuck me, she is one cool feline. An utterly gorgeous fetish model (among other things), a complete and total delight. A creative super-force; an angel. She's got tiger tricks, hip-hop hips, electric lips and those eyes… well, they just FIZZ!

Yup, everyone loves Ruta.

"Doll Daniel!" she gasps. "How ARE you? My, you DO look FABULOUS!" She holds me by the shoulders at arm's length and looks me up and down. I have to concur with her: I do look pretty darn fabulous in my paint-splattered jeans; grey dinner jacket with the words STAMP OUT YOUR CIGARETTES AND PULL DOWN YOUR PANTS! daubed on the back in acrylic paint of varying colours; my jet-black eye-shadow carefully smeared to look as if I've been crying; the sprinkling of glitter on my cheekbones and the slash of scarlet across my full lips.

"Why, thank you, baby sweetness!" I gushed back. "And I'm not the only one! Three snaps up to you, Dollface!"

We giggle and hug.

"Listen, honz," she whispered in my ear, "have you got anything? I asked Nicky and he's all out but said you might have something. Just a bump? I shoulda sorted myself out before I came but you know how it goes... sometimes you just forget..."

Well, of course I understood, and after all... THIS WAS RUTA. You just don't SAY *NO* to *Ruta*!

So we head into the toilets, lock ourselves in a cubicle and she has a couple of bumps of K off my wrist. Oh, and I give her a pill for good measure. As I told you, you don't SAY NO TO RUTA.

I do another bump of K and then back out into the club we go. Ooh, can you feel it, sugah? Can ya? Yes. YES! *YES!!!*

See, this is what I love; this is how it should be. There is no gay club; there is no straight club; there is JUST US.

Yes, uh huh, this is HOW IT SHOULD BE. No segregation; just integration.

Da Da Gods.

Oh fuck, but look... there's that twat: Artysmokes, he calls himself. Mm. We don't like him. Who does? He is this wanker who thinks he's one of us... but no way.

Ugly Southend Scumbag. Lives his life through a website journal that nobody reads!

S to the A to the D, or what?

Actually, he's been stalking Spectre of late; thinks she's in love with him; it's pathetic. Thinks he's it and a bit. But yeah, like I said – no way. Y'see, kids, it's like anywhere: you get your fair share of fuckwits 'n' fanny-faces.

That's right, it's not all gorgeousness, glitter, heels and hair.

There he sits, trying to chat up some poor unsuspecting barely legal wannabe on the plus velveteen sofa in the corner, sad cunt...But wait! No time for that. Oh, I love this one! It's Gene Serene with "Wicked". Oh, man I just gotta dance...

I grab Ruta and Spectre by the hands and haul them onto the dancefloor and we dance away...

Uh oh.

Uh-*fucking*-oh...

Thoughts of Jamie are rearing their pretty little heads. Oh no, starting to miss him... oh no... now... *what – should – I – do?*

Of course! The solution is simple, Sillies!

MORE DRUGS!

Ah.

Mmmm...

Little bit of heroin.

Lurveeeeeerrly...

There.

Now suitably off my tits, I can go back to it all and enjoy myself and forget – for the moment – all about Jamie.

Ruta, Nicky, Spectre, Lance, Louise, Paul, Bella... me... all of us taking it all, 'cos it's all for us...let's go...!

DA DA GODS...

Time goes by.

The seconds tick.

The minutes slip.

Finally the night is over and OH! what a night! Fabulousa, Darlink! MWAH!

Much booze and many drugs have been consumed by us all. But at last it is time to go.

We all say our goodbyes – thanks to much coke, E, heroin, K, speed, dexadrine and copious amounts of booze, my predicament with my beloved Jamie is for now far from my mind.

Spectre, Lance and I kiss our goodbyes to our darling compadres, and get into one of those MURDEROUSLY expensive black cabs. Well, honz, what do you expect livin' in our glorious capital.

We head off to Old Portland Street... got to pick up some fags. We can walk from the all-night offy to Spectre's. We get our stuff and proceed to walk home – but oh, *fuckety-fuck* – Spectre has gone and left her bag in the cab... along with her purse, cards, money and keys.

OH FUCKETY-FUCK, indeed!

What are we gonna do?

(Un)fortunately her neighbour is one of the Da Da Gods – Mr Jack

Divine – so off we head there…well, what else could we do, eh?

Mr. Divine must have the teeniest tiniest bedsit going… and Lance can't even bear to stay there, so he heads home to his own bedsit in Clapham, leaving Spectre and I at the toybox from Hell.

Oh well.

After about twenty minutes it becomes apparent that Jack is pissed as fuck. Louise is there also and he has shouted at her, making her cry, calling her a slut and telling her to get out.

"We'll go, too," says Spectre, pushing her blonde hair from her eyes.

"No," says Louise. "It's me he has a problem with. You stay."

Spectre and I huddle 'neath the blanket Divine has provided for us. We snort a small bump of K each from my wrist.

Jack, with his long red hair in the stinking pit of a bedsit, pushes Louise and tells her to GET OUT.

She goes.

Spectre and I, trapped in our respective K-holes, quiver.

CUNT, that's what J-Divine is, CUNT.

A while goes by. Perhaps it was ten minutes. Perhaps an hour. *Perhaps* a hundred years.

Who can say when you're on K?

(Ooh, that rhymes, too!)

Fuck, I'm missing Jamie. It's coming again. Yes, here it comes. HERE IT FUCKING COMES!

And now I know – *I know!* — that no drugs are going to help me this time.

"Yes, and YOU!" J-D shouts drunkenly – pissed as a fucking muffin – into Spectre's face. "YOU! YOU ARE A CUNT! YOU ARE A LEECH! A FUCKING DISEASED STINKING BITCH! YOU CUNT! YOU BITCH! YOU WHORE! WHORE! BITCH! YOU SUCKLE AT MY TEAT LIKE A FUCKING BITCH WHORE SLAG! BITCH! WHORE! SLAG! I FUCKING HATE YOU, WHORE!" He/It turns his/its head to me and spits, "AND YOUR FUCKING QUEER FRIEND. FUCKING QUEER!"

And Spectre just sits there and takes it. Just TAKES it. My FRIEND. My beautiful fucking friend just sits there and TAKES IT!

No.

"Hey, c'mon, leave her alone," I say. And I pull him by the shoulder.

But BOOM! He whirls on me, grabs me by the throat and rams me into the wall, smacks my head against the bookshelf and whacks me in the face several times.

Spectre is on her feet and pulls me by the arm. "Come on! Go! Go! Go! Come on! Come on!"

We run.

Out of the door, with Jack Divine screaming after us. On our way to Nicky Nuklear... he'll look after us.

Halfway there we stop 'cos we're safe and do a couple of bumps of K apiece. Then we collapse into giggles and get to Nicky's. Blood is pouring from my nose but we don't care; we're flyin' on K.

No, we don't care.

We get to Nicky's and yup! He takes care of us!

Nicky checks my face and I'm fine.

Shit, it's almost seven thirty and I have to be at work in less than an hour.

I'm still SO high.

Wish, I think to myself. *Wish and it will be.*

At least until morning comes...

I wash the majority of my makeup off and head to work. Thoughts of Jamie enter my head and I know that drugs won't take it away now. GOD, I MISS HIM SO MUCH. 'Cos I'm back now, back to reality.

When I get back to work, I am almost crying. Crying for Jamie. The night before, the drugs, the beating from Jack Divine, it seems so stupid and pointless it's ridiculous.

There is a voicemail from my friend Yvonne. My NORMAL FRIEND Yvonne. My non-drug addict friend Yvonne.

She's been talking to Jamie. He'll have me back if I sort myself out this time. Properly. If I book myself into rehab. It'll be fine; he'll have me back and things can be how they once were.

I email him to tell him I'll do it; that I'll get help.

My colleague Sue says to me, "Daniel, you look like shit. Go home. Go home, and get some rest. Go back to Fulham and see Jamie."

I know she's right. I know I look like shit. I know I am going to make the effort.

I get up to leave the office; the night before seems unreal, like a dream.

I make my usual checks.

Got my keys? Yup.

Got my fags? Yup.

Got my mobile? Yup.

I put my hand down into my sock...

Got my wrap of heroin?

Yup.

Wha...? Bu... Ah, come on, don't look at me like that. Hey, it's just for a pick-me-up, yeah?

'Cos after all, as I've said countless times:

I AM NOT A JUNKIE.

Yup?

Finding Danger Boy
Michael Wilcox

Finding Danger Boy
Michael Wilcox

Jim Briscoe lives with David Stow in sheltered accommodation in the East End of Newcastle upon Tyne. Jim has Down's Syndrome and David used to be a "special needs" student. They attended the same school, are the same age, 19, and have known each other since childhood. Jim works full time in a local supermarket. David works in a hotel kitchen. They are a well-known pair around the gay bars and clubs in the town.

I have recorded a series of interviews, with each of them on his own, over a period of weeks. Because of Jim's condition, he tends to talk in short bursts of concentration. He can become monosyllabic. Sometimes he retreats into himself and doesn't want to tell you anything. But he did want me to tell his story in his own words. So what follows is an edited transcription of what each wanted to tell me about their life together.

I've got to tell you about the bus, my bus, the one I wanted. My mam drinks – she's ill. Da's somewhere else. But the bus wasn't special. Not just for the school. Anyone can catch it – the public people. I'd been on it before – with someone showing me. It was the quarter-to-eight bus. How old was I? I don't know. Young. I was young then. But to get to my school – right across the town – my school was absolutely miles; I had to be on it. I was fed up with having to be taken. People make too much fuss of me – Heaven knows why. I hate fuss. I've never asked for fuss in my life.

So I went on my own to school for the first time. I suppose I was fourteen. A long time ago. But I wanted to do it myself – by myself, just me. And when I got to the bus stop, the bus – quarter-to-eight bus, my bus – it was off down the road. I'd missed it. I shouted. I waved. It wouldn't come back for me. That driver – he knew I had to catch it. But I was late.

He *didn't wait. Not a nice man.*

This is the mad part of my story. I thought only the quarter-to-eight bus went to my school. I didn't realise – if I waited, another bus with the same number on it would come along. It wouldn't be the quarter-to-eight bus, of course. I could have got there – just the same. No one explained that part of it. How could I know it if no one told me? So what could I do? I couldn't go home and say I've missed it. Poor me! I can't do it by myself. More fuss! Terrible! I couldn't do that. I'm not a failure, me. No way. But I am a stubborn cow. David says I'm the world's most stubborn cow. He's right. So – wait for it – I decided to walk to school. That's right across the other side of Newcastle. I thought I'd find it if I followed all the bus stops. I had two pounds in my pocket. I knew the first few bus stops. But there were so many. I got lost. Silly me. What am I like?

My first adventure was this woman. She was drunk. Like my mam. I knew what the matter was. And she was saying, "Buy us a cup of tea." And she was sitting on this bench. She was a smelly woman. Very smelly, as a matter of fact. I thought she'd shat her pants. David says she'd wet herself. I wanted to help her. I wanted to give her a pound. I said, "There you are." She wouldn't take it. I said, "Take it!" She looked at me and started to cry. That made things worse – in my opinion. Poor old smelly cow. Could have been my mam. I put the pound on the bench beside her. I said; "Get yourself a cup of tea – and a bath." There were people there – watching. I thought they might ask why wasn't I at school, so I left. Problem was, I only had one pound in my pocket after that.

I got away, but I didn't know where to go next. Then I saw the river. I know the river. And the Tyne Bridge. If I go there, I'll find myself again. It was so far! My legs aren't long enough for that sort of thing. But I wasn't going to give up. Then there was the attishoo man! He kept saying attishoo – I thought he did. David says he was selling the Issue or something. Didn't sound like that to me. And I was getting hungry and I said to him, "Where can I get something for a pound?" And he said, "I don't know. What are asking me for?" So I said, "I thought you would. But if you don't, you better carry on sneezing." That's one of my funniest jokes, by the way. The man just didn't get it. He carried on just the same. I was laughing. He told me to piss off. So I did. Then I had a stroke of luck!

*

I was wagging off school that day. I'll tell you why in a minute. Anyway, I was in this café with coffee and my favourite sticky bun and there was this face, staring at me from the street. And I thought, I know him. That's daft Jimmy. He was from our school but I didn't know him that well. So he came in and we had a bit laugh an' that and he told me about the bus. And he had half my bun – the best bit, with the cherry on. The reason I was there was the gongs! You remember them gongs at the Baltic? This massive art place down by the river. It had opened a few weeks before, and they'd taken some of us down there in the minibus to take a look round. And there was this huge room with hundreds of gongs hanging from the ceiling and you could wander round beating them. They made a fantastic sound. And each gong had a name like "peace" and "love" – crap like that. But the teacher got in a panic when she saw we were having so much fun – going wild an' that – and took us off before we were ready. Now I wanted to go back on my own to beat the shit out of those amazing gongs. So that's why I wagged school.

Jim wasn't on our trip, and hadn't even heard of the gongs, or the Baltic. But when I told him, he wanted to come with me.

David took me down to the Baltic – that's what it's called. It's free, which is good – in my opinion, anyway. Has he told you about the gongs? Right. David – he's different from me – different sort of boy. He wanted to hit the gongs as hard as possible. It really made my head hurt – bad-tempered bugger. David really is sometimes – he was then, not so bad now. But I said there's other ways of doing it – like this – and I did a load of little taps all together. I don't know how I knew., but I did. And the effect was amazing. The sound grew and grew with each tap into a great roar, like a jet plane, like taking off into the sky.

That was the day I realised Jimmy wasn't so daft. In that room, when we awoke monsters, from before history ever was, like terror, like the ghost of God haunting you – like forgotten secrets. Jim sees things from a different angle. He isn't simple at all. On his day, he can show you things you can't see.

Michael Wilcox

At school, we all used to keep clear of David. He was Danger Boy. If you got too close, he'd hit you. So you kept your distance.

I was on "special needs", what ever that really means. I couldn't read or write properly. I wouldn't let the teachers tell me what to do. I've wrecked more than a few classrooms. I was so uncontrollable, they wouldn't have me back. So I ended up at a different school, full of weirdoes. That's what "special needs" does for you. Why I was like that I don't want to tell you. I don't even know the answer, not entirely. Other lads had things worse than me, but they didn't go crazy. Something mad in me.

Doesn't hit me... only kind to me.

I thought I better take Jim back to the school. They'd never missed him. No way they could have contacted his mother, anyway. Could have sent someone round there, I suppose. She doesn't answer the phone. There is one in the house. She's frightened of it: might be her bastard husband wanting money. So when Jim and me turned up, they were more surprised than anything else. We just wanted to tell everyone what had happened – and what a good day it had been. It was me that took him home after.

I didn't want to get lost again, crossing the town. Danger Boy became my friend... lucky me.

What a state his place was in. His mam was pissed as a fart. The house was a shit heap. I told his mam that Jim was coming back to mine for his tea and I'd bring him back later. Had to, didn't I? I was away out later – even at that age.

David's dead tidy. If I leave anything lying about, he says put it away... It's always my mess, not his.

I used to hang about the gay bars while I was still at school. I was like a stray dog. They used to call us "Davy Bog Brush" and buy us drinks and sometimes give us jobs to do. A good laugh – made some pocket money. I used to sit in the corner of the bar and do my homework some nights. People would come over and help me and then I read my stories out loud if the bar wasn't too full – and they'd all clap. I called it my university. I did really well at school after that, and I never hit anyone – not at school, at least.

I got a job, down the road. No buses. It's great – supermarket. I'm boss of the trolleys. People leave them all over the place. What chaos! I make sure they're where they should be. In the car park – that's the worst. When it rains I get soaked sometimes. Once I scraped someone's car. They didn't notice, thank God!

When I became Jim's friend, I started taking care of him, seeing he was clean and looked after himself. To teach him how, I bathed him and washed his hair – did all the things he should have learnt at home but hadn't. We used to catch the bus together morning and nights. Because of the way we were together, the school and social services suggested we share. So here we are! When I'm not here – which is a lot of the time with my job at the hotel, an' that – there's a warden on call day and night if Jim needs help.

David takes me out at least twice a week. We see a film. I like films – some films, at least... Finding Nemo, my favourite, very frightening. I saw it twice. Then we go to the bar. I drink diet Coke. We have a laugh. It's a gay bar.

Jim doesn't get what a gay bar really is – or what "gay" means. It's a word he likes – like a happy word. I've tried to explain, but he just stares at me with half a grin on his face. In his own way he knows about sex, but he doesn't have any – I don't know how to put this – sort of... sexual response to anything. So we've never been lovers in a physical way... but we do love one another. We care for each other. We also have a life away from each other. I still cruise the bars and saunas. I have my affairs. If I'm away some nights, that's no problem. I let the warden know. Jim has lots of friends here.

Tonight David's taking me to the disco. I like dancing – good dancer, me.

Portrait of a King
Graeme Woolaston

Portrait of a King
Graeme Woolaston

Editor's note: The British Ambassador recorded the journal of his period in what he refers to only as 'the Kingdom' in a leather-bound, lockable diary, which after his death was deposited in the Bodleian Library, Oxford. What follows is approximately one-third of its contents, omitting many of his notes (almost invariably complaints) about meals, his surprising frankness about his amorous exploits with local ladies of easy virtue, and diplomatic material irrelevant to the principal purpose of his mission. Perhaps as a primitive security measure he refrained from using names, and although the locations and people involved have long since been identified, this mannerism has been retained in order to impart some of the flavour of his narrative. He was three years younger than the King he writes about.

GW

October 3rd. [18—]. Our journey here was in every way as unpleasant as we were warned it would be. The King uses the state of the roads as an excuse for the rarity of his visits to his capital, but of course that merely reinforces the complaints about his choosing to hide himself away – this is how his conduct is invariably described – in the mountains. Though I was in the capital for only three days, I was left in little doubt about how unpopular he has become.

Within less than an hour of our arrival I was, to my great surprise, summoned to meet him. My description of this must wait till later; dinner is to be served shortly.

October 4th. The castle dominates the village which lies just outside its walls. Its plan might be described as a figure of eight, squared off. Because of the King's aversion from photography I had only an approximate concept of its architecture, which is interesting, rather than either attractive or picturesque. The upper part of the 'eight' is the old castle, dating from the later Middle Ages, which the King has had fully restored. The lower and considerably larger part, the outer castle, was built for him, but in a style which attempts to match, on the whole successfully, the earlier work. This outer castle houses the military barracks, the school and lodgings for the choir and other musicians, stables, and lodgings for lesser members of the Court. One side of the yard is entirely occupied by the Chapel, the costs of which have aroused such hostile comment.

One enters the inner castle through an ancient gateway. The inner castle is the residence of the senior members of Court, the King's personal servants, including his gardeners, and of course visiting dignitaries such as myself. The King's own quarters, on the southern side of the yard, which include a second, private chapel, and his famous Library, are called 'the innermost rooms'.

But what is most astonishing about the inner castle is that its yard is almost entirely filled by a glasshouse which looks as if it had been sired by the Crystal Palace. It contains, of course, the King's collection of tropical flowers and trees and plants, of which he is so proud and which does nothing to increase his standing among his people, especially since it is no secret that he himself helps with its nurturing; indeed, cartoonists who are hostile to him routinely depict him in the garb of a peasant, and invariably draw him with dirty fingernails. The flower house, which is heated by some means which I do not understand, is connected to the main castle south and north by glassed corridors, for the King has a horror of cold and, in winter-time, walks only on a private terrace high on the Castle's outer wall and, on Sundays, to the principal Chapel.

As I recorded yesterday, he took me by surprise by a precipitate invitation to 'the innermost rooms'; but since dinner again is imminent (I cannot believe it can be as bad as yesterday's) I must once again postpone writing my notes.

October 5th. When the Chamberlain informed me that the King, having learned of my arrival, would be pleased to see me at once, I was horrified, for I had had no opportunity to change out of my travelling clothes, and my man had had no time to lay out my Court dress. 'That will not be necessary,' the Chamberlain said, with grave solemnity. 'His Majesty is most relaxed about such matters.'

I followed him through the humid atmosphere of the flower house into the south wing, and up the spiral staircase which leads to the innermost rooms, which are on the top, third floor. We had no need to knock: a manservant – of whose uniform, more anon – having obviously heard our footsteps (and possibly my panting), opened the door without bidding.

I found myself in a small hall, or even lobby, which might have been that of a suburban villa. A door, opposite that through which we had entered, opened as mysteriously as the first, and on stepping through, I found myself in the King's private sitting room. It in no way contrasted with the lobby. It could be the sitting room – the 'front room', indeed – of a City clerk.

It is quite astonishing. The King, whose reputation for extravagance has angered his people, troubled his ministers, given hope to his enemies, and which has spread across Europe, lives, in private, in no more luxury than any of his middle-class subjects, perhaps less. The room is furnished with simple armchairs and tables, there is a writing desk, there are photographs of fellow European royalty (to many of whom, of course, he is related), and there are a number of oils representing either scenery within his Kingdom, or his ancestors, including his father. There is no representation of himself, and there are no mirrors. There was a roaring log fire; I have since learned that he has a similar fire in every chamber. Several bookcases hold, bound in the finest leather, parts of his library. But the largest piece of furniture, which almost squeezes out the rest, is the King's piano, and beside his music stool, heaped on the floor, are piles of scores.

An inner door opened, and the King emerged. We exchanged the conventional courtesies; to my surprise he began at once in English, and continued in the language throughout the interview. His voice is light and most pleasant to listen to, and his English is almost flawless.

The instant impression of him which, I think, any visitor must have is how little he resembles the portraits which are seen everywhere. This is because they all show him as he was in the earliest years of his reign, before and just after he passed the age of twenty, and in many of them he wears the gorgeous chivalric robes of the various Orders of which is Head. No portrait of him has been painted since, and he absolutely forbids photography of his person; he even, once, attempted to persuade the Legislature to make this a crime, one of the many unwise actions which have contributed to his unpopularity.

So now one is confronted with a man a full quarter of a century older than any public portrait. His height, of course, remains unaltered – he is a good foot taller than myself – and he has continued the practice of being clean-shaven, which he has made so fashionable within his Court – I shall return to this subject later. But he is now corpulent (which can easily be explained by the food these people eat), and above heavy jowls his hair is becoming thin. Yet his eyes remain much more youthful than the rest of him and, as we talked, it was in them alone that I recognised the King whose accession at eighteen years of age caused such joy to his people.

A manservant brought in a tray with tea, ordered, the King informed me with a smile, from England. I could see that he partook simply to put me at my ease.

We spoke for about twenty minutes, but not once did he enquire why I am here, and not in the capital near his Ministers. I have little doubt that he understands exactly the nature of my mission.

October 8th. I have had two further informal meetings in 'the innermost rooms', and have twice walked with the King on his little terrace. All this Kingdom, and he has reduced his world to that! On the first occasion he played for me, and, though I am little of a musician, I have sense enough to recognise a prodigious talent. 'I no longer risk singing,' he remarked, with what I am beginning to realise is a characteristic self-mocking smile. It has been said, of course, that as a young man he was sufficiently gifted to have become an opera singer, and it is often added that this is the course in life he would have preferred to the Throne.

His love for music fuels the extraordinary school he keeps in this remote place. Not only are there choristers and orchestra to supply the needs of the most elaborate of High Masses in the principal chapel, selected musicians play trios, quartets, and quintets for him every evening as he dines – invariably alone.

On the second occasion we met, he led me through into the long room which houses the Library which has been so much written about, and showed me many of its principal treasures. He is in touch with booksellers and auction houses in every major European capital, and even in New York. He collects primarily from the past two hundred years, but none the less has acquired some very significant early books. Latin, Greek, Italian, French, Spanish, English, and of course his own language, are all represented on his shelves. He has a complete Scott, a complete Dickens, most of Dumas both *père* and *fils*, Dante, Cervantes, Homer, Vergil, Horace, Ovid... The list is endless.

His expenditure on this Library, and on his collection of flowers, of which he is no less proud, is another of the complaints most often made against him, though he has repeatedly said that on his death it will be bequeathed to his people.

Both of these meetings with the King, during which he spoke only in English, lasted scarcely less than an hour, which is most gratifying, but I note that the formal presentation of my Letters of Credence is being repeatedly postponed, on the most polite, but also the most flimsy, of excuses. I suspect I know why.

October 10th. My suspicions were correct. Yesterday the Ambassador of the Empire arrived, accompanied by no fewer than three secretaries. Perhaps he intends to send dispatches to the Emperor by the hour. Tomorrow we will present our Letters of Credence to the King in a joint audience. This, of course, will ensure that we have equal status among the diplomatic delegates here (though we are the only ones with the full rank of Ambassador).

October 11th. The Imperial Ambassador, who is a Baron and is invariably addressed as such, is everything which I detest about his nation. He makes no conversation in any language but his own, not even French. His voice is loud and his person unappealing. His arrogance might be that of his Imperial master himself. He has the repulsive facial duelling scars which his people so grotesquely consider an ornament on a man. Fate has made us inevitable enemies here, but I believe I should have hated him in whatever circumstances we met.

October 12th. Dinner, in the large and gloomy State Dining Room, is a most melancholy business, and not merely on account of the dreadful food.(They can usually manage soups with success, and desserts can be most satisfying. It is everything which comes between which makes me suffer. So far inland, we can perhaps not expect the best of fish, but frequently it is almost rank, and on Fridays, of course, we have nothing more substantial. As for the other days, I believe that, if the good Lord had not created pigs, this people would have died of starvation generations ago.)

The head of the table is reserved, of course, for the King, but, except on Sunday at midday, it is always empty. The Chamberlain and the Chapel Master, who despite his title is in charge of all music in the castle, are the principal lay officials. The King's Chaplain has a high placing, since he is a titular Bishop *in partibus infidelibus*. The colours of his robes provide what little relief to the eyes we have. We dine without music, except on Fridays, when the King denies himself that pleasure, though in truth the music which is played often seems to me merely to add to our melancholy. The wines, at least, are superb. Without them, and without the ladies of the guesthouse in the village, I believe this mission would be intolerable.

There are, of course, no ladies at table, since, apart from some washerwomen and a handful of scullery maids, all of whom reside in the village, not a single representative of the female gender is ever seen within the Castle.

October 13th. The anticipated assault from the Baron began tonight. Indeed, when he invited me to his rooms, offered me a choice of the finest cigars, banished his secretaries, and put his fat legs up on a footstool, I knew what to expect.

'The Imperial Government, Excellency, is greatly flattered that Her Britannic Majesty takes such an interest in our nation that she has sent her Ambassador to the King's private residence, rather than his capital.'

'I regret, Baron, that I do not entirely understand the reference to your nation. My esteemed colleague Lord — is honoured to represent us at His Imperial Majesty's court.'

He looked furious.

'You will not attempt to pretend, Excellency, that your presence here is unconnected with the proposal to complete the unification of our nation.'

'I will not attempt to deny, Baron, that Her Majesty's Government believes that the continuing freedom of this Kingdom and its people would be by far and away the most desirable outcome of the present discussions between your two nations.'

His face is always flushed; now he became puce.

'This, Excellency, is nothing but the most unwarrantable interference in the affairs of our nation.' The quarrel between singular and plural briefly threatened to become amusing.

'Baron, your Government knows that such a major revision of the boundaries of Europe requires at least our passive acquiescence, as one of the guarantors of the settlement of the Congress of Vienna.'

There now followed an historical argument too lengthy to be recorded here. The Baron cited, as I knew he would, the changes to the 1815 settlement to which we have raised no objection, including, as he rightly said, the growth of his native land to the point where it could claim the status of an Empire. 'And now, suddenly, England awakes, and has the effrontery to demand that a limit be set to our legitimate national aspirations!'

'But they are not legitimate, Baron. This is no consolidation of related peoples. This is the annexation of an ancient Kingdom into your Empire.'

I realised at once this was a mistake, and he seized on it: 'Ancient?' he spat out with contempt. 'It was only raised to a Kingdom by Napoleon!'

'Be that as it may, the King's ancestors have ruled here for seven hundred years.'

'And wouldn't rule here for another twenty, if their future depended on the present King.'

I stubbed out my cigar and rose: 'We have talked of these things enough for tonight, Baron.' I bowed.

As I let myself out, he spoke to me for the first time in English, and, moreover, in perfect English: 'You dare to come here to talk about the freedom of this Kingdom? What about Ireland, eh? What about Ireland?'

I left his rooms with the name of that damned people ringing in my ears. It is, of course, our Achilles' Heel at every turn of this attempt to prevent the Empire swallowing the Kingdom.

October 14th. Another wretched session with the Baron.

'Why cannot you admit that your sudden enthusiasm for the survival of the Kingdom has nothing to do with its people or, still less, its King' – I am beginning to loathe the way the Baron invariably refers to him with an edge of contempt – 'but rather, with fear of the Empire?'

'Why should we fear the Empire?'

'But why indeed! Is that not precisely the point I have laboured again and again?'

'We have no fear of the Empire. We shall always be at least equal to anything you can ever be, and probably surpass you. But such a huge revision of the boundaries of Europe cannot be permitted to proceed without our consent. And, at present, we are not minded to consent.'

He almost growled his next words: 'Because, in spite of everything you say, you are afraid of us.'

'We are not afraid of you, Baron, or of anyone. But we are afraid for the future peace and stability of Europe.'

Suddenly he was almost triumphant: 'Always England's policy! Always England's ancient policy! That no one power should be too strong in Europe. Admit it!'

'I admit it happily. It is no secret. May I remind you that it is scarcely two generations since our peoples fought together to defeat Napoleon?'

'And so, now, my Emperor is to be a new Napoleon?'

'Not him, perhaps, nor his present Ministers, but perhaps his successors, or the successors to his Ministers.' I leaned forward: 'If the proposed Union between the Empire and the Kingdom were to proceed, your boundaries would advance dramatically southwards, so much so that you would become involved in a whole region of Europe where at present you have no involvement. Why? You are a northern, Protestant people. Why do you want to absorb this southern, Catholic Kingdom?'

The Baron smiled.

'Have you seen the latest issues of the capital's newspapers?'

'Of course I have.'

My presence here is attracting much adverse comment from the mostly pro-Union press. The Protestantism of England is invariably mentioned, and, equally invariably, the Catholics of Ireland. I could wish ourselves rid of that useless island tomorrow, if that would free us to play our proper rôle on the Continent.

As I rose to leave, I said to the Baron: 'By the way, our policy of ensuring that no single power can dominate Europe has prevented any major Continental war for over half a century. That is why we shall continue to pursue it with every means at our disposal.' I left feeling myself to be unquestionably on my strongest moral territory.

November 4th, being the Sabbath. Today, for the first time, I attended High Mass in the great Chapel in the outer courtyard, standing at the back in the area reserved for Protestants at Court.

It is often said that the one aspect of his character for which his people are willing to forgive the King much is his undoubted piety. He hears Mass every day in his private chapel, observes all the fasts of the Church with rigour, and for Mass on Sunday he has caused to be erected this extraordinary building. The costs have caused much complaint, but it has a soaring, whirling, dazzling, bewildering Baroque interior – a brilliant imitation of the churches of last century for which the Kingdom is famous.

I am beginning to wonder if the King is really of our time, for the music he prefers, as well as the architecture, is almost all of last century – indeed, the Chapel Master tells me that his musicians are glad to perform for us on Friday evenings, because it enables them to play something other than Haydn or Mozart or Handel. But all the music for High Mass is from that time.

The Bishop-Chaplain in full pontificals; priests and deacons who are brought in, I am told, each week, from the capital; choristers and musicians; the swirling of incense; the elaborate, orchestrated movements of the ritual; the ancient Latin words; and, above all, the astounding, the breathtaking claim that weekly, daily, through this ritual the Son of God is again corporeally present – I wondered again if perhaps, despite all, Manning and Newman are right.

And, in the midst of all this, the sombre figure of the King. For High Mass he dresses in black, brightened only by the sash and glittering star of one of the Kingdom's Orders of Chivalry. He sits alone at the front and, when he goes forward to receive Communion, he does so alone.

The Baron was standing next to me. I discovered later that this was his first attendance at Mass in the Castle, too. He seemed as thoughtful as myself.

November 5th. Late last night, after I had written the above, one of the Baron's secretaries appeared to invite me to brandy and cigars and, despite the hour, I was so intrigued, I accepted.

Once the Baron and I were left alone he opened our discussion in a manner which greatly surprised me; he spoke almost wistfully: 'You realise, Excellency, that both you and I are wasting our time here? That we are not only in the wrong place, but the wrong country?'

'What on earth do you mean?'

'That the issue between us is not going to be decided by any influence on the King we can achieve.' He stretched his legs and sighed. 'No, Excellency, the most important man in this castle is the Bishop-Chaplain and, if you and I wanted to change the course of events, we should have taken ourselves to Rome.'

His words chilled me: 'You have heard something?'

'You have not heard from your own man in the Vatican?'

'Nothing.'

'I had a despatch yesterday. It is all but certain that the Pope will shortly declare himself in favour of the Union, and urge Catholics to vote for it in any plebiscite.'

If this is true, it is the death-knell of our policy. 'But we have always understood ...'

In what may prove to be his hour of victory, the Baron was surprisingly without an air of triumph; perhaps he is jealous that he is not, after all, to be the decisive emissary of the Empire: 'That Rome would choose to remain neutral – or, you must have hoped, oppose the Union?'

I shook my head: 'We have always realised that the Pope could not prejudice the position of Catholics presently within the Empire by active opposition. But' – I hesitated, and then saw no reason not to be frank – 'we did not anticipate that your efforts to persuade him to endorse your proposals to the Kingdom would be successful.'

'You underestimate both his stupidity and his greed for power.'

'Power? What will he stand to gain by seeing a Catholic realm disappear within an Empire which, even with its accession, would still have a Protestant majority?'

'I repeat, you underestimate his stupidity.' He drew on his cigar. 'We sent to the Vatican a Catholic who is nearly, though not quite, as stupid as the Pope. He has managed to persuade the Holy Father' – he spoke the phrase with undisguised contempt – 'that an historic opportunity now exists to reverse the Reformation.'

I could not suppress an oath of incredulity.

'Oh, yes, Excellency. Once the Kingdom is within the Empire, the tide of the true faith will roll inexorably northwards, till Luther's Theses are metaphorically ripped off the door of Wittenberg church.'

'But surely that is utter nonsense?'

The Baron smiled.

'Excellency, I can assure you, that if I suspected for one instant that it is not, I would become the most devoted supporter of the European policy of your Government.'

I sat for a moment or two in silence, trying to absorb the impact of this news.

'The King...' I began.

'Is a most devout Catholic,' the Baron concluded for me. 'One word from his confessor that the Holy Father desires the Union, and he would break his silence, not in the way you wish, but in the way we wish. And, of course, with every priest preaching for one outcome to the plebiscite, the Kingdom's electors will vote it out of independent existence.'

There was no possibility of denying the truth of all this. I made my excuses, and left.

November 18th. From Rome today I have confirmation of the accuracy of the Baron's report. My mission is now all but pointless, and will become completely so on the day the Pope issues whatever proclamation he intends to make.

November 21st. Relations between myself and the Baron had, in the light of the above, become slightly more cordial or, at least, less disagreeable, till tonight.

'What will become of the King, after the Union?' I asked him.

The question seemed to surprise him: 'Why, he will still be King, of course. Our Empire, as you well know, is a federation like the United States, not the United Kingdom. Much power will remain with the Kingdom's own Legislature, and the line of His Majesty's ancient family will continue.' He smiled a malicious smile: 'But, of course, through his brother.'

This is not the first time the Baron has made an implied reference to the worst innuendo which is thrown at the King.

'But he will be a King in name only!'

The Baron shrugged.

'So? He is a King in name only, now. He withdrew from all real involvement in the affairs of his Kingdom years ago. Why else are we having to endure this Purgatory in this place?' Once again he smiled maliciously. 'He will simply have even more time to devote to the passions of his life – his books, his flowers, his music, and, of course, his...'

'His what?' I asked, not believing he would actually say out loud what is spoken in the lowest taverns of the capital.

'His boys.'

I left.

November 22nd. I have been deliberately avoiding this subject, but I cannot do so any longer. The rumours began with the fiasco of his betrothal, a year after his accession, called off within a month (we had to work hard to prevent that becoming a *casus belli*). Since then his name has been linked with no woman's.

As I have noted, there are no ladies of quality in this castle. His servants are drawn from his military guard, and even my eyes can see that they seem to be chosen for their stature and their looks. They wear a uniform designed by the King himself, which combines what at school we called a bum-freezer jacket, black, with tight white breeches. They look more like hôtel page-boys than manservants, and, what is worse, it is all too apparent that they wear no underclothing. The obviousness of their masculinity is at times embarrassing to the point of indecency. The King's decision to remain clean-shaven even in middle age has set a fashion followed everywhere in this castle; there is not a bearded soldier to be seen, an absurdity which, not surprisingly, when combined with the entirely male personnel of the Court, has given rise to the innuendo to which the Baron referred last night with his customary crudity of manner.

Yet I cannot believe it. There is nothing effeminate in the King's demeanour, unless the politeness of a true gentleman is to be interpreted as such. And would the Bishop-Chaplain remain here for an instant if he knew, as the King's confessor, that there was substance to the rumours?

December 8th. I am recalled to London, as admission of our failure to persuade the King to make some effort to defend his Kingdom's freedom.

Today I had my farewell audience in the innermost rooms. As at my first, tea was provided, and the King spoke entirely in English; indeed, it has only been at his Sunday dinners that I have been obliged to converse with him in his own tongue.

'Excellency,' he said with a smile, 'I should like to remain in touch with you after your return home, in a private capacity. I shall write as' – the pseudonym he chose translated, to my surprise, as 'Mr Sorrowful'.

'Of course, your Majesty – if my superiors permit it.' He picked up several catalogues which had been lying on the floor beside him: 'I should like to use you as a spy on London book dealers.' He laughed. 'If I see books listed in which I think I might be interested, would you be willing to visit the dealer in question, and report to me if they are indeed worth the price asked for them? I have to tell you that sometimes in the past, I have been misled and disappointed.'

One does not, of course, refuse a King's request. But this reference to his hobby finally spurred me, as I was now able to do since my mission is over, to refer directly, without prompting from him, to its objective.

'Sire – does it not concern you that your Kingdom may shortly become nothing more than a province of an Empire?'

He smiled that winning, almost boyish, smile I have seen so often, but said nothing.

'Sire – even now, one word from you could change everything. If you were to return to the capital – address the Legislature in person, rally your people – they would, I am sure, follow you at once.'

Still he smiled, and still he said nothing.

'If you were only to refer to your ancestors – the seven hundred years your dynasty has ruled here – the history of your nation, its military victories, its long growth towards the granting of your Crown...'

At last he leaned forward, and, still smiling, spoke. 'Excellency – be grateful that I do not request you to visit Kew to report on plants for me.'

December 11th, in the capital. We leave for England tomorrow. The remarkable cheerfulness of the Foreign Minister, a man certain to lose his post as a result of the Union, has renewed my suspicions that the Empire has not failed to stoop to bribery to help secure its ends. In a café today I heard a man use a dialect word in reference to the King which I did not understand. Later I asked a waiter for its meaning, praying it was not indecent. From his explanation, I would say that the best English translation would be: 'barking'.

My mission has been a waste of time from the very beginning.

Editor's note: To this day there is controversy about the exact state of the King's mental health. A plebiscite confirmed the loss of the Kingdom's independence, but before the formal accession date he abdicated in favour of his brother, and it remains unclear whether he did so under pressure.

He continued living at the castle with a greatly reduced household, including the loss of all his musicians. High Mass was no longer celebrated in its great Chapel, and his military guard were a handful.

One morning the following winter his lifeless body was found at the foot of the castle's outer wall below his private terrace. It has never been established whether he fell by accident, committed suicide, or was murdered.

His funeral in the capital was lavish, a gesture widely interpreted as an expression of his brother's sense of guilt. His tomb remains the most elaborate of those of all his dynasty.

The Ambassador died in 1912, two years before the outbreak of the European war which he always feared would be a consequence of the Empire's aggressive foreign policy.

Because of its isolation, the castle where he spent a frustrating three months survived the Second World War undamaged, and it has become the Kingdom's principal tourist attraction. Today the image of its restorer and builder is found on everything from beermats to chocolate boxes.

A Boy's Book of Wonders
Ian Young

A Boy's Book of Wonders
Ian Young

In the early Eighties, when I told people I lived in Finsbury Park, they sometimes assumed I was sleeping rough, like Colin Wilson sleeping on Hampstead Heath while he was writing *The Outsider*. There *was* a park in Finsbury Park but I seldom went into it;Hampstead Heath and Epping Forest were my wandering places.

In those days, the district of Finsbury Park was a scruffy, working-class part of northeast London with a high quota of squatters, Indians, Rastafarians, old-age pensioners and young single lads. I moved there because I could afford the reasonable rent Russell charged for the big, top-floor room in his house, a Victorian mansion officially divided into "holiday flats" to get around the strict rent laws in case someone had to be quickly evicted. Fortunately, evictions were rare, as Russell, who had made his down-payment as a conman running a phony guide dog scheme in Australia, was a good judge of people, rented only to those who gave off the right vibes, and kept friction among the tenants to a minimum. He liked me, and I paid the rent on time. What I needed was a full-time job.

I had managed to land a temporary position at the London and Manchester Sanitary Packing Goods Company, located on the second floor of a crumbling turn-of-the-century office building on the dreary Holloway Road. The man I was filling in for was convalescing from some unspecified illness and would be returning in a month, or two months, or three.

In the meantime, the L&M suited me fine. My work answering letters, typing invoices and organising receipts filled most of the morning. After lunch at Ali's café, I could spend the afternoons writing articles and book reviews to supplement my meagre wages, and nursing the Byzantine filing system. The office was presided over by Mr. Bayliss, a gentle, quiet man with a dyed comb-over who spent most of the day sitting in his cubicle of walnut and frosted glass, warming his crippled, carpet-slippered feet by a small electric fire. The unofficial – and indispensable – office manager was my friend Rose Madder, a tiny woman who chain-smoked, always wore slacks and never went out without a beret. Her face was wrinkled and lined like an old chestnut. Over her favorite gin and orange at the Four Kings, she used to say she showed "all the wear and tear of them other three kings – smoking, drinking and fucking!" – and she would hack out a loud, rasping laugh at her own expense.

Rose was a painter – mostly of small, vaguely creepy abstracts that didn't sell. Long ago she had changed her original, ordinary surname to Madder, as she thought having the same name as a paint colour would be more memorable. It was, but it hadn't helped her sell her paintings. In the twenty years since she was hired as a clerk-typist, Rose had become indispensable to the efficient functioning of the L&M and particularly to Mr. Bayliss. And the L&M being one of those fusty, antiquated English companies that somehow mysteriously survived in spite of their avoidance of modern business practice, both Rose and Mr Bayliss would probably be there forever. But I would not. So I was keeping my eyes open for a new position that wouldn't leave me exhausted by the end of the day.

"You should talk to the Old Sarge," Russell suggested one morning as we collected breakfast eggs from the henhouse in the back garden. "Armed Forces Surplus, just off the Holloway Road. You never know. At least he'll sell you a cheap pair of pants."

The Old Sarge ran a shop with tables and racks of sold second-hand armed forces clothing, and equipment – British-army-issue khaki trousers, West German singlets, Yugoslav jackets, Canadian greatcoats, and an array of military shirts, boots, backpacks, rucksacks, mess tins and bits and pieces at prices affordable to the local workers, skinheads, punks, Rastas and other assorted denizens of Finsbury Park.

Sarge was a former British army quartermaster sergeant, a broad-shouldered cockney of about sixty with a ready laugh, a cough as bad as Rose's and a friendly mongrel dog called Soldier. After a few months and with a recommendation from his friend Boris, I was hired to staff the shop in the afternoons and early evenings. "You have all the qualifications for this job," Sarge used to say. "You're honest and you show up on time!" But, for the first few months, I was on the bottom of the call list for Sarge's scavenging trips. One or two nights a week, Sarge and a couple of lads would pile into Sarge's old lorry and troll around different areas of London looking for garbage to expropriate.

"Grab that chair, lads," Sarge would bark.

"What about the chest?"

"Too broken up, leave it –" and we'd move on to the next pile, which might offer up books, or china, or discarded appliances, or old copies of *Country Life*.

Sarge's crew usually drew on several local worthies: "the triplets" (Elliott and his identical brother Lionel); Yob and his friend Orbit, who lived in an abandoned house off the Seven Sisters Road; and a pale young hunchback with big dark eyes and a lopsided grin who called himself Piers Dragonheart, wore bright shirts and a Portuguese shepherd's capote, and, though he hung out with our gay crowd, only fancied the girls.

Riding with Sarge was a good way to make a little money, and, if someone couldn't be reached or didn't show up, I sometimes filled in on the scavenging team. On my first outing, I crouched in the back of the lorry with Orbit, a small wiry kid with a pinched, red face and a lazy eye. His wardrobe seemed to be supplied entirely by Sarge, except for a long, striped scarf, a Christmas present from Boris, who said he looked like a deserter from the gnomes' army. Sarge liked to have him along because he was surprisingly strong and could even lift quite large pieces of furniture by himself.

My memories of scavenging outings with Sarge have blurred into one another, but I remember my first trip very clearly because I was trying to reconnect with someone I'd met a few nights earlier – a mysterious young guy called Harry Telford.

In those days I often used to go to the bars and clubs around Earl's Court, usually on Saturday nights. If I was still alone by the end of the evening, and the weather was good, I would walk up Earl's Court Road, along Holland Walk to Holland Park Avenue and through Notting Hill to the West End. From there I could make my way by bus and by foot back to Finsbury Park. I always enjoyed those long night-time walks through the safe, familiar London streets, finally getting home to Turle Road by dawn, to sleep and laze through much of Sunday until it was time to go to dinner at my aunt and uncle's. And one summer night, on Holland Walk, I met Harry.

Holland Walk is a long pedestrian pathway lined with grass and trees, hugging the side of Holland Park between Kensington and Notting Hill. It was usually pretty deserted but that night soon after I entered the walk from Kensington High Street, I noticed a young man perched on the edge of the park bench. He had a half-length tweed coat, curly brown hair and a fresh, apple-cheeked look whose suggestion of innocence was belied by the smoke rings emanating from a rather large joint he was smoking. He grinned as I approached and, as I slowed down, he offered me a smoke. Without saying a word, we sat together under the lamps in the cool garden, I in my regulation leather jacket, he in his tweed and corduroys. My eager walk home interrupted by a silent, shared smoke with an attractive stranger, I soon lost interest in everything except the grass (which was strong but strangely mellow, as though mixed with damiana), the trees by the straight path and the face of my new companion, who had closed his eyes and seemed to be in a headspace of his own as his fingers rested ever so lightly on my arm.

Harry Telford lived with his much older sister, he said, in Camden Town, as far away from Holland Walk as were my Finsbury Park digs. And before we parted that night (for it was very late and we were both tired) we promised to meet again. When I got back to my room, I carefully copied his phone number into my book before I crawled into bed.

For several days, Harry and I played phone tag, getting no answer or busy signals or leaving messages with third parties. I was frustrated, and beginning to lose heart. And when I called – again – from Armed Forces Surplus, Sarge offered some unexpected advice.

I was helping him to sort a shipment of air force shirts and grumbling about not being able to get hold of my new friend. Sarge had been picking brass buttons out of a tin and sewing them onto a Canadian army greatcoat. Soldier slept in his basket beside the electric fire. Sarge suddenly turned to me and pointed a finger.

"You got to visualise harder!" He laughed quickly and coughed into his handkerchief. "I didn't say *'get* harder,' I said *'visualise* harder'!"

"Well," I said, "I've only met him once and... well, he's a bit blurry."

"A blurry boy?"

"Afraid so."

"Just concentrate," said the Sarge. "Concentrate on that handsome face, kiddo. *You'll* find him!"

That night I headed out with Sarge, Soldier and Orbit on the scavenger patrol.

We headed out around eleven o'clock and made for St John's Wood, a posh area where my bookseller friend Tim d'Arch Smith lived and where Sarge said the pickings were often good. As it happened, we rescued a big box of auction catalogues, a pewter jug and an old walnut table that took up most of the back of the lorry. And, towards the end of the run, we came across a paper bag with about a dozen old books in it. Most of them were mildewed or badly water-damaged but near the bottom of the bag there was one in surprisingly good condition. Oddly, I had seen another copy of it before, when I was a kid. It was a big book of illustrated stories for boys published in the 1920s called *A Boy's Book of Wonders*. The cover, in red imitation leather, showed an embossed drawing of the top half of a teenage boy, gazing upward towards an improbably dramatic shooting star. The picture was beautifully executed and the boy unusually attractive, with a slightly upturned nose, curly hair poking from under a tweed workman's cap, and a knitted turtleneck pullover with broad horizontal stripes. The book's raised design emphasised the knit of the pullover, inviting the reader to run his fingertips over the embossing.

We got back to Sarge's shop about one in the morning, and he was happy to give me *A Boy's Book of Wonders* instead of payment for the trivial amount of work I'd done. Orbit scuttled off to his squat with his pound, and I headed home to sleep; I had work at the London and Manchester the next day.

All the next day at work I tried to take the Old Sarge's advice to visualise Harry Telford. But, whenever I tried to picture him, the oddly similar face of the boy on the book cover kept intruding, until I could no longer tell them apart. *And* Harry still wasn't answering his phone. It was all rather frustrating.

"What's the matter, dear?" asked Rose as we finished work for the day.

"Communication problems," I said, hanging up the phone.

Rose laughed and gave her usual advice.

"Have a little drink, say a little prayer!"

I had dinner at Ali's that evening. Ali's was one of the few eating establishments in Finsbury Park – a workmen's café that did most of its trade in the early morning and in the evening after work. Ali was a beefy, bald, irrepressibly good-natured Indian. He liked me because I had heard of obscure Indian states like Faridkhot, Kishangar and Rajpeepla, and even knew where they were. One evening I'd shown him the stamps from my collection; his eyes lit up as though I'd brought him the Crown Jewels.

None of the usual crowd was in attendance that night but Ali was in a particularly expansive mood (his sister was coming to visit from the old country, he said) and he gave me an extra tin of lemonade to take home in my pocket.

I made yet another call to Harry Telford at about nine o'clock: still no answer. Idecided to walk to the Round House.

North on the Archway Road, the Round House had been built in the 1920s as a petrol station in the Art Deco style that was the latest fashion. It never recovered from the hard times of the Depression and the War and was eventually converted into a downmarket coffee bar with peeling paint and frequently blocked drains. But, as it had the virtue of being open late, it was frequented by lorry drivers and by young guys with motorbikes or scooters. Eddie, the owner, a refugee from alcoholism and the Earl's Court scene, was gay, and so were some of the customers – leatherboys, skinheads and even a few locals.

Monday nights were usually very quiet at the Round House and this one was no exception. I chatted with Eddie and a pair of leatherboys I knew, and after less than an hour, decided to head back down the Holloway Road to Tollington Way and home.

Halfway there, I saw him coming towards me. There was no doubt it was Harry Telford, and as soon as he saw me he ran forward, shouting my name.

"Did you think I'd forgotten you?"

"Well, yes!"

"Sorry. I've been working all hours. Got a few days off now." And he turned around and walked beside me.

And then I noticed. He was wearing a striped, knitted pullover and tweed cap, almost identical to the cover boy's outfit on the front of *A Boy's Book of Wonders*. My blended image of Harry and the imaginary boy from the 1920s had suddenly manifested in front of me.

"Like your jumper!" I said.

"I never wear it, it's a bit scratchy. Don't know why I put it on today."

I threw my arm around his shoulder and we walked quietly along together.

Harry had the bright, inquisitive eyes and boyish looks that I always found attractive, though I liked talkative people, and Harry seldom spoke, and then in brief outbursts punctuated with long stretches of silence.

Glad as I was to see him, I suddenly felt enormously tired. We arranged to meet at Sarge's shop the next evening. Harry caught a bus, and I finished my walk home alone, crashed into bed and quickly fell off to sleep.

Waiting for Harry after work the next day, I told Sarge what had happened. He finished rolling his cigarette, gave a little laugh and looked out of the window.

"There's only one Mind," he said. "The one we're using now!"

And he blew a smoke ring that rose very slowly above his head, and hovered above him for a moment, like a tilted halo.

Harry showed up right on time. As it happened, he turned out to be a chronic fibber withfar too many problems. And his sister wasn't really his sister. But that's another story. We did have some good times together. And for a long while I kept the tweed cap he left one night in my room and never did come back for.

Stealing Memories
Richard Zimler

Stealing Memories
Richard Zimler

In September of 1931, the French painter Fernand Léger visited the United States for the first time. He was fifty years old and already famous for his darkly outlined, colorful figures. In early October, while he was in New York, one of his lower molars became infected. At the time, my father did all the dental work for Marcel Berenger, the Madison Avenue gallery owner. One evening, Berenger called our home. Could his close friend and compatriot Léger come by that night?

Near midnight, Léger arrived wearing a tweed coat and cap. My father told me years later, "He had panicked eyes, and I knew he was going to be a difficult patient." In fact, he sat frozen in the dental chair and mumbled in French when my father didn't have his hands in his mouth. Was he cursing? Praying? My father spoke little French and couldn't say for sure.

"I remember that he sweated a lot and that he smelled of some peculiar floral soap," Dad told me.

The problematic molar was easily cleaned and filled. Léger shook my father's hands exuberantly and thanked him with great praise for his dental skills. In his awkward English, he confessed that the toothache had made him forgetful, and that he only had two American one-dollar bills in his wallet – just enough for cab fare back to his hotel. Of course, he had no checking account in America. If my father were willing to wait until the next day, he would mail a check drawn on Monsieur Berenger's account. My father said not to bother, that it was his pleasure to work on the molar of so talented an artist. Léger reluctantly agreed and parted a happy man.

Exactly three days later, however, a small flat package arrived by messenger. It was twelve inches square, wrapped with brown paper and tied with red and white bakery string. "I thought your Aunt Rutya had sent us some of her strange Romanian pastry," my father told me with a laugh. Inside the package, however, was a small painting Léger had apparently just completed and a signed, two-word note written in French: "*Avec gratitude*".

As children, my brother, two sisters and I called the painting, *The Woman with Stone Hair*.

It's a portrait of a young woman seated on the ground with long black tresses done in such a way as to make them look solid – like polished obsidian. She has the soft pink skin and dreamy face typical of Léger's female portraits at the time.

The painting was my introduction to modern art. It used to hang in my parents' room, above their bed. Years later, I realized that it must have been a study for Léger's famous work, *The Bather*, completed in 1932.

Both my parents adored the painting, and, after my mother's death, it seemed to take on the importance of an icon for my father. Sometimes, I'd find him sitting on the green armchair where he usually piled his dirty clothing, holding the canvas, daydreaming. Once, late at night, I found him asleep with the Léger on his lap. At the time, I had no idea why. Children sometimes don't understand the simplest things.

My mother died on June 6, 1954, of breast cancer. By the time the lump was detected by our family doctor, the disease had spread to her lymph nodes. I was thirteen at the time. I didn't understand why her hair was falling out. My dad explained that Mom was really sick but that I shouldn't worry about her: she was getting the best possible care.

Before I realized that she was dying, she was already dead.

My mother and I had been very close. During her illness, we played endless games of gin rummy after school. Sometimes she liked to draw portraits of me. I'd sit in her bedroom by the windows facing Gramercy Park where the light was strong. She'd sit on her bed with her box of colored pencils. She wore a bright-blue beanie to keep her bald head warm. Her eyes were large and brown. She smiled a lot, as if to encourage me. As she sketched, she nibbled bits of Hershey's chocolate bars; it was the only food she could keep down.

Sometimes, she and I would clear off the dining room table and paint together with the sets of Japanese ink that my father found for us at a tiny art-supply store on Hudson Street. Mostly she'd paint finches nesting in pine trees. I have two of these studies hanging in my office at Barnard College. Visitors always say, "Oh, so you've been to Japan..."

One strange little painting that she did hangs in my bedroom, however, over my bed. It's a finch, but it has human eyes – *my* eyes.

My mother was buried at Mt. Sinai Cemetery in Roslyn, out on Long Island. I refused to go to the ceremony and spent the afternoon alone, eating the rest of her chocolate bars in front of the television until I got sick and threw up all over an old Persian rug we had at the time.

After she died, I felt as if I'd been left behind on a cold and deserted planet. It was my father who rescued me. He let me come into his bed at night for a couple of months after her death, never uttered even a single complaint for my disturbing his sleep. Nor did he listen to my older siblings' warnings that a fifty-one-year-old man shouldn't share the same bed as his adolescent son. "Forget what they say," he used to tell me. "They don't understand." To get me to stop shivering and fall asleep, he'd rub my hair gently and tell me stories of his youth back in Poland. He spoke of demons from Gehenna, shtetls turned magically upside down, chickens with angels in their eggs. He took great pains to make all the endings happy.

On my insistence, he wrote down two of these stories and tried sending them to children's publishers, but all we got back were mimeographed rejection letters. Editors didn't regard dybbuks and Cossacks as fitting for American children. I still have the manuscripts at the bottom of my linen closet; maybe Jewish lore will come into fashion one day.

My brother and sisters were off on their own by the time my mother died; they were all in their twenties and married. So for the next six years, till I went off to college, my father and I lived alone in our apartment at the corner of Irving Place and East 20th Street. He was a good man, heartbreakingly lonely and prone to distant silences, but attentive when I needed him. After my mother's death, the pride which she'd taken in my smallest accomplishments was magically transferred to him, just like in one of his crazy stories. When I won my high school English award, he sat in the front row of the parent assembly with the tears of an immigrant father streaming down his cheeks.

When my father turned sixty-five, he sold his dental practice and moved permanently into a cottage in Hampton Bays out on Long Island. He gardened, watched New York Met's baseball games, and scratched out Bach suites on his violin. I spent every other weekend with him.

In later years, when New York winters forced him indoors for weeks at a time, he spent all of January and February with me at my apartment on 91st Street and West End Avenue. He'd read his magic realist novels in the bed that I set up in my living room, snooze, water my plants, browse in the local bookstores. When I'd get home from classes, he'd make me verbena tea. I used to make him jambalaya, his favorite dish, every Saturday.

In February of 1984, he suffered a minor stroke. In the hospital, he developed bacterial pneumonia. Then, something seemed to snap inside him and he grew delirious. One specialist said Alzheimer's disease. A couple others suggested various pathogens that could cause brain lesions. Tests were ordered, but none proved conclusive. It was agreed by default that Alzheimer's had set in, that he'd managed to keep it hidden until illness weakened him. He was eighty-one years old. I was the only child still living in New York. That spring, I took a leave of absence from my post in the Art History Department at Barnard and spent long afternoons in his cottage, keeping things clean, preparing meals, reading to him on occasion, and watching him snooze. He grew progressively weaker and would sleep most of the time, in the most cockeyed positions, legs and arms dangling over the side of his bed, his head twisted to the side and mouth open. One day, I dared to straighten him out and discovered that he was pliable, like a rag doll. I gingerly moved his legs together and placed his head straight back into the valley of his down pillow. He looked as if he were prepared for burial. So I took his right arm and laid it over the side of the bed and twisted his head. He looked much better that way.

Anyway, the important thing is that, after I arranged my father in his bed, I noticed out his window that the crabapple tree in the backyard had become a cloud of soft pink. And that a male cardinal had alighted there. Red feathers and pink petals – life doesn't get much better than that.

Now, a decade later, I still associate the cardinal and the crabapple with my father's illness. When he wasn't sleeping, he'd sometimes kick and scream, froth at the mouth, rant about being held hostage. Toward the end, during the few moments of lucidity that gave both of us a bit of peace, he'd reach for me. "Paulie, you're still here," he'd say. "When will it end?"

His grip was that of an eagle; talons biting into flesh.

Then he would begin to shout again. "I want out! Out! You can't keep me here against my will. I want to see the manager! Where's the manager?"

Pieces of the verbal puzzle I put together made it clear that he often thought he was being held captive in a hotel in San Francisco. At other times, he was convinced he was being dunked underwater by a Cossack marauder – and that his entire village of Jews was being butchered.

I found out that an eighty-one-year-old fights like a teenaged boxer to keep from drowning. His doctor recommended low dosages of tranquilizers. Half a five-milligram Valium usually did the trick.

Once, during a calm moment, I found him sitting on his bed facing the Léger, just like in the old days. We held hands without talking, and then he struggled to his feet to make us verbena tea as a treat.

All of us who loved my father knew he had been constructed of more fragile materials than most people – a man of balsa-wood with a rubber-band engine flying off to foreign lands inside his head. So dementia was not totally unexpected. In fact, my two sisters and brother all told me – independently of one another – that they were only surprised he'd stayed sane for so long. They said it easily, as if they were discussing a family pet who'd been gently weakened by an invisible cancer.

My own interpretation of the visions my father had that spring is that there was always a kind of fairy-tale landscape inside him that engulfed him completely in the end. It was a world of shtetls hidden deep inside the forests of Poland – a land of Talmud scholars and kabbalistic magic, but also one of Cossacks and pogroms.

For many years, he escaped such a world successfully, but then, when he weakened physically, it claimed him back.

As we reach the end of our lives, do we all return to our ancestral landscape? Will I, too, return to the threatening forests of Poland even though I've never set foot inside that country?

After he died, when I was sitting alone by his side, listening to the room exhale with relief, I began to tremble. There was no one there to make me verbena tea or rub my hair. No cardinal perched in the crabapple tree.

For about a week, I didn't feel anything but the gaping absence left by his death. My brother and sisters flew in for the funeral. They were willing to help by then because there was no one to nurse. They brought me barbecue chicken from the deli in Hampton Bays and cookies to nibble on in bed. Sometimes I'd go to Westhampton Beach, where I could walk down the strand and think about the past.

I didn't go to the funeral itself; that morning, my body seemed to give out, and I woke up shivering with a high fever and stomach cramps. I wasn't sorry; I was dreading having to share my grief with people who didn't help me take care of him.

Like my mom, the only thing I could keep down was chocolate. Real food tasted thick and stale.

Two weeks after my father died, I was alone in his house, beginning to inventory the Florida seashells, ceramic figurines, glass paperweights, and other *tchochkes* that he and my mother had accumulated over the years. It was then that I discovered that the painting by Léger was missing. *The Woman with Stone Hair* had been in his bedroom, of course, right above his nest of pillows. I'd seen it there every day for three months while nursing him. All that was left of it was a tawny square where the sun hadn't been able to bleach the wall.

I didn't panic. I called up my brother and two sisters to see if they'd seen it; they were the only people who'd spent any more than a few minutes at my father's house since his death.

I called each of them in turn, and they all denied knowing anything about the painting's disappearance.

I don't believe that my describing the personalities of my siblings will help anyone understand why they lied to me. What is important to know is that they hated my father for things that had happened many years before I came along, during their childhoods. After his death, they each made a point of telling me that he was a very different person when they were growing up: strict, unfeeling, vindictive. He didn't listen to them or our mother. They said he liked to humiliate the kids by slapping them in the face when they misbehaved.

They all mentioned these things to explain why they weren't visibly upset at his death. They spoke forcefully and slowly, as if they were prosecutors presenting the evidence against him.

Although it's hard for me to believe, I suppose that their portrait of my father may be accurate; after all, children grow up in different families according to their age. Also, parents often grow more tolerant as their youthful self-righteousness fades, and very possibly my father had changed his whole attitude toward child-rearing by the time I came along. Another possibility is that his relationship with my mother improved over the years; when I knew them, my parents were affectionate and playful with each other. Apparently, that was not always the case.

When I told my older brother Mark about the painting, he raised his eyebrows in a theatrical way. "I didn't even know Dad still had it," he said matter-of-factly.

Hard to believe he could forget a painting worth a few hundred thousand dollars, but I didn't say anything.

When I called Sarah, next in line in our hierarchy, she shouted, "You lost it? You lost the Léger?"

I replied, "It was right there all the time. And then it was gone. Someone stole it."

"How could they steal it?" she moaned. "You were living in the house."

"I wasn't watching every minute. Someone could have walked in, just picked it off the wall and carried it off. If you'll remember, I was pretty depressed at the time and wasn't thinking about such things."

"Well you should have been thinking about them, because now you've really screwed things up. You should have put it in a vault, goddammit."

Then I called Florence, number three in our line of descent. When I was a kid, I was close to her. She played baseball with me, took me to foreign films, taught me how to roller-skate in Gramercy Park. She had been bright and daring, had had thick dark hair, a quick smile, and long, elegant hands. After my mother died, however, she hardly ever came to visit me and my father. Now, she considered herself the only intelligent member of our family – the scholar. She taught anthropology at Oberlin College and spent her summers digging up Hittite tablets in Turkey. She had neither a lover nor partner – no children, no friends. Her conversations with me had grown more and more bitter over the years. She was like a never-ending winter whose days grow darker and colder with each coming year. Her particular brand of contempt for our father had mostly to do with his supposedly belittling her for pursuing an academic career. She hated me because I didn't hate him.

"That's just great," she told me when I informed her about the missing Léger. "Do you know how much money I make a year?"

"More than me, probably."

"Clever," she said. I could see her sneering. "I need that money," she continued. "We could've auctioned it and made a fortune. I was counting on it."

"So what do you want me to say?"

"You could start with you're sorry."

I let an angry silence spread between us to let her know that she'd reached the limits of my patience. She understood, and she spoke more gently. "Did they leave any clues?" she asked.

"None that I could find."

"So who could it be?"

"The only people who ever entered Dad's bedroom were me, you, Sarah and Mark."

She suddenly shouted, "If you're making this up... If you've hidden it so you can sell it later, I'll kill you!"

"Florence, what the hell are you –"

She was screeching at the top of her lungs: "I swear I'll kill you, I'll cut out your heart, and I won't give it another thought."

That was the first time I thought that something might be seriously wrong with her.

The police came twice to my father's cottage to dust for fingerprints and interview me. Florence even insisted on hiring a private detective. We each chipped in seven hundred and fifty dollars. But the painting didn't turn up. Until three weeks ago.

Meanwhile, within months of the painting's disappearing, we all stopped talking to each other. At first, Florence suspected me, Sarah suspected Mark, and Mark suspected Florence. It was like a bad imitation of Shakespearean comedy. Then things got really wild: Florence convinced the others that the villain could only have been me. After all, I was the only one who'd been at my father's cottage all the time. So I had far more opportunity to take the painting and find a buyer. As for my motive, that was harder for her to concoct, since I'd never been known to care that much about any inheritance. But she managed to come up with one. According to Florence, I needed the money to pay secret debts. Her diabolical reasoning went as follows:

I'd been promiscuous during the 1970s and had therefore caught AIDS. I'd stolen the painting because I didn't want to admit that I had the disease and desperately needed to make hospital payments. Of course, I could have used my Barnard medical coverage, but I didn't want to confess my illness to university administrators for fear of being ostracized, even fired. This was 1984, and that sort of cramped reasoning made some sense back then. Anyway, Florence claimed that she'd actually searched through my garbage and found bills for thousands of dollars that had been stamped overdue by Roosevelt Hospital. Naturally, she said, I couldn't admit that I'd stolen the painting or had such hospital bills because to admit either would be to virtually confess that I was tainted with plague.

I found all this out from Sarah's eldest daughter, Rachel, the only person in the family with the courage to call me up and ask if I was really ill.

Thanks to Florence's creative storytelling, my three siblings have never talked to me again.

It has always been hard for me to believe that reasonably intelligent and sensitive adults could behave like this, especially if they really thought that I had AIDS. But, as I found out, such things happen all the time. Since the end of 1984, I've never even received so much as a Christmas card or birthday call from any of them. And, until three weeks ago, I really did believe that they accepted Florence's story. I figured that they must have regarded it as an absolute miracle that I managed to live more than a few years.

During kind moments, I used to say to myself that when Florence started these rumors everybody was in a panic about the new plague striking America. And my father had just died. None of us was behaving rationally.

Occasionally, however, I speculated that Florence had stolen the painting and had accused me to cover herself. But mostly I didn't care. Dad was dead. I had a tenured teaching job that kept me fulfilled, good health and close friends. At a time when people really were starting to die in the long, drawn-out viral war that was just then beginning, these were the important things. As for the painting, I hoped that it had been sold to a museum where people could appreciate the nobility of the peasant girl with the obsidian hair. If I gave in to anger at times, it was only because I thought that the loss of the painting had somehow ripped out the very last page of my father's life story.

Then, one June day in 2001, I flew off to Porto, Portugal, to attend a series of lectures on French Twentieth-Century Figurative Painting at the Serralves Foundation, expecting not much more than seeing a few old friends. Martin Roland was there, the painter and professor of Art History at McGill University. The title of his talk was "Léger, the Female Nude and Solitude." I didn't know what this meant exactly, but I liked the way it sounded. During his lecture, he showed slides to illustrate his theory that Léger's women were fundamentally more isolated than his men – that they inhabited what he called *espaces fermées* – closed spaces. Additionally, Roland suggested that such an attitude was fundamentally new, the Classic and Romantic attitude being that women were far more in touch with the world – connected to the cycles of birth and death – than men. One of the slides illustrating Roland's thesis was of my father's painting.

When I saw it, I gasped; it was as if a loved one had risen from the grave. *So is she still here?* I thought; I realized at that moment that I'd imagined for many years that the young woman in the painting had died at the same moment as my father. Strange what the mind comes up with.

More importantly, I also realized that the young woman in the painting looked like my mother. How I could have missed that is beyond me. Maybe it was the trauma of losing her. Or maybe I needed to be older to see the subtle correspondence in their attitude rather than their physical form. There was no denying, however, that they had the same serene but knowing look in their eyes, the same inner elegance. Was this a coincidence? Or had Léger met my mother that night when he came to have his molar filled? Maybe he, too, recognized the similarity and offered the painting in tribute.

When Martin's lecture ended, I ran to him to ask about *The Woman with Stone Hair.*

"I got the slide from the Fondation Maeght," he replied. "I suppose the painting must be there, but I've never actually seen it in person."

From my hotel I called up the Fondation Maeght in Nice and spoke to a helpful young woman who told me that the painting in question was owned by a private collector in Princeton, New Jersey. She was a miracle worker and called me back later the same day with his phone number and name – Carlo Ricci.

When I spoke to Mr. Ricci from Portugal, he was friendly. Yes, he had the painting. It was hanging in his living room, over his couch. He remembered very well the circumstances under which he'd bought it. He voice was deep, his accent slightly British.

"At the time, I was collecting Léger, everything I could find," he told me. "I was in love with his scope, his size. A dealer in Boston called me one day. Jensen – Richard Lloyd Jensen. Do you know him?"

"I'm afraid not."

"Well, he called me up one day, out of the blue, and he said he had a lovely portrait in the style of *The Bather*, and that the people who owned it wanted to get rid of it quickly – that I could get it for a bargain price."

"Did he say who it was who was selling it?"

"Not that I recall."

"You wouldn't have Mr. Jensen's number, by any chance?"

"I have his gallery number. If you'll wait just a moment...."

But Ricci couldn't turn up the number; he'd stopped buying paintings years before and had moved on to antique cars.

When I got home a few days later, I managed to find Mr. Jensen through a series of phone calls to gallery owners in the Boston area. A man named Levine told me that Jensen was now retired, but still occasionally dealt in paintings. "His house is a treasure trove," he said.

When I got Jensen on the phone, I said, "Let me tell you a crazy story," and I proceeded to tell him about Léger's toothache and the history of the painting.

"I remember it very well," he said when I'd finished. "Personally, I didn't like it. But I knew Ricci, and I knew I could sell it."

"Do you remember who offered it to you?"

"I'm afraid not," he replied. "Ten years is a long time. But I still have my files. If you'll hold on..." I waited twenty minutes on the line. Twice he came back to tell me, "Don't hang up, I'm coming closer." Then, the third time, he said, "Got it... Mark Kumin and Sarah Halper."

"Both? You're sure?"

"It's right here – they both signed the forms."

"And no one else?" I was thinking of my youngest sister Florence.

"No one."

"Do you have the date of their contract with you?"

"June 17, 1987."

So they'd hidden away the painting for three years before putting it on the market.

"Do you mind telling me the price?" I asked.

"Oh, it was a bargain. Two hundred and seventy-five thousand.

Minus my commission, of course."

After I hung up, I sat for a long time with my head buzzing. For maybe a hundred thousand dollars each, Mark and Sarah had stolen our father's painting; been willing to let lies about me go unchallenged; and never spoken with me again. It didn't make much sense. And Florence? Had she been involved behind the scenes? I suspected so. She was clever enough to have developed the plan and found a way around actually signing anything.

I couldn't sleep that night. The sheets were icy, the bed too small. I watched TV and thought about the past as if I were searching for clues to a murder. At nine the next morning, I called Mr. Ricci back and asked if I could see the painting. He explained that he was an old man, seventy-seven, and was no longer in the habit of receiving guests.

"I'll come whenever you want and I'll only stay a moment," I said. He simply sighed, so I added, "I'll pay you five hundred dollars just to stand in front of it for a minute. "

"Oh dear, that won't be necessary," he answered in an apologetic tone. "How about tomorrow, say early afternoon?"

His granddaughter got on the phone to give me directions to his house. That night, I fished out my father's old medicines from the bottom of my linen closet and took a Valium in order to sleep. In the morning, I rented a car and drove to Princeton. I'd never been there before. Ricci lived in a wealthy neighborhood with towering oaks and perfect lawns about a mile west of the university. His house was English Tudor. When I rang the bell, a young woman answered. She introduced herself as the granddaughter I'd spoken to. She was tiny, with short brown hair. She wore jeans and a baggy woolen sweater. When I thanked her for giving me such good directions, she smiled warmly. "My grandfather is waiting for you with the painting," she said.

I'm usually quite observant, but I have no idea even today what the foyer looked like or how exactly we got to the living room. I suddenly couldn't seem to get my breath, and I was worried that I was going to faint. All I remember is my feet pounding on a wooden floor for the longest time. Then I saw Ricci seated in a wheelchair at the center of a large, brightly lit room, with all the walls painted white. He was bald and shrunken. A blue blanket was draped over his shoulders. He was holding my father's Léger in his skeletal hands. He smiled, and I remember his teeth were too large.

"Is this the painting, Professor Kumin?" he asked.

I nodded.

Objects must soak up memory and become aligned to certain events; looking at the Léger, I was overwhelmed with the feeling of being with my mother. It was as if we were about to play a game of gin rummy on her bed.

It was then that I understood why the painting meant so very much to my father, and why I'd discovered him once sleeping with it on his lap.

"Professor Kumin, would you like to take a closer look?" Ricci asked.

When he held it out to me, a hollow ache opened in my gut. I wanted to run my finger over her hair, but I was sure I'd burst into tears if I did.

"No, thank you," I whispered. "I think I should get going."

I turned and rushed past Ricci's granddaughter out of the living room. While running to my car, she called my name once, but I didn't turn around. I cursed myself for having visited.

At home I went through old photographs of my parents. I kept looking at my mother as if there were a mark I needed to find – later, I figured I was looking for the first sign of her cancer. Then I had this overwhelming urge to see her grave. I felt like a character in some feverish detective novel. So I drove out to Roslyn and found the Mt. Sinai cemetery. It was past closing time. The sun was setting, and the gates were locked. But the brick wall around the cemetery was only four feet high. On hoisting myself over, I found scruffy lawns, pink azalea bushes, and neat rows of white marble headstones. I rushed around like a trespasser till I found my parents' graves. It took less time than I thought, maybe a half-hour. By then, dusk had veiled everything a solemn gray.

Isadore Kumin, January 12, 1903 – June 18,1984

Gnendl Rosencrantz Kumin, December 4,1906 – June 6,1954.

I gathered pebbles and put them on their headstones and kept putting them there till there was no space left for anything. Then I put some more stones in my coat pockets till they felt heavy enough for me to leave.

When I got home, I typed one-line notes to each of my three siblings: "I know now for sure that you stole Dad's painting."

It seemed important to let them know that I had found out about their treachery, but not to say anything more.

Florence was the only one to write me back. She sent a typed, single-spaced, seventeen-page letter. She wrote about all the bad things my father and I had ever done to her. Eleven times she told me that I was a "queer without balls" and that if I'd had any courage I would have admitted years ago that I'd done everything I could to ruin her life. I had the feeling that she typed the letter with a hammer in each hand. A lot of incidents she referred to were totally invented: *"Don't you remember how you and Dad abandoned me after Mom's death. And then when you made fun of me for having an abortion when you knew I had no way of raising a baby... It was too much to ever forgive."*

The madness shrieking from her pages frightened me, but I couldn't stop reading. On page twelve, I learned more about why she, Mark and Sarah had stolen the Léger. She said that when she was in high school, they'd pleaded with our mother to leave our father and divorce him: *"Mom was so good and kind, but you weren't old enough to know. And Dad was evil, a secret man of silent plans whose very presence was toxic..."*

When their effort failed, and when our mother died, Florence realized that she couldn't bear to see our father keep *The Woman with Stone Hair*: *"We had to get the portrait of Mom away from him. He had her in life, but would never keep her in death. I had to make sure of that. And we knew you wouldn't agree, so we never told you."*

When I was growing up, I always thought that as an adult I'd be friends with my siblings, particularly Florence. I also thought that as we age we must each inevitably grow more accepting of our parents and their failings.

Over the last three nights, I've gotten calls at two in the morning, but, when I answer, no one is there. The last time it happened, I had enough of my wits to say, "Florence, if this is you, then please don't call again."

Sometimes, in my dreams, I see her trapped in one of Léger's *espaces fermées* – closed spaces. She kicks and screams, but she can't get out. Even so, I'm not taking any chances. I changed my phone number today and workmen are coming over in the morning to install a security system.

Further Reading

There are a vast number of anthologies of gay short stories and possibly just as many of gay erotic stories. What follows is a very brief checklist of some of the more essential titles. Editions cited are those on my shelf, not necessarily firsts:

Burton, Peter:
>   *The Mammoth Book of Gay Short Stories* (London, Robinson, 1997)
>   *Bend Sinister: The Gay Times Book of Disturbing Stories* (London, GMP, 2003)
>   *Death Comes Easy: The Gay Times Book of Murder Stories* (London, GMP, 2003)

Kleinberg, Seymour:
>   *The Penguin Book of Gay Short Stories* (London, Viking, 1994)

Manghel, Alberto & Stephenson, Craig:
>   *In Another Part of the Forest: The Flamingo Anthology of Gay Literature* (London, Flamingo, 1994)

Mitchell, Mark:
>   *The Penguin Book of International Gay Writing* (London, Viking, 1995)

Picano, Felice:
>   *A True Likeness: Lesbian and Gay Writing Today* (New York, The Sea Horse Press, 1980)

Sutherland, Alistair & Anderson, Patrick
>   *Eros: An Anthology of Friendship* (London, Anthony Blond, 1961)

White, Edmund:
  The Faber Book of Gay Short Fiction (London, Faber & Faber, 1991)

Wright, Stephen:
  Different: An Anthology of Homosexual Short Stories (New York, Bantam Books. 1974)

About the Authors:

Tim Ashley's first published short story appeared in *Death Comes Easy*; his first novel *The Island of Mending Hearts* was published earlier this year.

David Patrick Beavers' work has been variously anthologised; his novels include *Jackal in the Dark*, *The Jackal Awakens*, *Thresholds*, *The Colour of Green* and *Pathways*.

Geo C Bourne writes, 'I take the liberty of sending you .. the only piece of fiction I attempted... why? One. I am gay. Two. I was born in Brighton on 1923 but came to NZ on 1970. Three. I have a copy of *The Mammoth Book of Gay Short Stories*, which you edited.'

Perry Brass's work has been widely anthologised. His books include *Warlock*, *Mirage*, *Others*, *The Harvest* and *Angel Lust*.

Scott Brown's stories have appeared in *Bend Sinister* and *Death Comes Easy*.

Jeffrey Buchanan has published novels, short stories and academic work. His novels include two versions of *Sucking Feijoas*.

Peter Burton's books include *Rod Stewart: A Life on the Town*, *Parallel Lives*, *Talking to...* and *Amongst the Aliens*. He has edited six collections of stories.

Richard Cawley's books include *That's Entertaining*, *The New English Cookery*, *Green Feasts* and *Not Quite Vegetarian*. His first novel was *The Butterfly Boy*.

Bryan Connon's books include *Beverley Nichols: A Life* and *Somerset Maugham and the Maugham Dynasty*.

Jack Dickson's books include *Oddfellows, Crossing Jordan, Freeform, Banged Up, Some Kind of Love* and *Out of This World*.

Simon Edge has been editor of *Capital Gay*, written for the *Guardian*, the *Independent* and the *London Evening Standard*, and now writes for the *Express*.

Hugh Fleetwood's books include *The Girl Who Passed for Normal, Foreign Affairs, The Past, The Witch, The Mercy Killers* and *Brothers*.

Drew Gummerson's publications include a short story in *Death Comes Easy* and the novel *The Lodger*.

John Haylock's books include *See You Again, It's All Your Fault, One Hot Day in Kyoto, A Touch of the Orient, Doubtful Partners, Body of Contention* and *Loose Connections*.

Randall Kent Ivey's stories have been variously anthologised; his books include *The Shape of Man*.

Alan James's stories have appeared in *Bend Sinister* and *Death Comes Easy*.

John Sam Jones's books include *Welsh Boys Too* and *Fishboys of Vernazza*. His first novel, *With Angels and Furies*, will be published by GMP in 2005.

Francis King's books include *A Domestic Animal, Acts of Darkness, Voices in an Empty Room, Punishments, The Ant Colony, The One and Only, Dead Letters, Prodigies* and *The Nick of Time*.

Reuben Lane's short stories have been variously anthologised and he is author of one novel, *Throwing Stones at Jonathan*.

Simon Lovat's short stories have been variously anthologised; his books include *Disorder and Chaos* and *Attrition*.

David Mckintosh is a pen name of a writer who has been anthologised abroad (in translation); this is his first publication in the original.

Stuart Thorogood's books include *Outcast* and *Outside In*.

Michael Wilcox's plays include *Rents, Lent, Green Fingers* and *Mrs Steinberg and the Byker Boy*; his books include *Outlaw in the Hills* and *Benjamin Britten*.

Graeme Woolaston's stories have been variously anthologised; his books include *Stranger Than Love,The Learning of Paul O'Neill* and *The Biker Below the Downs*.

Ian Young's work has been widely anthologised; his books include *The Male Homosexual in Literature: A Bibliography, Year of the Sun, Some Green Moths, Common-or-Garden Gods, Sex Magick* and *The Stonewall Experiment: A Gay Psychohistory*.

Richard Zimler's novels include *The Last Kabbalist of Lisbon, Unholy Ghosts, The Angelic Darkness* and the recently published *Hunting Midnight*.

**If you enjoyed this book, why not one of these other books from
Gay Men s Press and Zipper Books?**

Erotica

Legion Of Lust	Lukas Scott	£9.99
The Last Taboo	Peter Gilbert	£8.99
Czech Mate	Caleb Ask	£8.99
Out Of This World	Jack Dickson	£7.95
The Masters File	Jack Dickson	£8.99
The Chain	Thom Wolf	£8.99
The Palace Of Varieties	James Lear	£8.99

Literary fiction

Attrition	Simon Lovat	£9.95
Fly On The Wall	Rupert Smith	£9.99
Adam	Anthony McDonald	£9.99
Sebastian s Tangibles	Anthea Ingham	£9.99
The Island Of Mending Hearts	Tim Ashley	£9.99
Bend Sinister	Peter Burton (Ed)	£9.99
Death Comes Easy	Peter Burton (Ed)	£8.99
Sucking Feijoas	J Buchanan	£9.95
Outside In	Stuart Thorogood	£7.95

Please add postage and packing:
UK: 1 item - £1.95   2 or more - £3.90
Overseas: 1 item - £4.25   2 or more - £5.95

Order By Phone: 0845 430 9113 (+44 20 77 39 46 46)

Order Online: www.prowlerdirect.co.uk

Order By Post: Millivres Prowler Ltd
                                        75B Great Eastern Street
                                        London EC2A 3HN

I enclose a cheque for £............ made payable to Millivres Prowler Ltd.

Please charge £............. to my VISA/MASTERCARD/AMEX/SWITCH:
Card Nos: ....
Exp Date: .... Valid From: .... Issue Nos: ....
NAME ....
ADDRESS..

POSTCODE..SIGNATURE...